CHESTNUT MARE, BEWARE

BY JODY JAFFE

Horse of a Different Killer
Chestnut Mare, Beware

CHESTNUT MARE, BEWARE

Jody Jaffe

FAWCETT COLUMBINE • NEW YORK

A Fawcett Columbine Book
Published by Ballantine Books

Copyright © 1996 by Jody Jaffe

All rights reserved under International and Pan-American Copyright Conven-
tions. Published in the United States by Ballantine Books, a division of Random
House, Inc., New York, and simultaneously in Canada by Random House of
Canada Limited, Toronto.

http://www.randomhouse.com

Library of Congress Cataloging in Publication Data:

Jaffe, Jody.
Chestnut mare, beware / Jody Jaffe.
p. cm.
ISBN 0-449-90998-0
1. Women journalists—North Carolina—Fiction. 2. Show horses—Fiction.
3. Charlotte (N.C.)—Fiction.
I. Title.
PS3560.A3125C48 1996
813'.54—dc20   96-16070

Manufactured in the United States of America

First Edition: September 1996

10 9 8 7 6 5 4 3 2

To my mother, Anne Isaac,
and my father, Phil Jaffe

"Why is it that a woman will forgive homicidal behavior in a horse, yet be highly critical of a man for leaving the toilet seat up?"—Dave Barry

Acknowledgments

Since this is a second book, I no longer feel the need to thank every human being who crossed my path in the past forty-three years. That said, there still are some people that I'd like to acknowledge for their help and support.

First to my agent, Rafe Sagalyn, the godfather of Nattie Gold. Thanks for everything, especially your above-and-beyond-the-call-of-duty caring about my books. And to Jenny Bent, of the Sagalyn Agency, for all your hard work getting the word (and book) out and for always being there to answer every single one of my questions.

Again to my editor, Barbara Dicks, for her gentle and astute editing ways. To her assistant Jennifer Scott, who continues to laugh at my jokes and is always on hand to help me. And to Joe Blades, your kindness and enthusiasm are much appreciated. To my publicist extraordinaire, the wonderful Rachel Tarlow Gul, whom I expect someday will be running Random House.

Once again to Peter Foley for his eagle-eyed copy reading skills, advice, support, friendship, general hand holding at horse shows and sense of humor about everything I've just mentioned. Of course thanks to my writing group, Vickie Baily, Abby Bardi, Len Kruger, and Rachel Carpenter.

For the amount of medical and psychiatric knowledge she provided for this book, Anne Sagalyn deserves to be put on retainer. But as luck would have it, not only is she a gifted doctor, but an extraordinarily generous best friend. Thank you.

To Sisters in Crime, both in the flesh and on AOL, thank you for all your sisterly support. To Raph Levien, Margot Williams, and Arnoud Galactus Engelfriet, many thanks for sharing your cybernautical knowledge.

I knew nothing about pathology before I started writing this book. Now I know a little thanks to the following doctors, Major Joseph Pulcini, of the U.S. Army Medical Corps, Angelica Oviedo, a pathology resident of the University of Washington Medical Center and Jeffrey Winters.

I also knew nothing about Jack Russell terriers. Betsy Branscome, a Jack Russell breeder and horse editor for the *Fauquier Times Democrat*, fixed that. Also thanks to Ronnie Klaskin for her Jack Russell stories. To Erin Harty, who covered the Chicago horse killing trials for *The Chronicle of the Horse*, thank you for double checking my facts.

To Gerri Pencola for her early read of this book and keeping my mother in line. And to Jasper Jensen for sharing his martial arts knowledge with me and keeping my father in line.

Jim Liles, thanks for helping me concoct the correct literary explosive.

To my friend Tom Scheve, whose light is a spiritual beacon to me, for his knowledge and guidance about finding the way.

To Tom Hardy for telling me about the tragic death of his cousin, Shelly Malone. *Chestnut Mare, Beware* is purely a work of fiction and cannot provide you any answers, but I hope and pray someday you'll find your own.

Thank you to Marge Kolb, secretary to the hearing committee for the American Horse Show Association for sharing her knowledge about equine drug abuse and sanctions. To the American Lung Association and Joe Cherner of Smoke Free Educational Services, thank you for your information.

To Alan Dynerman, for his architectural help and general wit.

My family gets a big round of applause, not only for sharing the printer, but for putting up with me—and too many dinners from Boston Market and the Thai Room—while I approached deadline. To my husband, Charlie Shepard, who has always valued my writing, even when it only generated eight dollars in five years. And to the two human beings who continue to put everything in perspective for me, my wonderful sons, Ben and Sam.

And most of all, to the readers of this book. Thank you very much for taking the time to invite Nattie Gold into your life.

PROLOGUE

Chestnut mare, beware. That's how it goes in the horse world. And Nobody's Fool was no exception.

She had a coat the color of a copper pipe, shiny and smooth with fourteen different shades of brown and yellow and orange bouncing around when the sun hit her right. She had a body that was sinewy and slinky with a neck that arched up to her head like a long, teasing C-slide on a saxophone. They called her Rita around the barn. Rita, for Rita Hayworth.

This horse could pack a squirmy ten-year-old over a course of three-foot-six-inch fences and make it look like poetry. When she wanted to. Which wasn't often enough. Because she was a chestnut mare.

Chestnut mare, beware. That's what they say in the horse world.

But Josane Leigh Ashmore wasn't listening. And she should have.

"Okay, Josane, canter her up the line. Nice and easy. Remember, this horse has a huge stride, so you don't have to worry about getting to the jump in time. Be definite in a soft way. . . ." The last part of the sentence Charlie Laconte muttered to himself. "And pray to God she doesn't duck out and send your ass flying to Outer Slovakia."

"How much leg does she take?" Josane Ashmore said.

Laconte slid his hand on his hip, rolled his eyes, and exaggerated each syllable of his sentence: "What color is she?"

1

"Chestnut," the woman said.

"What sex is she?"

"A mare," she singsonged.

"That makes her what?" Laconte said.

The woman swung her arm into the air and used her index finger to conduct the answer. In a trilling crescendo she warbled, "A chestnut mare."

"Very good, my dear. So you tell me how much leg she takes."

The woman smiled. "Not hardly anything."

"Right. Now go jump."

Laconte watched Josane Ashmore canter the big red horse up the outside line in six even strides, jumping both fences as if it were the winning trip at the National Horse Show.

"Now take her down the diagonal. And if that works out, go up the other outside line, down the diagonal again, and finish over the single jump."

No question about it, Rita was on the money today. Had been for the past two weeks. Laconte had been training on her every day, beating the crap out of her if she even thought about refusing. With this horse, sometimes the training stuck for a month, sometimes it didn't last an hour. There was no telling what Rita might do, which was why she'd been shipped to Laconte's barn—her fifth in as many months—to get sold.

The horse cantered the entire course, making it look so easy Laconte stopped holding his breath halfway through. Go figure it, he thought, put a green rider on a horse that's landed three pros in the hospital.

Laconte hadn't even planned on showing her the chestnut mare. He'd brought in an aged gray gelding for her to try. But she'd insisted on riding Rita. And after two years of training Josane Leigh Ashmore, Laconte knew he was wasting his time trying to get her to even sit on the gray.

Josane Ashmore was a quick learner: driven, focused, confident. And stubborn.

She'd taken one look at the gray and walked right by his stall, directly to Rita's. "Charlie, honey, Lord knows I'm no Margie Goldstein, but I want to try *this* horse. She sure is the prettiest thing I've ever seen. Just quit your worrying and let's get her saddled."

He did, reluctantly.

"Now take that look off that gorgeous face of yours and give me a leg up."

Laconte laced his fingers together and cupped them under the young woman's left calf. "Okay, here you go. One, two, three . . . I just hope you've got some of Margie's stickum in you." Margie Goldstein, the five-foot-two phenomenon from Florida. Not since Rodney Jenkins had a rider wowed the crowds like Margie. When she climbed on a horse, the animal seemed to sprout wings and fly.

". . . Let me know when you want to try the gray."

"Charlie, come on now, honey, have a little faith."

What he had was the jitters. The last thing he needed was another injury at his barn; not with that crazy father breathing down his back, blaming him for his little girl's death because Charlie'd sold them the pony that threw the child. One more accident and he'd have to sell a barnful of horses just to pay his insurance bills. But he wasn't about to turn down a potential client with a big checkbook. Which Josane Ashmore seemed to have. She'd come to his barn two years earlier. A rank beginner in custom-made Vogel field boots, toting a brand-new Butet saddle—close to four thousand dollars in horse equipment between her legs and arms alone. Said she'd been on a horse twelve times.

"I hear you're the best trainer around and I want to go to that big show they have in Washington," she'd said to him.

He'd laughed and so did she. But then she said "Hush now, I know you think I'm being funny. But I'm as serious as a heart attack about this. I'm a hard worker. How long will it take?"

Two years later, she could canter a horse around a course of three-foot-six-inch fences. Maybe not a complicated horse, but a packer—as in a horse who can *pack* anyone around—could take her where she wanted to go. The problem was finding the right packer. She'd already tried a barnful and not liked one of them. So when she got her mind set on Rita, Laconte thought, why not?

"That was fabulous, Josane," Laconte said as she walked the horse toward him on a loose rein. "You and Margie must have been separated at birth."

"Not hardly. It's this horse, she makes it easy." Josane patted Rita's neck and smiled. She had a big beauty-queen smile that showed lots of straight white teeth.

"See, Charlie, all that worry for nothing. I knew she and I were made for each other."

Physically, there was no question about it. The rider was as striking as the horse. Josane stood close to six feet, with the perfect leg proportions for an equestrian: long, slim thighs atop even longer and slimmer calves. Although individually her features were off—her nose bowed out a little too much at the bridge and her eyes were set deep into her face—everything together worked well enough to make just about any man turn as she walked by.

She slid off the horse and loosened the girth of her saddle.

"So, if we start showing now, can we still qualify for the indoor shows?"

"Let's not get crazy about this," Laconte said. "It's a possibility." Assuming the horse doesn't kill you on the way, is what he would have said if the promise of a five-digit check weren't staring him in the face. Rita had a $75,000 price tag on her head. That wasn't even wishful thinking on the part of the owner and all the trainers in the food chain who stood to pocket a ten-percent cut. More like foolish thought.

"I think the owners'll take sixty."

"I'll give you forty. The vet's coming in an hour to check her out. Just tell me who to write the check out to."

"Sure you want to do this? You've seen Rita on her bad days, she can be more than a handful. That gray horse won Virginia large junior hunter champion three years in a row. . . ."

"*Charlie*, that gray is older than Mrs. Alma May Cummins, the lady who plays organ at my mama's church, and I'd bet twice as crippled. I'd have to buy me a pharmaceutical company to keep that horse from toppling over. Besides, you saw yourself how good Rita just was. Come on now, you're the one who keeps telling me horses aren't machines. 'They have good days and bad days, just like us.' I know she can be a handful. What horse can't? It's like the Good Book says, 'Hast thou given the horse strength? Hast thou clothed his neck with thunder?' Job 39:19."

"And look what happened to Job. I hope the Good Lord blesses this union 'cause you might need a little watching over with this mare."

She handed Laconte the reins and laughed. "We're all being watched over, Charlie. We just don't know it sometimes. Be right back. I'm going to get my purse."

Laconte smiled, sort of. He looked at the chestnut mare he was holding. "Sweet Jesus, what have I gotten myself into? I'll be lucky if this woman makes it to spring still breathing."

Laconte was many things. Lucky wasn't one of them.

CHAPTER 1

I was hammering out the last part of my Sunday column, a riveting look at the history of underwire bras, corsets, and garter belts, when the little green letters flashed across the top of my computer:

NATTIE, IN MY OFFICE. NOW.—CANDACE

Whoever invented e-mail should be forced to wear all of the above *and* spike heels.

I tapped back: BE THERE IN A FEW MINUTES, JUST WRAPPING UP COLUMN—NATTIE. Before I had a chance to exhale, NOW! exploded across the top of my computer.

"Okay, okay," I muttered, "hold your horses, for crying out loud."

I slipped on my shoes—amber plastic jellies I wore canoeing down the Chattooga River—and headed toward Candace's office. The door was closed and I knocked, just below the red plastic laminate sign announcing her fiefdom:

CANDACE FITZGERALD

FEATURES EDITOR

THE CHARLOTTE COMMERCIAL APPEAL

Every other manager at the place had a black sign with white letters. Not Candace. She had to have red. She told her personal shopper at Dillard's—who couldn't wait to tell me—that red is the color of authority. Which explains why she's got at least seven different jackets in varying shades of authority. Today it was her cranberry bolero.

"What's up?" I said.

Candace smiled. She had a below-the-eyes smile.

"Get my message last night?"

"Message?" I said. "My machine records only when it feels like it. It was empty last night when I got back from riding my horse."

She looked at me like my fourth-grade teacher, Mrs. Wenzel, used to look at me during fingernail check. Every day she'd ask if I'd washed my hands that morning, I'd say yes, she'd give me *the look*, and then march me around the room as an example of poor hygiene. My fingers did look like hell, but it wasn't because I wasn't washing them. I was a rashy kid with rashy fingers. I always had my hands in dirt, digging for earthworms or building fortresses, which made my fingers even more rashy.

"Then get a new machine," she said. "Here's what I wanted. Got a great story for you."

I'd been at Candace's mercy for the past couple months. Payback for freeing me up from Features to let me work a murder investigation with a news side reporter. Even though the series we wrote stands a good shot at the Pulitzer, she's still spitting nails because all four stories ran on page one instead of 14C or 11B or 8A, whatever the features page was that day.

"As you know," she started, "the contingency budget hasn't allowed us to fill openings. That's left us precious few bodies and with you being in Metro so long, we had to run too much wire copy. Now that you're back, I'm counting on you to be an important player in the success of Features."

I nodded. She thought I was nodding in agreement; I was nodding because I knew what that was management-speak for: You're going to be working your ass off with no comp time. North

Carolina is a right-to-work state, a euphemism for exploited labor. I felt like standing on her desk, screaming "UNION, UNION, UNION . . ." until they carted me away or brought in Ron Silver to organize us.

". . . And as you know, this is the biggest time of year for the paper. Christmas, lots of advertising, a bigger paper with more pages and possibly even daily section fronts for us. I want Features to have a strong presence. So help me out on this, Nattie."

Uh-oh, more trouble. The minute an editor at *The Appeal* uses the words "help me out" with the reporter's name plugged in at the end, it means that editor has got that reporter's new assignment conceived, written, and edited in his or her mind. Not to mention promised yesterday at the ten A.M. budget meeting for the next day's paper. In my case, as the paper's reluctant fashion writer, it was probably a trend story about the revival of madras, due in twenty minutes.

"I'd love to, Candace. I've got a list of great story ideas. Remember I told you about that nursing home where—"

Candace cut me off with the slice of her hand. "Another time, Nattie. Write me a memo and drop it on my desk and we can discuss it next week. I've got something else in mind and I think you'll like this. . . . It's not fashion."

She got my attention with that. I'd been fashion writer for *The Appeal* for almost three years, two of which I'd spent trying to get off that beat and onto general assignment features writing. "Really? What's it about?"

I felt like a bass who'd swallowed a Lefty Deceiver. She was Lefty Kreh, father of that famous fly hook, in a power suit and pumps. Reel me in, baby, as long as it's not fashion, I'll bite.

"What sells papers, Nattie?"

"Kids and dogs. Preferably both," I said.

"Right," she said. "But that's old. We need something new. Something fresh. Something that'll make the readers know that the features page of *The Charlotte Commercial Appeal* is where they want to be every morning. That's when it came to me. This is the Christmas season. Families. Goodwill. Fond memories. Kids and fond memories."

Ouch, a jab from Lefty's lethal hook. Aside from Festival-in-the-Park stories, a dog of a story about an insipid and unfortunately annual crafts fair, holiday happiness assignments were the worst.

"You want me to find another Christmas miracle story? Last year it was the one-pound baby."

Candace puffed up. "Did that. No response from anyone but the mother. We need a grabber this year. Then it hit me. Dead kids. That's it. That's our ticket."

I looked at the five-by-seven on her desk. A four-year-old with a love-me-please expression. Her daughter, Christie, who spent thirteen hours a day at the Myers Park Childhood Development Center. Candace was never one to let personal feelings—assuming she had any—get in the way.

I took a deep breath because I knew where she was heading and I didn't want to go along for the ride. Not again. I'd done it once and it tore me up pretty bad.

I'd forced Candace to let me write the story in the first place, and when I did, we got a bucketful of letters and too many phone calls to log. I'd seen a little notice in the back of the paper: "Compassionate Friends, for parents who have lost children, first Thursday of every month. 7 P.M. . . ."

Candace refused to let me cover it because it conflicted with Bill Blass's big bash at Dillard's. I convinced her that I should interview the designer on the phone and then run the story the day of his show, thereby freeing me up that particular Thursday night. She bought it. I did a phoner with Blass, we ran the story, and I covered Compassionate Friends. Never in twelve years as a journalist had I been so affected by a story. I sat in a room full of hollow-eyed people as they poured their souls out to one another. When I wrote the story the next day, I could hardly see the screen through my tears.

"Compassionate Friends?" I said. "I already wrote that story."

"Exactly. And what a response. Rutger says that story comes up at least once a week over lunch at the Queen City Crown Club."

Rutger is Rutger Pearson, the silver-haired publisher of *The Appeal*, who looks like an aging Greek god and most of the time acts like one. The Crown Club, as it's known to its members, is a private dining and health club that just three years ago began accepting membership from anyone other than white Protestant males. It did so by inviting Harvey Gantt, the city's former mayor who came heartbreakingly close to booting Jesse Helms out of his senate chair. Gantt turned down their invite, so the club fathers went to the second black man on their list, Mugsy Bogues.

"That story ran nine months ago," Candace said. "We're still getting mail about it. And Fred told me yesterday that Miami's reprinting it in the annual report as an example of community service."

Everything became clear as the glass of all the editors' walls. Fred. Fred Richards, *The Appeal*'s editor who was referred to as the Shoe Salesman by both the reporters at *The Appeal* and other editors at our sister papers. In his utter lack of originality, Fred must have told Candace to tell me to do another story about Compassionate Friends because Miami noticed the first one. Jockeying for attention from Miami, the hub of our chain, was the name of the game for up and climbing editors.

"I don't know, Candace," I said. "How many times can I describe the ongoing hell these people live through every day? What more can I say that I didn't already say in forty inches?"

" 'Jingle Bells.' "

"What?" I said.

" 'Jingle Bells.' 'Frosty the Snowman.' 'Silent Night.' 'Little Drummer Boy.' I'm sure I don't have to remind you, it's Christmas. And they're having a Christmas party. Look."

She lifted a white piece of paper from a pile of seasonal red and green flyers and pushed it toward me.

In a no-nonsense no-frills typeface, it said: "Holidays are the hardest time . . . let's meet and help one another make it through the season . . . 4 P.M. December 24."

"It's not exactly a party," I said.

"Whatever," Candace said. "I want you there and the story written for the next day's paper. Bring Torkesquist, he's the best shooter we've got. Tell him to get close-ups when they start crying."

"That's Christmas Eve," I said.

"So? You're Jewish."

"I was going to see my mother in Greensboro."

"Well, she's Jewish too, isn't she?"

"Yeah, she's Jewish, but holidays are hard for her too. I don't know if you remember, but my stepfather died earlier this year, and it's been very difficult for her. . . ."

"Nattie, am I mistaken, or haven't you been begging to do nonfashion stories? If you want a general assignment slot, it seems to me the best way to get one is to do general assignment stories. Show us what you can do."

"I thought I did that with the horse show murder series."

"That was July. This is December. Nattie, I've got a meeting with Fred in five minutes. Can I tell him we can count on you? I don't have to remind you that your last review found you falling short in the team player category. . . ."

Team player. What the hell did she think this newspaper was, the Boston Red Sox? We both knew I couldn't turn it down, not if I ever hoped to be spelled off fashion in this century.

"I'll be there, with bells on," I said to Candace's back, because she'd already swiveled around to her filing cabinet and on to something else. All I could see was a very large triangle of cranberry wool. Despite numerous columns I'd written announcing New York had declared this unfashionable, Candace still believed in the power of shoulder pads—so much so, I wondered if she bought hers at Herman's.

I'd have liked to slam her door when I walked out or, better yet, slam her. But I'm trying to believe in peaceful resolution, so I went down to the cafeteria for a pack of Twizzlers.

I inserted two quarters in the slot and the machine ignored me. Before I could remember my resolve of peaceful resolution, I booted the shiny silver skirt of the candy machine with my right foot. A pain shot up my ankle right where a six-inch bolt of aluminum riveted my tibia to my fibula.

"Goddammit," I screamed.

"Nattie, do you think kicking metal with a leg that was just broken is a good idea?"

It was Henry. Henry Goode. The investigative reporter I teamed up with on the horse show murder story.

"As a matter of fact, Doctor Doom told me it was part of my physical therapy plan. Kick three candy machines a day and finish up on one six-foot-three-inch reporter."

"Nattie, I'm just asking about your leg, which, do I have to remind you, you broke twice in two weeks. What's wrong with you today anyway? Are you okay?"

"Candace! What the hell is ever wrong with me? Candace. That automaton they call an editor. Sorry, Henry, I didn't mean to explode in your face. It's just Candace and her half-assed Miami-will-love-this ideas."

"Let me guess," Henry said. "A fashion show in Gastonia."

And then he sashayed like a Seventh Avenue model past the belligerent candy machine.

"Okay, Vendella, enough," I said. "I don't feel like laughing,

I'm too mad. It's worse than a fashion show, and I never thought I'd be saying that. I'm not going into it now. Anything new with you? Perhaps a new blockbuster that might win you your third Pulitzer, assuming, of course, we walk away with the local reporting prize for our series?"

Henry smiled. He was one handsome man. Chiseled to perfection by a breeding program honed to flawlessness by generations of Mayflowerians. I couldn't help but admire his looks—as specimen quality only. We ended up squabbling about something every time we got together. Usually something pretty stupid, like where to park the car.

There was more to Henry than his looks. He had the unusual combination of being boyishly awkward, like someone who hadn't yet gotten used to his size—both metaphorically and literally—along with this solid lead core of responsibility and integrity, with an occasional dash of goofiness. Henry believed that life should be fair, that preachers shouldn't steal from their flocks, and that congressmen shouldn't prey on women. And it seemed to be his life's mission to make the world closer to the way he thought it should work.

"I don't know the scope of it yet, but I'm working on something that could be interesting," Henry said. Deliberate, precise, and accurate are the bylaws under which Henry operates, including the way he speaks. To anyone else, *interesting* is a three-syllable word. To Henry, it's four. "I've been getting copies of bizarre, somewhat threatening letters for several weeks, not that that's new in itself. What makes these interesting is the alphabetized cc list on a separate page the writer includes in all the envelopes. This person appears to be sending the same letters to some of the biggest who's whos in the Carolinas and Virginia, starting at A and ending at Z."

He pulled a letter from the inside of his rumpled sport coat. Henry's precision stopped at his closet. Though he was crumpled, the letter was neatly folded in thirds. There was no signature, no date, just words typed on some computer somewhere in anonymous land.

It said: FIRST YOU COUGH. THEN YOU DIE, BUT NOT RIGHT AWAY. THAT WOULD BE MERCIFUL. THAT WOULD BE AN ACT OF THE GOOD LORD. BUT THE GOOD LORD HAS HIS HANDS TIED. TIED BY YOU AND ALL YOUR KIND.

AND YOU'RE GOING TO PAY.

CHAPTER 2

Henry and I took a table by the large expanse of streaky glass looking out over the Firestone tire store on Stonewall Street. Streaky because the window washers had been put on hold, pending an upswing in our profits. Since *The Appeal* plays cash cow for the entire chain, the gray suits in Miami got hysterical when our profits dipped to 29.5 percent and tightened our belts to near suffocation. Never mind that the other papers don't even come close to 15.

"That's some letter," I said. "How very organized to alphabetize a hit list—just what the world needs, an anal-retentive psycho. It's a good thing there's no shortage of wackos out there, otherwise we'd be out of business. Has anyone on the list been threatened in person?"

"No, and no one's taking it too seriously. The other letters are more of the same; variations on the 'Good Lord giveth and taketh' theme. I spoke to Duffy Ritter, head of Carolinas IBM. He told me this sort of thing is part and parcel with being CEO of a major company. He just turned the letters over to his security people. So far there's been no contact other than the letters."

"Not yet anyway," I said. "I know you think I live for drama, but if my last name began with A and I was on that list, I'd be worried."

"As I recall," Henry said, "wasn't it you who once told me that's your normal state of being?"

"There's worried and there's *worried*. The first is just a general concern that the world's about to fall apart and all your loved ones will be struck by lightning, hit by a car and/or be the victims of heinous terrorist acts—that's just being Jewish. The second is real worry, when there's good reason to worry. Like when someone sends you threatening letters. There's something about that letter . . . I'm not sure what, but I'll bet you these guys won't be taking it so lightly after a while. Or maybe I'm just agitated about Candace. . . ."

Or maybe I was just plain jealous of Henry. Lucky Henry. He got to work on death threats while I'd be getting the chance to sob my way through Christmas Eve.

"I gotta go, Henry. Got to call Mother and tell her she'll be watching *Miracle on 34th Street* alone this year, thanks to Candace."

I drained the bottom of my coffee cup and started walking to the escalator. I took three limping steps—my ankle still smarted from my assault to the candy machine—and turned back to the table.

"Henry," I said. "What's the connection? What do Misters A through Z have in common? Are you Mr. G?"

He grabbed his notebook and started walking with me to the newsroom.

"No, the G on the list belongs to Booker Greene, a New York congressman who was born and raised in the eastern part of North Carolina, near Fuquay Varina. It's not me who's being threatened. Whoever's sending these wants publicity, and that's where I come in. I just started working on it, so I don't know much. The only thing that jumps out at me is many of them are quite wealthy. I'll do record checks on them to find out more, what the common denominator is other than money. I can't imagine that this letter writer's vendetta is about being rich."

"Maybe you're right," I said. "But money does make people

crazy. Remember Wally, our dead horse trainer friend who killed all those horses for insurance money? And he wasn't alone. Far from it. All those people who got indicted in Chicago, thirty-six of them and counting, some of the biggest names in the business, killing the very thing they started out loving, just for the bucks. Money, it's the worst thing we humans ever invented. Well, keep me posted. Oh, speaking of posted, where're these letters coming from?"

Henry held open the heavy fire doors separating the cafeteria from the bank of escalators. "I didn't see any return addresses on the top left corner of the envelopes," he said.

I slid under the arch of his arm and gave him a soft jab to the underbelly. "Very funny," I said. "You know what I mean. What were the postmarks?"

"One investigative story and you're asking about postmarks. Impressive. Gold, next thing you'll be asking to be moved out of lingerie."

Lingerie, the news side name for the features department.

"And if I'm really lucky," I said, "maybe the big boys in the glass office will let me play Carl Bernstein to your Bob Woodward. We're the right religions. Really, where were they postmarked?"

"The first from Greensboro, the others from various places around the state. He or she's probably from North Carolina, but you never know."

"No," I said. "I guess not. Maybe the wacko's got a thing against Tarheels too. Anyway, is there anything I can do to help?"

"Sure, maybe a new set of eyes would help. I have the cc list on my desk, come by and take a look or, better yet, I'll make you a copy. You'll probably recognize some of the names, tell me what you know about them. Thanks."

"Mone play-zeur," I said, intentionally massacring the French language. Henry was fluent in the subject after twelve years of instruction from Mme. Brooks of the New Haven Country Day School. I, on the other hand, took the subject in ninth grade at

Beeber Junior High School, a rough inner-city Philadelphia school where the teachers were more concerned about keeping the students alive than making sure we knew whether it was accent grahv or accent ageew.

"Remind me not to go to France with you, or tape your mouth shut," Henry said.

I laughed and put my arm around his waist, because that was all I could reach and I was reasonably sure he wouldn't sue me for sexual harassment. "Look," I said, "no hard feelings about me jumping on you before, okay?"

"It's forgotten," Henry said, and put his arm on my shoulder just as Kathy Powell, the pop-music critic, came down the escalator.

"Nattie, Henry . . . what's up, you two?" she said. I knew that smile on her face, it was her I-told-you-so smirk. Kathy and I were constantly going over the men options in the newsroom and Kathy was insistent that Henry should be a major one for me.

"I'd go after him myself if I weren't going out with Jim," she said.

"Henry and I were just planning a trip to France," I said as Kathy escalated past.

Her words trailed after her: "I told you so."

Henry gave me another puzzled look. "What was that all about?" Then it came to me, an updated major revelation about the sexes. The real difference between men and women isn't the Three Stooges—boys loved them, girls hated them. It's density.

"Nothing," I said.

We walked into the newsroom and Henry went his way—right in front—and I, mine; back to the catacombs of Features. Our department was stashed like yesterday's laundry in a faraway corner, out of sight and, much to Candace's fury, out of mind.

I sat down at my desk and before my rear hit the chair, Allison, the bridal editor and my new desk mate, swung the computer around to face me.

"Here, Nattie, I'll just move my stuff over to another desk. I can find a computer in Sports."

"Allison, calm down. Use the computer all you want. I've got some phone calls to make."

She swung it back around. Tentatively. File this under the be-careful-what-you-ask-the-gods-for category. Jeff, my old desk mate, had hogged the computer. I probably got to write on it six times in the two and a half years we shared one between our desks. Since Allison moved in, I had no excuse to wander around the newsroom looking for a spare terminal. I'd have given anything to be wandering the newsroom again, anything for Jeff to still be alive.

The phone rang, mercifully breaking my reverie.

"Are you coming or not?"

It was Rob. My trainer. Even when our series—"Murder on the A-Circuit"—cleared Rob of a murder-one charge, all he could manage to say to me was "When do you want to ride next?"

"I don't know," I said. "I've got a column to finish, a bunch of phone calls to make, then I've got to arrange with the photography depart—"

"I'll be in the ring at six. I have to be at Mrs. Pritchard's at seven to do her tree. That George Morris clinic is next week."

Click. I guess I'd be riding at six, if I wanted him to take my horse to the clinic, or anywhere else. God forbid Rob be late to Mrs. Pritchard's. Who would decorate her Christmas tree? As a Jew, I still hadn't gotten this whole Christmas-trees-by-Rob thing. Every year he spent the entire month of December running around like a crazy man from house to house, doing people's trees. I thought the whole point of the tree was gathering the family together, listening to Bing Crosby, joyously arranging gaudy orna-ments, and possibly even making mention of the man who inspired the entire event.

This put Hanukkah in a new light for me. As one who loves

flamboyance, I'd spent my whole childhood jealous of the Christian kids because they got trees and glittering glass baubles and tinsel and flashing lights, when all we got was the sober flame of a few candles and a story about perseverance. In retrospect, we made out pretty well: eight nights of presents, we didn't have to pay anyone to decorate the menorah, *and* my brother and I got to light the candles ourselves far before we were of the fire-handling age.

I called Mother and broke the news to her paralegal/best friend, Nora, a snappy lady who'd held my mother together after my stepfather died.

"Your mother's in court," Nora said. "But not to worry. You've got your job to do. If I have to drag her myself, I'll get her out of the house and make sure she comes to my house for Christmas Eve dinner. We've all cried enough. Now it's time to live."

Nora and my stepfather, David, had been best friends. She'd grieved as hard as any of us when he died.

While I was talking to Nora, another e-mail message flashed on my screen. I saw the name CANDACE at the end and didn't bother to read the beginning. What'd she want me to do next, a New Year's Day story about the poor, little, and highly photogenic puppies being gassed at the pound?

I called my Compassionate Friends contact, but there was no answer. I still had a stack of phone messages to return, mostly from readers who wanted to know what they should wear. My answer was the same to whatever outfit they'd concocted: "Just perfect." Even the mint-green leisure suit some woman's husband wanted to wear to his thirtieth high school reunion. My theory on fashion is simple: If you like it, wear it.

I had to e-mail Torkesquist about the shoot tomorrow, which meant I had to read Candace's missive first. TALK TO ME BEFORE YOU LEAVE. Not if I could help it.

I e-mailed Torkesquist and, just as I expected, he was in front of my face within minutes.

"Dead kids again? Kaaa-rist almighty. How 'bout if I just print up some of the old shots and you and me go riding? Come on, Wesley can use the exercise. I'll ride Hap."

"And what do I do for a story. Janet Cooke-it-up? Besides, I'm never sitting in one of your western saddles again. I couldn't close my legs for two weeks after the last time."

"That's just because you were fantasizing about how it would be with me, that's all. Come on, admit. You can't get me out of your mind."

Torkesquist was a fireplug of a guy. Short and wide. Bright yellow hair that looked like someone three sheets to the wind put a bowl over his head and started whacking away. Most of the rest of his face was covered by big, clear plastic glasses over ruddy pink skin. Minnesota born and bred, he talked with an accent so thick you could stand a stick in it. It sounded as if his words bypassed his mouth entirely and went right through his nose.

I knew Torkesquist had no interest in me that way. Though his genes got messed up somewhere down the line, he still had his ancestors' Viking taste in women. He liked them big and blond. The bigger and blonder the better.

"Yeah, Torkesquist, that's it. You're the man of my dreams. Let's get married on horseback and walk off into the sunset. Because that's about all your old nag, Wesley, can do."

"Come on now, be nice, you'll be old someday too."

Torkesquist and I made up the equestrian component of *The Commercial Appeal.* He had a place on the Charlotte side of Waxhaw, not far from where I kept my horse. A double-wide and fourteen acres of Carolina clay he called Tork's Turph. He shared his domain with two sweet old horses that followed him wherever he went, sometimes through his front door. And he also had Hap, a nasty brown Appaloosa who must have been abused as a child.

Nothing else could explain such a foul temperament except demonic possession.

Torkesquist found the horse at an auction, standing with his ears pinned back in the Chevalier pen, the leading supplier of horse meat to France and Canada. Who knows what Torkesquist saw in Hap besides a mean watch eye and a Roman nose. But he traded the meat man a photo shoot of his daughter's wedding for the ugly spotted horse.

I have to say, the horse could run. When Torkesquist and I went riding, we raced back to his house. By the time I got there, Hap was standing, his ears pinned back, in the pasture, the sweat marks already brushed from his back. And Torkesquist was nursing a sore arm from where the horse had bitten him.

I handed him the photo assignment. "Tomorrow at four, zoom in on the tears," I said. "It's for the next day's paper, so don't get lost on the way back."

In raw talent, Torkesquist was the best shooter at *The Appeal.* That was assuming he remembered to load his camera, had gas in his car, got to the assignment on time—or at all—and didn't open his mouth and start yakking his way into being thrown out of wherever he was. And that was assuming a lot.

"Torkesquist, keep a lid on it tomorrow, would you? These people are the walking wounded."

"What burr got under your saddle? 'Keep a lid on it.' Keep a lid on what? What have I ever done . . ." Torkesquist wadded the photo assignment into his pocket and stormed away.

If I'd wanted to continue down that path, I would have reminded him about the time he flashed the stump of his left ring finger under Barbara Bush's nose and told the first lady he got dismembered after his ex-wife bit it off during a fight. Then he elbowed the nation's grandmother and said, "Could've been worse, she could have gone lower." Or the time he pulled a horse needle from his pocket and asked the woman I was interviewing, a breast implant victim with leaky silicone, whether she wanted him to take care of the problem right there.

But I had other paths to walk down, namely my Sunday column, this week featuring the history of torture in lingerie.

"Underwire bras, corsets, and garter belts: the Marquis de Sade's take on what the well-undressed woman wears . . ."

Chapter 3

I finally wrapped up my column and looked around the room for a spare editor to mutilate my copy. *The Appeal* was top-heavy with midlevel editors who fancied themselves Writers.

Editing sessions at *The Appeal* aren't much different than going to the dentist, except you don't get Novocain. I found Jean, the most painless dentist around, a fiftyish woman who'd started at *The Appeal* thirty years ago as a copy kid. She had no pretensions of being a Writer, wasn't threatened by anyone who was one, and truly loved newspapers—the way they were when the big suits were the bad guys, not the owners.

Jean was smart about *The Appeal*, she knew which rules could be bent—and which ones couldn't. Alienation was an unbendable. She read my column, laughed at the right times, and apologetically excised the objectionable phrases, replacing them with euphemisms—"uncomfortable" instead of "excruciating" as in when the wire of an underwire bra escapes its nylon confines and bites into soft flesh.

She leaned back in her ergonomically correct chair and stretched. "You know as well as I how they are in the glass offices: 'Wouldn't want to alienate any of the undergarment companies . . .' "

We both laughed. That's *The Appeal*, all the news that's fit to please.

Jean sent my column along its merry way—first to Candace, then to Fred, who wanted to make sure I wasn't "burning any more bridges," and then to the back shop.

"See you tomorrow night," Jean said. "I'll bring the Kleenex."

Finally a stroke of luck. Jean would be my editor for the Compassionate Friends story. I'd been worried that I'd get stuck with Candace's squirrely little deputy, Ron Riley, a dangerously ambitious man short enough to limbo under the unofficial hiring height requirement laid down by our Napoleonic city editor. The problem with Riley's ambition was, he was just smart enough to cover up the fact he wasn't very smart, which put him on the fast track at *The Charlotte Commercial Appeal.* He was famous for undercutting reporters so he could look good to Candace and anyone else he could get to watch the Ron Riley show. As if that weren't annoying enough, before he edited your story, he'd take out his nail clippers, snip away, and then crunch on the crescent droppings like they were sunflower seeds. I didn't even want to think what he did with his toenails.

I was finished with fashion for the week—the only blessing in Candace's assignment—and almost out the door. Just a car ride away from the best part of the day: my horse, a sweet-tempered chestnut mare by the name of Brenda Starr. I had one more thing to do, try again to let Compassionate Friends know that Torkesquist and I would be there tomorrow. I called the woman who'd organized the Cabarrus County chapter five years ago. She'd lost her sixteen-year-old son in a car accident and was on her way to killing herself with booze when someone dragged her to a meeting. She said the group saved her life and now she wanted to save the lives of others like herself who couldn't find a way back. That way, she said, her son's death would have had a purpose.

I've found few heroes in my life. She's one of them.

I was sure there'd be no problem about another story. The first one had gotten the group close to $1,000 in contributions from moved readers—and writers. I'd sent them a check for $100.

Just as I was about to leave, another message popped on my screen. NATTIE, COULD YOU PLEASE STOP BY MY DESK ON YOUR WAY OUT TO PICK UP THAT LIST WE TALKED ABOUT EARLIER? HG

HENRY BE GOODE—BE THERE IN A FLASH, I messaged back. I shoved my notes in a drawer and locked it. I was new to the anal-compulsive approach, but it was part of my pre–New Year's resolution. I figured it would last another three days.

I swung the computer around to face Allison's desk. She was sitting in Sports with a foot-high stack of bridal announcements.

"It's all yours now," I said to her as I walked by.

"Are you sure? I don't mind sitting here."

"Allison, for God's sake, take charge of your life. You can use the computer now. You can *even* use it when I'm there. Stand up for yourself, do our sisters proud, you know, 'I am Woman, hear me roar' . . ."

"Oh, yeah, *Batman*, Michelle Pfeiffer."

I shook my head. Kids.

The problem with being a baby boomer is that after spending a lifetime as the official younger generation and being slapped with a moniker that never lets you to be anything but, it's hard to remember you're not anymore.

"Close," I said. "Run a computer search on Helen Reddy."

Henry had his ear glued to the telephone and his fingers tap-dancing across the keyboard. He glanced down at a couple of pieces of paper and without missing a beat, motioned my way with his head. "Thanks," he mouthed.

I scanned the list as I glided down the perpetually moving stairs. I knew the second one, B for Benson, Jim Benson. I competed against him, if that's what you call riding against someone who has no job, buckets of money to spend on horses, and a full-time live-in trainer. He was an heir of some sort who liked to call himself a cow-calf farmer. His idea of farming was to hire a full-time farm manager and pet the baby cows once a month. Mostly what he did was ride horses in the amateur division and ride them very well. A classic sham-ateur, he was a professional in everything but declaration. Him, I wouldn't have minded being

26

put out of action. That way I might finally win a blue ribbon at a Virginia show.

C, I knew or, rather, knew of. Who didn't? You'd have be dead not to have heard of Christopher Carey, the '90s answer to Charles Bronson. But what could a he-man Hollywood star have in common with a bunch of rich Billy Bobs? Henry'd have to do some creative record checking to find that connection.

I knew the next one, but didn't know how. D for Duncan, Outerbridge Duncan. I felt sorry for the poor guy, getting saddled with a last name like that for a first name. A case in point of some overzealous southern mama getting a little too carried away with this heritage bit. Surely he had an uncle John or Grandpa Joe he could've been named after. Outerbridge Duncan. I knew that name from somewhere, but where? With a name like that, who could forget it? Obviously, me.

My eyes slid down the alphabet, stopping here and there at familiar names. Some I recognized from the high society parties I'm forced to cover. A couple of others I knew along with Benson, from the horse show circuit. They were big-buck daddies who kept their kids supplied with a fresh set of $200,000 horses. Like M. M for Mr. Santee Mundell. He was an industrialist/entrepreneur of the zillionare kind. I don't know how he made his money, but he had plenty of it. His daughter, Topping Mundell, was an amateur rider, who, like Jim Benson, had no career other than cantering her expensive horses over fences. Her, I didn't care about being put out of horse show action. Unlike Benson, she had as much riding talent as a stick of wood. Even when Daddy paid $250,000 for a six-month lease of Rox-Dene, the winningest horse in hunter horse show history, she couldn't find the jumps. Not that that arrangement lasted long. Topping left out a stride and the horse ended up crashing through a big oxer fence. Everyone by the ring rushed to the horse, leaving Topping standing there alone, bewildered and broken. While Rox-Dene was being examined with a magnifying glass for injuries—she suffered "grass stains to the nose," according to published reports—Topping collapsed in pain from a broken shoulder. And that was it for Topping and Rox-Dene. The owners refused to let her ride the mare again and were more careful the next time they leased the horse, this time to a young woman from California who went on to become the youngest Olympian in equestrian history.

I was thinking about what it would be like to ride the horse of the century as my eyes continued scanning the list. The floors slipped by and I was still riding Rox-Dene when my eyes ratcheted on O, O for Osborne. John Knights Osborne, the man who broke my heart in eighteen pieces. My body may have been on the escalator, but my mind was in New Paltz, New York, at the Northern Lights restaurant, crying over corn chowder as John was saying good-bye. I never got to replay his explanation. Just before he got to the "didn't feel the tingle anymore" part, I was jolted back to Charlotte, back to *The Appeal,* and most definitely back to the escalator, which I'd hit the end of. Literally. My feet jammed into the bottom, sending me rearfirst onto the step. Of all days, this was the day I'd chosen to wear a pair of vintage jodhpurs, the kind with three extra yards of fabric for the balloon thighs. There was so much excess twill jutting out of my thighs, it was an easy grab for the side teeth of the escalator.

"Ahhhh," I started screaming, "I'm caught. Someone help or I'm gonna be Isadora Duncan here in a second."

The guard—we now, finally, had guards at *The Appeal*—luckily happened to be standing by the little red emergency button that seizes control of the escalator. He froze me in mid-bite before I had the first recorded case of escalator liposuction. My jodhpurs were hopelessly chewed up. I pulled hard, but was still caught. The guard came over with a pair of scissors and not nearly enough concern for my personal well-being. I'd almost been eaten by the escalator and all he cared about was getting the thing moving again. That was taking this team-player bit to extremes.

I grabbed the scissors, said a curt "Thank you," and surgically removed myself from the metal steps. I looked down at my pants, or what was left of them. Damn, sixty-five bucks down the drain. On the good side, however, this would give Candace and Fred one less article of my wardrobe to bitch about. They expect me to look like their idea of a fashion writer, which doesn't include old clothes, silly shoes, and Day-Glo socks.

I walked out with as much dignity as one can with a gaping hole in her pants. I hadn't thought about John for a long time, and I didn't much like dredging up all that pain. After my father left, I swore I'd never let a man inside my soul again. Four years later my mother married David. Big, boisterous David, who barreled into our lives, funny and warm and loving, and made us love him back. I started feeling the world might be a safe place. Then along came John, promising he'd never do anything to hurt me. Promises come and go, and so did John. I've felt that kind of hurt three times in my life—and that's three times too many. No more.

Damn, John had torn a hole in my heart and the escalator had torn a hole in my pants. What a day. And what was John Osborne doing on that list anyway? He was an artist. He was going to be the next Edward Hopper and I was going to topple a president or at least a senator. Now look at me, writing fashion columns about underwear. He couldn't possibly have strayed that far.

I forced him out of my mind and brought the list back into focus.

Twenty-five names in all—no Mr. X. I reread the letter. FIRST YOU COUGH, THEN YOU DIE . . . What makes you cough and die? Coal mining, asbestos, tobacco, cotton dust . . .

. . . YOU'RE GOING TO PAY. Pay what?

CHAPTER 4

"God, Nattie, Brenda was great tonight. You didn't miss a spot or pull up once. Poor Rob had nothing to yell at you about."

It was Gail, my best friend and the barn manager of February Farm, where we both kept our horses. Hers was a big, beautiful blood bay she called Allie, short for "All Dressed Up."

She was right. Brenda had been great. A regular jumping machine. We sailed over four courses of three-and-a-half-foot fences in sheer syncopation. I should only get along with a man—or an editor—as well.

When it went right with my horse, which it did frequently because she was a wonder horse, it made me feel like my insides were pressing up hard against my outsides. Bigger, fuller, more there. Better than any of the chemical highs I'd tried in my youth. Too bad it took me so many fried brain cells along the way to figure that one out.

I slid off Brenda and walked her to the wash stall. The wonders of southern living. Here it was, almost Christmas, and I could hose down my horse's back without turning her into a Popsicle.

"What can I say, Gail? I've been blessed by the equine gods with a miracle. And her name is Brenda Starr."

"Stop it, stop it, you're making me sick. I can't stand the, what do you call it, 'schmootz'?"

They didn't come any more shiksa than Gail—tall, flat butt, straight nose, thin thighs, big boobs, long yellow hair—but hanging around me, she was becoming an honorary Jew and quickly approaching my command of Yiddish.

"It's schmaltz. Schmaltz, as in 'schmear me hunk of rye with schmaltz.' Speaking of, want to go to Morrison's for dinner? We can do the southern version of rye and schmaltz: Parker House rolls and oleo."

"Can't. Got a meeting tonight."

"I thought that was last night?"

"It was. And probably tomorrow night too. Holidays make me want to drink."

I put my arm around her. "Gail, I don't want to get schmaltzy, but if it means anything, I'm proud of you. I know how rough a go it's been."

"It could have always been worse, Nat. You know, with Allie. If it weren't for you, he wouldn't be here, and if something happened to him . . ."

I hugged her hard and I was glad I was a woman. I can't imagine two men doing the same, unless, of course, they were horse trainers.

"Hey," Gail said, "did Rob tell you his new joke?"

"Get real," I said. "Rob barely talks to me. What is it?"

"What does a gay man bring on the second date?"

"I give," I said.

"*Second* date?"

Poor Rob was right. At least he could still laugh about it. Since he broke up with his live-in, Wally, the now thankfully dead murder-for-hire horse trainer, Rob had been through a slew of first-onlys. Not that he shared that information with me, but on the show circuit gossip flies faster than a coked-up racehorse.

Gail handed me a sweat scrape and I ran it across Brenda's back, pulling off the excess water. It ran off clear.

"Good thing she's clean," Gail said. "You better keep her that way until your big day with George."

She was talking about the riding clinic I'd signed up—and paid a month's wage—for. But how often do you get a chance to study under the person who literally wrote the book on your passion, in my case, showing horses in the hunter divisions? I'd eagerly emptied the balance of my savings account to George Morris so he could scream and humiliate me for a solid four hours.

Gail pointed to a splotch of dried-up dirt I'd missed on Brenda's leg.

"Take her like that," Gail said, "and you'll be out on your ear in five minutes. I heard he threw a rider out because her horse had a manure stain on its butt, screaming all the way across the ring, 'That *is* a gray horse underneath that filth, isn't it? When you learn how to clean a horse, you can ride one with me. This isn't a sport for housewives.' The woman never came back. With your horsemanship, Nats, you're lucky Brenda's the same color as this nasty Carolina clay. You *are* still going to the clinic, aren't you?"

"Wouldn't miss it for my life," I said. "I could use a little more torture before the show season gears up. Having Rob scream at me once a week isn't enough. I'm like bread when it comes to riding instruction—I need to be punched back every few hours. What the hell, I can take it. Everyone who's survived his clinics says they can ride a zillion times better by the time they finish."

"Just be sure to take notes so you can tell me everything."

"I'll let you know about every last scream," I said.

I wiped down Brenda's freshly washed back and tucked her in bed for the night with three flakes of alfalfa that smelled so sweet, it made me want to be a horse.

"Try not to get so worked up about things tomorrow, Nat," Gail said to me as we headed out to my car.

Gail had nursed me through my stepfather's death and watched me fall apart after the first Compassionate Friends story.

"That's like telling me to try not to have red hair."

We laughed and I left, into the dark night. I stood outside for a few seconds and breathed deeply. After twenty years of owning horses, the smell of a stable still stopped me in my tracks and filled me with happiness. Tonight it was particularly intoxicating. Between the new load of hay and the soggy fields heavy with freshly spread manure and pine shavings, the thick Carolina sky around me was swelled riper than the Guess girl. If air molecules had seams, they'd have been bursting tonight. I closed my eyes and saw it: crests of deep mahogany, tipped in cream and hazel, undulating slow and easy. I've been seeing smells all my life. It wasn't until college, when my best friend was tripping on acid and became amazed that she could see the smell of her Shalimar, before I realized not everyone could do the same—without chemical enhancement.

I took another breath for the road and headed off. The ride home was uneventful, though I did think about stopping at my friend Tony-the-cop's house. I was starting to feel a bit blue; holidays, my stepfather, Compassionate Friends, it all made me sad. Tony, with his slow drawl and obtuse colloquialisms, always made me smile. The fact that I was friends—very good friends—with a cop still made me laugh at myself. Twenty years ago, when my entire wardrobe consisted of Indian print bedspreads and fringed leather vests, anyone with a blue uniform and a gun was the Enemy. Tony was far from the enemy—hell, we'd almost consummated our friendship, in the biblical sense. Had it not been for Sharon, his on-again off-again wife who couldn't decide if she wanted to be married, we might have. But truth be told, I'd just as soon have Tony as a good friend with none of the complications sex brings into the picture, even if that picture does include the best butt this side of Lake Norman.

I wasn't sure what Sharon's thinking was this week, and I didn't want to walk into the middle of Lucy and Ricky reuniting, so I turned right instead of left on Route 16. I arrived home to an apoplectic answering machine. It was sputtering and beeping at the same time. Playing back my messages was a joke. But it didn't matter because I recognized the bits and pieces of voice—Mother. Then, just as I was about to toss the worthless mass of fried circuitry in the trash, I heard a voice I didn't know. It was a woman's. Either she was crying or the answering machine was adding sound effects along with cutting and editing where it pleased. I could barely piece together her words. "Is this . . . tee gold? This is . . . nee . . . shmore . . . anes . . . other, you rememb—miss . . . ticut? She's . . . ead . . . she . . . was murdered . . . and I . . . get any . . . nsers from anyone. Help me. . . ."

CHAPTER 5

The garbled message bothered me from the moment I woke up, which was good. That way, I didn't have to think about my upcoming assignment. I called my voice mail at work, hoping the mystery woman might have checked in there.

She hadn't.

I had a message from Henry saying he was sorry he missed my call last night and what I'd had to say about the names on the list was very interesting. I'd left out the broken-my-heart part about John Osborne, leaving it at an old artist friend from Upstate New York.

The other message was from Candace, about why she'd wanted to talk to me before I left, which I didn't, because she was in one of her many meetings. Her sister, Diane, was taking part of her psychiatry residency in Charlotte and wanted me to talk to her about where to board a horse. Candace had a sibling? I didn't know that model came in a series.

I had to call Candace anyway. A four P.M. assignment meant I wouldn't get home till after the last edition went to press, around midnight. To me, that meant the morning off. Who knew what it meant to Candace. Rather than find out, I waited till I knew she and her short shadow, Ron Riley, were firmly entrenched in their daily suck-up exercise: the ten A.M. budget meeting for the next day's paper, where all mid-level editors try to impress Fred with their reporters' productivity and then jockey for power by lobbying for above-the-fold page-one play for their stories. I left a message on Candace's voice mail telling her I'd be happy to talk to her sister and that I'd be at the office after the Compassionate Friends meeting. Then I made a beeline for the door.

The air had cooled some from yesterday. But it was still warm enough that I didn't need to cushion myself against assault with the feathers from a gaggle of unfortunate geese. All those years I spent shivering. Silly me.

I headed south on Providence Road and went into mental cruise control. After three years of the same drive, day in and day out, you know the curves of the road like the curves of your body, which, unfortunately, were both changing. Development was seeping south—on me and in Charlotte. Ten years ago, size twenty-six riding britches and I were on speaking terms. And from what I'd heard about the Queen City, ten years ago the southern stretch of Providence Road was flanked by blankets of green. These days, it's cheek to jowl redbrick colonials and I'm lucky to squeeze into size twenty-eight britches. Time for aggressive development zoning—for both of us.

At least I didn't have to deal with rush hour traffic. At ten in the morning, it was just me and the moms on their Harris Teeter runs. I wished them all well, and hoped I wouldn't be seeing any of them at the meeting tonight. Before I knew it, I was driving down the crunchy gravel road to February Farm. Gail and Allie were in the ring.

"I'm just working on my lead changes until you're ready to go on trail," she called to me.

"I'll be right there," I called back. And I was. I grabbed my tack and saddled up Brenda in what might have been a new record even for me, the queen of cutting corners. Thank goodness Rob wasn't around to see my shoddy horsemanship. But Brenda was clean enough and I was ready for a trail ride, ready to stop feeling blue. Nothing would make that happen faster than a spin in the woods.

I climbed on and felt myself sink into her and it felt good, like I'd come home. I was ready for the magic.

I met Gail by the ring and we headed to the green wall in front of us, both of us silent. I looked up; it was one of those giggly skies filled with boisterous puffs of white, the kind where you feel like you could cloud-hop your way to China. Gail was smiling and so was I. Not a word passed between us, but I knew what she was thinking and I'm sure it was likewise. What else can you think when you're about to ride out into a day so perfect you know heaven can't be any better? Nothing else, but glory be.

I offered a silent prayer of thanks to whoever was responsible for such splendor.

We finally did start talking. I unloaded about Candace, and Gail about her alcoholic mother who's been bothering her again with drunken calls at three in the morning. Her tales put my childhood wounds in perspective. At least I never had to drag my mother to her bed or clean up her vomit or spring her from the drunk tank. My mother's great parental sin was youth—she'd been too damn young to have me and my brother, Larry, and never cottoned to the idea of motherhood. While all my friends' mothers were helping them with homework, cooking big meals, and keeping the house clean, my mother was talking on the phone to her girlfriends, going on dates, and keeping the books at a shoe factory to keep us fed, or her idea of fed, which was either overcooked steak or five bucks for me and Larry to walk to Barson's on Haverford Avenue for tuna fish sandwiches and cherry Cokes. The steaks were horrible, but Barson's had the sweetest fountain drinks in all of Philadelphia. Compared to Gail, I didn't have it that bad as a kid.

Next, we moved on to the topic of men. I didn't mention anything about John, because I didn't want to think about him. There's some hurt even horse magic can't help. Since neither of us had any beaus at the moment, it didn't take long to exhaust the subject. I'd broken up with my television reporter talking head months ago and hadn't found a replacement—or particularly wanted one. Up until then I'd had a steady and quick stream of love interests, so I was just as happy spending some time by myself. Gail, on the other hand, had had only one date in the last four years. And it was a fix-up of my doing with my old desk mate Jeff, the lothario loud-talking but lovable TV critic. She'd fallen for him hard. Unfortunately, he not for her. After their first tumble in the sack, she was calling the moving vans to bring her stuff over and he was calling me to get her out of there. That's what sent her over the alcoholic edge into a three-day binge. Unlike her mother, she had some reservoir of self-preservation and dragged herself to a dry-out clinic.

After that fiasco, I swore I'd never fix her, or anyone else, up again, even if it did go against my genetic structure. But listening to her talk and hearing the loneliness in her voice, I was back to my old tricks, scanning my mind for available and, this time, suitable men.

"You know, Gail," I started, "there's this new business reporter. He's got a great—"

Gail obviously didn't want to hear about his great anything. She sliced me off mid-sentence.

"Don't say another word, Gold-ilocks, or I won't feed your horse tonight."

I made a peace sign and shut up.

A few minutes later we were back to chattering. This time about something we could talk about for hours, centuries maybe. Horses, horse show gossip, and more horses. Before we knew it, we were back at the barn.

"Gail," I said. "A second ago we were heading out and now we're back. I don't know, maybe we should take up skeet shooting, make our lives last longer."

Gail hopped off Allie. "Skeet shooting? What the hell are you talking about, Nattie? You hate guns. Why would you want to do that?"

I slid off Brenda's back reluctantly. "What were you doing in the sixties? Sleeping? Didn't you read *Catch-22*? The guy in the book, Yossarian, has this theory that life goes slower when you're bored, and there's nothing more boring than skeet shooting. . . ."

"Yeah," she said, "then he should've tried cleaning stalls. I've got a barnful of them waiting. I guess that'd be a three-year afternoon ahead of me by his way of thinking. Thanks just the same, I'd rather live fast and happy."

"Me too," I said. And happy I was. After an hour in the forest on top of the best horse in the world, I was ready to face anything.

Even Candace.

Or so I thought.

CHAPTER 6

I was a bowl of feel-good jelly by the time I oozed myself home. Like a fool, I had to go and ruin the moment as soon as I got there by checking my voice mail at work. This electronic communication stuff is as addictive to me as horses and almost as expensive. Any more monthly hours on America Online and I expect they'll be changing the service's name to Nattie Online.

I punched in my retrieval code—217, even I couldn't forget that one, it's the month and day of my birth. I recognized the voice instantly and should've fast-forwarded through her, but my marginal respect for authority and continued need for a paycheck wouldn't let me.

"Nattie, next time you take a morning off, you better clear it with me. FIRST. I needed you to do a phoner with podiatrists for a local insert about laser bunionectomies. I had to ask Allison to do it and then walk her through every step of the way. I don't have time for this. Just who do you think you are anyway, Madeleine Blais? Win a Pulitzer, then make your own schedule. Got it? And another thing . . ."

Blah, blah, blah . . . I should've just gone to the meeting and let my voice mail messages talk to each other. But this mystery crier was eating at me. She still hadn't called back. All I got was Candace, ranting. Her MBA power voice made my hand twitch. I felt like Dr. Strangelove, holding down one hand with the other so I wouldn't reach out for the telephone and tell her exactly who I thought I was. Mercifully, the little man in my head screaming "Don't shoot yourself in the foot *again*, sister" won this battle. Instead of calling, I ate a piece of herring.

Granted, I'm no Maddy Blais, the best in the business who won the first Pulitzer for feature writing, but I *was* doing Candace's cockamamie story on Christmas Eve when other people were happily eating turkey with their families. Or was it ham?

Speaking of which, that's what they had at the Compassionate Friends meeting. A Carolina baked ham with a thick crust of crinkly brown sugar and pouffy biscuits by Bojangles. They could have saved themselves the money. No one was eating except Torkesquist, who motioned me over to his post by the food table.

"Nattie, got any Baggies on you?" he said between and during bites. "They said I could take what's left of the food. Great, huh? What's a matter anyway? Don't these people eat? Maybe they're all of your persuasion."

"Torkesquist, I was raised on bacon. These people aren't eating because they're crying. Look around, you idiot. They've got other things on their minds besides free ham."

There were about thirty-five people gathered in the room, an upstairs dormer office at the Cabarrus Savings and Loan. They were sitting on chairs, the stackable kind hotels use for weddings and dental hygienist conventions. These chairs were pressed up against the walls, like it was a waiting room. Which in a way it was. A few people were talking to others, but mostly they were just sitting there, waiting. Waiting for something that could never happen.

I spotted Christine Motley, the woman who'd lost her sixteen-year-old son and then started this chapter. She saw me and smiled. I did a double take and my heart jumped. Christine was standing next to a man who was wearing a dark brown corduroy sport jacket, tan turtleneck, and had a pipe gripped between his teeth. For a second I thought it was my stepfather, David.

Try not to get so worked up. Any more worked up and I'd be skittering across the teal tin roof.

Christine excused herself from the man and walked over to me. "Nattie, it's always a pleasure. Thank you for coming. I made an announcement before you got here that you'd be writing a story for *The Appeal.* I hope that helps."

"Thank you, Christine." I hugged her and asked how she was doing, wishing I could right the world's wrongs. I'd have started with her son, Landon.

"Nattie, what can I say? It's one day at a time. One hour at a time, one minute at a time. But guess what? Molly has discovered boys in a big way. . . ."

Molly was her younger child, a startlingly mature girl who'd called 911 on more than one occasion to come get her mother, drunken and dying after swallowing fistfuls of sleeping pills. The girl had been at the first meeting I covered, gripping on to her mother, afraid to let go. She'd told me, "The hardest part about losing a brother is that you lose your whole family too."

"Well, give her a big kiss and tell her I've discovered boys in a big way too and I'd be more than happy to share my tips with her."

Christine smiled again and it was good to see.

"Come on, I'd like to introduce you to some of the new members before we start."

She took my hand and led me to a clump of people near the door. Three women and two men. Introductions were made. Reserved chitchat followed. The balmy weather, expansion on Lake Norman, the congressional race. I was just about to pull out my reporter's notebook and start asking real questions, when I felt a tap on my shoulder.

"Miss Gold?"

I turned around and looked into the face of an older woman, sixty-five or seventy. I knew her, I just couldn't remember how I knew her. The problem with moving around so much is that when I run into people I've met before, I can't remember from which before. I searched her face for a clue.

"Did you get my message?"

"Message?" I said.

"On your answering machine."

It took a second to register. I was so consumed with the task at hand—covering this meeting—that I'd forgotten about my dysfunctional answering machine and the mystery message.

"That was you?" I said. She nodded and I forced my brain into hyperscan, feverishly trying to place her face. Nothing came up.

I apologized, explaining that my machine was kaput and died during her message.

"I don't know if you remember me."

I apologized again.

"Well, it was a long time ago. Ten years, be eleven this week. Atlantic City, the Miss America Pageant? I'm Reenie Ashmore, Josane's mother? I know I don't look much like I did then. . . ."

Much like, how about anything like? I flashed on a face that didn't match the woman standing in front of me. I remembered joking with that Mrs. Ashmore that I couldn't tell who was running for the crown, her or her daughter. Sure I remembered her, her daughter—and the story I'd met them on. How could I forget? I was working general assignment on a small daily in Upstate New York. They barely had the budget for gas money to town council meetings, let alone a trip to Atlantic City.

I paid my own way down because I knew there was a big story about to happen. I just didn't know how big. That was the year of the first black Miss America: Vanessa Williams. The pop star, the Broadway star, the TV star Vanessa Williams, who a lifetime ago was forced to give back her tiara after some raunchy photos of her surfaced.

I'd gone down to Atlantic City four days before the big night. My editors gave me the time off if I agreed to flood the paper with stories, sidebars, quotes, you name it. Which I did. One of the stories was about Josane.

"Miss Connecticut? Right?"

The old woman nodded. I'd met Josane in the media briefing room, where reporters get to ask contestants questions about their chosen platforms. Josane's was handicapped children (for or against?), pretty standard for a beauty queen, but it wasn't her canned platform that intrigued me. It was her drawl.

"Miss Connecticut, how'd you get that southern accent?" I'd asked. The pageant chaperones shot me a poisonous look. Josane was smooth as her Vaselined legs.

"Well, I'm from *southern* Connecticut," she'd said without breaking her smile. Everyone laughed, including me.

I may have been just out of the journalistic gate back then, but I still knew a good story when it hit me in the face. I tracked her down after the press conference. Seeing as the Misses never went anywhere without their personal chaperones, I had to wedge myself between a formidable battle-ax of a woman and the towering Josane. Just as the official chaperone/bouncer was about to do her bouncing, Josane put her arm on my shoulder and walked me to an empty corner of the room, the chaperone following behind.

"Quit your worrying now, Miz Butelle, this reporter means me no harm."

Either Josane was especially naive to the ways of the media or the best chess player this side of Moscow.

My vote was on the latter. She had me eating and writing out of her hand by the time she was finished. Yes, she was from the South—a small mill town in North Carolina—and yes, she'd moved to Connecticut recently. Why? For a job, of course. Which was exactly the way I reported it.

My story was accurate. The problem was, it wasn't the truth. Accurate but not the truth, the bane of a journalist's existence. We search for truth, but ultimately can produce only accuracy. It took me ten years to figure that one out.

I was accurate when I wrote that a job brought Josane Ashmore to Connecticut. And I was accurate when I wrote that she took a job with a Connecticut cosmetic company. But truth was, which I learned days later, that Josane Ashmore moved to Connecticut for a different job—the job of Miss Connecticut.

Since her first crown, Little Miss Baby Cannon Mills, Josane had devoted her life to the penultimate tiara—Miss America's. She'd tried four years in a row for her homestate crown, Miss North Carolina. But in the South, pageants are the girl version of Little League. The best she ever did was second runner-up. She was starting to age out of the beauty business and knew she had only one last shot—and she didn't want to take aim in a competitive market. Connecticut is a small state with small pageants. A pro like her blew away what little competition there was.

Of course, my story said none of that. Mine was your basic puff piece, southern girl moves north, calls her worried mother every night, has her car radio stolen, but realizes her rhinestone dreams. I wasn't angry at Josane. She'd played the game well. I was annoyed at myself for being taken in so easily. My problem as a journalist was—and still is—I want to believe people tell the truth. That's why early in my career I moved over from the hard side of news to the soft side, Features. Also, having a disgruntled telephone employee who hated a story I'd written threaten to throw lye in my face made the career choice an easy one.

As part of the pageant package for my paper, I did a story on the contestants' parents. What I remembered most about Reenie Ashmore was how she and her daughter looked like a matched set of Valkyries. That, and her determination. She put a second mortgage on her house to buy Josane the obligatory body-grabbing bugle-beaded gowns custom-made by the preeminent designers in the beauty pageant business: a couple of guys from Spartanburg, South Carolina, who also made dresses for drag queens.

"How is Josane?" I asked. The words came out just as I remembered where I was.

Mrs. Ashmore's eyes got heavy with tears and I knew what was about to come next.

"I lost Josane. Up to Virginia, where she was living. I read your story in the paper about this group and I kept meaning to come. But I couldn't make myself. It's coming on four years since Josane . . . It got me to thinking and I called Mrs. Motley, asking when the next meeting was. She told me about this one and said you'd be here again, writing another story. That's why I came, I wanted to talk to you."

I was about to tell her, if there was anything I could do, just ask. But Christine Motley walked up, put her hand on Mrs. Ashmore's shoulder.

"Reenie, we've got to start now. The bank wants the janitors to be able to clean up early tonight because it's Christmas Eve. Would you mind taking a seat?"

I looked at Josane's mother and all the other mothers and fathers in the room. I hoped like hell there was a plan I'd know about someday, something that explained all this suffering.

"Mrs. Ashmore, we'll talk afterward. Okay?" I sat down and Mrs. Ashmore sat next to me.

Christine Motley walked to the center of the room. She was of average height, which to me is tall, and on the slim side. Her hair was a deep dark brown, the color of old but well-kept riding boots. She wore it short, cropped in a boyish cut that skimmed her face. It was a face with good strong bones that looked like they could weather the worst of storms.

She was approaching that used-to-be age. But there was nothing used-to-be about her. She'd borne two children and buried one. Then the demons tried to take hold. She'd stared down the devil and won, and you could see the triumph in her walk. The death slump was gone, in its stead, the wary confidence of a warrior. Straight back, muscles taught, ready for another go-round with the enemy. Of which there had been plenty.

And Christine Motley's face bore the scars. There were small hollows beneath her cheekbones and lines creased at the corners of her eyes and continued halfway up her temples. On anyone else they'd be called crow's-feet. On Christine they looked like the sun's rays, or battle cries. And they made her face seem even more like an intricately forged mask of an ancient Mayan goddess.

Maybe a man wouldn't see her this way, and it'd be easy to say that's the problem with men, but I thought she was beautiful.

She welcomed everyone, made a few business announcements—next meeting, items for the newsletter, a psychologist offering free services—and then asked, "Who'd like to start?"

For the next couple hours, mothers and fathers took turns talking about the children they'd buried. One little boy was crushed when he climbed in a ditch that caved in. Several car accidents. Leukemia, cancer, cystic fibrosis. And one suicide.

I took notes and smeared away my tears with the back of my hand. Torkesquist was on his best behavior and, I have to say, as unobtrusive as a two-hundred-pound Swede with three motor-driven cameras could be.

Reenie Ashmore didn't say a word. According to Christine, some people never talk at the meetings. Just coming, she said, is a step to living again.

I looked at the clock. Six-twenty. I was ten minutes past first edition deadline. Candace wanted the story for the second edition. If I didn't head back to the office now, I'd never make it. I scribbled a note to Mrs. Ashmore: *I've got to write this story for tomorrow's paper. I'd be happy to talk to you another time.*

I placed the paper on her lap and ducked out of the room with

47

Torkesquist behind me. Just as I was about to get into my car, I saw Mrs. Ashmore rushing toward me.

"Nattie, I know you're in a hurry, just a second. Here's my number, could you call me tonight after you finish your story? Please."

"It might be late," I said.

"Not to me. I don't know what's late or what's early anymore."

I told her I'd call, and got in my car. She stood there looking so sad I couldn't pull away.

"Mrs. Ashmore, is there anything I can help you with now?"

"I think my daughter was murdered."

CHAPTER 7

It's hard to leave someone who tells you her daughter's been murdered. But I had no choice. I promised her I'd call the second I finished. Torkesquist and I raced back to the office, he to the darkroom, me to my desk. I closed my eyes and thought of the first thing that came to my mind. The little boy in the ditch and his mother's quiet cries. "No one calls me Stevie's mom anymore." That was my lead and the story wrote itself after that.

Some reporters struggle over leads. They hadn't the good fortune of working with my old editor, Stuart Rimowitz. He told me early on, after he'd seen me agonizing over a lead on an infertility story: "Quit sweating it, kid. Close your notepad, now tell me what sticks out in your mind about the story. There's your lead. Go with it, quit fighting it."

It always worked.

I sent my story to Jean, she cleaned up the typos, asked me a few questions, handed me a tissue, took a few for herself, and sent it to the back shop.

"I hope this satisfies Candace once and for all," Jean said. "I can't take another one of these dead-kid stories. They keep me up at night, worrying that it could be me. Then I have to go into Nellie's room every hour to make sure she's alive. She's seventeen, a little old to be holding a mirror under her nose so I can see the glass fog up."

Nellie was her daughter, who'd started running copy in the newsroom a few months ago. Like mother, like daughter.

"Makes me not want to have kids," I said. "Why put yourself out on the line just to get crushed?"

Jean looked at me and said, "Want the *New York Times* answer or the *USA Today* answer?"

I could tell she was feeling philosophical, and this was as good a time as any to philosophize. The Compassionate Friends story had put us both in sober moods.

"We've got nothing to do until the art comes out," I said. "Let's go with the old gray lady. Pontificate away."

She smiled, a slow, heavy smile like she was just warming up. "Have you noticed the run of miracle stories coming across the wires? Candace had me replace a wire story on soda pop for dogs we were going to run and plug it with a girl-grows-leg story the day after Billy Graham spent twelve inches talking about the glory of the miraculous. Then she wanted the damn thing localized, so she had Allison call all the ministers, priests, and rabbis in our, quote, new penetration areas, unquote, looking for a local miracle. The closest that poor kid came was a water stain on the outside of a Circle K store that the midnight-to-eight worker claims turns into the Virgin Mary crying."

We both laughed. "Let me guess," I said. "Candace called Photo and made them send a shooter to camp out in back of the Circle K?"

"She tried," Jean said. "Photo conveniently didn't have anyone available. So we ran the story with file art of the Virgin Mary. Everyone's looking for a certifiable miracle. They want concrete evidence, documentable stigmata, analyses of the water at Lourdes. They want hard data, scientific proof. If that's what they want, all they have to do is go to a labor and delivery room and watch a new, separate human being emerge from another human being. That's a documentable miracle. Have a baby, Nat, you'll understand."

Jean usually wore a pretty calm expression on her face and

wasn't one to force her opinions on anyone. Unless it came to motherhood. I'd seen this same look flash across other mothers; even the most dispassionate people ended up looking like Elmer Gantry when it came to talking about Junior.

"I hope that understanding doesn't come anytime too soon," I said. "The only miracle I'm looking for these days is that Candace finds herself a heart."

Jean laughed. "Some things are impervious to the miraculous. I wouldn't wait on that one."

"Speaking of waiting, need me for anything else?"

She nodded. "How about some help on the cutlines? Could you stick around until Torkesquist comes out with the art?"

"I'll be here, got a phone call to make."

I dug out Mrs. Ashmore's telephone number and dialed. She picked it up in one ring.

"Nattie?"

"Sorry I couldn't talk earlier. I've got a piranha for an editor. Tell me about Josane."

"It's a long story and I'm wanting to show you some things. Is there any way you could come by my house? Tomorrow?"

"On Christmas?"

"Christmas? Lord, you're right. I forgot. The next day'd be fine. That's the twenty-sixth, right? Just not the day after, that's the anniversary of Josane, you know, and I'm going to spend the day with her. 'Sides, I'm sure you're wanting to be with your family. . . ."

"Where do you live?"

"Not four miles off I-85, just outside Kannapolis."

That was directly on the way to Greensboro. If Reenie Ashmore wasn't gathering around a tree, I didn't see any reason why I couldn't stop at her house on the way to Mother's.

"I can do it tomorrow. Is ten too early?"

"Like I said, early, late, it makes no never mind to me."

She gave me directions and I told her to take care.

"Take care of what? Nothing left to take care of."

I slipped the phone into the cradle. Cradles, babies, death, go figure it. Is someone up there playing Monopoly with our lives? *You landed on Park Place, two hotels; that'll be three sons, two daughters and a stepfather. . . .*

"Nattie, come look at these pictures. Torkesquist's outdone himself."

It was Jean, calling me over to her desk. In front of her were a stack of eight-by-tens, close-ups of the parents. I don't know how Torkesquist did it, but each one looked as if he'd taken a picture straight into their haunted souls.

I helped her with cutlines and then called it a day. Thank God.

CHAPTER 8

My stomach was complaining and I remembered I'd for-gotten to eat. I didn't have much at home, but what I had would have to do. I wasn't about to go solo to a restaurant on Christmas Eve. And I refused to do the fast-food thing. Despite feelings of abandonment, I am still my father's daughter and he's a registered new age flake/vegetarian/Fit-for-Lifer/food activist.

I made do with tomato soup and a stack of saltines. I shouldn't have even eaten that since I was heading to dreamland and dream-land for me is usually pretty weird. When I add a full stomach to the equation, I'm dancing in Fellini country—in my worst underwear.

I thought about reading; I had Alice Hoffman's new book in paperback and I'd been waiting a year for that. She's the queen of American magical realism and I am her most faithful subject. But I was just too damn spent.

Sure as the red in Candace's closet, I had a whopper of a dream. I saw Josane Ashmore, bugle-beaded from head to toe, shimmering like a hidden pond on a late August afternoon. She was riding a big chestnut horse with a blaze down its nose and waving to me in the beauty-queen way, like she was atop a Cadillac convertible in a ticker tape parade. Then Nana Greenburg came into the picture, the grandmother of my best friend in sixth grade. Dead about twenty-five years. She's the one who told me I had something extra from God besides my red hair, something that made me know things I had no way of knowing.

"Nana," I said in my dream. "Nana, I'm over here. My hair's still red, see?"

She was waving at me too, that same beauty-queen wave, which looked a bit odd coming from an eighty-year-old Litvak babushka. She was waving and smiling and singing. The words were in a strange language and I listened closer. Suddenly I could understand Polish or Hungarian or whatever language she was singing and I heard her thick Slavic words telling of Mother Mary coming to her.

I couldn't figure out why an old Jewish woman was singing a Beatles song about the Virgin Mary, but I started singing along with her and together we sang the refrain, "There will be an answer, let it be, let it be." Just as we were about to get to the next verse, a chorus of white-robed redheads entered. They were carrying placards painted in blood and chanting, "First you cough and then you die. Prepare to pay."

Being that a horse will spook at its own shadow, Josane's chestnut just about imploded and exploded at the same time when it saw the white-robers and their waving signs. The big horse reared straight up and Josane plummeted straight down. Right when Josane's butt slammed against the horse's butt, something very peculiar happened—and it's the reason I hate to go to sleep sometimes—Josane wasn't Josane anymore. She was me. And I was catapulting backward. As I tumbled, I saw my old boyfriend, John Osborne. He was sitting at an easel, drawing cartoons.

I willed my eyes open before my head splattered on the road. It's not true what they say about dreams, that if you die in a dream, you die for real. A while back, before I learned dream management, an evil thug named Howie pressed a gun to my head and, much to my chagrin, pulled the trigger. The bullet exploded and everything went black. Then it was as if I were watching a Disney movie, the kind that opens with a book written in fancy calligraphy with lots of trills and loops, and has voice-over narrating the words. My voice-over, a deep baritone a little too chipper for the occasion, was saying, "And Nattie died on a cold winter day. . . ."

It was too weird the first time it happened and I sure as hell wasn't going to sleep through a rerun. I looked at the clock. Four-thirty. Enough with these strange dreams. Why couldn't I spend my sleep time on the beach, or, even better, my horse?

I fell back asleep and, thankfully, remembered nothing else until my phone started ringing. I grabbed it and pressed it to my ear.

"Nattie, it's your mother."

I grumbled something into the phone.

"Are you all right?"

"A strange dream," I said. If anyone knew about my dreams, it was my mother. She'd spent many a night wrapping her arms around me, rocking me, cajoling me, trying to shake me loose from whatever terror had taken over. Till this day she swears the dreams started when my father left. What I didn't know until years after it happened is that she told him to leave.

Whatever the cause, I've learned to exorcise the nightmares for the most part. A psychologist friend taught me the trick: If someone, or thing, was chasing me, confront him and tell him to get lost, that it was my dream and I was in charge. Hokey, maybe, but it works. Getting rid of demons and big, bad men named Howie is one thing; nothing can control my overactive imagination. My dreams are still wildly surreal.

"Look, I don't want you driving here if you're tired. I've got enough to worry about. I can't take—"

"Mom, Mom, calm down. I just woke up. Don't you sound a little foggy when you first wake up? I'll be fine. I'm stopping at this lady's house first, so I probably won't be there until two or three."

"Drive carefully, okay?"

"No, I'm going to drive like a maniac and get myself killed just to see how much stress you can take. Of course I'm going to drive carefully. Stop worrying. I'll see you this afternoon. Oh, yeah, Merry Christmas."

"Nattie, we're Jewish."

"So was Jesus," I said, and hung up. I think I even heard a small laugh from her end.

After David died, I worried I'd never be able to really let loose and laugh again. It came back slowly for me. For my mother, that was another matter.

I got dressed and found my mother's Hanukkah presents, which I always give her on Christmas. I'd splurged and blown a small fortune—for me that's $125—on the first: a half-year membership to the health club near her house. She'd become a hermit in the last six months and I had to do something to get her out of the house on weekends. I figured it was worth the 125 bucks to dislodge her from her bed and the remote control. The second was a book of lawyer jokes. I hoped it would put a smile on her face, but judging by the jokes, that was questionable: What do you do when you see a lawyer on a beach, buried up to his neck in sand? Find more sand. Hardee-har.

Outside it was another one of those not-too-crisp Carolina winter days that made me glad to be a Tarheel transplant. My idea of heaven is wearing a T-shirt in December. And today was heavenly.

I opened my windows wide and headed my Rabbit north, straight up I-85, with Harry Chapin crooning at full blast. Twenty-seven cars with red and green wreaths tied to their grilles and thirty minutes later, Kannapolis was coming my way. I exited toward the City of Looms. That's what Kannapolis supposedly means in Greek. But if you ask me, I think it was James William Cannon's fancy way of naming a city after himself without seeming like an egotistical megalomaniac. Cannon, as in Cannon towels, sounds suspiciously like Kannapolis to my untrained-in-the-classics ear.

James William was the guy who started the whole shebang back in 1887, when he was just a thirty-five-year-old whipper-snapper cotton broker. Back then, cotton went north, at a mere five cents a pound, to be milled into towels and sheets. When it returned to the land of cotton in its transformed state, the price was bales away from its nickel-a-pound origins. Who knows what set the lightbulb flashing in Cannon's mind, but somewhere along the way, he must've figured, "Time to stop shipping to them Yankees and make our own selves some money." And that he did.

He opened the first mill in Concord, a small town about twenty miles north of Charlotte, and the demand was big enough for him to keep expanding. Eleven years later, his venture was so successful he'd bought up six hundred nearby acres of an old cotton plantation and called it Kannapolis, built a few more mills and lots of mill houses for the workers to live in.

Three-quarters of a century later, the powers that be transformed Kannapolis yet again. In the great American tradition, they turned a sagging downtown into an outlet village, this one with an ersatz Colonial Williamsburg spin.

I cut a path through the empty downtown and pulled the directions from my pocket. Right on Cannon Court, left on Mill Way, and left again on Spinner Drive.

The run of redbrick ramblers was so similar I had to edge my car down the road slowly, counting houses just to make sure I didn't miss it. Each one looked like the next, set halfway up neatly trimmed rectangles of green with foundation plantings of tightly pruned azaleas. Frank Lloyd Wright must be banging his head against his coffin right about now. When he came up with his ideal of affordable but artistic houses for the masses, he presented America with one-floor, basementless living with interesting roof angles and sweeping flows. I'm reasonably sure he had no idea his design would spawn a countrywide outbreak of these McRanchers.

Fifth house on the left. I pulled into the driveway. Even if all the houses did look alike, this was the place, no doubt about it. On the lawn was a wooden cutout of a farm girl and boy leaning over, with the farm girl's polka-dot bloomers showing. Between them they held a sign that said: THE ASHMORES, THOMAS, DOREEN, JOSANE, THOMAS JR.

I turned Harry off just as he was lamenting that his son had grown up just like him. At least he'd had his son. But then he had to go and die, smashed himself to smithereens on the Long Island Expressway.

Reenie Ashmore was waiting by the door. She was wearing dark green slacks made from some miracle fiber she probably spun herself on the nine-to-five shift and a beige shirt with thin red stripes, starched and pressed. Southern women always look presentable, regardless of anything. I've noticed it at the supermarket, where I'm the only schlep in dirty jeans and frazzled hair. And I noticed it at both Compassionate Friends meetings, where women who'd just about lost their lives still looked like they could walk into a job interview at NationsBank.

"Nattie, I don't know how to thank you." Mrs. Ashmore put her arms around me and hugged me. She smelled of Lysol and I could see why. Her house was so clean, I expected the white tornado to come careening down her hall any second.

"I haven't done anything. So no need for thanks," I said.

"You came on Christmas, didn't you? I know your people don't celebrate it, but I'm sure you had other things to do today."

Here we go again, even the most well-meaning Southerners find a way to bring up my religion. I never mention it and it's not like my last name is Goldberg or Silverstein. But, still, they know. It's some kind of Jew radar they've got, like they're born with a Jew-dar receiver programmed directly to their brains.

"We celebrate everything," I said, and left it at that. It's hard to be mad at a woman who'll spend the rest of her life grieving for a lost child.

Her living room was small and meticulous. Pushed against the far wall was a cornflower-blue couch with little red rosebuds merrily making their way across the nubby fabric; end tables at either side in glossy knotty pine and a matching coffee table in front. To the right, a gray velour recliner with a knotty pine magazine basket next to it and a television set tucked away in the corner.

The other wall was a shrine to Josane. The only thing missing was incense. Dead center was a huge gold frame with lots of gee-gaws and curlicues featuring a life-sized oil portrait of the reigning Miss Connecticut wearing a sparkling beaded gown, her state sash, and crowning tiara. Flanking the picture were knotty pine shelves brimming with trophies, crowns, badges, banners, dried corsages, and framed beauty-pageant programs.

There was enough trophy metal on that wall to set the house lopsided and the foundation cracking. There must have been better than a hundred of them, ranging in size and shape from a six-inch fluted column with a golden rattle on top and loopy script on the bottom that said LITTLE MISS BEAUTIFUL BABY AT EAST-LAND MALL, FIRST RUNNER-UP to a three-and-a-half-foot-tall candelabrum-looking thing with black and white checkered flags sticking out the sides. MISS CHARLOTTE MOTOR SPEEDWAY it said in large block letters.

"Your daughter was a beautiful woman, Mrs. Ashmore," I said. I didn't know what else to say, and it was the truth.

"Yes." She nodded and looked away for a few seconds. "Call me Reenie. Would you like some tea?"

Had she meant real tea, as in boiling water, a bag of Lipton, and a slice of lemon on the side, I'd have said yes. Tea here in the South means iced with a sack of sugar in it. I declined and said I'd already tanked up on caffeine.

"Any more," I said, "and you wouldn't be able to get in a word edgewise."

She offered a small laugh, that same small laugh as my mother's.

We sat down on the couch and Reenie started talking. I started to reach for my pad and pen, when I remembered I wasn't working. One of the problems with being a reporter is that you always feel like you should be taking notes when someone talks. It felt good to just sit and listen.

Big surprise: It turns out Josane lost her allegiance to her crown state just about seconds after the Miss America Pageant. She fled south and commuted north to fulfill her Miss Connecticut duties: visiting schools for the handicapped, opening JCPenney stores at malls, and riding in town parades.

"She was wanting to get back to where she felt comfortable," Reenie said. "She never felt at home up north with people talking so fast and being pushy. Not that you are, but you know what I mean. Everything moves so fast for y'all up there. 'Course, she didn't want to come home. Not to Kannapolis anyway. Nothing here for her excepting the mills. She was Miss Connecticut, she had plans for herself."

Those plans apparently included moving to Middleburg, Virginia, a horsey upper-crust kind of place where Jackie rode to the hounds from when she was Jackie B., K., and O. Reenie was kind of muddy on what brought Josane there. Possibly a man. Probably a sugar daddy. Reenie didn't know his name.

"She said she met an older gentleman; he called here once when she was trying to decide what to do. He sounded like a foreigner from Europe or something. He kept talking up Middleburg to her, saying a girl like her would feel right at home there."

From what I knew of Middleburg, it took a big bank account, not a pretty face, to feel at home there. Of course, there were those who could parlay one into the other. Which apparently Josane had done.

"Then she got it in her mind she wanted to ride horses. As a child she never paid any mind to them. She was busy with her pageants. I told her, 'Now, Josane, you be careful on those horses. You could get yourself hurt.'

"She said, 'Don't you worry yourself, Mama, I found the prettiest horse you've ever seen and I'm taking lessons with the best instructor around. He teaches senators' children how to ride. I expect you to come watch me at the Washington International Horse Show when I get there. And you know I will, Mama.' I knew she would; when Josane gets to setting her mind to something, it happens."

Poor Reenie, still talking about her daughter in the present tense, same as my mother talks about David. I tried to ask as delicately as possible how Josane afforded "the prettiest horse" and lessons with "the best instructor around."

"She said she was doing real good at her cosmetics company."

That'd be a hell of a lot of lipsticks: at least fifty bucks a pop for each lesson and no telling how much she'd ponied up for a horse that could take her to the big indoor shows like the Washington International.

"And that little store of hers," Reenie said, "she said that was becoming real popular in town."

"Store?" I said.

"Yes, ma'am, that's my Josane, never resting when she could be working. Always doing something. When she was a little girl, she was always busy, making garage sales, running bake sales. By the time she was ten, she had herself her own bankbook with forty-six dollars of her own money."

"Where'd you say this store was?" I said. I knew Reenie could talk for hours about Josane, but if I let her, my mother would start calling the hospitals, looking for a dead daughter.

"Right in Middleburg. Right in the middle of that main street in town. She gave the store a cute little name, Daisy Cutter, except

61

she spelled it funny. D-a-z-e-e Cutter and she sold little horsey things, knickknacks and whatnot and some clothes I think too. Dazee Cutter—isn't that unusual? She told me why she called it that, but Lord if I can remember now."

"Daisy Cutter makes sense," I said. "It's what they call really good moving horses in the hunter world. I guess she got into hunters in a big way. Do you remember who her trainer was?"

"Do what?"

"Her trainer. Her riding instructor."

"Oh," Reenie said. "Let me see now, he was a handsome fella, looked like he stepped out of one of those magazine advertisements. And neat, I never in my days seen a man that neat, his boots shinier than a mirror almost. Every time I saw him, he was polishing them. . . . His name, his name . . . what was his name?"

She'd just described half the hunter world. "Was it Tony? Tony Workman?"

"No, it was more of an American first name. Goodness, for the life of me, I can't think of it now. . . ."

"That's all right, Reenie. When you remember, give me a call. By the way, did Josane ever make it to the Washington show?"

"She would have. I know she would have. Like I said, when Josane gets her mind to something . . ."

"What happened, Reenie? What happened to Josane?"

"I told her to be careful on those horses. 'Josane, honey,' I said not once if I said it a thousand times, 'those are big animals that could do you harm.' She always just laughed and said, 'Stop your worrying, Mama.' "

A riding accident. My mother's worst fear too. Like Reenie, she's told me once, if not a thousand times, that the horses will be the death of her because she can't stop worrying about me. And I've given her good cause: one broken leg, a separated shoulder, ten stitches in my head, five broken toes, and too many concussions to count. "Riding's a dangerous sport," I said. "I don't know any rider who isn't put together with nuts and bolts. How'd it happen? Was Josane wearing a helmet?" I wondered how Reenie could figure a riding accident to be murder. After all, that was what this was supposed to be about.

Reenie straightened the magazines on the coffee table—a few *Guideposts*, some *Family Circles*, and a *TV Guide* with Kathy Lee Gifford smiling it up—not that they were out of line. "Oh, they said it was the horse, and I believed them at first. They said she'd gone riding in the woods by herself and her horse got scared. They said it was a crazy kind of horse to start with, that everyone was just waiting on something like this to happen. I know *that's* not true. Josane told me it was a good horse and I know she'd have the good sense not to buy herself a crazy animal."

I looked down at the table, wanting to straighten the straight magazines myself. Anything to avoid seeing Reenie's eyes. Blank, shell-shocked, taking her back to a time I know she's been playing over and over and over in her mind. I didn't want to be there with her. Being there myself, and then with my mother, had been bad enough. So I scanned the magazine covers: "The All-New Mango Papaya Diet!!" "Kathie Lee: I just love being a mom!" "Jesus and Me: A true love story." Then I noticed the dates. They were from four years ago, when Josane was still alive. That's when I started crying.

"Nattie, are you all right?" Reenie saw me wiping my tears with my bare arm.

"I'm sorry, Reenie," I said. "I have what they call 'thin boundaries.' I heard about it on a talk radio show. I feel everyone's pain. And I'm sure I don't have to tell you, you've got more than your share."

Reenie nodded her head. "You've got that right. 'More than my share.' But what I can't figure is, my share of what? Who all decides what the shares are? I've lived a good Christian life. For what? I used to think I knew how the Good Lord worked. Since Josane, I don't know anything. Why me? Why take my Josane away?"

Reenie and I sat there crying. The two of us, together in tears.

I saw a blurry 12:23 on the clock by the TV. I'd told my mother I'd be back on the road at noon. I had to crank things up if I had any hope of making kugel for her. That's about all that brings her pleasure these days. That and going to Las Vegas.

"Reenie, what makes you think it wasn't a riding accident?"

She untucked a stiff white handkerchief from beneath her shirt cuff and dried her eyes.

"On the phone they told me it was a riding accident, a real bad one. The horse trampled her and she hit her head hard enough to kill her. And then no one knew where Josane was, so they couldn't find her in time. I know that's not what really happened. Not hardly. I found that out when I went up there to get her things. Everyone acting so strange, happy and laughing and drinking beer like it was a big party at her house. Excepting all of Josane's things were already gone. That boyfriend of hers, I didn't like him the first time I met him before what happened to Josane. He was a smart-alecky kind of fella. When we were there, he told me he and his friends put all of Josane's belongings in big black plastic trash bags and hauled them up to the dump. They were drinking beer and laughing like nothing happened. Nothing happened excepting my baby girl was lying in the ground and they were having a party. That got me to thinking something was wrong, throwing out Josane's things fast, like they're going to tell a story they don't want told. Then at the hospital I found the nurse who saw Josane that day. She said she didn't look hardly stepped on at all, like they told me she'd been, and she had a funny smell to her. I talked to the police, but all Josane's friends, if that's what you can call them, come from those rich families up to Middleburg. So the police weren't interested in talking to me about Josane being murdered.

"But someone murdered her. Lord knows why or what for. I know something else happened out there in those woods, something no one's talking about. . . ."

"Reenie," I said, "can you think of anyone who had a grudge against Josane, someone angry enough to kill her?"

"That's what I go over in my mind every day," Reenie said. "Everyone loved Josane. She was always winning the Miss Congeniality at the pageants. I can't figure who'd want to hurt her. The only thing I can come up with is that girl she hired to watch the store when she couldn't be there. Josane had to fire her for stealing from the cash register. She called me the day she told that girl to leave. 'Mama,' she'd said, 'that was the hardest thing I've ever done in my life. She was so mad when I told her take her things and leave, I thought she was gonna take a knife to me.' Three weeks later I got that call about Josane."

"Do you remember her name?"

"Yes, I do, can't hardly forget it if I wanted to. Lannie Post. I told the police what Josane said about her thinking Lannie was mad enough to kill her. The police said that girl wasn't in town that day. Then I found out they never even talked to her. Something's wrong. Real wrong. And the funny thing about that girl was, when I met her up to Josane's store, she followed Josane around like a little puppy dog looking for a petting. Then she went and stole that money. It doesn't make sense. Not one part of this makes sense."

Reenie's tears had more than dried by now. Nothing shoves sadness back inside faster than anger. I looked at her sitting on the couch, her spine straighter than a plumb line, her face taut and her dark brown eyes that had a softness to them when I met her the first time now hard as frozen chunks of tea.

"They never even talked to her—imagine that. I don't know if it was that girl or not. But I know something wrong happened out there in those woods and that's what I'm wanting you to find out. I've got some money I could pay you. Not much anymore, 'cause I already paid two thousand dollars to a private investigator from Charlotte and all he came up with was this report here that says he couldn't find any evidence that it happened any other way than what they say up there. But I've got enough for you to get up to Middleburg and maybe a few meals and—"

"Reenie, whoa, just hold on a minute. I don't want your money. I'm a reporter, not a private eye. Besides, you already had it investigated. By someone who knows what he's doing. What more could I do?"

"You know that world of rich people and horses up there. I know you do, I read those stories of yours in *The Appeal* and I read that little thing the editor wrote about you, saying that you ride show horses and that's how you and that fella got to the bottom of that story about the horse trainer that got hisself killed. You know those people, Nattie, you know how they can close up aside themselves and not let anyone in to know the truth if that's the way they're wanting it."

What was going on in Reenie's mind was pulling the skin across her face tighter than a canvas stretcher. I thought she'd rip herself right off her cheekbones if she didn't calm down. No question where Josane had gotten her drive and determination. And no question that I'd be walking out of there agreeing to look into Josane's death. It's hard for me to say no under the slightest pressure, and this was the barometric equivalent of Hurricane Hugo.

I put my hand on Reenie's shoulder; it, too, was as taut as a trampoline.

"Reenie," I said. "You're going to work yourself up into a stroke. Take a few deep breaths, better yet, chant a few *ohm-nahmah-shee-viya*s."

"Do what?"

"*Ohm-nahmah-shee-viya*, it's an Indian chant, my crazy father's cure for everything. He kept repeating it to himself before he went in for a quadruple bypass, says it worked better than Valium. I know it sounds bizarre, but I've tried it a few times myself and it's surprisingly calming."

"Nattie, I don't want to be calming down. I need to be finding out who killed my daughter. I've got to find out, surely you understand that. When you lose a child, you lose your future, that's what that lady at that meeting told me last night. So you see, it's not for me. I don't have a future. It's for Josane. I've got to find out what happened, I promised her I'd do that for her. That one last thing."

CHAPTER 9

Well, I suppose it's good to know yourself.

By the time I left Reenie's—which was late enough to get my mother twitching—I'd agreed to everything. Go up to Middleburg. Snoop around and pull in all my horse sources who knew Josane, talk to her friends, her trainer, track down the disgruntled employee, and find that horse who allegedly did her in.

"One final question," I'd said as I stood to leave. "Josane's horse. Do you have a picture of it or know what it looked like?"

Reenie's eyes teared up again and I was sorry I'd asked. She told me she'd just be a second and headed down the hall. More than a few minutes passed and I was doubly sorry I'd asked. Finally she came back with a fresh handkerchief and a framed eight-by-ten photo.

She handed me the picture facedown. "We packed these away afterward. . . ."

I turned it over and saw Josane. Sure enough, she was standing next to a big, gorgeous chestnut with a big white blaze. The horse in my dreams.

"Can I keep this?" I asked, and knew the answer. Reenie Ashmore couldn't even look at the picture. I was sure she didn't want it.

I walked out with that photo and a bunch more, the PI's report, a stack of newspaper clippings, a couple of scrapbooks, and a heavy heart. Whatever I found out, Josane would still be dead and Reenie Ashmore would still be spending her nights looking at that life-sized portrait of her daughter and staring at out-of-date magazines.

File this under the life sucks category.

I found a pay phone and called Mother.

"Where are you?" Her voice was edging into panic.

"I'm not mangled," I said. "I'm just running late. That interview lasted longer than I thought it would."

"Just drive carefully. Oh, by the way, I forgot the cottage cheese. Can you make it without?"

"Kugel without cottage cheese? That's the glue, Mom. I'll stop and get some." Easier said than done on the birthday of the savior of half the free world. Finally I found a Circle K with an Indian guy behind the counter.

"Cottage cheese? Got any?"

He nodded and pointed to the glass-doored dairy case, where I found a tub of Light n' Lively, expiration date, Dec. 24. Well, it was also Hanukkah, and if a little drop of oil could burn for eight days and eight nights, then surely a clump of cottage cheese could make it twenty-four hours past its shelf life. I paid way too much for it and left.

Back to Harry and the road. After a few notes I pushed the eject button. There was just something a little too plaintive in Harry's voice for me now. I needed uplifting. Time to take back the day. Time for Tina Turner.

Before I knew it, I was at the Holden Road exit screaming "What's Love Got to Do with It" and heading toward Mother's. But heading there slowly. Only a fool or a newcomer goes over thirty-five on Holden Road. The Greensboro cops have so many speed traps set, it must be the city's biggest source of traffic revenue. I counted three different cruisers with their radar guns pointing my way. Why weren't they home unwrapping presents?

Mother was standing at the door as I pulled up, just as Reenie had been. And just like Reenie, my mother was dressed with a capital D. Jewish style. Calvin Klein jeans with a knife-blade crease pressed down the middle, Cole-Haan penny loafers with freshly minted copper pennies smiling up from the slots, navy blue Ralph

Lauren sweater with an American flag woven onto the front, and just a hint of J. G. Hook white oxford collar peeking out. This was her casual attire.

For me, casual attire *meant* casual: a pair of broken-down jeans, frayed and fringed at the bottom from where I'd hacked off the excess six inches, and threadbare and splitting at the inseam from fat thighs and lots of riding; beat-up Nikes with green horse manure stains, and a crumpled T-shirt.

Needless to say, I've been a big disappointment to my mother since the day I took a pair of shears to a brown satina romper suit. I was three and the elastic around the legs and arms was all wrong—it was too tight.

The only thing I really care about in clothes is that they're comfortable and that I can write snide things about their designers. But lucky for my mother, her son, my brother, Larry, lives to dress and even married a woman whose in-laws own Boston's toniest haberdashery.

My mother's opening remark: "Nattie, have you lost weight?"

She's been monitoring my poundage since I was ten, when she saw me reach for the Oreos. "A fat child makes a fat adult," she'd told me. Easy for her to say. She was built like a Barbie doll, and still is.

"Not that I know of," I said, and we hugged.

Christmas/Hanukkah dinner came and went. Just Mother and I, two boxes of Banquet frozen fried chicken, a large can of Le Sueur peas, and the noodle pudding I made with the out-of-date cottage cheese.

We cleared the plates—blue Styrofoam—and tossed them in the trash. Paper plates and fried chicken may not sound like much in the way of a holiday meal. But this was a big effort for my mother. Since David died, she'd been eating dinner—a bowl of instant maple cinnamon oatmeal—on her bed in front of the TV.

I was wrapping the kugel in silver foil, when she took a hunk and popped it in her mouth.

"I could eat it all," she said. "You know what, leave me the recipe. Maybe I'll make it one of these nights."

"Mom," I said, "you cook? Get real, you don't even know how to make the Cuisinart work."

She laughed and so did I. We knew the underlying joke, that she'd made David put in a fancy $25,000 kitchen and she hardly did more than boil water in it.

She asked me again for the recipe. Who knows, maybe she was having a three-quarters life crisis and wanted to reinvent herself. If she wanted to learn how to make kugel, who was I to stop her? Trouble was, it was my grandmother's—her mother's—recipe and my grandmother came from the *schiterzein* school of cooking; in Yiddish, a little bit of this, a little bit of that. And since they'd stopped talking a couple of months ago—the Jewish way to resolve disagreement—she couldn't get it from her. So I wrote it down as best I could:

> Esther's Kugel: Mix this stuff together in mixer, blender, or if you ever figure it out, food processor—10 eggs, 1 lb. cottage cheese, a couple tbsp. butter, $1/2$ pint sour cream, $1^1/2$ cups or so of sugar, 1 cup or a little more of yellow raisins, 2 or $2^1/2$ grated apples, 1 (but I use 2) grated oranges, 1 grated lemon (rind and all for citrus), 2ish tsp. vanilla, a couple pinches nutmeg. Whiz until soupy. In big bowl mix this goop with 1 lb. cooked wide noodles and turn the whole mess into a greased baking dish. Sprinkle with cinnamon and sugar and bake around 350 until brown.

My mother looked at the recipe and puffed up. "Looks easy enough to me. I'm sixty-one years old. I went to law school. I passed the bar. I can make a kugel for God's sake. Just one thing, how do I grease the dish?"

I snatched the paper away from her. "Mom, forget it. When

71

you get a yen to stop up your arteries with this, let me know and I'll make it for you and FedEx it up. Okay? Time for presents. If you don't use the first one, I'll tell everyone in Greensboro you spend more money a year on your clothes than you make."

I handed her the envelope and the book of lawyer jokes. She gave me a shirt I'll never wear, a blue pinstripe J. G. Hook thing with a matching bow tie—hope dies hard.

My mother settled in with the joke book and I picked up the newspaper that was rolled up on the kitchen counter. I unrolled it and pulled up a chair next to hers. Out of habit, I carefully filleted the sections. David, although a wonderful man in every other regard, had been psychotic about having his paper intact. Now I could leave it out of order, pages turned back, crumpled in a ball if I wanted to. I didn't want to. I carefully lifted the front section from the piles and started reading.

"Mom," I said. She was chuckling over the bad lawyer jokes. "When'd you start reading *USA Today*? Where's the Greensboro paper?"

She looked up from her book. "That is the Greensboro paper. They said they've redesigned."

Oh, man, another one bites the dust. When I hear the *redesign* word, it makes me cringe. To the rest of the world, redesign is an innocuous concept that means move a few things around, but to a newspaper person it means readership surveys have indicated that the reading public wants shorter, more colorful stories, and plenty of them. In a word—or two—*USA Today*.

"Shit," I said. "Soon we'll all be reading comics and calling it the day's paper."

"Nattie, enough with that mouth."

"Okay, okay," I grumbled, and started reading the short, sprightly stories. There was so much going on on the front page, it made me dizzy. I read the whole thing in less than two minutes and turned the page, hoping for more meat inside. Fat chance.

The stories were just as short, but a name caught my eye in one of the twenty-three headlines on page 12A.

Hinton Allard Dies in Car Crash.

I read the story. It didn't tell me much, of course. What can you say in six inches of copy? Allard crashed into an underpass on Route 40 outside of Greensboro; there was an open bottle of Jim Beam in the car. It also said he was a Winston-Salem attorney.

"Hey, Ma, did you know a guy by the name of Hinton Allard? A lawyer over in Winston-Salem?"

She thought for a second, then shook her head. "No, but I can ask around if you want. I can call some of the people I went to law school with at Wake Forest."

"Nah, it's okay," I said. "Don't bother. His name rings a bell, but I can't remember how. . . ."

I folded the front section back into place as if it had never been read. Then it hit me.

"Holy shit, Ma, how soon can you ask around?"

CHAPTER 10

My mother, who has never said anything worse in English than damn—Yiddish is another matter—looked up at me. She was not amused.

"Nattie, that mouth of yours. I don't know where you get it from. And that look on your face. What's about this Hinson All-bright anyway."

"Hinton Allard," I said. "I just remembered how I knew the name. He was Mr. A on Henry's hit list. And now he's dead."

My mother looked at me like I was taking drugs. And why not? She's got plenty of clients more coherent than I was right now who do. I filled her in on Henry's wacko letters, leaving out any mention of John. After he dumped me, she and David were ready to send a hit man after him.

I called Henry pronto, but got his answering machine.

"Mom, I've got to make a few more phone calls. Do you have any contacts at the state troopers who will talk to me?"

She wrote down a few names and, of course, none of them were working. The ones that were would supply only the official "No comment, you'll have to talk to our public affairs liaison when the office reopens after the Christmas holiday."

I was hoping to find it had just been a drunk-driving crash—plain and simple. I know I told Henry I thought the letter meant business, but I didn't think this soon or this serious. Just because I hated John for breaking my heart didn't mean I wanted him dead—anymore.

74

Besides, the idea of a psycho picking off twenty-five human beings one by one made me sick to my stomach. And not just because I didn't want to see twenty-five people die. I'm sorry to admit I'm a small enough person that it made me even more jealous of Henry and his job. Because if the listees did start dropping like flies, it meant Henry, once again, gets the story of a lifetime. Another late-night dance with Ted Koppel on *Nightline*, another picture in *People*, another pop at the Pulitzer.

Putting my petty nature aside, I scanned my brain for my cop connections. How could I be so dense? Must be an extra Y gene lurking around the twists and turns of my DNA helixes. Tony, I'd forgotten about Tony. I dialed, hoping he, not she—assuming the Mrs. was in today—would answer.

I was in luck. "Hello, darlin'," Tony said to me. "How you've been? Are you having yourself a good holiday?"

I lied and told him I was happier than a bloodhound in a health club on the day after Thanksgiving.

"Well then, that makes two of us," he said. "And that's a pretty good saying you just made up for yourself. Why, if'n I didn't know better, I'd say you have some grit blood in you."

"Pure kasha blood in this girl," I said. "Anyway, I hate to bother you on Christmas, but I've got a favor to ask you."

I didn't tell him about Henry's list, because even though Henry had come to like and trust Tony, he was still wary of working with the police. I asked him to find out more about Hinton Allard's crash and the possibility of it being something more than just a drunk losing hold of the road.

"Something like murder, you mean?" Tony said. "Nattie, you got your nose in someplace it doesn't belong again? I know nothing I say will make you stop whatever it is you're doing. Just do me one favor and be a little more careful than you were last time. No midnight rides to the barn to capture murderers by yourself, okay?"

"Yeah, yeah, yeah," I said.

"I'll call you back when I find out something about your Mr. Allard. Got to go." I heard why. Sharon was calling him. I guess the Mrs. was home for the holidays. Good for Tony. That's what he'd asked Santa for.

While I had the telephone in my hand, I called my office to check my voice mail.

"Gold, thanks for the compliment." It was Torkesquist. I'd left a message on his machine, telling him how moved I was by his pictures. "Moved to where? Cincinnati? Or the bathroom? Do you still want me to take some pictures of that Thoroughbred nag of yours? Holiday rates this week. I'm home with nothing to do but think about giving you rug burns. I might just go over there and snap a few shots of her later today."

Then a string of messages from readers about my Compassionate Friends story. ". . . Cried while I read it" ". . . So thankful for my blessings" ". . . So beautifully written." Blah, blah, blah. Candace may be an unfeeling robot, but she knows how to push the reading public's buttons. Rarely do reporters get any response to a story unless you spell a person's name wrong or inadvertently add a few years to an age. I stopped counting at twelve messages and fast-forwarded until I heard something else besides ". . . Today's story was so . . ." It was from a reader in Rock Hill, S.C.; I could practically hear, the *warning, warning, key penetration area* alert. She wanted to know why designers end their fashion shows with a wedding gown. I took down her name and number so I could give her the official *Charlotte Commercial Appeal* Fashion Writer answer. If I didn't get back to her, she might call Fred to complain, and that would be like burying my performance rating in concrete shoes and sending it for a swim. Last year I'd slipped down to a seven. A complaint from Rock Hill could plummet me to a four.

I couldn't even blame Candace for this act of corporate suck-up-tee-tude. It was her predecessor who came up with a brilliant numerical rating system. She figured out a formula where you take the number of stories written, add the length in inches and all the sources quoted, and then divide by the number of days times a constant. "Press the button," she'd said proudly at the unveiling, "and you have that reporters' productivity rating." The paper got heavy with padded stories full of irrelevant quotes, so she switched to a secret formula, which stayed secret for about eleven minutes. It was basically a grown-up version of the old on-a-scale-of-one-to-ten and it pitted all the reporters against each other. Which was probably the idea.

Wedding dresses at fashion shows—who cares what the ditzes on Seventh Avenue do? Apparently Miss Key Penetration Area did. I'd have to call her first thing next week. I pressed number five on the phone to forward me to the next message. It was from Gail.

"Hi, I'm at the barn, celebrating Christmas with Allie. Rob invited me up for dinner and, can you believe it, I said yes. I think I should hose off before I walk upstairs to his apartment and if I spill cranberry sauce on his white rug I guess that's it for me at February Farm. He says supper will just be a few things he can get together because he's worn out from doing all those trees. But knowing Rob, it'll be china, silver, and goose. Brenda's fine. I gave her a Hanukkah carrot for you. Call me when you get back, I gotta go sweep the aisle. Love to your mother. Oh, by the way, a very strange guy came by the barn to take pictures of Brenda. He asked me to marry him."

Oh, no, I'd forgotten to warn Gail about Torkesquist. I hoped he didn't pull his pants down and show her his surgery stitches.

After Gail's came a message from a Diane Harding. "Sorry to bother you on Christmas, but my sister said she told you I'd be calling." Diane Harding? Sister. Then it clicked. Candace's sister-the-shrink. The last thing I wanted was Candace's sister spying on me at the barn. I'd tell her about High Lake Stable, a run-down lesson barn on the other end of Charlotte. "I know it's an imposition and there's no telling what my alexothymic sister has done to you. Whatever it is, I'm sorry. We're nothing alike. I'm moving to Charlotte and I'd like to find a good barn with good trails. If you could help me out, I'll tell you what we all called Candy as a kid, the name she made everyone in the family swear we'd never tell anyone."

There was an empty stall at my barn. . . . Could be interesting.

I forwarded past the electronic talker telling me the time and day until I heard a human. I knew who it was instantly. There was so much music in her voice, just listening to her say my name was like hearing an old, faraway folk song. "Nattie? Nattie? Is that you? Lord have mercy, these machines doin' everything nowdays. I got a little something I want to give you. I know, I know, you say it ain't your business, 'not my holiday.' But we all the same underneath and we got to be celebrating the Good Lord just so's he won't be forgettin' what he done started down here. When you coming anyway? Tomorrow? I ain't doing nothing but going to church in the morning. You better be bringing that tall boy with you, hear? I bet you and him still fighting like a couple of banty cocks. Lord, girl, if your head ain't as hard as that old mule standing out in the barn."

It was Dorothy, the Bladstones' maid. I'd gotten to know her when I was reporting the horse show murder story and we clicked right off. Maybe because I was a red-haired Jew and she a green-eyed black—Nana Greenberg said God gave special gifts to both our kind because of what happened to our mothers' mothers.

Since the story, I'd been visiting Dorothy regularly and calling every week to make sure she was all right. She was pushing seventy-five and still working forty hours a week. Not that she was the least bit worried about dying. On the contrary, every time I saw her she told me she had some business to settle with God and was looking forward to the time she could meet him face-to-face and ask him right out, "Like'n how come he take my babies from me?

Then when we get that settled, I got me some more things to say to him, things about this mess down here. Peoples killing one another for no good reason; fighting about what name to call him. Like it done matter if you pray to Jesus or God or what they call him over where all those people shooting at each other all the time. How come he don't just tell everyone he don't care what you call him? What's he doin' up there, lookin at the ladies? He got to know there's some fixing needs to be done down thisaway, or else 'fore long we all be dead. Then what's he gonna do? All us up there with him, no one down here? That's what I be telling him. Then I'm gonna go see those babies he took from me an' wrap my old black arms around them. I been waiting half my life for that. . . ."

I replayed her message. I could've listened to her talk forever.

CHAPTER 11

For a Jew, nothing's lonelier than Christmas except the day after if it falls on a Sunday in the South, where all the stores are closed. My mother and I were sitting around with nothing to do but look at the leaves that still needed to be raked.

"Let's go," I said, grabbing her by the hand.

"Go, go where? I can't go anywhere, I've got a million things to do."

"What, watch *Jeopardy!* at three and *Wheel of Fortune* at four? This house is like a tomb, you don't raise your shades, you don't open your windows. You smoke and watch TV. I feel like a salmon on the way to becoming lox. Come on, the fresh air'll do you good. We're going to Camden to see a friend. You'll like her."

I had to drag her, but she came finally. We took her car—a new blue Lincoln with a white ragtop she had to have. Blew more money on that than she made the whole year before. At least it made her smile.

A couple hours later we pulled up to the Bladstone house and my mother did the same thing I did the first time I saw it. Gaped in disbelief.

"L. M. Bladstone of Bladstone Tobacco, that's where he lives? A redbrick ranch half as big as my house?"

"And," I said, "you should see what he drives. Half as big as the car we're in and ten times as old."

We walked up to the door and knocked. At least the 139 stray dogs were gone, gone with L.M.'s now ex-wife, Lucy. We waited some more and I knocked again. Finally I heard scuffling sounds moving toward us. Dorothy opened the door and threw her arms around me.

"Oh, Lord, child, I'm so glad to see you. Where's that boy I tol' you to bring?"

I stepped forward and pointed to Mother.

"I brought her instead. We get along better, for the most part. You know as well as I, Henry and I can't be in the same room without fighting."

Dorothy laughed. "'Course you can't. That's cause you two so stirred up about each other, it scares the skin off your hides."

I hugged her again and handed her a Christmas present. I'd gotten her a white leather photo album embossed with flying golden angels. She'd once shown me pictures of her two children who'd died. The old photos were stacked in a box that was starting to fall apart.

"This is for all your pictures of Willie and James," I said.

She ran her fingers over the angels. "Just what I've been asking the Lord for, angels watching out for my babies . . . You and your mama wait just a minute. I got to go get yours."

The place had certainly improved since Lucy's departure. The furniture was still years beyond its shelf life, but it didn't smell of dog feces anymore. It was as clean and neat as Reenie Ashmore's place, with the magazines piled in orderly stacks on the coffee table just like Reenie's. My mother was looking around; she'd shut her mouth from the wide-open gape, but the look of disbelief was still there.

"*L. M. Bladstone?*" she said.

I nodded. I'd seen the place before, so I didn't have to catalogue its utter lack of extravagance. I took the top magazine, an old *Vanity Fair* with a cover shot of Demi Moore oozed up next to the large-print teasers of inside stories.

Dorothy came back in carrying a small present. "These old bones don't move me as fast as they used to."

She handed me a box wrapped in silver foil. I shook it and it rattled.

"Dorothy," I said, "would you sit for once, it's making me nervous you standing there."

I knew she wouldn't. She'd been standing around sitting white people for seventy-five years, she wasn't about to start sitting now.

"Well, go on," she said, "what you waiting for, child, open it."

I did. I took a quick breath in surprise. It was far more than I'd expected. Sitting on a puffy bed of white cotton was a necklace as pretty as anything I'd ever seen at those expensive craft shows where everything starts in the three digits and keeps climbing. I lifted it off its cushion and looked at the delicate purple shells interspersed with small blue and green stones.

I stood up and hugged her. "Dorothy, it's beautiful. But I don't want you spending your money on me."

"Hush, now, I can spend whatever I want to spend. But I ain't spent a dime on this. My mama gave it to me 'fore I got married, called it a happy man weddin' necklace. Her people down 'round Kiawah made things like that. She tol' me it would make the mens like me and then keep my man happy forever if I wore it on my weddin' day. It sure enough worked. Not more'n a month pass 'fore Willie Campbell done ask me to marry him and I never seen him even look at another woman in the forty-three years we were together. Not once.

"Girl, ain't you getting close to forty years old? Time I was your age, I done borne me two children. I'd a been almost finished raising them too if— No time for that kinda talk. Here, put that necklace on and start getting yourself your man."

She looked over at my mother and said, "Then you let your mama wear it awhile. She's too young and fancy to be buryin' herself up like an old dog fixin' to pass. Ain't that the truth?"

Even my mother laughed.

I couldn't stand me sitting and Dorothy standing. I knew the only place she'd ever sit was in the kitchen, so I steered us all that way. We shared tea, fruitcake, and talk for better than an hour. I could've stayed the afternoon, but I knew my mother wanted to get back before dark. Over Dorothy's protests, I cleared and washed the dishes, then headed to the door, stopping by the coffee table with the magazines.

"Dorothy, can I take this?" I held up the *Vanity Fair.* "It's a couple years out of date and there's a story I'd been wanting to read."

"Take any of those nasty magazines you want. I never have seen Mr. Bladstone pick one up. They were hers."

We both knew who she meant. She'd hated Lucy.

"In that case, I'll take more. I love old magazines."

I grabbed the top half of the pile. It'd give me something to do on the way back to Mother's.

At the door, Dorothy and I hugged. Then she hugged my mother.

"This here a special child. You tell her to take care now and stop fighting with that tall boy."

"Dorothy," my mother said, "in thirty-seven years of life I've never been able to tell Nattie anything. They don't come any more stubborn than her."

Dorothy laughed, then said, "Sure enough. Wonder where she got that from? You still smoking those nasty, filthy, stinking cigarettes? You worrying those lines deep into that girl's face, you are. Keep doing that, she'll never find herself a man, happy man weddin' necklace or no happy man weddin' necklace."

"All right, all right," my mother said. "Six months and I'll stop."

She's been saying "six months" for thirty-seven years and probably more. I tossed the magazines onto the seat and we

headed back to Greensboro. I shuffled through the magazines to
see what I'd gotten. Between the second and third *Vanity Fair*s, I
found something that wasn't a magazine: the Bladstone company's
annual report. A smiling L.M. was on the cover handing out ten-
year service pins to happy-at-least-in-this-picture employees. I
slipped it back in the pile and picked up the next one, an old copy
of *Spur*.

We got home before dark. She settled in with the television and
I, the telephone. Just one message on my voice mail. From Henry.

"I guess we're on for an extended game of phone tag. Good
job on the Christmas story, Nattie. I know you hated doing it,
but I have to say it was a compelling read. As a parent I can
appreciate . . ."

I heard little voices screaming in the background and Henry
saying a muffled, "Chet, Hank, I'm on the phone. Stop that
fighting, NOW. Hank, don't you ever hit your brother in the pri-
vates again, young man, or you'll spend the rest of the day in your
room with no toys."

The screaming died down and Henry resumed his message to
me. "Sorry, Nattie. They're overstimulated. Last night a neighbor
gave them Coke, which kept them up. Now they're tired and
hungry. They refused to eat breakfast until they tried their new
computer game. Anyway, I just wanted to say good job. Oh, I
probably don't have to say this, but should you talk to your old
friend, the one that's on the list, don't mention anything. In case
this does turn out to be a story, the fewer people that know about
it, the better. By the way, I got another letter. I think you'll find it
very interesting."

More screams in the background with Henry assuring them
he'd be off the phone in a minute. "I'm driving the boys to Washington to leave them with their mother for Christmas break. Since
I'll be up there, I thought I'd take the opportunity to do some
record checking in Virginia. At least half of the people on the list

live there. If you can, call me before I leave. I'm taking the boys to a movie, I'll be back around nine. Thanks. Oh, and happy holidays."

The wheels in my head started spinning, maybe as fast as James William Cannon's had spun a century ago. The big difference between the two of us—other than maggots—was expectations. While he wove himself into the very fabric of American commerce with his textile empire, I was looking for more modest gains. Three days, a week tops, sprung from the daily grind of calling podiatrists for local inserts and absolution from my Sunday fashion column.

I was up against tough odds. Had Jimmy Bill been forced to square off against Candace, he might've died a poor cotton broker.

It made perfect sense. I was heading up that way next week for the clinic with George Morris. Candace had reluctantly approved the time off, not that she had a choice. It was the last of my comp time—*The Appeal* had long ago stopped paying overtime—and I had to use it by the end of the year. I'd planned to catch a ride with Rob, my trainer who was hauling up Brenda and a very rich client's horse. He wasn't charging me anything, he was generous that way. But sitting in a truck with a man who's never had a normal conversation with me wasn't how I wanted to spend eight hours.

And I didn't want to take my car. It had groaned and moaned all the way to Greensboro. I couldn't expect it to take me clear up this state and three-quarters of the way up another without a major tantrum. When my car throws tantrums, it leaves me walking to the nearest gas station or stranded by the side of the road, live bait for the next truck-driving psychopath rolling by.

Henry was driving up to Virginia. I could catch a ride with him, we could discuss his prepare-to-pay list, and I could tell him about Josane and pick his brain for strategies. I could arrive earlier at Annie's, my old college roommate who'd gone home to her mother's farm after her marriage fell apart three years ago and never left. It was outside of Upperville, which was outside of Middleburg. Hell, from what I remembered of the homestead—all 832 acres of it—they'd have enough spare rooms for Henry and his entire extended family.

Perfect. Except for one thing. Candace. I'd have to convince her there was something in it for her. I didn't have much of a backup since I'd used my wild card a few months ago for the horse show series. Just as she was getting ready to yank me back to fashion, I paid a visit to my only ally in management—Gary Stockwell, the managing editor. He was short, attractive, and smart. The first was why he was probably hired by our city editor, a short man who never hired anyone taller than himself, which explained the growing ranks of little people like myself and Candace's creepy deputy. I'm sure he didn't notice the second part—Gary's looks—because our city editor's thing was for young, short women. And he should've taken note of the third part, Gary's smarts, because Gary quickly leapfrogged over everyone—including the city editor—to the ME spot.

Gary was a fan of mine, and I, him. Maybe even more than professionally. As I said, he was smart and there was something appealing about him, but he was also married. And that's where I draw the line. He's always there for me in a pinch. The trick was choosing my pinches carefully.

So this had to be good.

I picked up the phone and started dialing information, looking for Candace's home number. I disconnected before James Earl Jones welcomed me to Bell Atlantic. When the dial tone came back, I tapped out *The Appeal*'s WATSline. A free call—it was worth a try. I was sure it would be a dry run; even Candace couldn't be working on the Sunday after Christmas.

I keyed in her extension, and as it rang I started to lip-synch her prerecorded message: "This is Candace Fitzgerald, features editor of *The Charlotte Commercial Appeal.* You, the readers, are what our newspaper is all about. So please leave a message and I'll get back to you promptly. That's a promise. We care what you think."

I bet she got at least fifteen MBO points for that one, with a possible extra five bonus points for the you-the-reader baloney. Our chain rules its managers by the old carrot and stick, corporately updated and renamed Management by Objective, aka MBO. It works like this: Managers meet with their managers and come up with a list of I-promise-to-dos; if they meet all of them by the end of the year, everyone—except the reporters who actually do the I-promise-to-dos—gets a big fat bonus.

On the third ring, her phone picked up and I singsang along with the message: "This is Candace Fitzgerald, features editor of *The Charlotte Commercial Appeal.*"

I wasn't really listening and went off into a baroque rendition of the "You, the readers, are what our newspaper is all about." It wasn't until I started trilling my voice that I realized I was singing solo.

Then from the other end of the line I heard, "Who is this?"

Someone opened the adrenaline spigot inside me and sent my heart slamming around my rib cage pretty good. What to do? Hang up? Hope she hadn't recognized my voice? Own up to my mockery? Blame it on Manischevitz?

"Nattie, is that you?"

Decision one, made for me. Chalk that up to the all too easily identifiable remnants of a Philadelphia accent.

"Candace, yeah, yeah, it's me. My mother and I got a little wild with the wine. I was just feeling happy to be alive, got a little carried away."

When in doubt, blame the demon rum. Hopefully Candace wouldn't remember my drinking habits could qualify me as a card-carrying member of the Women's Christian Temperance Union.

"Candace," I said. "What are you doing at the office? It's the day after Christmas. Why aren't you home putting batteries in walkie-talkies?"

"Only here half the day. Came in to see what kind of response your story got. Thirty-nine calls so far, about half of them from our new penetration targets: Gastonia, Rock Hill, and Kannapolis. Hell of a story, Nattie. Great read. Nice mix with all the Christmas feel-good stories on the rest of the page. Looking forward to getting the final tally on number of calls."

Candace was so consumed by the glory of reader response, she'd forgotten, ignored, or didn't even hear my operatic parody of her voice mail message. She was charged, no question about it. I could tell by the way she was talking. She'd slipped into power speak, a peculiar verbal tic of editors at *The Appeal*. When they go into the robo mode, they start dropping the I's out of their sentences as if they're just one big mass of editorial flesh. The ultimate team players.

"I got a bunch too," I said.

"Terrific. Total them up and memo it to me. If any of them came from the three new penetration zones, give me a subtotal on those. Got a call from Fred after the second edition. Loved the story and said our pages would be the best read. Good job, Nattie."

Now was the time to hit.

"Candace," I said, trying to figure out what tone to take in my voice. Firm and decisive? I didn't want to threaten her. Obsequious and cajoling? I didn't want to seem like a dog, rolling over and showing my underbelly. Carpe diem. Time to seize the day. Go for firm and decisive with an underlay of team player and an emphasis on her dearly beloved dead-kids theme.

"If you think the Compassionate Friends story made the readers cry, wait'll you hear this idea for a story. It's got it all: a mother's love, a child's death, fame, beauty, beauty pageants, deceit, and possibly murder."

I laid out the whole Josane story, grabbing her first with the murder theory. You've got to hook an editor the same way you do a reader. By the time I got to Reenie Ashmore rearranging four-year-old magazines, I could tell Candace was mine. Before I hit her up for the time off, I threw my last hardball.

"And guess what?" I said. "Josane Ashmore grew up in Kannapolis—didn't you say that was one of our new penetration zones? *And* her family still lives there."

I heard a little gasp from the other end of the phone; Candace having a newspaper orgasm.

"When can we run it?" Candace said. Was it my imagination, or was she breathing heavily?

I had to play this one carefully. "Well," I started, "I already spent two hours with the mother. Five, six days in Middleburg, a week at the most, and then two or three days for research down here, three or so days to write it. I don't see why you can't run a few Sundays from now."

"Shit, three fucking weeks? Are you crazy? What am I supposed to do around here, fill the pages with wire copy?"

My hardball was turning into a wild pitch. I had to be careful here. Time to rein her in.

"I'm sure I can tighten that up. Give me a few days in Middleburg—not counting the two comp days you already approved—to snoop around, talk to her trainer and friends. I'll skip the other research and write it fast. Two weeks tops. You can put it in my year-end review if I go beyond. That's two weeks to a completed story. Written, reported, edited, cutlined."

"One week, and you can bet it goes in your review if you're an hour late. One more thing, take a laptop and phone in your fashion column. I have to go, the other phone is ringing."

She was from the Rob school of telephone conversation endings: click.

I'd gotten the week. Now, to hitch a ride with Henry and everything would be perfect.

CHAPTER 12

"I want to sit in the front. You promised. Chet sat up there last time. You promised I could."

"Come on, dorkface, just get in the car."

"Stop pushing me. I'll get in when I'm ready to get in."

"Yeah, well, I think you're ready now."

Push, slam, punch. SCREAM.

"Dad, Chet hit me in the head."

"That's because you tried to strangle me."

"That's because you called me a dorkface and pushed me in the car."

Henry pulled a tangle of screaming boys from the backseat. I could tell this wasn't going to be the trip I'd envisioned.

"That's enough. I'll take away your computer privileges if you don't stop."

The boys made a grab for each other and Henry peeled them apart.

"This is your last warning. If I count to ten, I'm throwing out your new CD-ROM with eighty games on it."

That shut the boys up fast. They glared at each other and climbed back in the car.

Henry turned to me. "Sorry, Nattie, they're just excited about the trip."

"No problem," I said, and mustered a smile. Not that I hadn't been warned. I'd had to convince Henry I could take eight hours of two boys in a small car.

"They can get pretty rambunctious," Henry said to me on the phone when I'd called him from my mother's, looking for a lift to Virginia.

"Come on, Henry, it'll be fine. They can play road bingo or whatever it is kids do in a car, and we can talk about our stories. They're nine and six years old, it's not like they're screaming babies who need their diapers changed."

"I only wanted to let you know, in advance, that traveling with two children can be stressful at times."

Henry, master of the euphemism. *Stressful at times.* The kids were banshees.

"Settle down NOW!!!" Henry blasted from the front seat.

We'd barely made it forty-five minutes out of Charlotte and already stopped twice. First a pee break and then a lemonade stop, which surely would necessitate another pee break. At this rate, we'd make it to Middleburg when the azaleas started blooming.

Sure enough, a little voice piped up from the back.

"Dad, I gotta go to the bathroom. Now." It was Hank, the younger one.

"Me too," said Chet.

I turned around and said, "I thought boys could pee in a Coke bottle?"

This scored a big hit. Chet and Hank guffawed and elbowed each other, which started them tumbling into one another. Hank grabbed his brother's pants and started to pull them down.

"Pee in a Coke bottle," Hank said between giggles. "Yeah, let's do it!!! You first, Chet."

"There's just one problem," Chet said, laughing even harder than Hank. "Dad doesn't let us drink Coke."

Then both boys chimed together an imitation of Henry: *"Too much caffeine."*

We all laughed, all four of us, and after that the boys and I got along like three pigs in a poke. I'd aced the gross-out test. I wasn't about to rest on my laurels, not when there was an opportunity to capitalize on my newly earned respect.

"Now," I said, "for the PEEEEEEEE-ayce de résistance, I bet you guys can't hold it in for another thirty minutes."

A urinary challenge—the penultimate dare to this scatological duo.

"You're on," they shrieked in utter joy.

To my chagrin, they bettered my bet and we made it all the way to Greensboro before I heard another word about the bathroom. For the most part, they settled down; Chet was into his book and Hank stayed happy as long as his father pitched him intricate math problems.

"I think my eyeballs are turning yellow," Chet finally said.

"There's a Bojangles two exits up," I said to Henry, and drifted back three years to when David and my mother took me to that Bojangles for cinnamon biscuits to celebrate my new job at *The Appeal.* Stuart Rimowitz tracked me down at my parents' house and called me at ten o'clock on a Sunday night to break the news that they'd chosen me to be the fashion writer. Ten o'clock on Sunday night in Greensboro—the town locks up at eight P.M. on Friday. Bojangles was about the only place open. So it was celebratory cinnamon biscuits or nothing. And David loved a celebration. Anytime, anywhere.

Again a little voice from the back. This time it was Hank, and I thought he was going to chime in on how badly he had to go. Instead, he said, "I like parties too."

"What?" I said. Who called Dionne Warwick's psychic line?

"Nothing. Something just got me started thinking about parties."

Chet peered over the pages of his book. "Parties, who's going to a party? Dad, is Hank going to a party I'm not?"

Henry shook his head and smiled. "You boys could fight over the color of the sky. Anyone ready to tap a kidney?"

With that Henry exited the highway and pulled into the Bojangles.

The boys scrambled to the bathroom and I ordered us a round of hot cinnamon biscuits, yet another reason to move south of the Mason-Dixon line. Balmy weather in December; cushy biscuits oozing white rivers of sugar glaze; glorious springs that showed you what God intended by pastels, and cheerful supermarket cashiers who intercepted leaking cartons of milk and called you by your first name—I do believe I'd found myself a chunk of heaven. Now, if only I could just get one southerner to laugh at a joke of mine or affix a specific time, date, and address to the ubiquitous "You'll have to come by sometime."

I walked over to the table where David and I had sat a lifetime ago. I wondered if I listened hard enough, could I hear remnants of his big laugh? I'd been reading books on quantum psychics lately, all part of my spiritual quest to make sense of tragedy. It seems time experts think we've got it all wrong. Time's not a line dance like we think it is, with a permanent past, present, and future. It's more, they say, like a waltz where everything's swirling around and around.

I listened carefully, but all I heard were the skittering feet of two boys. Chet saw the bag of biscuits first. He started jumping up and down.

"Cinnamon biscuits!! My favorite. Thanks, Nattie. Did you get some for Hank too?"

Underneath the fart talk and wrestling with his brother, Chet was a sweet kid. He was a big galumph of a boy who could have passed for twelve, even though he just turned nine a month ago. Precocious wouldn't even start to describe Chet's verbal and writing abilities. Henry would rather die than brag about himself, but when it came to his kids, you couldn't shut him up. He told me Chet started reading chapter books at four and was now zipping through *The Canterbury Tales*—in Old English. When he wasn't reading—or pummeling his brother—he wrote poetry about withering roses falling to the frozen earth and the bittersweet joy of fireweed.

Of course Henry carried copies of Chet's poems in his beat-up leather satchel and, of course, he'd asked if I'd like to read them. It's hard to turn down a man with a look of absolute devotion in his eyes, even if that devotion isn't pointing my way. Chet's astonishing poems were well beyond his years, and in my way of thinking, well beyond his life. The only way I can explain such prodigy is that he'd been Keats or Yeats last time around and hadn't finished his writing when he'd died.

Then there was little Hank. Henry and his ex obviously bred well. Their younger son was as gifted in math as Chet in English. In the few quiet moments on this trip, when Chet had been reading, Hank was working long division problems in his mind and giving us the answers, all of them correct.

I gave the boys the biscuits and they wolfed them down pronto. Chet looked like he'd been tarred and feathered or, rather, sugared and napkined. Henry sent him back into the bathroom to wash off. Hank, on the other hand, had finished his biscuit with not a trace of glaze anywhere but the napkin.

The little guy flipped his wrist and looked at his watch. "It's eleven twenty-seven. That means we'll be in Virginia in a hundred and ten minutes. Right, Dad?"

I was ready to take out a pad and paper to figure it out.

"Thereabouts," Henry said. "I may go a little faster on this stretch. I think the speed limit goes up. Hanky, you sure are the mather-man, aren't you?"

Henry scooped the little boy in his arms and hugged him. He was still at the age where that was not only acceptable, but welcome.

Henry and I didn't get much of a chance to discuss Josane,

the hit list, or Hinton Allard's unfortunate rendezvous with the underpass and what Tony found out about it. On the upside, however, the boys weren't tearing each other's throats out. We all played Mad-Libs using only bathroom words, so the Mad-Libbed stories turned out to be one variation of fart joke after another. We sang some songs, played a few rounds of twenty questions in which I stumped everyone with "air," and finally, right around the North Carolina–Virginia state line the boys fell asleep. Hallelujah!

It doesn't take a welcome sign to know you've left the Tarheel state and entered the Old Dominion. You can feel it in your bones—literally. The last stretch of North Carolina highway is a mishmosh of teeth-rattling concrete patched here and there like an old pair of pants. Right about the time your fillings are about to shake loose, you glide into Virginia and the road turns into a smooth streak of black asphalt, a quiet hum of a highway.

Henry looked in his rearview at the sleeping lumps of boy.

"My guess is that they'll be out at least an hour," Henry said. "Okay, tell me exactly what Tony said about the crash. And thanks for spotting Allard's obit in the paper. I'd have never heard about his death, thanks to our new obit policy."

"Ain't that the sad truth," I said, referring to *The Appeal*'s new pay-for-space obituary plan. Hard to believe, but *The Appeal*, once the foremost newspaper in the Carolinas, now charges grieving families by the inch to run stories about their loved ones' final newsworthy event. "Speaking of sad truths, apparently Mr. Hinton Allard tipped the bottle one too many times before getting behind the wheel of his taupe turbo Mercedes. My mother found out he'd gotten at least two—and possibly three—drunk-driving offenses expunged into oblivion. The perks of being a well-connected lawyer. So the question is, who was he connected with? My mother's tracking down his client list for you.

"And according to Tony, Allard's blood alcohol level was

point eleven, not exactly rip-roaring underpass-crashing drunk for an old-line souser like him, but enough to make him woozy. Woozy enough to crash? That's anyone's guess. So far no one's suspicious of anything except why he was still driving with a valid driver's license. Tony and his brethren were just as happy the guy smashed himself up. Or, as Tony put it, 'He was more dangerous than a cross-eyed moose in a schoolyard full of screaming babies.' "

"A cross-eyed moose?" Henry said.

"You know Tony, the bard of Waxhaw. Didn't he tell you he used to want to be the next Faulkner? Anyway, what do you think? That lowish blood alcohol level is curious, and don't hard-core drinkers need a lot of booze to be really drunk? It's possible your nutcase knew about his drinking and planned a car crash for exactly that reason. To make it seem like an accident."

"Gold, what you lack in physical stature you make up for in imagination. I'm not ruling it out. It's certainly a possibility. Thanks for all your digging—and thanks to your mother too. Here, take a look at the latest letter."

He rooted around in his satchel and pulled out a piece of paper, the same kind of cheap copy paper as before: flimsy with no sheen to it and the color of my white laundry that's gone too many washings unsegregated.

The mystery maniac was feeling more chatty this time around:

HE DIDN'T HAVE TO DIE. HE WOULDN'T HAVE DIED IF IT HADN'T HAVE BEEN FOR YOU AND YOUR KIND. YOU WILL PAY. THE LORD AND I WILL MAKE SURE OF THAT.

HAVE YOU EVER HURT SO BAD, DYING SEEMED GOOD? THAT'S WHAT HAPPENED. FIRST HE COUGHED, THEN DIED. BUT IT TOOK SO LONG. SO LONG. A HUMAN BEING SHOULDN'T HAVE TO SUFFER LIKE THAT. AND THERE ARE OTHERS, JUST LIKE HIM, TAKING SO LONG TO DIE. SO LONG AND HURTING SO BAD.

THE LORD SPOKE TO ME AFTERWARD. HE SAID, "THEY NEED TO

BE PUNISHED. THEY NEED TO BE STOPPED SO MORE DON'T DIE LIKE HE DID."

YES, LORD, I HEAR YOU. THEY WILL BE STOPPED. I'LL DO AS MUCH AS I CAN DO FOR YOU.

"Yikes," I said. "This is scary stuff, Henry. We're talking major delusions here. Whoever wrote this thinks he or she's got a direct line to the almighty. And it doesn't look like this almighty is all-forgiving. Someone's looking for retribution. The question is for what?"

"You're right, that *is* the question. Intriguing, isn't it?"

"I'll say. . . . HURT SO BAD, DYING SEEMED GOOD. Somebody died a horrible death, that's for sure. Coughing and dying. Could be anything. Cancer, emphysema, black lung, brown lung, tuberculosis, and probably an assortment of other respiratory diseases we never heard of. Now all you've got to do is find out who, what, where, when, and why—before your nutcase gets a call from God, assuming Hinton Allard wasn't the first direct dial. Good luck."

"I might need it. But I'm hoping things will start to gel when I see what the people on the list have in common. The ones that stick out most are Christopher Carey and your artist friend. A Hollywood movie star and a New York artist amid a list of well-connected Carolinians and Virginians? Maybe the records check can turn up something. By the way, thanks for telling me what you know about the others. Is that right, that Santee Mundell leased his daughter a horse for *two hundred fifty grand* a year?"

"Not a year." I said. "A *half* year. Six months, fourteen hundred a day. Do you mean right in the moral sense? Hardly, and that's the low-end guess. Don't look at me like that. I'm not going to apologize for the wretched excesses of my sport, because they're just that—wretched excess. Some people just have too much money. And I think a person who pays more money to rent a horse than some third world countries make in a year just so his pea-brained little girl can try to win blue ribbons is just too damned rich."

"There's always basketball," Henry said. "Tell me about that woman who thinks her daughter was murdered."

I sketched out the story for him and told him my plans, what there were of them—talk to all the horse people I knew, find the boyfriend, the employee, the nurse, corner the cops, and maybe even track down the horse and ride it to see if it really was the killer beast it was cracked up to be.

I watched Henry's face, looking for signs of anything. Approval. Disapproval. Life. If newspapers go the way everyone thinks they will—into the Smithsonian as "the way it was"—Henry could easily pursue a backup career in gambling. He had the best poker face I'd ever seen. Trying to read anything off his puss was like looking for depth in television news.

Admittedly, I was edgy about my so-called plan. I know my strengths journalistically, and my weaknesses. I can write: I've made readers cry and laugh and just plain get to the end of a sixty-inch story—no small feat for the USA Today-ified redesigned readers who think twenty inches of copy is War and Peace. And I can interview. I don't know how I do it, maybe it's because as a short woman I look so nonthreatening. People open up to me and tell me their secrets. Feelings, intimate details of their sex lives. You name it, they've spilled it. One woman told me how she did handstands after she and her husband had sex so she could help the sperm along their way. And that was just for a puff-piece Mother's Day story. Another person, an upstanding suburban career woman, told me how she shoplifted bottles of Fire and Ice nail polish because it made her feel alive. Then there was my coup: Jessica Hahn's parents. After weeks of deluge by reporters, it was I her parents finally let into their tiny Massapequa rambler. It was I with whom they finally broke their silence about their daughter and Jim Bakker. I ended up staying four hours, sipping homemade lemonade with her mother while she showed me old pictures of little Jessica and her baby brother, Danny.

As for my weaknesses, what I can't do is organize and plan. I get the same reaction internally when I try to read maps—panic mixed with nausea. So you'd think I'd be grateful for any help in that area. Maybe in another twenty years, when I've matured some and had my brain completely shrunk by the Good Doctor Grass, the unofficial newsroom shrink the one who wears a bad toupee and tells me I should be able to have sex with my father because it is only a primal act.

Henry's face continued to show nothing except concentration on the road. He was silent for a while, cogitating. I'd learned from the last time we worked together that Henry is a ruminator of the tenth degree.

Finally, eight miles later, he spoke. "Running around Middleburg and riding horses is probably not the best use of your time. I think you should do some record checking on her finances. Money, that's where you catch people. How they make it and how they spend it speaks volumes. Also, find out who the man was. Or men. Dig around about that store. Middleburg's in Loudoun County; the county seat is in Leesburg. I've got to go there myself to do background checks. I'll show you how to work the books. It's not difficult, you just have to get organized and focus on what you're looking for."

I could feel the spat brewing. I hate it when people tell me to get organized, no doubt because I can't do it. I may be an immature idiot sometimes, but I'm an analyzed immature idiot.

"Henry, I guess I didn't mention I've got Candace breathing down my back to get this story in fast. I don't get months off to do research like some investigative reporters who shall remain nameless. I may not be as organized as you, but I'm plenty focused and I'm focused on talking to people about Josane, not wasting a day in the stacks."

"I wouldn't call looking through financial records wasting a day. People leave behind enormous paper trails, and if you're diligent, you can find out almost everything about someone through his or her records."

"Henry, spare me your 'rewards of records searching' lecture you give to all the eager-beaver Bob Woodward wannabes at the IRE conferences. I'm not one of your groupies."

Someday I'll learn to control my temper. Maybe around the time I learn to organize.

The truth was, from what I'd heard from my friends who'd watched Henry deliver his spiel at the conferences for investigative reporters and editors, he was funny, contagious, and captivating on the subject.

But I didn't feel like being captivated. I sunk into my seat and Henry flipped on the radio. Frilly classical music trilled around the car, and I zoned out, trying to rein in my temper. What works best is riding; when that option's not available, I move into the make-believe and imagine perfect courses on my horse. After a few of those I'm usually ready to face the world again.

"Henry," I started. "This organization thing drives me crazy, and I just wanted to say th—"

Henry put his hand up to my mouth. "Shhh, just a second." Then he turned up the volume. I'd been too far out in the riding ring to notice the music had changed to news. He pointed to the radio as if the announcer were sitting between us.

"They just promoed a story I want to hear."

I listened, as instructed, wondering about the existence of an electronic collective unconsciousness between radio and television reporters. How else to explain the same tired clichés?

"In the picturesque little village of Markham, Virginia, home to an apple orchard and an old stone post office, the tranquillity of a Shenandoah Christmas season was shattered with the apparent execution-style slaying of one of its own. Residents here had hoped to escape such big city–style violence, but it seems even in these placid rolling hills, sixty miles isn't enough of a buffer from the mentality of the war-torn streets of the nation's capital.

His name had been Jim Benson. He was a prominent Markham cattle farmer who was found late Christmas day by well-known Virginia horse trainer Charlie Laconte. Benson had been shot twelve times in the head and neck.

" 'I heard shots and thought it was deer hunters. The property is posted, but that doesn't stop anyone,' Laconte said. 'Then an hour or two later I found him, blood everywhere. That's the kind of thing that happens in Washington, but out here? Never, I don't know who—' "

"Holy shit!" I blurted out. Henry was about to shut me up again, but I got there faster. "Jim Benson. B for Benson!! Number two on the list. That's the one I know—or knew. I show against him all the time. He's that faux farmer horse pro I told you about, the one who rides as an amateur. Still think Mr. A was just a car crash?"

Henry was about to say something. But he'd been right before, what I lacked in height I more than made up for not only in imagination, but speed. Again, I got there first. "Looks like your wacko got his or her marching orders—again. I know you started out thinking it was just a bored little old lady with nothing better to do than write poison-pen mail. There was something about those letters, something too Old-Testamenty to take lightly."

I took a breath and let Henry in.

He said, " 'Old-Testamenty?' "

"You know, when God got mad at Charlton Heston and blasted the Ten Commandments out of his hands with a lightning bolt? Like I said before, that letter writer seemed too righteous, as if he or she had been anointed the acting hand of God while God was busy settling other business."

"Maybe you're right. I thought all this story would come to would be a few threatening telephone calls, more letters, cheap vandalism, but not likely a murder—or okay yes, possibly two murders. People send crazy letters all the time, I must see five a week and they never end up in murder."

"This one did," I said.

"It's still hard to believe. But when I heard the promo on the radio about the Christmas Day murder story in the country with Benson's name attached to it, I knew we were headed for trouble. I just hope things don't get worse."

"Don't count on it. I've got a bad feeling this is just the start. And it's not my heightened sense of drama flaring up. This one I feel in my bones. Misters C, D, E, and so on ought to be worried."

I was glad John's last name started with O. Surely Henry would catch the killer by at least M.

"You might be right. What've we got for C and D?"

Henry handed me the list and I moved my eyes down to the cc list. "How could I forget? C is for Carey, Christopher Carey, *People* magazine's new sexiest man alive. You know I have an old friend who's in the film business out in L.A. I'll e-mail him and see if he knows anyone in Carey's camp, see if the blue-eyed hunkola's being bothered by anyone. Let's see, D for Duncan. Outerbridge Duncan. This guy's name has been eating away at me since I saw it. I know I know him, I just can't remember how. I hate this feeling, it's like picking a scab."

"A scab? Well, should it come loose, let me know. I don't know if I told you, but I had an interview set up with Benson tomorrow. I suppose I'll be going to his funeral instead. I'm wondering if he told anyone about the note."

"The person to ask is Charlie Laconte. The 'well-known Virginia horse trainer.' That radio reporter didn't finish his sentence. It should have been, 'Charlie Laconte, well-known horse trainer, and longtime significant other to Jim Benson.' Those two were practically married and probably would have been had it not been for the Commonwealth of Virginia's frowning upon that kind of thing. That and Benson's roving eye and other body parts."

"Benson and Laconte? Nattie, are there any straight men involved with horses?"

"A few," I said. "Mostly western riders. But then there's that big gay rodeo. No, I'm joking, not about the rodeo, about the hunter guys. I guess there are some straight ones. Let me think, there's Keith Rollings, remember him, the South Carolina pedophile? And then Johnny Tugsten, the best rider this sport has ever seen. He's been married around 534 times, about the same number of times he been in detox. Then there's Billy McCabe, he's kind of an old dimwit; his child bride, a former junior rider of his, started romping around with their groom, then the groom started up with one of McCabe's new junior riders, then McCabe's wife put sugar down the gas tank of the car owned by the mother of the junior rider and left town with all of McCabe's tack, including three Hermès saddles and five custom bridles. Can't forget Joe Reading, the Mafia homophobe who calls all the gay trainers 'girls' and isn't allowed within a hundred yards of a horse show anymore because he hired a moron thug to kill two of his well-insured horses who stopped winning ribbons. Last but not least, there's the subcategory of married men who are really gay but want to put up a straight front. At least a handful of the biggest names in the business operates that way. One of them has two children. Gail heard they were turkey baster babies.

"The bottom line is, Henry, if you're a straight woman, you're sure as hell not going to find your soul mate on the A-circuit. As a gay trainer friend says, 'It's not exactly the heterosexual man of the year pickings out by the show ring.' And the good ones, the few and far between, get snapped up in about three seconds by the beautiful blond heiresses looking for someone just like Daddy. Like Lucinda DuPont, who married—"

"Stop, stop," Henry said. "It sounds like *All My Children*."

"How would you know what *All My Children* sounds like?"

"I started watching it in college."

"At Harvard? You were watching soaps at Harvard?"

Henry puffed up, proud in his ability to be one of The People. "As a matter of fact, everyone on my floor at Lowell House watched. I still tape it on occasion to find out what number husband Erica is on."

"Well, I'll be a monkey's ass," I said. "And speaking of, I sure was one about the records checking stuff. I can't see that a day in the stacks will kill me. You name the day, I'll tag along."

"It'll depend on Benson's funeral. I think I should be there," Henry said.

"Then consider me your shadow, because any person I needed to talk to will be watching Benson take his final jump—the big ditch."

I heard movement from the back and then a voice, "Who's a big bitch, I can say it if she just said it, who's the big bitch?"

Henry craned around to see the sleep status. It was Hank, looking confused but invigorated by a curse word.

"Hanky, shhhh, don't wake up your brother," Henry said. Was that a note of emotion in his voice? Perhaps panic? "No one's a bitch. Nattie said 'ditch.' Now go back to sleep. I bet your mother will let you stay up late tonight if you take a long nap."

Hank burrowed back into the official children's sleeping-in-a-car position: slumped into the corner with the neck bent at an unnatural angle.

Then Henry did the most un-Henry thing; something readable flashed across his face. Annoyance, hurt, concern, something along those lines. He muttered, "She'll let you stay up late even if you don't get a nap. And that'll be after she gives you Coke and chocolate ice cream at nine o'clock."

"What?" I said. I didn't know if I was supposed to be hearing him grouse about the former Mrs. Henry.

"Nothing," he said. His face went back to concentration on the road.

I guess The Former was his business.

CHAPTER 13

W e pulled into Washington, D.C., a weary and crumpled bunch, the four of us. Eight hours in a car under the best of circumstances can be challenging to body, mind, and soul. And I have to say, after that first horrible hour, Henry's kids were gems. We zipped straight up I-95 with nary a fight and only one stop. The boys, road savvy to this route after a couple years of the joint-custody shuffle, knew the landmarks by the time left to get to Washington.

"There's the death stick building that fills our graveyards with corpses," Chet announced solemnly as we passed Philip Morris in Richmond. He was referring to the tobacco company's architectural totem to cigarettes, its research and development building. The tall building had strange tubelike columns, which may have been the architect's idea of modernism, but to me looked like a giant stuck his giant-sized cigarettes on the front of the building. "That means we've got only two hours to go. Whew."

Twenty miles later, Hank spotted a big purple sign. "Yes!!! Kings Dominion, an hour and a half or ninety minutes or fifty-four hundred seconds!!! Yippee, we're almost there. Chet, you think Mom will take us to that place for fried chicken?"

Henry answered, "Remember to take off the skin if she does."

A while later we passed the ugliest and biggest office building known to humankind, a full twenty-nine acres of squat concrete. I knew that one.

"Hey," I said, "anybody know what that big, ugly thing on the right is?"

The deeper of the two voices. "The Pentagon," Chet said. "That's where all the warmongers are."

"Right," I said. "On both accounts. Say, Henry, who's been teaching this kid, Angela Davis?"

"Close," he said. "You'll see."

We crossed the bridge with the big golden horses and wove around the streets of Washington. After everything I'd been reading about our great nation's capital, I wondered if I'd be ducking stray bullets anytime soon.

"Henry," I said, "my mother couldn't take another death. Sure this is safe?"

"It's fine," Henry said in his full-blown Daddy voice of authority, which is exactly what I wanted to hear. "We're three blocks from the Watergate building and ten minutes from the kids' grandparents' house. It's as safe as any place in Charlotte."

I believed him, mostly. Not that it made me feel entirely secure. Charlotte's been home to some pretty awful crimes lately. Part of me stayed on high alert looking for sudden eruptions of big-city violence.

The city looked pleasant enough, and, in parts, downright beautiful. He exited onto the Rock Creek Parkway, a winding stretch of blacktop that snaked through woods, streams, and past the back entrance of the National Zoo.

"The zoo!!!" shrieked Hank. "Three minutes and twenty seconds if we hit the light right."

I looked at the digital clock on Henry's dashboard and sure enough, by the time we pulled up to the curb and parked, three minutes had passed.

The kids blasted from the car and catapulted up the steps, three long sets of them leading to a large blue stucco Victorian in bad need of a coat of paint. The front door swung open and I heard bits and pieces of some country-western singer. Who knew which one? They all sound alike to me; tears in their voices and twangs in their hearts. But it did clear up any question regarding the names of Henry's children. I'd have thought Henry would have gone the family route and I was reasonably sure there'd been no Chet Goodes along the way. So Chet must have been The Former's idea and Hank, which probably started out as Henry, his.

I looked up the stairs and caught my first glimpse of the first Mrs. Henry Goode. I'd assumed she'd be like Henry; tall, blond, and beautiful. Assume, as they say in the newspaper business, makes an *ass* out of *u* and *me*.

From my perspective, three flights below, she was short, dark, and sure as hell not going to win the Miss Universe contest anytime soon. I got out of the car and started walking up the steps. At closer range, I could see better what she looked like. She wasn't ugly, she wasn't pretty. It was hard to tell what she was. I'm not a believer in tons of makeup and fancy clothes, but she made me look like Divine. She was wearing a dowdy maroon paisley dress, dark hose, and much too sensible shoes. Her hair, somewhere between brown and dark brown, was pulled back in a ponytail. No makeup, no jewelry. She was probably my height, but wiry as a twig of thyme. Her eyes were dark, her nose—we Jewish girls always make a visual beeline for that—was straight enough, a little on the wide side, but nothing to run to the nose doctor for. She was a little pale, probably from all that New Jersey air she'd been breathing. That's where she lived and that's why she and Henry didn't live together.

We were eyeing each other like two nervous tomcats staking out territory. I had no turf to claim in this matter, so I stuck out my hand and smiled big.

"Hi, I'm Nattie Gold, a colleague of Henry's at *The Appeal*. I did that horse show series with him this past summer. Now we're working on another story, some kind of death threat list where there's already been a death. And he's helping me with a story of

109

mine, a mother who thinks her daughter was murdered, but she's probably wrong. It was probably nothing. Henry and I are just friends."

No turf to defend? Why was I blathering on and on like an idiot? What made me say that crap about Henry and I just being friends? It was none of her business what I was with Henry. Sometimes words pass through my lips that startle me as much as the listener. This was one of those times. I forced myself to stop talking. Not that it mattered; her attention was, mercifully, elsewhere.

Saved by the boys, who were climbing all over their mother looking for love. Henry, on the other hand, had heard everything I'd said. And while I couldn't be sure, I think I saw a hint of a smirk on his face.

"Hi, Martha," Henry said to the woman. "How are things with the Teamsters?"

"Very interesting times," she said. "I'm working around the clock, and good things are happening. Finally. When we have more time, I'll fill you in."

Henry nodded. At best, it was a noncommittal nod. I'm guessing that nod translated into the private language of couples meant Henry would have time to talk about Martha's job when cows started flying. We hadn't discussed his marriage and what went wrong, but from what I heard around the newsroom, they'd had a shaky one to start with, and when she got offered the job with the new Teamsters in Newark, that was it. He refused to move, she refused to stay.

"Martha," Henry said, "I realize you think I'm overbearing on the subject, but go easy on the sugar with the boys. Don't forget Hank's speech exercises and Chet's movement stuff. He's up to—"

"Henry, relax, the boys and I'll be fine. They're out of your control now. We're going to have the best time, aren't we, guys?

Ice cream for breakfast, lunch, *and* dinner!!! Wait'll you see what Grandma baked you, espresso brownies."

Chet and Hank started whooping and hollering. Henry started to redden around the neck.

"Got you? Didn't I, Henry?" Martha said. She laughed and then I saw what Henry must have seen in her. She had a great, earthy roar and big, homey smile. "Just kidding. Henry, I know what to feed the kids. I *am* their mother. I promise not too much sugar and don't even say it about the skin off the chicken. Henry, go to Virginia and be Bob Woodward. This is my time with the boys."

Henry hugged and kissed each little Goode and reluctantly walked back down the steps.

"Wait, Daddy." It was Hank. He was standing on the top step, holding his mother's hand.

"What, Hanky?" Henry said. The little boy ran down to his father and put his arms around Henry's waist.

"I just wanted to say good-bye again and be careful driving," Hank said.

"Hank, your job is to have fun, not worry," Henry said. "Okay, little guy? I want to see a big smile. No, that's not a big smile. Bigger. That's better. We made it *all* the way up here from North Carolina and we're fine. See? Nothing's going to happen, I promise."

Martha called to him. "Come on, Hank-man, I think Grandmom's got something for you."

"Bye, Daddy." Hank dashed up the steps and Henry seemed incapable of moving. And I thought Hank was having trouble separating.

Henry needed a distraction, so I offered to treat for dinner.

"I thought you were bouncing checks?"

"That was last week," I said. "This is now. My treat, your choice. You know this town better than I."

"How hungry are you?" Henry said.

"I could eat a cow—if I ate cows."

"Not at this place," Henry said.

"Oh, please, no more tofu. It's bad enough I have to put up with that from my father."

"Trust me, you'll like where I'm taking you."

I did. It was a little place with peculiar semicircular vinyl booths and purple pop beads hanging from vases. Can't judge a restaurant by its decor. I had the best Indian food I'd ever had in my life. Not that I've had a vast selection of opportunities in Charlotte.

It must be difficult to leave your kids for a couple of weeks, even if you're leaving them with their mother. I could tell Henry was having a hard time with the arrangement, because he was distracted enough that he didn't even want to talk about just what you do in a room full of musty records. So instead of story strategies, we talked kids and life and marriage over our mango lassis.

"I lived with someone once," I told Henry. "It was the classic rebound thing. I bounced into him so fast and furious, we moved in together two weeks after we met. That's as close to marriage as I ever got, and it wasn't too much fun after the first five minutes. He used to take the towels I'd folded, unfold them in front of me, and then show me the proper way to fold. I knew I couldn't live with him the rest of my life, or even much longer. But I didn't know how to get out, or maybe I was afraid I'd hurt him, so I ended up staying with him another year."

A sad smile came across Henry's face. "I know what you mean. It's hard to let go of a relationship, especially one where you've got a history together. Then, if you add children to the equation, well, it's absolutely the worst. Anything you do seems wrong *and* you have these two little lives dependent on you."

I was about to ask what went wrong with the Henry-Martha

union, but the check came. Just as well, Henry was feeling sad enough without me doing a root canal into his personal life.

Henry wanted to go back and say good night to the boys. It was getting late, we still had an hour to go, and I didn't think Martha would appreciate it.

"If Martha did that to you, would that annoy you?" I said.

"Good point," Henry said, and pointed the car toward Virginia.

Too bad it was too dark to see the sights. From what I remembered, the land around Upperville, where my college roommate lived on her family farm, was spectacular. The stuff of hunt country picture postcards. We'd see it tomorrow, on the way to Jim Benson's funeral, assuming he was having one.

"That's it," I said, motioning to the fieldstone pillars and brass sign that announced, MUCH ADO FARMS. "That's Annie's. Go slowly, the driveway's twisty."

Twisty, long, and steep. A driveway to her, a country road complete with babbling brooks to anyone else. At the end of it was an old stone house that made my heart beat fast. Before my father left us for good, he promised me he'd come back and take me to live in a fieldstone farmhouse. The closest I ever got was when David, my stepfather, married my mother and moved me, my brother, and his bride/my mother into a little rambler in North Jersey with a rock facade.

"Nice house," Henry said.

"I'll say, wait'll you see the inside." It was more a manor than a house. I banged the knocker, a brass fox head. Steps followed and the door swung open.

"Nattie!! Nattie!! Nattie!! It's so good to see you."

Annie and I threw our arms around each other and hugged. She'd been my roommate in college and, though we were as different as ragweed and orchids, we'd been good friends as well. That's something I'd have never expected when I first met her twenty years ago.

From the get-go, Annie intimidated every cell in my body. She was everything I wanted to be: tall, thin, refined, silky-haired, perfect-nosed, rich, horsey-ed, poised, and Wasp. She wasn't exactly beautiful, but close enough for me. At seventeen, I was too young to know that was just the wrapping, and she wasn't any happier with hers than I with mine. One night the girls in our dorm wing were playing a dumb board game called Therapy. Annie got a card that asked, If you could be anyone, who would it be and why? She didn't even have to think about it. "Nattie," she'd said. "I'd be Nattie. She's funny, she's full of life, she can wear anything and look like a kid instead of a thirty-year-old matron, she's got a heritage that embraces her, and she says whatever she feels like saying without worrying what people think of her."

That was my first big Life Lesson. Too bad it didn't stick. It took another wallop in the face to get it down pat. About ten years later I was once again struck by idol envy. This one being in roughly the same shape as Annie: tall, thin, poised, etc. She, like Annie, was also gregarious, smart, and genuinely nice. I found myself wishing I could be just like her, measuring myself against her and failing miserably. Then one gorgeous fall afternoon my idol walked into the woods, put a Glock to her head, and scattered her brains across the fallen red and gold leaves of a maple tree. I got the message, finally.

"Annie, Annie, Anniebannannie, how *are* you? Single life suits you well, you look spectacular." She did. At eighteen, her face and body did look a little too old to house a kid. But at thirty-seven her age had finally caught up with her looks. She was what most people except my mother would call a handsome woman. But then again, my mother's role model in the beauty department is Cleopatra, or, if forced to tone it down, Sophia Loren.

Annie was a study in subtlety. Her hair was highlighted just enough to look like she'd been sunning in Palm Beach, and her body was slender with no sudden turns or shouting curves of womanhood. She was dressed straight out of Ann Taylor: impeccably tailored black wool slacks, black patent leather flats, and a starched white shirt. On me that getup would scream busgirl at Bennigan's. "Oh, hon, couldja bring some ketchup and another diet Coke?" On Annie it whispered *Town and Country*, as in this month's cover matron. Even in college, when we'd fancied ourselves hippies, she'd never been a jeans kind of gal. Her biggest act of rebellion hadn't been in the fashion arena. When she acted out, she did it with her choice of men. Annie went for bad boys in a big way.

"Nattie, you look terrific yourself."

"Annie, it's me, Nattie. You don't have to be polite. Say what you think, that I look like I've been run over by an eighteen-wheeler. I've just spent the last eight hours locked in a car with two boys, age nine and six."

She laughed. "All right. But not an eighteen-wheeler, maybe just a pickup."

We hugged again and I introduced her to Henry. I knew Annie well enough to know she was holding back her charms, which are considerable when it comes to men. Not that Henry would have interested her for more than ten minutes. Henry and Annie looked like bookends and that was the problem. Annie went for her own kind about as often as I did, which was never. Unless, of course, they were felons, about to be felons, or class-A schmucks.

When I'd called to ask if Henry could stay, I just said he was a reporter from the paper. I was too busy to explain anything else. Annie probably thought Henry and I were more than what we were.

As we stood there, exchanging hellos, a paler version of Annie walked in. It was her mother, who was working on her fourth or fifth marriage. I'd lost count years ago. I didn't know what last name she went by these days, and since I'd met her when I was still officially a kid, she'd always be Mrs. something to me.

"Nattie, how delightful to see you," Annie's mother said.

I didn't know how to respond, seeing as I didn't know her current name. Just as I was about to fudge it, a man walked in. He was the same style as Annie's mother—high Wasp, well groomed, quite attractive in an Abercrombie-and-Fitch, just-got-off-my-sailboat kind of way. But he was definitely not of the same vintage. While Annie liked her boys bad, her mother liked her men boys. This one was definitely older than the other ones I'd met, but still not in her decade. I'd have guessed at least a fifteen-year difference, though it was difficult to tell, given all the plastic work Annie's mother has had.

Annie stepped forward. "Nattie, I don't think you've met my mother's husband. Let me introduce you all. Nattie Gold, Henry Goode, this is Outerbridge Duncan."

Outerbridge Duncan!! Holy mother of Methuselah, I knew I knew that name. Outerbridge Duncan, Mr. D, number four on the psycho's hit parade.

CHAPTER 14

I shook the man's hand as if he were just the newest in a series of stepfathers of an old friend. It took all my restraint, but that's all I did. Just a handshake, a "Hello, nice to meet you," and "Great bow tie," which it was. Red, with small white dots. I admired traditional men who wore bow ties. They were dancing on the outer edges of straight-man fashion. And it was yet another reason to be happy I had both X chromosomes. We women may get screwed in every other way in the workforce, but at least we can dress with a sense of whimsy without being considered a fop or gay.

"Oh, that's right, Annie tells me you're the fashion editor for the Charlotte paper."

Hoisted by my own petard.

"Not exactly," I said. "I write a fashion column on Sunday, but I do other stories the rest of the time."

I quickly shut up after that. Not another word. Nothing about what other stories I might be working on such as helping Henry with his death threat list. Nothing about Jim Benson's riddled body or "Watch out, you're next."

This was Henry's story, and he had the right to play it however he wanted.

Annie's mother—now I had a name to her, Mrs. Duncan—moved us into the living room. We didn't even know we were being directed and managed, but before I knew it, I was sitting in a chintz chair with a glass of red wine next to me.

What the hell, it'd been a long day. I took a swallow. I judge wine by how little it makes me grimace. This one was pretty good, I barely twisted my mouth. I hate the taste of anything alcoholic. But I do like how it makes me feel.

I took a few more sips and sat back, waiting to see what Henry did after we made our way through the polite pleasantries of host-guest chitchat. Even I, Ms. Talk First and Maybe Think Later, knew you couldn't burst right in with a "Hello, nice to meet you and is it true you've been getting threatening letters for the past three weeks?" So we talked weather, their house, our trip.

Mr. and Mrs. Duncan sat on the sofa, close enough to let me know they hadn't been married all that long. Now I remembered. Annie had written me last year, telling me her mother had married—again.

This one's only moderately horrible, she'd written. *A man by the odd name of Outerbridge Duncan. You know how we Wasps can't let go of family names regardless of how dreadful they are. At least he's better than the last one, who was barely out of diapers and only wanted to play polo while Mother supported him. Number Five seems to be fond of Mother. Here's the big news, he's actually old enough to remember World War II and he has a job. She met Number Five at the . . ."*

That's why I hadn't remembered his name. She'd written it only once. Thereafter he was always referred to as Number Five.

I took another sip and this time my lips barely twitched. My head was starting to buzz and I was getting that warm, glittery feeling like all my blood vessels were wrapped in velvet heating tape. I sank deeper into the down, silently offering thanks to the fifty-four flocks of geese who gave their lives for my comfort.

I reached for the wine, and thought better of it. Any more woozy and I'd end up calling Mr. Duncan "Number Five" and/or possibly rubbing up against Henry like a cat in heat. Not that that would be so horrible. Okay, I admit it, I've had a fantasy or two about him. Possibly even three.

One in particular, where Henry and I are out in the woods on a rainy day. There's a creek, we take a dip, then—

"Nattie, oh, Nattie, are you with us?"

I shook my head to clear the fog. Annie was talking to me.

"Sorry, Annie, I was out in the ozone. You know how well I handle wine."

"Yes, I do. Put that glass down so I can find out why you two are in Virginia. What's this story you're working on?"

Josane Ashmore would have to wait. I smiled and looked at Henry.

"Take it away, Hank," I said.

"Hank?" Henry said.

"Oh, you know who I mean, tell them, tell them why you're here before I do. I've exercised more restraint in the past ten minutes than I have in thirty-seven years of living."

That got everyone's attention, including Henry's. I couldn't tell if he was annoyed, flustered, or getting his thoughts in order. I had no idea how he wanted to introduce the list, but I was tired of waiting. If he didn't tell Mr. D he'd better be watching his butt, I was going to.

And this is why I don't drink much. Alcohol is to my superego what water is to the Wicked Witch of the West. I could practically hear the little man in my head shrieking "Help, I'm melting." Any thoughts of professional courtesy to Henry were gone by the second swallow.

Just as I was about to say "The list, Henry, tell him about the list," I saw Henry fishing around in his satchel.

"I hadn't planned to spring this on you so suddenly, but it seems Nattie can't wait another second. Does this look familiar?"

Henry handed the letter to Mr. and Mrs. Number Five.

Duncan scanned the paper quickly and an amused yet dismissive look spread across his face, which now that I looked at it more closely and under the influence of alcohol bore more than a passing resemblance to Jack Kennedy. "This?" he said. "*This* brought you all the way up here from North Carolina? What's the matter, have they run out of preachers raiding the collection plates?"

For the rest of his life, Henry would be known as the reporter who brought down Jim Bakker. Not bad, considering my legacy to American journalism would probably be the time *Newsweek* picked up my lead to a fashion story and quoted me: "Ralph Lauren, in search of the shiksa goddess . . ."

"As long as there's religion, I'm sure there'll be scandal," Henry said. "However, one minister is enough for me for the time being. About the letters, I assume you've been getting them?"

"Well, yes, I have. Those and others too numerous to count just like them, enough to fill a trash bag, which is exactly what we do. So?"

"Look at this other page. Did you also get the cc list?"

"Cc list? I couldn't be certain either way, though I don't believe so. What does it matter? We get these letters all the time. People blaming us for everything from the depletion of the ozone layer to their car not starting in the morning. Last week we got one from a woman complaining about her dog's mood swings."

"Mr. Duncan," I said. "Take a look at that list."

He did. And so did Annie's mother. It was she who gasped first.

"Oh, my God," she said. "Bridge, the second name is Jim Benson."

That paled up his ruddy complexion a bit.

"Oh, dear," he said. "I see your point. But Jim Benson? What did that television news report say he did? Cow farming? That was it, right? The only thing I know about cows is that they make an awful racket in the early morning. Benson and I have nothing in common other than we both live in northern Virginia. Why would I be on a list with him?"

"That's what I'm here to find out," Henry said. "What you have in common with Benson as well as the rest of those people on the list. You mentioned 'other letters like this' and being blamed for everything. What do you mean by that?"

Number Five leaned back and smiled big. It was the expansive smile of privilege from someone who's grown up with plenty of it or married into it.

"My dear boy, you're looking at the pariah of the free world, the whipping boy for the world's woes, Satan in the flesh."

"Let me guess," I said. "Jesse Helms's campaign manager?"

"Now, that, young lady, depends on your perspective," Duncan said. "Mr. Helms can get a little carried away at times. That silly business about shooting the President. Can no one take a joke these days? However, he certainly has been good to us."

"Okay," I said. "I give. Who's us?"

Outerbridge Duncan reached inside his sport jacket, a muted charcoal tweed with a hint of aubergine, and pulled out a pack of Benson & Hedges.

"The great golden leaf," he said, smiling as he slipped a polished fingernail under the cellophane tail of the wrapper and pulled. "Years ago they called it the divine leaf. That name has unfortunately given way to other, less flattering terms. Coffin nails. Death sticks, and so on. In Latin it's known as genus *Nicotiana*. In English, tobacco. I am the founder of the American Smokers Council and Research Group. Care for a cigarette?"

CHAPTER 15

Tobacco. That's what makes you cough first then die. If I remembered correctly from a World Health Organization story I'd read recently, cough and die to the tune of three million people a year. I took out my calculator. That's 8,219 deaths a day, 342 deaths an hour, 5.7 deaths a minute.

In just the time I'd been sipping wine at Annie's, more than a hundred people had coughed their last breath, leaving behind a raft of crying daughters, wives, husbands, children.

Suddenly the wacko didn't seem so wacked out.

I'd watched my grandfather die a long, horrible death from colon cancer. After three years of that, I'd have liked to wipe away the responsible party. However, taking out the beef industry seemed excessive and not entirely fair since I'm sure the big fatty slabs of roast beef my grandfather wolfed down every Friday night weren't the only things that caused his cancer. He also smoked cigars.

"Well," I said, "you *are* Satan in the flesh. You got a pair of horns back there?"

"I like a young woman with a sense of humor," Duncan said.

I laughed, but then said, "I'm not entirely joking. I don't believe in Satan. But that doesn't mean I think what you're doing is right. My mother smokes three packs a day and swears she's as addicted as any crack addict."

I could feel the tension rise in the room. I should've just shut up. I was a guest in their house and I'm sure Henry wanted to ask him some questions before we got thrown out. Between the wine and my worry that I'd be one of the crying daughters soon, I was having a hard time reining myself in.

"By the way, what about this nicotine stuff anyway?" I said. "How could the tobacco companies crank up the nicotine levels just to hook in more smokers? Don't you guys have any conscience?"

This is where breeding shows itself. Duncan smiled graciously.

"That is certainly a topic of great debate," he said. "And I would love to discuss it with you in as much detail as you like. Perhaps at my office?"

He handed me his card, and that was clearly that. Annie's mother, well schooled in the art of people-management cues, glided over to the wine bottle and topped off everyone's glass.

"Mother," Annie said, "don't give Nattie any more. She'll start telling you what she really thinks about your decorating."

I looked around.

"Annie," I said, "this place is gorgeous. I'd kill to live here."

Silence. A few throat clearings.

"Oops," I said. "Just a figure of speech, probably the wrong figure of speech given what happened to Jim Benson."

I looked at Henry, who wasn't laughing. He was getting easier to read by the second. If I hoped to salvage anything of our friendship—forget any fantasies—I'd better lock up my tongue for the night.

I sank deep into my chair and shut up.

Henry asked Duncan more questions about the letters. Yes, he'd first shown them to his security people, but that was standard procedure. No, there'd been no telephone calls or person-to-person threats. And yes, he knew a few of the names on the list, primarily from social occasions.

"I have met Christopher Carey once," Duncan said, "at the

opening of that western he starred in with Julia Roberts. Lovely man and much smarter than one might imagine."

My head was starting to bang and my eyes droop. It was time to put this day to an end. I tapped Annie and whispered, "Where am I sleeping?"

She got up to lead the way.

"Mr. and Mrs. Duncan," I said, "thanks in advance for your generous hospitality. Sorry my mouth got out of control. It's been a struggle my whole life."

"Not to worry," Number Five said. "Smoking brings out the passion in all of us."

It does? I thought, but thankfully, didn't say. Phlegm, maybe, but passion?

"Henry," I said. "See you in the morning."

"It's been a long day for me too." He stood up, thanked his hosts, and walked with me and Annie upstairs.

"You two choose which room or rooms you want," Annie said. "Behind either of those two doors you'll find a guest room with fresh linens."

Annie hugged me again. "Good night, Nats. It's wonderful to see you again. It's good to know some things stay the same—you namely. Don't worry about Number Five. I give him another six months at best, less if he doesn't behave himself. Mother has a short attention span. Henry, good to meet you. Nattie can be a handful, but she's worth it."

Henry blushed! And then stuttered. A lot of I's and uhs. I finally rescued the situation.

"Annie, you've got it all wrong. I'm here not as Henry's love interest sidekick. I'm working on a story also. A different one. I was too drunk to tell you about it. And now I'm too damn tired. I'll just give you a headline now until tomorrow morning. Josane Ashmore, ever hear of her?"

"Nattie, everyone knows everyone around here. Of course I

knew Josane. It's terrible what happened to her. But I'll tell you this, it was bound to happen. She wouldn't listen to anyone. That horse of hers was crazy and everyone tried to warn her. I feel sorry for Charlie."

"Charlie?" I said.

"Charlie Laconte, her trainer. A year or so before Josane died, a little girl at his barn fell off her pony and died. Then Josane had that accident on that horse Charlie didn't even want to sell her, then his barn burned down, and now Jim. This man has had a terrible run of bad luck."

"Yeah, well, it seems Josane's had the worse luck," I said. "She's the one dead. So what was she like?"

"Josane?" Annie asked. "Bubbly. Effervescent or any other adjective in the gregarious line. She actually reminded me a little of you. Except when it came to men. Not that you don't have your own compelling way with them, but Josane was a man killer. Every man she met wanted her. It wasn't just her looks; she was high-spirited and men found that tantalizing. At least they did with Josane. She was a lot of fun, but toward the end I heard she was traveling with a fast crowd . . . coke, things like that. Nattie, you look exhausted, I'll tell you more in the morning."

She kissed me on the cheek and headed off down the hall. Before she got to the end, she turned.

"Another thing about Josane. She was headed for trouble, one way or the other. Years before she moved here, I dated her boyfriend. I stopped because he became abusive. One black eye was enough for me, but from what I heard, not her. See you in the morning."

This was too much information for one drunk brain. I looked at Henry. "You know," I said, "there really are only four people in the world. I can't take any more coincidences tonight. Door number one or door number two?"

Henry pointed to the first, said a quick and chilly good night, and walked into the room. He closed the door, I knocked. He opened, I walked in. Pretty nice digs. Heart of pine floors, hand-hooked wool rug with little horses trotting across, probably very old and very expensive, a big four-poster, joyously exuberant in its fluffiness. At the head was a tumble of cushy white pillows—six of them—and the rest of the surface was covered by a marshmallow of a comforter with deep, curvy squares of softness. It looked good enough to toss my poor drunken body on and be swallowed up for the night.

However, it was clear Henry wasn't up for sharing his bed. Not with me at least. On the chest of drawers—a heavy, dark piece of mahogany that quietly asserted "I am an important piece of furniture, don't fuck with me"—was a stack of white towels. I picked one up and started waving it.

"White flag of surrender," I said. "I hope you're not angry."

"Angry? Angry because you forced me to tell Duncan about the list in your time frame rather than mine? Or angry because you started mouthing off about the tobacco industry and could have cost me a source? You tell me, Nattie, which one should I be angry about?"

"Well, if it were me, both, I guess. But then again, I must be a more forgiving person. I don't hold a grudge after someone says 'I'm sorry.' "

Henry turned away and walked toward the bed. "Funny," he said. "I didn't actually hear the words 'I'm sorry.' I must have missed it when you said, 'Henry, I'm sorry I trampled on your story.' "

I'm sure this is why people smoke, so they have something to do with their hands when they get nervous. All I had was the towel, which I stopped waving and started folding. To my horror, I realized I was folding it the way my live-in compulsive love had taught me years ago. I shook it out and let it puddle to the floor.

"Now that you mention it," I said, "I guess I did forget to say those actual words to you. So are you listening now? I'm sorry I trampled on your story. I really am. I was an oaf. An absolute, utter oaf. Oh, God, listen to me. An hour around these people and I'm starting to talk like them. Shoot me when I start wearing corduroy pants with embroidered whales. Listen, Henry, I was an ass, pure and simple. Second time today. Friends?"

I walked over to the bed, next to Henry. I stuck out my hand and so did he. We shook.

"All right, on one condition. No more wine when we're working."

I reached up and kissed his cheek. "Thanks, sweetie, you're a pal." With that I walked out of his room and through door number two. I looked around. Henry chose the right door. This room was okay, light-years nicer than my place, but it was missing the princess-and-the-pea bed. My room had two canopied twin beds, each with one pillow at the head and antiquy-looking quilts across them. Pretty, most definitely pricey, but not cushy.

I opened a door and found a bathroom behind it with Henry standing at the sink, sans shirt. Damn, I wish I hadn't been ovulating. Between the wine and nature's way of insuring the continuation of the human species, I was ready to dig my fingers into his flesh.

"Excuse me," I said. "I guess this means we have a connecting bath."

He smiled. I smiled and stood there feeling thirteen.

"Well, good night," Henry said, and stood there, I hope feeling thirteen.

This was stupid. All wrong. Henry and I can't agree on the color of the sky. I forced my hand to close the bathroom door in front of me.

"Well, good night," I said to Henry beyond the door.

The wine was starting to wear off and the drive was starting to wear in. I felt as if I'd wound up on Mars or Uranus or wherever it is with a gravitational pull a thousand times greater than ours. I needed to get horizontal, fast, while it was still my choice. I slipped out of my clothes, into a T-shirt, and between the cool white sheets. Within seconds I was back in Fellini land.

I don't remember what weird dream woke me, but I had to pee in the worst way. I knocked on the bathroom door, just to make sure Henry and I weren't on the same urinary cycle. He wasn't. I thought about peeking in his room to see what a sleeping Henry looked like, but all thoughts ended when I tried his door. Locked. I slid back into bed and closed my eyes, waiting for sleep to claim me.

Twenty minutes later I was still waiting. Nothing worked. How many times could I visualize riding my horse over a course of three-foot-six-inch fences? After thirty-seven perfect trips, even I was bored. My eyelids popped open. I was awake.

I got out Alice Hoffman's book *Second Nature* and started reading her dreamy wolfman love story. I forced myself to read slowly, to make her words last. She isn't what you'd call a showy writer with big, fancy words and clever phrases. It was her simplicity that sucked me in. She writes about ordinary things with such magnification and crystalline clarity, they become magical. And I'm a sucker for magic in any shape or form.

I just got to the part where the wolfman's real life princess rescues him, when I heard a slight knock at the door. Henry? Were the same fantasies tumbling around in his brain as mine?

I looked down at the stretched-out Charlotte Hornets T-shirt covering my body. Even I had to admit it wasn't too enticing, unless you were as much a Muggsy Bogues fan as I. Talk about magic. Whoever told a little guy like Bogues he could play pro basketball? No one but himself, and that's why he was my man. He's stands an inch taller than me, which makes him five-three, yet he's one of the best players in the country. If he could shoot hoops against giants, I could do anything.

But it was still just a T-shirt and there was a knocking at my door. I've never been the pink-satin-negligee and marabou-mules type. What the hell. The shirt was clean.

I walked to the door. "Henry," I said as I opened it. "I couldn't sleep either."

Except it wasn't Henry standing there. It was Number Five without his bow tie. He was wearing some kind of brown paisley robe. Silk probably.

"Mr. Duncan?"

"Oh, please, call me Bridge. I couldn't sleep and was heading down to the kitchen for a drink. I saw the light on under the door and thought it was Henry's. I'd been thinking about that list, and a few more things came to me that I thought would be helpful. However, since you're awake and Henry isn't, why don't we continue our talk about the tobacco industry?"

He was pushing, ever so softly, against the door. Insistent but mannerly.

"Now?" I said. "You want to talk cigarettes in the middle of the night?"

"Well, you seemed quite passionate about it downstairs."

He walked over to the bed and sat on the edge. Great. My old friend's mother's new husband was sitting on my bed in his bathrobe with me in nothing but a T-shirt with a sly-eyed, teal and purple hornet buzzing across my body.

"Mr. Duncan, I don't want to—"

"Bridge, call me Bridge."

"Okay, Bridge. I don't want to talk tobacco tonight. Or really ever again, for that matter. I said what I had to say, and the only thing you could say back is your industry propaganda, which I won't believe. We'll both get annoyed and then I'll feel even more uncomfortable and ungracious than I do now."

"Well, you certainly don't mince words," Number Five said. "However, I'm sure there are some interesting facts I could tell you about how the tobacco industry has been manipulated by the government to appear to be the villain."

I shook my head and gave him a get-real look.

"So be it, not another word about tobacco," he said. "Then what shall we talk about?"

"I don't think we should talk about anything. It's three in the morning, I'm thinking about sleep, not conversation."

Duncan wasn't moving off the bed. He was just looking at me in a funny way. Christ, did my T-shirt have a hole in it somewhere embarrassing?

"You are quite the ball of energy. I wonder what it's like to be inside that much fire."

"Excuse me?" I said. I was about to tell him to head back to Mrs. Five's room lickety-split before I did, when he got up from the bed, put his hand on the back of my head, and pushed me into a kiss.

"Yuk," I said as I broke through. "You taste like the floor of the Greyhound bus station. Even if I did want to kiss you—WHICH I DON'T—I'd sooner clean a toilet with my tongue. Yech, smokers."

I spun around, stormed into the bathroom, and slammed the door behind me, from which I could faintly hear his words. "Nattie, perhaps you misunderstood my intentions."

CHAPTER 16

Did I actually see the bathroom door handle wriggling? Could that oversexed, undermoraled idiot really be trying to get into the bathroom with me? It wriggled some more.

"Nattie, I think we should discuss this before we both walk away with the wrong idea."

I leaned against the door and hissed, "I think you should know I came in second in the Philadelphia-wide 'Hi-oh, Silver, away,' screaming contest. And I was only six. Get out of my room before I wake up all of Upperville."

He tapped on the door. "Nattie, this is quite unnecessary."

"Here I go," I said.

"All right, all right, no need to get upset. I'm leaving. Good night, then."

I heard footsteps across the heart pine floors and the faint closing of a door behind it.

What a day—and night. I still tasted that disgusting man in my mouth. I grabbed the tube of toothpaste and squeezed hard, piling an industrial-strength dose of the stuff on the pink and white bristles of my toothbrush. I scrubbed and scrubbed. Real or imagined, there was still an underlaying of Benson & Hedges beneath the Colgate. I found a bottle of Listerine in the medicine chest and took a big swallow. I stool there swishing until it burned out all taste in my mouth.

Then I heard a tapping on the other door. Henry's door.

"Come in," I said, or tried to say with a mouthful of mouthwash.

"Did I hear you talking to someone, and why are you holding on to that bottle of Listerine like that?"

I looked at my hand and realized I was white-knuckling the Listerine. "Oh," I said, and then told him what happened.

"What a pig," Henry said. "I'm sure he won't be coming back. Just in case, I think you should sleep in my room and I'll take yours."

He got the first part right. I was too tired by now to fix the second part.

"Fine," I said, and headed into Henry's bed, sans Henry. The bed felt as good as it looked and I didn't have to wait long before sleep claimed me.

The next thing I knew, someone was touching my shoulder. I reached up and slammed the hand on my shoulder.

"I told you I was the second-loudest screamer in Philadelphia and I meant it." Then I opened my eyes. It wasn't Number Five. It was Henry.

"Oh," I said groggily, "I thought you were him."

"Sorry, Nattie. I didn't mean to startle you, but it's getting late and I think we should get going."

"Get going? Where?"

"Benson's funeral is tomorrow, the funeral home has visiting hours today. I think we should go there and talk to whomever we can, get a feel of who's who."

"Sounds good to me. Let me just hop in the shower."

Reluctantly I left my marshmallow cocoon.

"Muggsy Bogues?" Henry said, looking at the back of my T-shirt.

"Yup," I said. "He's my hero. I love sleeping with him, even if it's just his signature."

"Well then, he's a lucky man."

I looked at Henry and I'm not sure who looked more surprised, me or him.

His face actually flushed. "I meant that he's a lucky man to have such a devoted fan."

So he felt thirteen, too. "Whatever," I said, and popped into the bathroom. "I'll see you downstairs."

I was showered, dressed, and do-ed in less than ten minutes. Finding Henry should have been so easy. After unintentionally exploring the entire downstairs, I made my way to the kitchen. That's where I found him, along with the rest of the happy household: Annie, Mr. and Mrs. Number Five, and their indentured servant, Rosalita, who was working the stove like a short-order cook at HoJo's.

"Omelet?" Number Five said to me as if last night never happened.

I glared at him.

Henry intercepted. "Nattie doesn't eat in the morning. Her body is in the, let me see if I remember this right, 'elimination cycle' which, as I recall, becomes interrupted by food. Or have I gotten it reversed?"

"Right the first time," I said. "Good memory, Henry."

Henry was smiling. So was Annie.

"Nattie," Annie said. "Does this have something to do with Lou?"

Lou, my father, the new age flake who drifts in and out of my life between trips to his latest ashram or colon integrity institute.

"You got it," I said. "At least it's better than macrobiotics. Or that electric cow prod he came down with a while back. He kept walking behind me and zapping me with it, saying something about cleansing my chakras."

I was surprised Henry remembered I didn't eat anything until after noon. It had been months since I'd told him about the Fit for Life diet my father wangled me into.

Food, I could give up in the morning. Coffee was a different matter. Rosalita handed me my morning dose and Henry, two eggs over easy.

Annie's mother pulled out the chair next to hers. My cue to sit. "Nattie," she said, "Annie tells me you're working on a story about that girl Josane Ashmore."

"Well, that's the plan," I said. "Did you know her?"

"Of course. We all knew *of* her and what happened. And then, after that unpleasantness, her family came up here. Everyone did whatever they could to help them. We all rallied together. Not that it was appreciated in the least. Nothing short of handing them the keys to Jack Kent Cooke's farm was good enough for them."

Unpleasantness? As in death? I wasn't drunk, so I held my tongue on that one.

"I thought her mother just came up here briefly to collect Josane's things," I said.

Annie's mother laughed politely, in a well-bred fashion that would have translated into Jersey street talk as "what kind of stupid f'ing idiot are you?"

"They stayed here forever. All they cared about was making sure they got every penny Josane had ever collected. I'll tell you, it was embarrassing to watch. They were absolute vipers. The commotion they made about Josane's jewelry. Within twenty-four hours they started accusing her friends of stealing Josane's rings and necklaces and furniture. Then, when no one listened to that, they went to the sheriff, first about the jewelry and then about the circumstances of her death. I heard they were demanding a homicide investigation. A homicide investigation? How ridiculous. The girl was trampled by a horse. Anyone who rides knows accidents are part and parcel of the sport. We've all had our share of spills and tumbles."

"Josane's accident was a little more than a tumble," I said.

"Of course it was. That horse was too much for her. Ask anyone in Middleburg or Upperville or The Plains, they'll all tell you the same thing."

"Anyone in particular you suggest I ask?"

"Her trainer, Charlie Laconte," Mrs. Duncan said. "Though I can't imagine he's feeling up to talking to a reporter right now. Annie, what's the girl's name who runs his barn? Karen something. Do you remember? She'd be a good person to talk to. Then there was that boyfriend of hers, Flip Nilson. Didn't you go out with him for a while, Annie? And she was quite friendly with the Mundell girl, Santee's daughter. Try them. As for others, I'm sure Annie and I can come up with a list of people, though I can't imagine what kind of story you could write. It was a riding accident. Unfortunate, certainly. But that's all it was."

Henry was getting edgy to leave. But I had a few more questions to ask.

"You're probably right, Mrs. Duncan," I said. "Let's just hypothesize for a quick second. Can you think of anyone who disliked Josane? Maybe enough to kill her?"

Mrs. Duncan started laughing. "Who disliked Josane? Any woman over fifty who was married. Josane had a, what would be the best way to describe it, let's see, she had a predatory and economic interest in any man who was of heart attack age as long as his bankbook was large enough to warrant her attentions. How do you think she got that store?"

"I was wondering that," I said. "How did she?"

"I shouldn't be saying any more. Suffice it to say, it was a gift, a rather large gift from a man whose heart wasn't up to Josane's acrobatics. They found him with her the same way they say they found Nelson Rockefeller. Except the ambulance got to him in time and he lived."

A different kind of riding accident.

"Oh, Mother," Annie said. "You don't know that for certain. Nattie's a newspaper reporter. She's looking for facts."

"I'll take rumors," I said. "I can always chase it down to find out what's true."

The phone rang and Mrs. Duncan went to answer it. Henry

looked at his watch. "Nattie, I think we should go to the funeral home. Visiting hours started about an hour ago."

I took a final gulp of coffee to chase away the clouds from last night's wine.

"Mrs. Duncan," I said, "you've been very helpful. That list sounds great, and anything else you and Annie can think of about Josane, let me know. We should be back in a few hours. Annie, I'll talk to you later."

It was cold outside and I wasn't used to it. After three years in the South, my body had grown accustomed to nature's pampering. Now anything under forty-two degrees sent my circulatory system into revolt. Already my feet were starting to freeze up.

"I can't stand this Yankee weather," I said to Henry, who was scraping the frost off his windshield.

"This is still technically the South," he said.

"Is that like a technical virgin?" I said. "There you go again, confusing accuracy with the truth. We are in *northern* Virginia, go try to find a plate of grits or someone who says y'all. Better yet, order tea at a restaurant and I'll bet you dinner it doesn't come iced."

Henry slid into his car talking about the exact whereabouts of the Mason-Dixon line. The last thing I wanted to do was sit on freezing cold leather. So I started jumping up and down to thaw my feet while Henry warmed up the car.

Except I was the only thing jumping. Henry's engine was deader than Jim Benson.

Henry got out of his car and slammed the door. "Goddammit."

An appropriate thing to say, though it did sound odd coming from cool, calm, collected Henry.

"I just had this car tuned up. I bought a Japanese car so I wouldn't have these problems. I can't understand this."

"Cars and women," I said. "Consider us a Buddhist koan."

136

He looked at me like I was talking Russian. "Cones? My car won't start, why are you talking about religious pine trees now?"

"Must have missed Philosophy 101 at Harvard," I said. "A koan, like what's the sound of one hand clapping? Or how can you understand cars or women? The unanswerable questions you meditate on to clear your mind of chatter. Forget it, let's meditate on getting us a ride out of here. How about calling Triple A, you are a member, aren't you?"

He nodded. Of course he was a member. I'd have bet my bottom dollar that Henry, Mr. Plan for Every Eventuality, was an in-perpetuity member.

We made our way back up the driveway to the house. Inside we found the nearest phone and called Triple A. Henry was not pleased.

"Three to four hours,"he said. "That's the soonest they can be here. In three to four hours the funeral home will be closed. Great. Just great."

"Let's rent a car," I said. "I'll ask Annie for a lift to Middleburg or wherever the closest Hertz or Avis is."

"Rent a car? What for? Is something wrong?"

Henry and I turned around. The Duncans were standing by the door, looking at us.

Henry told them his car woes and asked where the nearest car rental place was.

"Don't be ridiculous," Number Five said. "I'm not going anywhere, take mine. It's by the garage. The silver Olds. You can't miss it."

Henry and I both said no about a million times. But Duncan kept insisting. Finally Annie's mother said in her firmest people-management voice, "Enough, we won't take no for an answer."

So Henry and I headed to the garage with the devil incarnate's keys. He was right, his car would be hard to miss. The only silver

Olds in a small fleet of Mercedes. But that wasn't the giveaway. His tags were: ISMOKE. I got in and held my nose because he did—smoke. I hate the smell of leather and cigarettes; it reminds me of too many unhappy car trips to Atlantic City with my mother pulling at one Chesterfield after the next while she and my father screamed at each other. I could only not breathe for so long. I took a breath, and to my surprise, even I of the bird-dog nose couldn't detect a hint of tobacco in Duncan's car. And to my further surprise, there wasn't a butt or an ash in the ashtray. Then I realized why. It was a new car.

The only good thing I have to say about cold weather is the air. From inside a heated car, cold air is beautiful. It adds a shimmer to everything. You can practically see the molecules dancing when the air is thin and cold and the sun hits the world just right.

I was drinking in the scenery, and there was plenty of it to drink. Annie's house sat at the top of a knoll that sat at the back of their property, which went on like a Faulkner sentence, forever. We were winding our way down to the main road and I was tingly from the beauty of it all. I loved the spunk of the pines, their glossy green needles adamant in their verdantry, happily impervious to anything nature could throw their way. They were the Muggsy Bogueses of the plant world. What they lacked in the summer grandeur of their showy deciduous cousins, who now from a distance looked like rolls of steel wool lining the countryside, they more than made up for in their winter explosion of color.

"Henry, what's your favorite tree?"

He didn't answer and I figured he must be formulating his funeral-home strategy. It was a dumb question, so I didn't bother to ask it again. Besides, I was too busy looking out the side window, imagining what it would've been like to grow up here.

"Maybe next life," I muttered. It was then I realized this life was passing a little faster than I liked.

"Hey, Henry, slow down a little. This is too beautiful to rush."

I looked over at Henry. For someone who doesn't register emotion on his face, he was looking awfully concerned.

"Henry?"

The concern was turning to panic, and then I saw his foot pumping the brakes. Hard and fast. Which was how our car was now careening down the road.

"Henry. What's wrong?"

A very stupid question when the driver's face is turning red, his foot is stomping the brake pedal like he's being attacked by fire ants, and he's white-knuckling the steering wheel.

"Is your seat belt on?" he said, and he said it so flatly, I knew we were in bad trouble.

"Of course my seat belt's on. What do you mean, is my seat belt on? I always wear my seat belt. What the hell is happening? Tell me, for Christ's sake."

The pine trees were whipping by so fast, I felt like I was on one of those motorcycle arcade rides. Except I knew when we crashed, it wasn't going to be a matter of putting another quarter in.

Henry was fighting the twists and turns as if he were wrestling a bobcat. He'd already geared down to first, and that did nothing to slow us up. I saw a sharp turn coming up that Richard Petty himself couldn't have made.

I closed my eyes, whispered, "Mom, I'm sorry for this. Be strong," and waited for the crash. I didn't feel anything and thought I might be dead. I opened my eyes to see heaven.

What I saw was a green blur. Whoosh. Our car zoomed right between a break in the trees and blasted into the woods. We bounced and bumped our way over, around, and through rocks, trees, and gullies. The underbrush slowed us down a little, but we were still traveling through the woods faster than the woods are designed to be traveled through.

"Hold on," Henry shouted. He flung his right arm straight out across my chest like he was a human seat belt, and I saw why.

It was the end of the road, or, in this case, the woods. Straight ahead was a pretty steep bank. There was no way out this time. We were going to crash—into the creek.

I would have liked to close my eyes. I don't know why I didn't. But I didn't and the weirdest thing happened. The car, me, Henry, the scenery, we all went into slo-mo, the same way it happens when I fall off my horse. It seemed to take an hour for the car to reach the bank. I was wondering if I'd be hearing from David again, my dead stepfather, when I felt a slam.

A soft slam. Blessed are the air bags.

I looked around. There we sat. Henry and I, in the creek. Not exactly the way I'd fantasized it.

I felt around for blood. The only thing sticky and wet was the sweat dripping down my forehead.

"Are you okay?" Henry said.

I nodded.

"You?" I said.

He nodded.

"Good," he said.

"Yeah," I said.

We both sat there, monosyllabic.

Finally, I strung together a few more syllables. "What just happened?"

Henry took a deep breath, then said, "The brakes."

"I figured it was the brakes," I said. "What about the brakes? Are you sure you're okay?"

"Fine, I'm fine. I can't believe it, but I'm fine. I had no brakes. At first I thought they were soft, but I assumed that was just this car. But the more I drove, the softer they became. Until they were just gone . . ."

Henry was still gripping the wheel with his left hand. I reached over and unpried his fingers. His hand stayed in mine and we sat that way, silent and holding hands.

Finally I said, "Someone was watching out for us today; we could have been killed. And just maybe that's the point. This car barely has the sticker off it. It still smells of new cowhide. Duncan hasn't even had a chance to stink it up yet with his cigarettes. So you tell me, what's the likelihood of brakes breaking in a new car? About one in a million, I'd guess. I'm no mechanic, Henry, but I think someone cut the lines."

CHAPTER 17

"**. . .** Cut the brake lines? Are you sure? How could that be? I can't believe it, there must be some other explanation."

Annie's mother was talking. Her pale skin had paled down a few shades more after we walked back, yet again, into the house with even more dire automotive tales of woe.

Henry told her again exactly what happened and ended with "I think you should call the police."

That's when Number Five jumped in.

"I'd rather we didn't. Let's get the car towed to my man over in Marshall, have him take a look at the brakes, and see what he has to say. He knows automobiles. I think we need the voice of an expert, not one of wild speculation. After all, the car is just a machine. Machines break all the time."

"Well, that machine smelled brand new to me," I said. "And new cars just don't lose their brakes all of a sudden. I say someone cut the lines, someone who wants you as dead as Jim Benson."

Number Five's face hardened. "I'm calling the mechanic, if you'll excuse me."

He and the wife exited stage left, leaving me and Henry in the entry hall.

"I guess that's how Wasp hotheads act," I said. "But who'd have thought it, given last night's performance. When I launched into the tobacco industry, he was a regular Mr. Smoothee."

"He's used to that attack," Henry said. "He has the armor for any ammunition you could hit him with. Duncan's a professional soldier in that war."

"Why, Henry," I said. "How metaphorical of you. Our crash must've sent your brain waves skittering to the right side of your head. Do you have an overwhelming urge to go outside and smell the pines?"

"Very funny, Gold," Henry said. "I happen to love evergreens, though my favorite tree, since you asked, is a sugar maple. By the way, I'm glad to see the crash has obviously done nothing to temper you and your tongue."

"Much to the dismay of all the editors at *The Charlotte Commercial Appeal*. Nothing short of a lobotomy could do that," I said, grinning and still pleased as punch we were both alive. "I know what you mean about Duncan. Pull his antismoking string and out comes the we-are-just-victims-of-overregulation bullshit. A regular tobacco industry Chatty Cathy doll. But this car business snapped his strings. Did you see his face? He was mad. He's lying about something. He knows more about the list than we do. Mark my words."

"Possibly," Henry said. "Possibly. However, we'll never know if we don't get out of here and do some reporting. I'm calling a cab."

Twenty minutes and a couple of fights later about which cab company to call—I wanted a Checker Cab and no, I didn't care that out in the boonies of Virginia they probably weren't the old boxy kinds with fold-down seats, and Henry wanted a Yellow Cab because he claimed that company always carried receipts—we were sitting in the back of a Joe's Taxi Service cab—a compromise—taking us east on Route 50. Annie's farm is a good way west of Upperville toward Paris and the Ashby Gap, where the hills are more steep than rolling. We headed east toward Middleburg and the land stretched out into long, gentle curves, as if its creator had said "Take a deep breath and relax."

We finally got our chance to see the picture postcards come to life. Four-board fencing ran up and down the soft hills, undulating with the land, defining who owned what by occasional low stone walls and rock pillars with brass name plates announcing ROKEBY or ATOKA or FOXLEASE or whatever that estate was called. Way far in the distance you might be able to make out the houses, grand stone structures like Annie's, but mostly it was vast expanses of what would be bright green fields in another few months. Closer to the road, just beyond the blackened fences, were the horses, wrapped in blue Gore-Tex turnout rugs and gathered around giant rolls of sweet hay. Eating and staying fat and shiny for the upcoming show and breeding seasons.

We passed through Upperville, as quaint and pretty a town as little towns get. The old stone houses hugged the road close enough so you could see inside. I wondered what secrets lay beyond those *Country Living* windows, through the filter of thick, settled glass and lacy white curtains. Did anyone here know Josane? Had they been to her shop, seen her riding through the fields on an unruly horse? Did they even remember the tall woman with the beauty-queen smile and a penchant for rich older men?

We passed the Upperville Horse Show grounds just east of town. I watched it drift by and was glad I was sitting in Joe's taxi this time around. Hell would freeze over—or even more improbable, *The Commercial Appeal* would go off contingency budget—before I showed my horse there again.

Not that I hadn't been warned. I had to force Rob to take me, as much as I can force Rob to do anything. He said it would be a waste of money because the courses were set in hilly grass rings with trees in the middle of them. But I had to go. I'd been reading about Upperville for years in *The Chronicle of the Horse,* a weekly magazine that crazed hunter enthusiasts like myself ruin their eyes over just to see who won what at which horse show. *The Chronicle* reports show results in the tiniest agate print imaginable.

144

Upperville. Upperville. Upperville. Just saying the name made me feel like a legitimate horse person who fit into the show world. When I moved south, I swore I'd make it to Upperville. Which I did, but you know what they say about expectations.

It was even more beautiful than I'd imagined. If horse show grounds competed in beauty pageants, this one would be wearing the tiara. Rolling green hills with necklaces of freshly darkened board fences, an old-timey wooden grandstand that looks like an Edward Hopper painting come to life, and large grass show rings with towering oaks in the middle, just like Rob said.

Then when the hunter barns put up all their fancy stall fronts with truckloads of potted plants and custom-made draperies and the merchandisers set up their striped tent-front stores with tack, antiques, and pricey clothes, it ends up looking like a Broadway stage set of what a country fair is supposed to look like.

There might be snazzier, more modern show grounds around. But Upperville, started in 1853, making it the oldest horse show in America, has what people empty bank accounts for when they buy antiques—a patina; the sheen, glow, and aura of fantasized times gone by.

I should have stuck with my fantasies. Upperville turned out to be the scene of the second most humiliating experience of my life. And what a place to make an ass of myself. It's about as tony as horse shows get. The blood is so blue or wannabe blue, the participants practically bleed midnight ink. Not that there's much bleeding. It's six days of one perfect trip after another and another and another. That's especially true in the upper ring with the professionals sailing their green machines over the immaculately groomed fences. They call it the green hunter division. Green, as in inexperienced or new to the game. Ha. Those horses are about as new to the game of horse showing as Michael Jordan was to basketball when he left Carolina for the Bulls. In the horse show world, green hunter, as in successful green hunter, means a

$100,000 plus animal who's pounded around a different horse show every weekend of his life for at least the past two years.

The worst part is these allegedly green horses pop up in the amateur division, bought by someone who thinks $100,000 or $200,000 is a reasonable amount of money to pay for an animal. Then they compete against me and my bargain-basement horse, Brenda Starr.

I showed at Upperville shortly after Christopher Reeve's horrible accident. Since I'm old enough to know I will die someday—that's the difference between amateur and junior riders—I didn't want that day to be the day I took Brenda in the Upperville ring. But it was hard to think about anything else. Everywhere you turned you heard or read stories about Reeve and how dangerous jumping a horse is. That can tug at a brain. And ask any rider—it's all a mind game anyway. Ride with authority and confidence and you can nail a winning trip. Start doubting yourself or, worse, your horse, and you might as well take off the saddle and take up bowling, which I should have done that day.

Simply put, I was spooked. From the second I entered the ring, I saw Christopher Reeve strapped in a wheelchair. Every breath my horse took wasn't hers, but the artificial whoosh of Reeve's ventilator. My mind was clearly elsewhere than in the ring and on my job, to get my horse around the course. We ate the first fence, because I let her die around the corner. A course is only as good as its corners. If you don't have the pace around the turn, it's pretty hard to find the right spot to jump from.

Eating the first fence meant I had to gallop up the line to make it to the second fence in the correct amount of strides. Brenda's as stretchy as a training bra. I pressed my leg into her sides and she lengthened out and got to the second fence with room to spare. No problem for her.

I was still thinking about Christopher Reeve and did the same stupid thing at the next fence, which was mercifully only a single jump. We cantered around the turn to the in and out, two jumps set one stride apart. I looked up and realized I had a dog of a canter that might get me over the first fence, but we'd surely run out of gas in the middle. She jumped the first fence and then I committed the worst sin known to horse showing: I pulled her out of the line of jumps. I could have let her take an extra stride, but I was so discombobulated that I fell back on my old bad habit—pulling out into a circle. I circled back around to the in and out and did the same thing again. Pulled her out between the two fences. I saw Rob, my trainer, standing by the rail, his head buried in his hands. I had one last shot before I was excused from the ring.

My horse had no reason to jump the in and out after I'd pulled her out twice. This is why I've turned down every offer I've gotten for her. I stopped thinking about poor Christopher Reeve and concentrated on getting her through the in and out. I got the right canter before the turn and kept my leg on her all the way. I saw the spot five strides before and just kept pressing. Brenda sailed through both elements as if there were no other options.

Here's where it gets embarrassing. The crowd around the ring started clapping because we'd finally made it. I was mortified. As I turned for the final line, I saw that Rob was no longer there. I didn't see him until the next day—and then he refused to speak to me.

"Nattie, we're here."

"Huh?" I said. I was lost in thought.

"In Middleburg," Henry said. "I don't know where you were, but *we* are at the funeral home. Remember?"

I looked outside the window of the cab. He'd pulled it up in front of a flat-faced redbrick building. We could have been in Charlotte, which surprised me. Middleburg is a town full of old stone and stucco buildings, so what was this plain Jane doing here?

Oh, well, Benson wouldn't know he was being said good-bye to in a characterless building. At least there were plenty of cars outside. Big money, horse show cars. Mercedes. Range Rovers. Suburbans. Lexuses. Duallys. Lot of high-dollar automotive heft here. But it was an old red Toyota that caught my eye. Not only was it out of place parked among these big buckaroos, but its license plate made my skin shiver. I felt like I was seeing a ghost. Josane's ghost.

Clear as a new autumn day, it said DAZCUTR, the name of Josane's store.

CHAPTER 18

I walked up to the car to peek in the windows. So much for the preternatural. Josane wasn't going to be driving this vehicle in any lifetime. She'd have been chewing her knees, the seat was pulled so close to the steering wheel. A shorty like me was the operator, and she'd be as easy to spot inside the funeral home as a Shetland pony at the Olympics.

I turned back to see what was taking Henry so long. He was making the cabbie sign a piece of paper attesting to the fact he'd just shelled out twenty-three of his own dollars to get us from the other side of Upperville to Middleburg.

Let those guys haggle it out. I thought I'd be polite and wait for Henry. So I looked down the street to check out the sights. I could have been in a Dickens book, with the old cottages, red velvet bows and evergreen garlands wrapped around everything. I expected Tiny Tim to be popping out of a window.

"What kind of taxi doesn't have receipts?" Henry muttered as he double-stepped the stairs. "I'm going to call their office and complain. How difficult would it be to carry around a pack of receipts?"

"Henry," I said, "save your energy for something important. Your problem is you expect the world to follow rules just the way you do. Taxis should have receipts. Everyone should park between the yellow lines. Bills should be paid on time. Let me be the one to tell you—life ain't like that."

"These words of wisdom coming from the woman who's got three collections agencies after her?" Henry said. "Next time we're taking a Yellow Cab."

"I had every intention of paying those bills, but I lost them. And then they went and sent their big dogs after me before I could find the bills. Fine about the cab. If you want Yellow Cab, we'll go Yellow Cab. Just don't get in a huff about it."

I opened the heavy door, and a pillow of hot, sweet air pushed into my face. Perfume. Lots of it. I stepped inside and slid my parka down my arms. I took Henry's coat and headed for the hangers. Both coatracks were full, so I stuffed ours underneath.

The place was packed wall to wall with tall, leggy blondes and men dressed better than the women. The horse show crowd. I looked around and recognized plenty of faces, though when my eyes traveled down, the pictures didn't match. It's always a shock to see horse people in civilian clothes. Especially the men. I must have counted eleven bald heads I never knew existed. Another reason for hunt caps.

"Henry, want to tag along with me or mill on your own?"

"Let's meet by the casket. An hour?"

"Sounds good to me," I said.

Henry headed toward the casket, and I, the other way, to a group of three women, one I recognized and knew well enough to ingratiate myself into their conversation. She was a fellow amateur owner rider by the name of Peggy Eames, who'd been around forever. When I was still kissing pictures of horses as a toddler, she was winning blue ribbons at the National Horse Show in Madison Square Garden.

Things have a way of equalizing—years do that to you. Last year I aged out into her division, older amateurs, ungenerously known as the Flying Fossils. Peggy may be old enough to get the discount tickets at the movies, but she still has that no-miss eye of hers and the ferocity to keep galloping to the fences regardless of anything. That's what makes her so good. The best riders know you have to gallop forward to get the good jumps, not hold back. She and her husband, Tad, have a small farm outside of Middleburg where they breed horses and reclaim junk horses from over-rated pros who've either ruined the animal or can't do anything with it from the get-go.

When they're not riding, they're judging horse shows. The big ones. Devon, Ox Ridge, Harrisburg, the National. Peggy and Tad, known to all who care, are the original horse show royalty, the reigning king and queen of the equine prom.

By horse show standards, Peggy's been pretty nice to me. We weren't best friends or anything, but every time she saw me, she actually said hello, remembered my horse's name, how we did at the previous show, and congratulated me when I won a ribbon. Sometimes she was downright chatty. Maybe it was because she was short like me and figured we were sisters in inches, or maybe it was because she was a genuinely nice human being. It's hard to know in the horse show world.

She was standing next to Sprinkle Rusk; Rusk as in Rusk's, the biggest clothing conglomerate in the free universe. Sprinkle used to board all of Daddy Rusk's horses at her thousand-acre trillion-dollar farm until she doubled-billed him. Daddy didn't like being bilked and sent the whole barnful to his other daughter. A regular King Lear on horseback. The most amazing thing about Sprinkle, other than her chutzpah and her name, was her hair. It was a solid brown helmet of something that looked like a lacquered rattan armchair had landed on her head.

Next to them was a woman I'd never seen. She was about the same age as Sprinkle, anywhere from fifty-five to sixty-five depending on who you asked, but better coiffed. Of the three of them, this was the one with style. Her silver hair was swept back into a French twist and she wore a snappy black swing dress, black hose, and black pumps.

"Hey, Peggy," I said.

"Nattie? I thought you lived in North Carolina. What brings you here? Did you know Jim?"

"I do—live in North Carolina—and I did know Jim. Not well, but enough to know not to show where he showed," I said.

"Isn't that the truth," Peggy said. "What a rider he was. It sounds so awful to be speaking of him in the past tense. I just can't believe this happened. Of all people. Jim Benson. And so horrible. I can't imagine how Charlie's going to manage. . . . Nattie, you know Sprinkle, don't you?"

"Not officially," I said.

Peggy did the introductions, first to Sprinkle and then to the French twist. ". . . And this is Breezey Mundell."

Topping's mother. Now that I looked, I saw it. Same face, different hair. Color in the white locks with coppery red, stand back twenty feet, and Breezey could've passed for Topping.

"I know your daughter, or at least I know of her," I said. "I used to show in her division. Now I have to compete against this riding machine here."

"Oh, please," Peggy said. "I couldn't have been worse at Upperville."

"You must've missed my trips, then," I said. "I set a new standard for couldn't have been worse."

"As I recall, the next month you were champion at Culpepper," Peggy said.

"Good memory, Peggy," I said. "That was more luck than anything else, plus the fact you weren't there. Anyway, so who did it?"

Peggy looked surprised for a second, the same way Will Smith's brother looked after I'd met him at a society event I was covering. It was during his brother's infamous Palm Beach rape trial. We shook hands and I'd said, "Did he do it?" He looked like he just tasted kumquats for the first time and couldn't decided whether they were a yay or nay. Then he smiled and said, "No one's ever asked me right out like that. Of course he didn't do it." He stayed by my side for another twenty minutes, carping about the media coverage and talking about the strain it had all been on The Family. Needless to say, I got a great story.

Peggy paused a second and then said, "That's what we'd all like to know. Charlie especially. This is the last thing he needs right now, and it's the last thing our industry needs. The insurance fraud business was bad enough. *The New York Times, The Washington Post, People, Time, Newsweek*—they all had stories about George Lindemann, Barney Ward, and the rest of them killing those poor horses."

I have to admit, having the world read about the scummy side of horse showing didn't do much for the sport. Ward and Lindemann weren't exactly equine ambassadors. But Lindemann was an Eagle Scout compared to Ward, a short and bulky former semipro football player with thighs the size of mutant watermelons. Ward played pimp for Tommy Burns, matching the horse-killing cretin who confessed to offing fifteen horses with owners who wanted their mounts dead. He got caught when another horseman offered to wear a wire to trap Ward because he'd heard him talk about doing away with the aforementioned Burns—who considered Ward a father figure. Ward thought Burns was stooling on him. He was also charged with extortion after threatening the wife of a famous rider he'd put a bullet through her head *plus* kill one of her horses if she didn't lease him space for his horses at the Palm Beach Polo and Country Club. Ward's an old hand at the justice system. Two years before that, he was convicted of defrauding a customer out of $100,000.

Lindemann's less showy in his wretchedness. A twerpy little guy who stands close to the same height as Muggsy Bogues but has none of his class. He was barred from the jumper ring after the indictments came down for having his horse Charisma killed. No problem, he had Daddy—owner of Cellular Farms—slap a $1 million lawsuit against the ASHA, the association that governs horse shows, tying their legal hands. They countersued and baby George, not wanting to miss the show season, started competing in dressage instead of show jumping. One thing you have to say about George. He can ride. And he can afford Olympic-caliber horses. The combination of the two won the horse killer an all-expense-paid scholarship slot on the United States dressage team to compete internationally.

None of it made for good publicity. And it's not as if horse showing has a good name to start with. At the Spain Olympics there was a big brouhaha about the cruelty of eventing, the most grueling of equestrian sports, where horses jump off cliffs, into lakes, down banks, and over huge, indestructible hurdles like trucks. Then, at the Olympics before that in Los Angeles, one of the American riders said something snide about his newly won medal, like he was just going to toss it into the closet. The wires picked up his remarks and loaded the story with lots of John Q. Citizen outrage responses.

"Jim didn't kill any horses," I said. "He never had to, he was never out of the ribbons. What could his death have to do with the horse industry?"

"Hopefully not a thing," Peggy said. "But you never know. Someone told me that the father of the little girl who died at Jim and Charlie's farm might have something to do with it. You know she was riding a pony Jim sold to her when it happened. The pony bolted, the child fell and hit her head on the mounting block, and died right there and then. It was a freak thing because she was wearing a helmet. The father never got over it. A couple of months ago the police were asking all sorts of questions about him, thinking he might have had something to do with the fire. That pony died in that fire."

Another dead kid and an avenging parent.

"I see what you mean," I said. "Wait'll the tabs get hold of that. Even if it's not true, wait'll they get hold of it. Better hang on tight, Peggy. Speaking of horrible riding accidents, did you know Josane Ashmore?"

Breezey Mundell looked at Peggy and Peggy looked at her. Something passed between them, but I didn't know what. Sprinkle, meanwhile, was scanning the room, looking for something. Who knew what. From what I'd heard about Sprinkle, she'll talk to you as long as she's interested, which isn't too long. Then her eyes start wandering, looking for something or someone else. It'd be easy to assume she was social climbing, looking for a higher vantage point. But given her last name, that was doubtful. In this crowd she wasn't going to find any rungs higher than herself. So it was either a prehistoric case of attention deficit disorder or simply chronic ennui. Whichever way, it was clear she'd already checked out.

"I knew her," Peggy said. "Though not as well as I knew her horse, Rita. The foal was born and raised on my farm. She was the ugliest thing you've ever seen right off. Sickle hocked, skinny neck, bumps on her legs. She outgrew everything except for those damn bumps, never did know what they were and tried everything to get rid of them. But that foal grew into the prettiest animal I've ever seen and she could jump. Jump like a dream. And what a mover, she'd have won the hacks at all the indoor shows if she'd have ever gotten there. She had the talent to be another Rox-Dene, but not the mind. I've never seen a mare cycle as hard as she did. Even Regu-mate couldn't settle her down."

Equine PMS. When a marish mare ovulates, watch out. She pins her ears, kicks, bites, screams, and generally says screw you to anyone who comes near her with a saddle. She's got one thing on her mind, and it isn't that kind of riding. If you're lucky, a daily dose of Regu-mate, a synthetic hormone that tricks the body into thinking it's pregnant so it won't ovulate, can smooth out the hissy fits. Luck, apparently, wasn't on Rita's side.

"Where's the mare now?" I asked.

Peggy shook her head and the hair on my arms rose. I knew what was coming next. I have a sixth sense when it comes to horses. Luck sure as hell wasn't on Rita's side.

"She was in the barn with the pony. No one could get to her in time; even if they could have, she wouldn't have budged. You know as well as anyone fire makes a reasonable horse crazy and that horse was crazy to start with."

Now it was my turn to shake my head. One insurance fraud story was enough for me, at least when it came to torturing horses. How many times can you cry over a keyboard?

I said, "Shades of Wally Hempstead?"

That brought old Sprinkle back into the loop. "Now I remember your name. Aren't you that reporter who wrote about Wally Hempstead?"

She didn't have a smile on her face, so I was pretty sure she wasn't about to shake my hand and say good job. I shook my head yes and steeled myself for the assault.

"The ASHA should have barred you from the show ring along with Lindemann and the rest of them. Someone I know read your stories and said your facts were wrong and you made us out to be a bunch of spoiled rich people who do nothing but kill horses."

I'd have liked to say something about the shoe fitting, but she was already starting to look away. I was as sure as my name is Nattie Gold that all the facts in those stories were right. Henry had insisted we triple-check down to every comma. At the time it made me want to choke him, but now I could have kissed him for it. As to her complaint about her people's portrayal, it was a straight reporting job. Henry and I went to the mat on that one too. I wanted to make it snappy, more like a feature. But he won. There wasn't a snide swipe or nasty remark in the series, though there were plenty of opportunities. It even passed through Fred's will-it-offend-anyone-even-the-janitor? screen.

I fished in my purse for my card, found one, and scribbled Fred's name and number on it.

"Here, give this to your friend who reads," I said. "Tell her to make a list of everything I got wrong and call Fred Richards, the editor of *The Appeal*."

"Oh, don't be ridiculous," Sprinkle said. This time her body wandered off with her eyes, in search of more stimulating turf.

"Don't pay her any mind," Peggy said. "She'll forget about it before she goes home. But about Wally Hempstead, don't even say his name in the same breath as Jim Benson or Charlie Laconte. You couldn't be further from the truth. It wasn't anything like that. After Josane's accident, Charlie couldn't even donate that horse. No one wanted her. The family couldn't afford the board, so Charlie got stuck with the mare. No one killed that horse to make money. He couldn't have insured her if he wanted to. The insurance companies are a lot more careful these days."

Two dead horses, two dead children. No money trail. What to do. I'd have to mull this over with Henry, whom I caught out of the corner of my eye looking very engrossed in conversation with Topping Mundell. I had to admit it, she was a looker. Of course she was tall and slim, she was a rider. But there was more to her than a perfect body. She had an unusual face, midwestern broad like the plains, eyes set a little farther apart than expected, a nose to match her goyishe thighs, which is to say Dr.-Diamond-perfect, and those pouty, full lips that men fantasize about. Then there was the hair. Long and red like mine, but that was where the similarities stopped. It was perfect girl hair, the kind I used to dream about in fifth, sixth, seventh—well, all the way up to college—grades. The kind that never needed to be rolled on orange juice cans, sizzled flat with a hot iron, or fried with hot rollers to smooth out the kinks. Topping's tresses looked like liquid amber tumbling down her back.

Okay, so she was a looker. Pretty is as pretty does. And from what I knew, that wasn't much of anything.

Josane was a looker and look where it got her. Dead, possibly murdered.

"What'd you think of Josane? I met her at the Miss America Pageant, she couldn't have been nicer. . . ."

"Well, that *was* her job, wasn't it?" Peggy said.

I had a feeling if I said something positive about Josane, Peggy would feel it her duty to set the record straight eventually. But I hadn't expected such quick and snide results. I could practically see her back arch. Meow, with a capital M. I didn't know old Peggy had it in her. The word on Peggy was that she was the quintessential southern matron, meaning she was raised to smile, be gracious, and never say anything unkind about anybody unless it was General William Tecumseh Sherman or one of his kin.

Josane must've pushed something inside Peggy that shorted out her imprinting. But not for long. She smiled at me and said, "Now, I'm not wanting to be ugly about it, but Josane Ashmore was a *beauty queen*." Peggy said beauty queen in exactly the way the Miss America people cringed at and fought to change with their this-is-a-scholarship-pageant shtick. Judging by Peggy—and the rest of the pageant-watching free world—it wasn't taking one bit. They needed to hire the Kentucky Fried Chicken people or a lesson in spin control. The pageant's on-air vote confirmed exactly what kind of a pageant they were running. More than a million people paid fifty cents apiece to make sure the T and A component—politically correctized to the new name of fitness—of the "scholarship pageant" stayed. Fitness, that's as funny as green horses. I'd seen it firsthand; those young women are so padded and taped together up top, even the flatties of the bunch walk down the runway looking like the *Baywatch* babes.

"So what was underneath the smile?" I said. "Something that made someone want to make her stop smiling for good?"

"Nattie, you must have murder on the brain," Peggy said. "Breezey, what do you think? Did Josane make anyone mad enough to kill her, other than that crazy horse she bought? Did Toppy ever say anything about Josane getting into a fight with anyone, a fight bad enough to get her killed?"

There was current flying between them, I just couldn't read the charge.

Breezey Mundell gave me her old-money smile, not too big— don't want to overemote—and said, "I guess anyone could anger anyone enough. But certainly not in this case. I understand everyone was very fond of her, so why would anyone want to harm her? I'd heard that she and my daughter rode together, but we never discussed what happened. If you'll excuse me. Peggy, I'm going to talk to Charlie."

Oooh, baby, someone hand me a sweater. This lady could be her own air conditioner. And was it my imagination, or did I hear a twist in the words "everyone" and "very" when Breczey said *everyone* was *very* fond of Josane? I needed footnotes for this conversation and unfortunately Peggy wasn't supplying them. Though I did try. Peggy was as mum on that subject as she was when I tried to flesh out the truth behind the Josane I'd heard about from Annie's mother, Josane the older-man eater. Peggy's lips were locked; it appeared the beauty-queen remark was as good as it was going to get.

"Is there anything else you can think of about Josane?"

"Nattie," Peggy said, "you ride that wonderful mare of yours the same way you ask questions. You just don't give up. You can dig all you want, you're not going to find anything other than a riding accident. But I know that's not going to stop you. So if you're bound and determined to ask more questions, I guess I'd start over there."

I followed her eyes to a man standing by the door. Mid- to late thirties, not too tall, probably five-nine or ten and on the slender side. White-blond hair parted in the middle, a small ponytail at the nape of his neck. Very blue eyes. All he needed was a herring in one hand and a bottle of Aquavit in the other, and he could have been a travel poster for Scandinavia. Anyone who liked the type might have called him handsome. Anyone but me.

I don't find anything attractive about women-bashers, even ones that look like Norse gods.

"That was Josane's boyfriend," Peggy said. "Flip Nilson."

CHAPTER 19

"**D**on't believe anything you've heard about me."

I'd hardly gotten past my name and I'm-a-friend-of-Annie's and Flip was already denying his reputation.

"What should I believe?" I said.

"Everything you hear from me," he said. He was used to wowing women. I could tell by his smile; wide and easy like he knew just where to touch you.

"Okay, then," I said, not smiling back. "Let's start with Josane Ashmore."

That wiped the grin off his face. He was either a very good actor or just the mention of Josane's name cracked his cocky veneer. The let's-do-it-baby look in his eyes gave way to such a look of hurt, even I wanted to wrap my arms around this Neanderthal and say, "There, there, it's okay."

"Why do you want to know about Josane?" he said. "She's dead, there's nothing more to say other than when they buried her, they buried part of me. Why are you asking questions? Does this have something to do with that crazy mother of hers?"

I handed him a business card and did my official *Commercial Appeal* introduction that Richards insists we do.

"I'm thinking about doing a story on Josane and yes, I did interview her mother who—"

Flip started to walk away. I grabbed his arm.

"Wait, just hear me out," I said. "I am looking into her death,

161

but I don't know what happened out there. For all I know, it could have been a bad riding accident and Josane's mother just can't let her go. You of all people should understand that. You say they buried part of you with Josane? Well, they buried just about all of her. Just a few minutes of your time."

Flip stopped. I took my hand from his arm.

"Not here," he said. "This isn't the place. Tomorrow morning at eight, the Rail Stop in The Plains. I'll answer your questions on one condition. Get her mother off my back. Tell her I loved Josane, I'd never do anything to hurt her."

I couldn't help thinking what Annie had said about his hitting her, and it must have showed on my face.

"You're a friend of Annie's," he said. "So why should you believe me? What happened between me and Annie happened a long time ago. There's nothing I can do to change that. But I was a different person then. Josane was my wake-up call. Do you know what I mean by that?"

I shook my head. "Not exactly."

"I'll tell you tomorrow," he said. "For right now, let's leave it at this—a day doesn't go by that I don't feel it right here in my heart."

He balled his hand into a fist and punched himself in the chest. He hit himself hard, maybe even harder than he'd planned.

"Four years and it still hurts like it happened yesterday."

His eyes filled and he turned away.

"I'll see you tomorrow," he said as he walked toward the door.

Whoa, me feeling sorry for him? Time for a dose of reality. I walked by the coffin, mercifully closed, and remembered there were two dead bodies, both suspiciously made that way. Smarten up, Nattie, every criminal on death row insists he or she is innocent.

It was curious that Nilson was even here. This was a horse show crowd, and other than his association with Josane, I couldn't see him fitting in. The guys were mostly gay, so I couldn't see Nilson-the-ladies'-man palling around with a bunch of men drooling over him.

Put that on the question list for tomorrow. What was Flip Nilson's connection to Jim Benson, and how did he get that silly name anyway?

I scanned the room for Henry, hoping to catch his eye. It looked like the only thing I'd be catching from Henry anytime tonight was a joint cab ride home, and that was questionable. He was still talking to Miss Topping Mundell, and I could practically see the energy dancing between them. He smiled, she smiled, he smiled, she smiled, and I turned away, looking for someone to interview or at least looking for something to keep me busy until they were finished smiling at each other.

I felt a tap on my shoulder and turned around. I was eye level to a very large set of breasts. I looked up to the owner of that formidable chest to see a woman about my age, shoulder-length brown hair, hazel eyes, and a big enough smile to make me think she wasn't about to throw me out for crashing a wake or a viewing or whatever it was called.

"Hey," she said. "You're Annie Hoskin's friend, right?"

"You've got that right," I said, smiled, and extended my hand. "Nattie Gold, how'd you know?"

"Annie said 'short, long red hair, and looks she's not afraid of anything.' " She shook my hand.

"Well, she got the first two right," I said. "Put me near an oxer and I'm a quivering mass of cowardice. Okay, so you know me. Who are you?"

"Karen Rose, I run Charlie's barn. Annie said you'd be looking for me. And wanting to ask a bunch of questions about Josane."

"As a matter of fact, I am and I do," I said, and caught the Bobbsey twins—Henry and Topping—out of the corner of my eye, still talking AND smiling. The hell with him. If he wanted to play smiley-face with a beautiful pea-brain, that was his business. I had a story to report and a monkey on my back by the name of Candace-the-automaton.

I grilled Karen for the next thirty minutes about the barn, Charlie, Jim, Josane, and the little girl who died. Karen loved to talk, that was for sure. And she seemed to have an opinion about everything.

About Josane—she was obviously a fan.

"I remember the first day she came to the barn," Karen said. "I wanted to hate her because she was so goddamned beautiful plus she had a way about her that made men stupider fools than they already are. Then it turns out she's a lot smarter than any beauty queen I'd ever met. I tried, but I couldn't hate her—she was as nice as she was beautiful."

Her take on Josane's death was the same as everyone's up here—pure and simple, a nasty riding accident waiting to happen. She said she'd seen that horse dump Josane any number of times. "I stopped counting after I'd used up my fingers and toes."

Karen laughed. She had a ditzy giggle to her that might have made you think she was an airbrain. But in the course of our conversation, it came out that she spoke five languages, was working on her sixth, checked the NASDAQ—and even knew what it stood for—every morning to track her investments, and read German novels *in* German.

"Don't get me wrong," Karen said, "Josane wasn't a horrible rider. She was fine on any normal horse. But Rita wasn't exactly normal. She was like one of those freaky, brilliant kids who become doctors when they're nine. Smart and talented as all get-out, but underneath the brains, screwed up. Deeply screwed up."

I asked Karen to walk me through the day Josane died, step by step. I was looking for anything. An inconsistency in the police report, a pertinent detail not recorded. Something, anything. I didn't know what.

It went like this: She'd watched Josane groom and saddle up

the mare as they talked about her latest man problem. Karen's, not Josane's. "Josane's only problem when it came to men was too much. She could have had anyone—and from what I saw, did. Her cup definitely ranneth over, again and again. Speaking of which, that girl was amazing when it came to the Bible, she could quote you any passage. Said her mama made her memorize half the good book by the time she was ten."

A Bible-spouting femme fatale whose nose was no stranger to the white stuff and enjoyed a wide array of male companionship. Josane had been a bundle of contradictions—and to me that only makes a person more interesting. I was getting sorrier and sorrier that I'd never get a chance to really meet her. Interviewing someone who's running for office or crown doesn't count.

I shifted back to the topic—Josane's final ride—and was wondering if a change in tack might have made the horse explode. A different bit that irritated the already cranky mare or a new girth? No luck there either. She'd used the same custom-made Jimmy's bridle with the same egg-butt bit she used every day. The saddle was the same—her pricey Butet—even the saddle pad was the one she'd used the day before. I guess Charlie was a little more relaxed than Rob. At my barn, if he caught me using the same saddle pad from the day before, that'd be worth at least five minutes of telling me what a slob I am.

"And if I remember right," Karen said, "she rubbed Rita's legs down with some kind of bump medicine and then put galloping boots over the top. Josane wanted Charlie to ride Rita in Green Conformation Hunter in the worst way. As if that mare could be conformation anything. Her legs were bumpier than a roller coaster. And I don't have to tell you conformation hunters can't have a blemish anywhere, let alone bumpy legs—might as well light a match to your entry fee money. But you know Josane, or I guess you didn't know her, when she got her mind made up, you could have saved your breath for all the good it did."

I had to admit that Annie was right about one resemblance

between me and Josane. I could challenge a mule to a duel of obstinacy and win.

I asked Karen about Josane's mood. Maybe she was upset about something and the mare picked up on that and flew with it.

"Are you kidding?" Karen said. "Josane was as high as a kite that day. And it had nothing to do with drugs. Though if you're going to ask about that too, I might as well tell you now if you haven't heard already. Josane ran with some cokeheads. From time to time she used. Nothing crazy, just a little partying every now and then. But that day she was high on life. High, high, high. She was flying, really flying. On a normal day Josane was what you'd have called a bubbly person. That day she was ready to pop. She'd spent the morning with a lawyer in Warrenton about her divorce. I guess that went well—or something after that went even better—because by the time she got here she was giddy as all get out. Giddy, you know, giddy like someone who'd just rolled out of the sack with someone new. And if I had to bet, I'm sure it wasn't that pretty-boy Karate Kid she'd been seeing."

Divorce? Reenie hadn't mentioned anything about nuptials *or* divorce proceedings. I'd have to find out why she was mum on the matter. Even I know the first person to suspect is an ex. Karen was right on the money, though, with her suspicions about Josane's sex life. I remembered something in the police report about a semen check and at the time thought it strange that they'd done one. But they had and Josane had had sex in the last few hours of her life. It was too late to find out whose, laboratorically speaking. I'd have to rely on the old-fashioned method—asking questions.

"Flip? You mean Flip? Why not him?"

"They were on the outs," Karen said. "He might not have known it, but they were. She told me he smothered her."

"Interesting choice of words," I said. "Smothered as in killed?"

Karen laughed again and I watched her chest heave up and down and knew she must've had welts the size of licorice ropes from where the bra straps sliced into her shoulders. I know a big set of mammary glands is attractive to men, but I was glad I didn't have to haul around all that extra flesh hanging off my front.

"Annie said your imagination was as big as your hair," Karen said. "Murder? Jeez, I don't know. . . ."

I went into my let's-just-suppose mode. As in let's just suppose *someone*—and we'll leave that blank for now—followed Josane out on the trail, or knew where she'd be and was waiting for her. And suppose that someone spooked the horse big-time, maybe waved a sheet or a plastic bag right as she turned a corner, but did it loud enough to make the horse really go bonkers, which from what I understand about Rita, wouldn't take much. The horse explodes. Josane, no Margie Goldstein, falls off. And let's suppose the accident isn't bad enough to really hurt her. So the person finishes off the job and smashes Josane in the head with a rock.

"Boy, oh, boy, you do have an active imagination. You should write for television," Karen said. "I guess that's possible. Shit, anything's possible. I don't want to tell you your job, but with all this supposing, don't you have to have an idea who you're supposing about?"

"Well, what about Flip?" I asked.

She put her hand on her chin and arched her eyebrows. "Flip? I know Annie's told you what a creep he was with her and I'm sure you probably also heard what a jerk he was about other men with Josane. He couldn't stand to see her look at a man, let alone talk to one. And back before Josane died, he spent a lot of time bragging that the sheriff said he should have his hands registered as weapons. He's big into karate. But murder? Like I said, I guess anything's possible. But I've always thought he was basically harmless. He's certainly harmless now that he's found Jesus, or whoever it is he's found. Even back when he was with Josane, I thought he was a lot of bark and no bite. I'll have to think about that some more. In the meantime, let's play your let's-suppose

167

game. Suppose he didn't do it? What've you got? Everyone I know luuuuuved Josane, except for maybe some of the wives whose husbands were gaga over her. But I can't see any sixty-year-old Middleburg lady hiking through the woods in her little Gucci espadrilles, looking for a rock or something big enough to bash Josane in the head with. Can you?"

She had a point, but there was always murder for hire. If twenty-three people could find a cretin like Tommy Burns to kill a horse, surely someone could find another lowlife to kill a human for a couple more zeros at the end of the paycheck.

Karen didn't buy my murder-for-hire scenario. Said the horse world was too small, there'd have been talk, and the lowlife would have surfaced by now. But not one to close doors, she said anything's possible and she'd ask around for me. I was out of questions about Josane and thought I'd help Henry out on his story and dig around about Jim Benson. I brought up the barn fire and the little girl's father.

Karen wasn't smiling when she talked about him.

"Talk about troubled," she said. "That man's dangerous. He's gonna spend the rest of his life trying to find someone to blame—and pay—for his kid's accident. We call him the Fireman around town. I know the police say he didn't burn down the barn. I say bullshit to that. I just hope they nail him to the wall for Jim's death.

"Suppose he didn't do it?" I said.

"Not a chance," Karen said. "Who else'd want Jim dead?"

I couldn't tell her about the list. "I don't know, you tell me?"

"No one, that's who," she said. "They didn't make them any nicer than Jim, and just forget about Charlie killing Jim. First of all, he was at the barn when it happened. I know that because *I* was at the barn the same time. But even more so, Charlie wouldn't have ever done anything, and I mean anything, to hurt Jim. Sure they had their ups and downs—you tell me who doesn't. But they were like Ozzie and Harriet basically."

I hadn't really considered Charlie a suspect. If he had been, the police would have been all over him and arrested him by now. But if Josane ran with a fast crowd, that crowd could have easily included Jim and Charlie. They wouldn't have been the first horse show people to have snorted half their bank accounts up their noses—or the first to get wiped out for a drug deal gone bad. I asked as delicately as possible; it was clear Karen was Labrador-retriever loyal to Jim and Charlie.

"Oh, man, now you're starting to piss me off," Karen said. "I know you're just asking questions. But it's these kinds of questions that get the wrong kind of talk going. So put it to rest right here. Jim and Charlie didn't have a dirty bone in their bodies and their noses were as pure as fresh snow, no pun intended. They knew Josane was hanging out with a rough crowd, and not two weeks before she died they'd talked to her about it. They were ready to kick her ass out of the barn. When it came to drugs, Jim and Charlie didn't want any of it at their barn. From anyone. It didn't matter how much money Josane had or whoever it was that had it and was giving it to her."

The money trail. I'd forgotten all about it. Give me an F in investigative reporting. It's the first place to look for clues, and I'd just about walked away without asking.

"Okay, okay," I said. "Not another word about Jim and Charlie unless it's how wonderful they are or were. One more thing about Josane. She obviously had big bucks. Where'd they come from? Surely not from that little store of hers?"

Karen laughed again and I was glad she wasn't one to hang on to her anger.

"You mean the Dazee Cutter?" she said. "Ever see Middleburg on Saturday? It's a running stream of tourists going from shop to shop looking for ceramic cows. And Josane had plenty of them, along with all her horsey stuff. She made good money there. Enough for that girl who worked for her to steal half of it before

169

Josane ever noticed. But that's the point, that store was just something to keep Josane occupied, not pay the bills. She had a bigger source of income that made what she took in at the Dazee Cutter seem like mad money."

I started to say "what," but Karen cut me off at the "wh."

"Like I said, her cup ranneth over. She had herself an older man who thought the sun rose and the moon hung over her. She never would tell me who it was, but whoever he was, he had a bankbook the size of Kansas and wasn't afraid to spend it on her. That's how she bought Rita."

Either Josane really never revealed the identity of her patron—the polite term for sugar daddy—or the Middleburg Mafia was closing up and protecting Daddy Bigbucks. Whatever way, it was clear no one was going to come right out and tell me who he was. That meant the dreaded records check. At least a day in the stacks with Henry, oh, boy.

I asked Karen what happened to Lannie Post, Josane's itchy-fingered helper. Not much, was her answer. Josane never pressed charges, just told Lannie to stay away from her.

"Far away," Karen said. "Toward the end, Lannie was giving Josane the creeps and Josane was just as happy to have a reason to distance herself from Lannie. I don't think she stole that money for the money. That's the creepy part, and I know it sounds strange. But it wasn't money that Lannie wanted. She wanted Josane's attention and I think stealing was her sick way of getting it. Lannie had a thing for Josane, I'm not saying either one of them was gay. Sure as hell not Josane. It was more complicated than just plain sex. Josane kind of took Lannie under her wing. Taught her how to use makeup and how to wear the right clothes. Lannie didn't look like the same girl after a while. Shit, it's amazing what makeup can do. Josane dolled me up once with all her paint, and even I looked like a fuckin' movie star. But Lannie, she was kind of a nutcase if you ask me. Turning up at Josane's door at all hours, calling her all the time. Even dressing in the same outfits. She'd wait for Josane to show up at the store, see what she was wearing, make an excuse to leave, and then come back in a black skirt and blue blouse—or whatever it was Josane was wearing that day. It was too weird for me."

Now it made sense, in a sick sort of way. The car and the tags. I'd have bet my life savings, if I hadn't already spent it all by buying Brenda, that Lannie Post was the driver of the DAZCUTR. But she'd have to be a shortie. No one taller than me could've fit behind the wheel with the driver's seat cranked up that far.

"How tall is Lannie?"

Karen looked at me like I'd just asked the stupidest question on earth.

"Huh?" she said. "You want to know how tall she is? What does that have to do with anything? God, you ask some strange questions. About your size, maybe an inch shorter, ten pounds heavier."

I cleared up the whys to the height question when I told her about the car, the vanity tags, and the pushed-up driver's seat.

"So there is something underneath all that hair," she said, and laughed. "I figured as much and Annie told me anyhow. I don't know what kind of car Lannie drives and it wouldn't surprise me one bit if that's hers. See what I mean about creepy? I gotta go talk to someone. Call me if you have more questions."

Karen was writing down her phone number on the back of a funeral home card. Something was nagging at me and I couldn't remember what. "Reach," I said to myself, because I didn't want Karen to think I was delusional. It sounds odd, I know, but it works. Lose something, say "reach," and nine times out of ten you remember where it is or what it was. My father's girlfriend taught me the trick, her new take on it being that saying "reach" acts as a request to your all-knowing-everything-including-where-you left-your-keys spirit guides for a nudge in the right direction. I said it again and I didn't know which would come first, my answer or her departure.

Just as she was pivoting, I remembered. My hand caught her shoulder in mid-turn.

"One last thing," I said, "then I'll stop bugging you for tonight. If Rita was such a crazy horse, what was Josane doing going out alone on the trail?"

Karen laughed again. "You should know by now, no one could tell Josane anything she didn't want to hear. That wasn't air or gray matter between her ears, it was concrete."

CHAPTER 20

I guess Henry finally dislodged himself from Topping's side. When I looked up she was talking to someone else.

Now to find Henry. I scanned the room and saw him standing in a clump of men. I caught his eye and motioned to the nonexistent watch on my arm as if I had someplace to be. An hour had passed and the agreement was to meet now by the casket.

So I walked that way and planted myself by a very large spray of something white and waxy. Between the perfume and flowers, I'd practically had to do a breaststroke through the air to get there. Another difference between Jews and Christians. Dying. I hate funerals, especially when I'm crying my heart out; however, a few sprigs of something pretty would be nice. Jews don't get flowers when they die. We get rocks—no kidding. When you visit a Jewish cemetery, you place a rock on the headstone to show you've been there. And if you're really on the Judaic track, not only don't you get flowers, but you end up in a plain pine box, wearing a simple white shroud. No flowers—plain pine box and a scratchy cotton shmata. We're talking spartan, as opposed to today's event. At least five florists must have emptied out their refrigerators on Benson's coffin. And what a coffin it was—no pine box for this boy. He was taking his final snooze in an ornate dark wood casket so shiny you could see your tears roll down your cheeks. Big brass fasteners, brass hinges, and an inside that I can only guess had more aqua satin than three New Orleans whorehouses.

Henry joined me by Jim.

"So," I said, making sure my voice didn't betray me, "what'd you find out? Anything interesting? Was that Topping Mundell you were talking to?"

I finished the sentence in my head, ". . . for three hours."

"As a matter of fact, it was," Henry said. "She knows you and your horse. She's very impressed with what a good rider you are. Nattie, you've been underplaying your riding abilities."

"Really? Talk about anything besides me? Perhaps the subject at hand?"

I placed my hand on the coffin and smiled.

"Of course we talked about Benson. Why else are we here?"

I continued to smile and pinched my hand so I wouldn't say it. "Okay," I said. "Spill."

I had to admit it, Henry had gotten a good bit of information from Topping. It made me second-guess my read on things. Maybe Henry had just been conducting an interview. And just maybe jealousy had clouded my judgment, which is why I say stay away from newsroom romances. Not that I've ever been one to take my own advice. The night after I moved to Charlotte, I found myself driving across the state line into South Carolina with a tall, lanky reporter from Tennessee who'd swooped down on me in the newsroom with hawklike grace and speed. I was enchanted with the lyrical cadence of his accent and his poetic soul. Storytelling was in his bones, and I could've listened to him spin tales all night. If he'd wanted to. Unfortunately for me he had other plans and they weren't of the verbal nature. And unfortunately for him his poetic soul was the only thing I was attracted to. So we parted friends; he moved on to the television clerk, and I to a short reporter from New Jersey who was as lyrical as Sylvester Stallone but too cute for words. Like my father, Lou, I think with the wrong part of my anatomy when it comes to the opposite sex.

As it turned out, Jim Benson had a connection to tobacco. A

big connection. His family not only owned what Topping called "that little cow-calf farm" where he was murdered, but a good chunk of the lower Virginia Piedmont, where they don't grow cows. They grow crops. The killer crop. Benson's fortune came from tobacco farming. It seems Granddaddy Benson got himself a market share of the tobacco allotments the feds were handing out in 1946. That was when the government stepped in and started paying tobacco farmers to grow how much they told them to grow and not a stalk more. By controlling supply, they controlled demand, and by controlling demand they could keep the prices jacked up high as the good senators from North Carolina told them to.

From what Topping told Henry, the Benson acres have been keeping the Bladstone cigarette machines rolling for years.

"The interesting thing about Benson is," Henry said, "he never smoked and couldn't stand to be around anyone who did. There was no question he enjoyed the revenue from the tobacco farm. Toppy said he was an extravagant spender and apparently there was plenty to spend because he was the only child. But she said he was almost apologetic about where the money came from."

I ignored the Toppy this and Toppy that and listened to the rest of what he'd learned about Benson. Such as that Topping had seen him the day before he was murdered and said he seemed pre-occupied. Such as he'd had a troubled relationship with his father, an overbearing tomcat of a man who'd never approved of his son's lifestyle and was constantly threatening to disown him and cut him out of the will.

I guess that meant Benson's father fancied himself the ladies' man and couldn't accept the fact that the product of his manliness turned out to be gay. I wondered how he would accept the fact that his only child was now dead. I was glad I didn't have to spend the night in that man's mind.

Then it was my turn to tell Henry what I'd found out. I told

him about the other father, the Fireman, who'd never come back
from the death of his daughter. Henry and I agreed the poor man
probably had nothing to do with Benson's death, but still it needed
to be chased down. You never know where a lead will take you.
Maybe the Fireman did take a final act of revenge and just maybe
Benson's death had nothing to do with the letter-writing wacko.
Stranger things have happened.

Someone had to talk to Benson's parents, and I was glad it
wasn't me. I figured old man Benson must be really wrestling with
his demons right now, and I didn't want to be referee, participant,
or observer. I'd done that enough when I worked newsside. Even
though I'm a reporter, I hate my profession and all those in it when
I see one of my brethren shove a mike in front of the tearstained
face of a mother who's just been told her entire family has been
killed by a madman.

When I worked newsside I had to make too many of those calls
and I always felt dirty afterward. I don't care what the editors
say—and they'll say just about anything to make you do it,
including the old saw that down deep families really like to talk
about their newly departed kin—it's an invasion of privacy and the
public's right to know means doodly-squat when someone is
grieving.

I can't say Henry was keen on talking to them either, at least
not at the funeral home. He hemmed and hawed and finally
decided on a plan—that he'd call them later in the week. Good
decision, Henry.

"So," I said. "What about Topping?"

"*What* about Topping?"

It was then I knew for sure Henry had other things on his mind
than a newspaper story.

"I'm not asking if you two have plans for New Year's Eve. I
mean what about Topping and the M connection. You know, her
father, Santee Mundell, Mr. M on your psycho's hit parade?"

"Oh, that," Henry said. "I didn't tell her about the list. I don't want too many people to know about it and I didn't see any reason to worry her. She's very close with her father. I don't know if you know this, but after her mother left, Topping stayed with her father, from the age of eleven on. She's crazy about him. So what would be the point in telling her someone might be trying to kill her father, especially since no one's sure of anything right now?"

"No point," I said, and mustered a smile. "What about the tobacco connection? What did Topping say Daddy did for a living? All I know is that he's got some kind of company that brings in dump trucks full of money."

"Mundell Industries," Henry said. "An industrial chemical company. I don't know yet what and if there's a tobacco connection. Toppy said her father's company has many subsidiaries all over the world and it was possible one might concern tobacco, but she didn't know. By the way, I think you had her pegged wrong. She doesn't only ride horses. Did you know she founded and administers something called the Mid-Atlantic Therapeutic Riding Program, apparently one of the most successful of its kind in the country?"

"No, Henry," I said. "I can't say I knew that. That's impressive. Those programs do wonders for kids. I guess Topping's a redheaded Mother Teresa without wrinkles, what more can I say?"

He gave me a funny look, like he wasn't sure whether I was being serious or sarcastic. I'd had enough of death for the day and enough of hearing how terrific little Miss Mundell was. Next thing I'd know he'd be telling me she wasn't the pea-brain I'd said she was, that she'd gone to his alma mater, Harvard.

But I did need to talk to her. According to Karen, Topping and Josane had been close friends and constant riding companions. I looked her way and she was engrossed in a conversation with three matching Middleburgers—tall, thin, hair tastefully pulled back in taut little ponytails like their taut little behinds, and well, if not particularly excitingly, dressed. Just looking at them made me feel exactly the way I do at the horse shows—like I'm from the planet You-Don't-Fit-In-And-Never-Will. I wanted to break into that bunch as much as I wanted to have another late-night go-round with Outerbridge Duncan.

Besides, my stomach was grumbling loud enough for Henry to look down at it a few times. It was well past twelve and the elimination phase in my body was over. My body, trained like a Pavlovian dog, knew it was time to chow down on something real. I'd catch Topping later in the day, maybe at the barn.

"Henry," I said. "Let's grab a bite to eat and figure out what to do next. Okay?"

He looked at his watch and glanced around the room. "That sounds good. Just give me a second."

Like a torpedo, he zeroed in on Middleburg's very own saint of troubled children and walked over to her. I couldn't lip-read because they were both facing the side and I didn't want to stare. But I did see her write something down on a piece of paper.

"Let's go," Henry said. "I asked Toppy to join us, but she's leaving now to go ride. In this weather—you horsewomen are crazy. She recommended the Coach House."

"Then the Coach House it is," I said in my most magnanimous voice.

CHAPTER 21

Of course the DAZCUTR car was gone by the time Henry and I walked out of the funeral home. What did I expect, a gift from the investigative-reporting gods, perhaps Lannie Post sitting in the front seat of her car with a deranged look on her face, carrying a sign that said POSSIBLE MURDER SUSPECT?

Forget it, this story was going to take work. And a lot of it. The question was, would I have the time? I still had to find something to write a Sunday fashion column about—and then write the damn thing.

The Coach House was just down the street in one of those old charming stucco buildings decked out with more pine garlands and red velvet bows than a North Carolina interstate of wreath-nosed cars. Inside it was even more Christmasy. Bells on the doors, lights in the window, carols on the airwaves. And I thought Charlotte took this decoration thing seriously.

We ordered. Henry a burger; me, vegetable soup and salad. I guess the apple doesn't fall far from the tree. I've been an on-and-off-again vegetarian for the past twenty-five years, since my favorite cousin stopped being a junkie and started being a macrobiotic. He got the whole family hooked on the vegan way. My father was living in his basement at the time, so Sunday visitation was always the same: a trail ride through Fairmount Park, followed by brown rice and vegetables at Aunt Shirley and Uncle Artie's. If Aunt Shirley was up, she'd be sitting at the table, jabbering away nonstop. If she was down, she'd be sitting on the pink velvet vanity stool in her bathroom, alone and in the dark. Regardless of Aunt Shirley's mental state, after dinner Uncle Artie would tap-dance across the black and white linoleum squares of the basement floor and pull quarters from my ear. I never said my family was sane.

The soup was warm and soothing, just like soup should be. Henry downed his burger in three bites and left a smear of ketchup on his chin. This always presents an interesting problem—do you tell the person he's wearing his lunch or talk to him like he doesn't have a face full of ketchup? I'd want to know. I motioned with my fingers and he got the message.

"I'm a sloppy eater," Henry said. No embarrassment, no pride, just statement of fact.

"So," I said, "what's on your schedule? I need to go to Charlie Laconte's barn, track down Lannie Post, write a Sunday fashion column, find out the identity of Josane's mystery sugar daddy, talk to Josane's divorce lawyer, track down her ex-husband, find the nurse at the hospital who said she had a funny smell, interview Josane's old boyfriend, talk to Topping, and figure who, what, where, when, and why Josane was killed. By Friday. Any suggestions?"

Henry laughed, took a bite of French fry, and checked his chin for flying food.

"You're clean as a whistle," I said. "Didn't you go to deportment classes or something?"

"That was years ago," he said. "No retention. I've got Toppy's number. Here, call her for an interview. She's very approachable."

"So I saw," I said, and took the piece of paper he slipped me.

"As for all the rest," Henry said, ignoring my last comment, "I think you've got to call Candace and tell her it's going to take more than a few days to break a four-year-old murder case. In the meantime, what about going to Leesburg tomorrow with me to look through the books? That'll be the most efficient way to find out where Josane's money came from."

I started to nod yes, then remembered Flip.

"Can't," I said. "I've got an interview first thing with Josane's old beau."

I told him about Flip and then we talked about Josane for a while. He, too, was intrigued by Lannie Post and her fixation. He wasn't the least concerned that I'd be meeting with an alleged woman-basher tomorrow morning. What did I expect? He wasn't my mother and he wasn't Jewish. Henry's worry threshold is about 175,000 times higher than any of my people. I'd seen it in action last time around when I got threatening phone calls at the office. He was certain the calls meant nothing, I was sure I'd be buried the next day. The truth lay somewhere in between, with me splayed out in the woods, broken, battered, and learning the power of prayer firsthand.

"How about the day after for records? That'll at least be a two-day gig for you, won't it?" I said.

Of course it would be. With Henry, it could turn out to be a weeklong excavation. So we were set for the day after tomorrow for my first lesson in reading the fine print.

"Want to meet for dinner later tonight?" I said.

"Actually," he said, and I knew what was coming next, "Toppy arranged for me to meet her father tonight for dinner at her house."

"Oh," I said. "Gee, that's great. Take notes on the mansion for me."

I'd have said something more nasty next. But I was saved by the waitress, who wanted to know if we wanted dessert.

Henry went for the homemade peach cobbler and it was tempting. I live for sweets, but being in the Land of Tall and Thin does something to a woman's appetite. Especially a woman who's climbed to Jupiter on the Stairmaster and still has a set of thighs twice the size of her waist.

"I'll pass," I said to the waitress. "Just a cup of hot water with lemon."

Dessert came and went—fast. And we had to decide what to

do next. It was clear our stories would be taking us in different directions. The question was how. Henry worked the pay phones, looking for a rental car company, and I, knowing Candace would rather cut off her right arm than foot the bill for a rental, called Annie. I still don't know how Henry finagled himself an expense account, permission for a rental car, and unlimited long distance. In the features department we're not allowed to call directory assistance without written permission from Candace or her squirrelly little deputy.

Annie had offered me a vehicle when I'd called last week to ask if we could stay there. Now I took her up on it.

"No problem," Annie said. "You can take the Suburban. I'll leave the keys on your dresser."

Music to my ears. A Suburban, the car of my dreams. I've been mooning over that vehicle for the past twenty years. Someday I'll own one. Or should I really strike gold, I plan to plunk down the sixty grand for my ultimate dream machine—a Hummer.

"Find a rental car company here?" I said to Henry.

"Right down the street," he said.

We paid the bill, I left a bigger tip than Henry wanted, and we walked outside. Who turned up the air-conditioning? I thought it was cold before. Now it felt like I was being slapped, as they say in the South, "upside the hay-yed" with a frozen two-by-four. We aimed ourselves toward the gas station. In the middle of the block Henry saw a newspaper machine. Talk about junkies. In these arctic conditions, Henry had to fish around in his pocket, looking for quarters, just so he could read the news of Fauquier county in the *Fauquier Times Democrat*, possibly the only newspaper in America with a full-time horse editor. Meanwhile, I was jumping up and down like a pogo stick trying to jackhammer blood back down into my brittle toes.

"Come on, Henry," I said. "I'm freezing my buttinskies off. Let's hoof it, that gas station looks heated."

The wind was really blowing now, grabbing my hair and whirl-pooling it around my face, flapping and snapping Henry's hood like it was a flag having seizures. He got his paper, I grabbed his coat and started pulling him toward the street.

"I can't stand another second of this," I screamed over the roar. "Let's make a run for it, the gas station's just across the street."

We started to dash. We ducked our heads and pushed into the wind. My right foot leapt into the air and onto the street. That's when I heard it.

"STOP."

The same voice I'd heard almost twenty years ago, my freshman year in college. I was standing at a stoplight, holding my bike in front of me, waiting to cross the street. The light turned green, I pushed my bike forward, and stepped onto the road.

"STOP." I'd heard it in my head: a quiet, insistent, and deadly serious voice. My left foot froze mid-step, and just as I was about to put it down, a purple van blasted through the red light, tearing with it my bicycle and the other two pedestrians who'd been by my side.

"STOP." And I did. I grabbed Henry's coat for all I was worth and swung him back out of the street with enough force to send him flying on the sidewalk butt-first. Just as I pulled him back, I felt the cold whoosh of air blast by and saw a stream of metal, close enough to touch—or kill—had we been one step further.

"Jesus H. Christ," I said. "We'd have both been knocked over like bowling pins if I hadn't've stopped. What the hell is happening here? Twice in one day is a little too much for this girl. I don't know about this investigative-reporting stuff, maybe I should stick to shoulder pads."

Henry stood up, looked around, and must've been gathering his thoughts. 'Cause he didn't say anything right away. Me, I was blathering a mile a minute—my reaction to stress, and I think being the target of attempted murder two times in less than three hours counts as stress.

"Did you see that, Henry? Someone tried to kill us. AGAIN. Who's stirring this bees' nest, you or me. Or both of us?"

He was brushing dirty gray snow from his rear. "You're much stronger than you look, Nattie. That's quite a right back swing you've got."

"Henry, let's not talk about my physical fitness. Who the hell is after us?"

"It was probably a drunk, still celebrating the holidays, who didn't see us crossing. We were jaywalking, you know."

"Jaywalking? You're talking about us jaywalking when someone just tried to kill us? Henry, we need a reality check here. Someone just tried to run us down, do you agree to that statement?"

"I won't say yes or no. It's possible, but not likely. Now, let's walk up to the light and cross, like we should have done in the beginning. Okay?"

I opened his coat and tapped his chest. "Hello, anyone home in there? Didn't that make your heart beat just a little faster?"

Before he answered I laid my hand on his chest. What Henry said wasn't what Henry felt. His heart was slamming hard against his blue oxford.

"So you are alive," I said.

"Come on," he said. "Let's go."

We made it to the gas station without further incident. Neither of us had gotten a good look at the vehicle, what with the wind flapping and me hurling Henry down to the ground like I was a sumo wrestler. But the man at the gas station said he thought he'd seen a light-colored pickup racing by "too damned fast for anybody's good."

The question now was, who drives a light-colored truck that wants to put me and/or Henry out of question-asking action?

CHAPTER 22

Henry and I went our separate ways after he dropped me off at Annie's. Everyone was gone, except Rosalita, who was cooking up some delicious concoction with enough garlic to keep the vampires—and hopefully Outerbridge Duncan—away. I found the Suburban's keys on the bureau, made a few phone calls, and got behind the wheel. This time I tested the brakes first—in the parking lot before I hit the twisty driveway. They were as good as any Suburban brakes, which isn't saying much. I love the car, but the brakes need work. Try to stop, and you practically have to jack your foot out the door and drag it down the road to grind it to a halt.

So I drove slowly.

My first mission, to talk to Lannie Post. She wasn't listed in the phone book or directory assistance. Karen had said she thought she'd gotten a job at a feed store in either Marshall or Warrenton. I'd called the Warrenton store, they'd never heard of Lannie Post. I'd struck paydirt in Marshall. The man there told me she'd was due back anytime now, just as soon as she finished delivering bags of grain to some farms out by Middleburg and The Plains.

I followed the Zulla Road from Middleburg to Marshall, and what a road it was. The gentle hills roll on out to the horizon, a soft sea of fields framed by old stone walls and planked coop fences for the foxhunters to jump. From what Annie tells me, this is Middleburg's answer to Charlotte's Queens Road, the highest-dollar stretch of real estate in a town full of high-dollar real estate. Even the tenant houses here were better than anything I'd ever lived in. I followed it to where Marshall starts and reality begins.

A long, graceful sentence of a road, it ends with a formidable period: a looming three-story white cinder-block building that looks right off the movie set of *Dick Tracy* or *Batman*. Big black art deco letters announce FAUQUIER LIVESTOCK EXCHANGE, INC.; jabs of rust stains from the tin roof icicle their way down the front of the building, and in the back are long, rambling pens where hundreds of animals wait before being run through the small auction ring. On Tuesdays it's cows that are doing the running: heifers, calves, bulls, whatever the farmer's got to sell. But I know the place from its second-Saturday-of-the-month activities—the horse and pony sales. Annie took me there years ago when I was visiting. I'd never been to an auction before, and after that experience, wish I never had. These are the forgotten equines one step from someone's dinner table, and if they can't catch the eye or heart of some kind soul in the audience, that's where they end up. In the Chevalier pen, the meat man. Every time the auctioneer said "Sold to Chevalier," it felt like I'd stuck my finger in the socket. Finally, about the tenth time, when a cute little pinto pony was led away to Chevalier, I turned to Annie and said, "Let's go. I can't take this anymore."

I drove past the auction house, across the railroad tracks, by the Farmer's Coop, and on into Marshall. It's hard to believe Marshall and Middleburg are both called towns—that's about all they have in common.

Marshall is to Middleburg as field hunters are to show ring hunters. They start off with the same premise, but along the way get so ungapatchkeyed up, you'd be hard-pressed to see any resemblance. Show ring hunters are supposed to be the personification of field hunters: real working horses that gallop hell-bent through woods and fields, toting pink-coated horn-blowing huntsmen and women who are chasing the hounds who are chasing the fox. That was the intent—about a million years ago, when the father of the sport, George Morris, barely needed to shave. Father George's beard is probably more white than brown now, and the sport he perfected—show hunting—couldn't be further from its roots. Back in the fifties, when George swooped in and won all the riding awards, show hunters galloped on outside courses over big—really big—substantial fences, just like what field hunters would jump on a real fox hunt. Now the only time a show horse walks outside is if he's being led to the ring, where he's supposed to canter around a sand ring over fences that are about as naturally occurring as Michael Jackson's nose.

Like the field hunter, the town of Marshall works for a living. I drove down the main street. Two hardware stores, an IGA, a furniture upholstery shop, a post office, and an auto parts store. Not a tchotchke store or a nylon flag with kittens or cows or Christmas bells in sight. I turned left on Frost Street and saw the feed store. Sure enough, out in front of the yellow clapboard building sat Lannie's old red Toyota with the DAZCUTR plates. There were a couple other cars parked there, which left only one small space. Besides bad brakes, the only other drawback to Suburbans is parking. You either get really good at squeezing yourself in without dinging the thing up, or you get lots of exercise from parking a mile away. I opted for the latter, since it wasn't my car to ding. I found a place big enough for the boat across the street in an empty gravel lot.

Just as I was fishing out my notepad and pen from my purse, I heard a vehicle drive up and come to stop by the side door of the feed store. I looked up and saw a white pickup.

The door opened and a short person in a big green parka ran from the truck to the building. Lannie must like the cold weather as much as I.

A white truck. And she'd been making deliveries in Middleburg the same time Henry and I almost became roadkill. . . . This was too easy and I'm not what you'd call a lucky person. There are some people to whom things have always come easily; they glide through life like they've caught hold of a jet stream. Me, I usually catch hold of turbulence. So it was difficult to believe my first crack out on this story and I had the answer. But you never know, maybe I'd repaid my karmic debts and maybe I was about to snag my first jet stream.

I scribbled a few notes in my reporter's pad—descriptions of the feed store, the truck Lannie drove, the funny green building I was parked in front of, the veterinarian's office next door, and if I wasn't mistaken, the name on the shingle was the same Jennie Waldron who was the world-class endurance rider—anything and everything that caught my eye. It's the details that bring a story to life. The hard part is in knowing which ones to use.

I took one last look around and readied myself for the assault. When I was fully wrapped in down, wool, and polar fleece, I made the same dash Lannie had. Except my run was for the front door.

Lannie was standing behind the counter, helping a lady with a yipping Jack Russell find the right collar for her obnoxious little terrier. Pardon me if I can't find a nice word to say about this par-ticular breed of dog. But the last Jack Russell owner I talked to had her lip stitched together after she and her dog got into a disagree-ment. I know the dog was bred to fight to the finish, that that was Parson John Russell's intent when he invented the breed more than a hundred years ago in merry old England. Farmers needed some-thing to kill the foxes that were killing the chickens and lambs, and daily foxhunting on horseback with a pack of hounds was out of the question—who could take that much riding? Plus, foxhunting on horseback is just not that efficient; the fox is usually smart enough to slip into one of his holes when the going gets tough. So the good pastor bred down his hounds to produce a dog small and aggressive enough to beat the fox at its own game. Enter the Jack Russell Terrorist. Somewhere along the line, though, things got out of hand and the dog started getting known as a feisty little troublemaker who'd just as soon kill your pet cat as he would eat a bowl of kibble. Jack Russell breeders say it's a case of too much inbreeding, kind of like the old joke, "I'm so southern, I'm related to myself." Maybe, but what'd they expect to happen when the specific intent of a breed is to annihilate its quarry—and to an untrained Jack Russell, its quarry is the world—a fox, rat, groundhog, cat, German shepherd, you name it, a Jack Russell will take it on. If the golden retriever is as *Washington Post*'s columnist Tony Kornheiser says "the bimbo of the dog world," then Jack Russells are Muggsy Bogues on mean pills.

I stood by the bags of sweet feed and watched. I didn't feel like moving yet. It was cold outside and just breathing in the gooey amber smell of the molasses and corn made me feel warm—which is what eating sweet feed does for horses. In the winter you switch to a sweeter, heavier feed with lots of corn to keep the horses' furnaces stoked high. I've been eating it myself for years—granola for real women.

Lannie had gone through a handful of leather collars. The woman was just as fussy as her dog and it could be argued even looked like him. She was short, long-bodied, and pointy-nosed. You have to be careful when you choose a dog for exactly that reason. Someone once wanted to give me the cutest basset hound–German shepherd puppy. What a combination—how'd he ever reach? I had to pass. A short, squat dog with an overaggressive personality? No thanks. I'd spend the rest of that dog's life with everyone thinking how cute it was that I looked *and* acted just like my dog.

The lady's little nipster took a hunk out of Mama's hand and that was a good diversion for me. Lannie was busy attending to the bleeding woman, so she couldn't see me staring at her, freezing her image into my brain. I'd be hard-pressed to see any resemblance between Lannie and Josane in this incarnation. When Josane died, so, too, must have Lannie's look-alike program. She was as drab as Josane was sparkling. In every way. Starting with her clothes, an assortment of those Gap mud colors I hate: gray-blue, gray-red, gray-white, gray-brown, and gray-gray. I worship at the altar of color and anything with gray or brown makes me feel down-trodden. Which was exactly how Lannie looked: tired, beaten, just waiting for the second she could become one with her nubby brown plaid sofa and watch *Oprah*.

Her light brown hair hung halfway down her back in hair spears, the hair god's way of telling you it's time for a trim. She didn't wear a dusting of makeup and could've used a hefty schmear of concealer around her eyes. As first cousin to Rocky Raccoon, I know from dark circles and the wonders of concealer. Yves Saint Laurent concealer stick number two to be exact. Just two half-moons of Yves's number one (she didn't have my mother's Sephardic olive skin genes) and she'd look a lot happier.

Of course her mud-color plaid flannel shirt didn't do anything to perk up her looks, which weren't bad. She had biggish brown eyes, a decent nose that was straighter and shorter than mine would ever be, and smooth skin. Her face was on the round side, and I could see the tips of her ears jutting out from her hair.

I'd bet my lunch they called her Dumbo as a kid. I know first-hand how cruel kids can be. Between a headful of unruly orange hair, a face full of freckles, teeth as bucked as Francis the mule's, and a screaming set of parents who divorced when divorcee meant trollop, I'd been on the receiving end of taunts my entire child-hood. I can't remember how many times the popular kids screamed such witticisms my way as "Hey, girl, your hair's on fire!" "Better dead than red in the head," "Beaver mouth," and "Freckle face." Or the number of times I heard them hiss "Your mother's a tramp." My brother Larry only made matters worse by calling me Fatalie my entire childhood.

Braces fixed the teeth; my mother refused to let me Summer

Blonde my hair into popularity; Porcelana, lemon juice, and cleanser—nothing faded my freckles except time; and I developed a pretty good fist that I planted in the faces of more than a few taunters who questioned my mother's morals. I slimmed down to a size five on good days and Larry, he got his own payback. He's no stranger to the treadmill and still can't get rid of his spare tires.

When you don't look like everyone else, you've got to be tough to make it through childhood with any semblance of self-respect. And it looked like Lannie didn't make it through with much.

I wanted to walk up to her, push my hand into the base of her slumped spine, and say, "Stand up for yourself, girl." I could see why Josane took pity on her. She was as pitiable as any sad-eyed puppy I've seen at the pound. However, there still was that little matter of the white pickup and the possibility that she'd just tried to kill me.

The lady with the dog collar finally chose a raised and laced leather affair that looked like an aborted attempt at bridle reins. Expensive bridle reins. Even from across the room I could see the soft suppleness of the caramel leather. A good set of reins like that can run over a hundred bucks. I'm guessing that collar probably set that woman back at least half that. Then I saw her reach around and grab a miniature version of a Baker horse blanket, distinctive by its navy, beige, and black glen plaid. Next was she going to buy booties for Fido?

Booties for Fido. Bingo!! Yes!! It hit me: the answer to my weekly fashion column panic, what the well-dressed animals were wearing.

I could whip it off in no time. A few phone calls to feed and tack stores and a couple of quotes from owners about how they'd never send their precious Jack Russells—the official dog of the horsey set—outside shivering. I could even contact a store or two in our new penetration zones just to get Candace's motor running.

The dog-dressing lady finally finished buying her pooch's

winter wardrobe and left. As I walked up to the counter, the phone rang. Lannie answered and I had a chance to look at her up close. I love horses as much as the next horse-crazed female; however, I've never been one to decorate my body with them. Which wasn't the case with Lannie. She was horse from head to toe. Little silver horse heads peered out from her earlobes; around her wrist, a silver horseshoe bracelet; on her mud-green shirt beneath the flannel shirt, two tiny galloping horses racing above her heart where on any Charlottean would have been a cheeky alligator; on her left hand, two silver rings, one a horse head, the other a horse butt; and around her neck, a gold charm of two horseshoes hammered into a heart with a glittering something inside. Had she been Annie or Topping or any of the other rich show girls, I'd have assumed it was a diamond. But Lannie worked in a feed store and before that stole money, so the only thing I could assume, which I knew would probably make an ass out of me, is that she didn't have the bucks to afford a real rock that size. That's why God invented zirconium.

She looked up at me and smiled. "Just a second," she mouthed.

Unlike Henry, I hadn't really planned my attack. I had a general idea of what I was going to say, but I had to see how she reacted first. Some people hate talking to reporters, and you have to cajole them into talking. For others, standing next to a member of the media is like turning on a faucet and you can't shut them up. I guess they figure we're the express ride to their fifteen minutes of fame.

I did my hello-I'm-Nattie-Gold-a-reporter-from-*The-Charlotte-Commercial-Appeal* introduction spiel and handed her a business card. She had a blank look on her face, so I knew she didn't know what was coming next. When I got to the part about how I'd been interviewing people for a story on Josane, it looked like someone punched her in the gut.

I couldn't believe the way my luck was running. What was she going to do next, confess on the spot and then call the cops on herself? You know what they say about something being too good to be true?

It was.

What came next was so far from a confession—and so confounding—I knew I still had many years left of karmic debt.

"A story about Josane?" she said. "Oh, my God, you're not going to put in the bad things about the men, are you? You said you were in Middleburg interviewing? Who'd you talk to so far, those fancy Middleburg ladies? No, never mind, I bet I can tell you what they said. I bet all they could talk about was the men, how all the men *just* loved Josane and how she *just* loved them back. Except they didn't use those words, did they? I've heard the talk before. They didn't know I was listening, but I was. I bet they made Josane sound like she was nothing better than a whore. It's because of the way she looked. Not just that she was pretty. Josane was more than pretty, she made them all look like a bunch of used washrags. So they were jealous. Jealous because their husbands walked around with their tongues hanging out around Josane. I bet they didn't tell you the good things about Josane, did they? I know the kind of story you're going to write. It won't be right, doing a story like that. I know what you newspapers want, things about drugs and sex. Doesn't matter if it's true. . . ."

It looked like Lannie was about to launch off into Rush Limbaugh land.

"Hold on, hold on a second," I said. "I don't work for a tabloid. I work for *The Charlotte Commercial Appeal.* We've won two Pulitzer Prizes for excellence—and, I may say, accuracy—in reporting. I'm not looking to do a smear job on Josane. I'm looking to find out if she was murdered."

Well, that shut her up pretty fast.

"Murdered?" she said in a small voice. "Josane had a riding accident. A riding accident. No one would ever want to kill Josane.

Those Middleburg ladies were probably just as happy their husbands weren't bothering them. Other than them, everyone loved Josane. Everyone."

"Including you?"

Lannie stiffened and looked at me. I recognized the look, the same look my horse Brenda gets when she walks past a rock or a plastic bag or new shadow that she's convinced is going to do her bodily harm. "God, you newspapers always bring everything down to that."

"Down to what?" I said. "I'm just asking if you loved her. I love my best friend and it doesn't mean I'm anything but a person who loves her best friend. I'd do anything—and believe me, I about have—for her. I know how strong the bond can be between friends."

Lannie relaxed. "It'd be hard not to love Josane. She was perfect, but not so she knew it or was obnoxious about it. She had everything. And I don't only mean the way she looked. She was happy and fun. Just being around her made you feel like you were happy and fun. Know what I mean? Have you ever known anyone like that, where just being in the same place with them makes you feel more alive? When you hang around with Josane, she's having such a good time, you end up having a good time. . . ."

It looked as if Reenie wasn't the only one who couldn't lay Josane Ashmore to rest. Lannie was talking about her in the present tense, just as her mother had. And like Reenie, Lannie could've talked about Josane all day. Which she was starting to do.

I decided to let her keep rambling before I steered toward the stolen money and where she was the day Josane was killed. Some interviews you shape and decide where and when to take them, others—and I think the ones that reveal the most—you let the situation that develops take you along for the ride. This situation was that Lannie wasn't finished talking about Josane and that was fine. With each story Lannie told, Josane was becoming clearer to me. Also, I'd have to back gently into the theft and firing business.

For better than an hour Lannie reminisced. I asked a few questions, but mostly tried as unobtrusively as possible to scribble down everything she said. I was surprised to hear she'd met Josane at the barn, and that she'd been a groom there. Karen, the barn manager I'd just talked to at the funeral home, never mentioned Lannie worked for her.

From the way Lannie told it, she looked after Josane's horse, Rita, like it was her own baby girl.

"You wouldn't believe the shine I worked up on that mare," Lannie said. "When I got finished with her, her coat was as shiny as Josane's hair. You can't tell in pictures, but Josane had this kind of brownish-blond hair that shined like you wouldn't believe. When she was standing in the sun, it was sort of like her hair was sparkling. Then when she stood next to Rita, you've never seen anything like it. They looked so gorgeous standing next to each other, like they could have been on a calendar or something. I used to hate it when Josane put her hunt cap on."

What I said earlier about best friends is one thing, this was becoming another. I love Gail as much as any woman loves her best friend, but I don't moon around over her shiny hair. Lannie's thing for Josane was getting weirder by the second. Weird enough for murder?

Maybe. The world's full of strange people who do strange things. Just read any newspaper any day of the week, it's like one big nonstop News of the Weird column.

Lannie kept talking and talking. She was clearly on a roll, and for the first time I saw some color in her face, heard some enthusiasm in her voice. She went on and on about Josane and Rita and how most times the horse was good, but every so often the mare would be as rank as any horse she'd ever seen.

"That's when Charlie'd have to get on her and teach her a lesson," Lannie said. "But sometimes that didn't work. If it went on for a few days, especially before or at the shows, he'd Ace her up and keep her that way so Josane could get on her."

Not surprising they went the pharmaceutical route. What was surprising was Lannie's big mouth. Everyone does it, but does it with little or no talk. You'd have just as much luck finding a kid who grooms her own horses on the A-circuit as you would a trainer who hasn't reached for a syringe and a bottle of Ace—the horse industry's answer to Valium. The problem, other than the moral implications of drugging a horse, is that Ace is illegal at the shows, so the trick is not getting caught, which isn't a big trick at all. There are plenty of A-shows where the drug testers never even show up, and when they do, most people know—sometimes in advance.

That's not to say no one ever gets caught. The best part of *Horse Show,* the American Horse Show Association's magazine, is the last few pages, where they run a list of suspended horses and people. Just last month, Tommy Kutter, aka the Pharmacist, one of the biggest trainers in Georgia, got slapped with a $2,500 fine and a six-month suspension after his champion green horse, Speak to Me, tested positive for Dormosedan, a tranquilizer so powerful, just the residue of the drug on a needle is enough to make a wild-eyed lunatic canter around like a docile lesson horse. This makes Tommy's second appearance on the bad-boy list. Once more and the ASHA hearing committee could theoretically throw him out of horse showing for good.

Of course that's in theory only. And that doesn't mean good-bye to making lots of money in the horse business. Look at Paul Valliere—he's still buying, selling, and training horses like he never confessed to killing a horse for insurance money or wore the wire to trap his fellow horse-killing horseman, Barney Ward. One set of happy horse show parents even took out a full-page ad in *The Chronicle of the Horse* thanking Paul for all his hard work getting their daughter to the indoor shows. Amazingly, the horse show community continues to associate and do business with this lowlife as if he just made one teeny-weeny little mistake. *The man had his horse electrocuted.* He should be booed out of the horse world, or, better yet, snap an alligator clip in his rear and plug him into the wall to show him how it feels to be fried from the inside out, just like he had done to his horse.

Talk about warping out into Rush Limbaugh land. This horse-killing business makes me see red, worse yet, it makes me start talking like a Republican.

I took a deep, calming breath and refocused my attentions on Lannie. She was still talking about Josane and Rita. She blew hot and cold on the horse. One sentence, Rita was the most beautiful thing since Aphrodite, and the next, she was "that stupid piece of shit."

"I don't care what you or her mother think," Lannie said. "I know that Josane'd still be alive today if it weren't for that mare— and Charlie Laconte. If anyone's guilty of murder, it's him. He should be the one lying in the casket, not Jim. He should've never sold her that horse. All he was thinking about was his bank book. Ask him about that, ask him how Jim was about to break it off and leave him with a big stack of bills. That's why he pushed Rita on Josane."

Now, that was a new spin to check out. I asked where she got her information, from Josane? No. She said Josane would've never said anything bad about Charlie, that she just knew it happened like that. Uh-oh, the just word.

Beware the words *just* and *but.* I learned that, along with being able to hold my pee for acrobatically long stretches of time, in est. Years ago my father, Lou, popped for the $350 tuition for those two weekends of bashing your way to enlightenment. That was a few years after he paid for me to chant my way to nirvana with transcendental meditation—$75, student rate. Neither seemed to advance me much on The Path, but I did learn that when people use either "but" or "just," forget about reasoning with them. "But" negates everything that comes before it and 'just" means I don't care if you have scientific proof the world is round, I *just* think it's flat.

I didn't pursue Lannie's information source further. There was *just* no reason to. . . .

I was curious how she went from groom to retailer. Her sticky fingers were why she was working at the feed store now. I wondered if another reckless part of her anatomy—her loose lips— were responsible for the previous career change in her life: from the barn to Josane's store.

"Why the job change?" I asked. "Any problems at the barn?"

She shook her head from side to side. "Nope," she said. "I'd have stayed forever if Josane's assistant at the store hadn't fallen from her horse."

Apparently Lannie'd overheard Josane telling someone on the phone about the accident. With more spunk than I could envision in Lannie, she walked up to Josane and asked for the job.

"As soon as she hung up, I did it," Lannie said. "And you know what Josane did? This is what I mean about her being so kind and everything. I was just a groom, but it didn't matter to Josane. She put her arm around me and told me the job was mine if I wanted it. So long as Charlie didn't get mad at her for what she called 'stealing me away.' 'Stealing me away,' can you imagine that? I was just a groom and she made me feel like I was a big hotshot worth stealing away. That's Josane. You felt special when you were around her."

I didn't know how much longer her boss would let Lannie stand here and talk. Finally I had to do it. Ask her about the money. She'd just spent more than an hour talking about Saint Josane and she seemed as pliable as a horse who'd spent the morning doing shoulders-in with Olympic dressage rider Robert Dover. Shoulders-in is a suppling exercise where you make the horse walk down a track with its hindquarters going straight and its shoulders tipped in to the ring. Strangely enough, making the horse walk crooked makes him more flexible and thereby malleable to your requests.

No matter how malleable Lannie was, I still had to be careful. The way I figured it, Lannie was still lighting incense by Josane's picture every night, that's how much she idolized her. But then again, she did rob her idol blind.

How to ask the tough question? I thought for a minute while Lannie went on about how Josane used to fix her up and a couple of times they even double-dated.

"Not that it ever worked," Lannie said. "I liked one guy all right, but it didn't work out. But it was still fun, even with Flip being a jerk, like he was most of the time. Josane made everything fun."

Lannie was quiet for a minute, probably playing her own private tapes of those nights in her mind. I let a few more seconds pass and then eased myself in as gently as possible.

"Lannie, I've got to ask you something and please don't get mad at me. If you were me, you'd be asking the same qu—"

I didn't even have to finish the sentence.

"You want to know about me stealing from the cash register, right? And then Josane firing me?"

I nodded.

"I did and then she fired me," Lannie said. "She had to. What choice did she have? It wasn't her fault. She had to fire me. She had to. Wouldn't you have done the same?"

I didn't know what to say to that. I hadn't expected the mea culpa bit.

"Why?" I said.

"I already told you," Lannie said with enough of a snap in her voice, I thought I might be losing her any minute. "She had to fire me. It wasn't her fault."

"No," I said. "I don't mean that. I mean why'd you take the money? Weren't you worried you'd get caught? Especially by Josane, whom you obviously cared a lot about."

Lannie grabbed a rag and started wiping down the counter

199

with about twenty-three times more elbow grease than the job required. Okay, so the Jack Russell opened up his owner's hand enough to spill a little blood on the Formica, but Lannie was scrubbing the counter like she was Lady Macbeth.

"I don't know," she said, and wiped even harder. "I don't know. I took the money. I told you I took the money. What does it matter why? I took the goddamned money, okay? Is there anything else I can help you with? They don't like it when I talk to the customers too long."

She swung around and started rearranging the dog collars hanging on the back wall.

I wasn't going to be getting much further here. She'd shut down.

"One last question," I said. "Where were you the day Josane died?"

She spun around with such speed, I felt the air tunnel past my face.

"Oh, so you think I killed Josane? Just because I told you I took the money, now you think I killed her, right? If anyone killed Josane, it was that crazy boyfriend of hers. Ask him about his 'lethal weapon' hands. Ask him about that, why don't you. And his temper. Better stay away from him if he gets mad, which he did plenty around Josane. Just for your information, I'd have sooner cut off my hand than see anything bad happen to Josane. If you must know, I was home sick that day. I had a stomach bug and was puking every two minutes. Satisfied?"

"Well, the police said you were out of town," I said.

"Well, they were wrong."

The phone rang and that was that. Lannie buried herself into the conversation like it was Josane calling from the beyond.

CHAPTER 23

No such luck. AT&T hasn't connected there yet. Though I hear it's only a matter of time and patents, according to a client of my brother, Larry-the-lawyer.

Larry has carved out quite the legal niche for himself: defending alternative healers the government is trying to make go away. One in particular, a last-chance doctor to kids with inoperable, unradiatable brain cancer. He saves the ones everyone else gives up on; the patients' traditional doctors shake their heads over and tell the parents it's time to say good-bye. Though Larry's doctor/client has turned many of those good-byes into welcome-backs, the FDA and judicial system continue to pursue him with such ferocity, you'd think he was Charlie Manson's eviler and medically licensed twin brother.

That's not to say Larry doesn't have his share of lunatics: the Reverend Dr. Miguel Del Jesus, who treads AIDS patients with chicken dung and whale sperm massages and if that doesn't work zaps them with the ozone generator machine that shoots toxic ozone gas into their systems either through a vein or rectally. Then there's the many-Ph.d.ed Peterson Scott, the mad botanist who rearranges plant DNA and claims he's bioengineered a time-release superpotent hybrid of marijuana, echinacea, and American yew that cures cancer with only one small side effect—weight gain from an aggravated case of the munchies. And we can't forget Mr. Twilight Zone himself, the guy who wants Larry to patent his interdimensional communicator. That's the telephone to the beyond. Larry says he tried it once but kept getting a busy signal. The inventor swears it'll be only another year or so before he irons out the glitches.

Too bad I didn't have the time. I could have used a direct line to Josane. Ask her what happened to her that day in the woods. While I was at it, I'd have placed a call to my stepfather to find out if the vision I'd had of him after I fell from Brenda and snapped my leg in two was just my overactive imagination endorphically enhanced or a near death experience even though I wasn't.

But on second thought, I'd have just told him how much we all miss him and skipped the part about whether my vision was real. It was real to me and that was enough. I like thinking he's there, watching over me. I don't care if it's scientifically documentable. Sometimes the truth is what you make it—or want it to be.

That was surely the case with Josane. Everyone had their own truths. About who she was and how she died. I, unfortunately, agreed to the no-win job of finding out whose truth was accurate.

Lannie was looking more and more like a bona fide suspect. Nevertheless, I walked out of the feed store with the same heavy heart I left Reenie Ashmore's with. It didn't seem as if Reenie would ever be able to piece back her life, and as for Lannie, if she were innocent, what kind of life did she have to be pieced back? When Josane was alive, Lannie was one big as if, *as if* she were Josane. Now that Josane was dead, she'd gone from as if to so what.

What a depressing day this was turning out to be, and steeling myself against the combative weather wasn't helping my mood one bit. I needed to do something frivolous. I can take only so much despair and sadness before I start worrying about being springboarded into deep depression. Not that it's ever happened, but I'd be a fool not to be concerned given my father's family predisposition to severe—and hospitalizable—manic depression. Seven out of ten Gold siblings have wrestled with the big dark bear—and lost. So when I slip into sad thoughts, I can't help but wonder if the slip will turn into a major fall and I won't find a way back, just like my Aunt Shirley or my Uncle Maury, who spent his last night on earth tucked up tight to his Chrysler's exhaust pipe.

What could be more frivolous than fashion? I'd get Candace off my back and sadness off my mind. A couple of calls to dog owners and pet shops and I'd be chuckling my way through anything, even more interviews about Josane.

I drove back to Annie's the way I came and started feeling chipper the minute I hit the Zulla Road. I'd have preferred to be on horseback—even with the bad weather—but it's hard not to be happy when you're looking at gorgeous curves of landscape for eight undulating miles. By the time I got back, Aunt Shirley and her dark days were far from my mind.

"Henry, the man you came with. That's his name? Yes? Four times his little boy calls. I hope nothing is wrong."

It was Rosalita. She met me at the door with a worried look on her face. I thanked her and she gave me the piece of paper with the telephone number on it.

"Your mother, she also called," Rosalita said, and left.

I had no idea where Henry was or when he'd be back. I did the only thing I could: I called his voice mail at *The Appeal* and told him to call his children ASAP. Not two seconds after I put the telephone down, it rang. This not being my house, I didn't answer it. But Rosalita did. She came back into the library with the same worried look on her face.

"His little boy is calling again. You take it?"

I picked up the phone and said hello.

"Is my dad okay?" All little kids sound the same to me, but if I had to guess, I'd have bet this voice was littler.

"Hank?" I said.

"Is my dad okay?"

Stubborn as his father.

"He's fine, he's fine," I said. "Is this Hank or Chet?"

"Hank. If he's fine, then where is he?"

"Doing his job, Hank. He's out interviewing. What's the problem there? Is there anything wrong with you or Chet?"

I asked the last question into a void. A few seconds later a female voice came on. Martha's.

"Is this Maddie?"

"Nattie," I said. "What was that all about?"

"Oh, just Hank. He was convinced something happened to Henry. Nothing I said would make him feel better. That's why he's been calling. Are you sure everything's all right?"

"Everything is now," I said. Then I told her about our morning brushes with death.

"Well, that's not the first time something like this has happened," Martha said. "But if you ask Henry, he'll discount it to coincidence. Hank's a funny child. In many ways he's like Henry—analytical, emotionally contained. But unlike Henry, Hankie's got a whole other side to him. Has had it since he could talk, I don't know how to describe it. He was always playing with imaginary friends and then, when his grandfather died, he started talking to him. . . . I know it sounds crazy."

"Not to me," I said. "But then again, Henry thinks I'm a major flake because I believe in all that stuff."

Martha laughed. "I know exactly what you mean. I was a big stretch for Henry because I preferred Chet Atkins to Beethoven and I'd skip a class or two, when he attended every last one of them. Once I surprised him and took him on an unplanned birthday trip to Graceland during the middle of the semester. Well, let me tell you, missing three history lectures was the most impetuous act he'd ever committed in his life. I'm sure you've figured out that spontaneity doesn't come easily to Henry. I still think his blinders need to be expanded a little, don't you?"

We both laughed. I heard the boys yelling in the background.

"It sounds like you've got your hands full," I said. "Tell Hank to stop his worrying. Or better yet, if he gets any more weird feelings, have him call *me*. I'll listen."

"You've got yourself a deal," Martha said.

I liked her. Henry had good taste in women. Or had up until today. What was this business with Topping Mundell anyway? It was just as well. Like I said, phooey on newsroom romances.

Besides, I had more pressing things to do than ponder Henry's love life. Namely, call Mother and then write my Sunday fashion column. I busied myself at the telephone.

"Nattie," my mother said, sounding more animated than I'd heard her sound in six months. "I found out more about your Hinton Allard. Nora and I went up to Winston-Salem and snooped around. That law firm I told you he was a partner in? Allard was their big-gun litigator. He has a reputation, or, rather, had one, of brilliance before the bench. He supposedly could get anyone off anything. I heard rumors he was a silent adviser to Johnnie Cochran. Also, from what I've been hearing, the rain in Allard's firm comes from Bladstone Tobacco. I know, they've got an army of in-house lawyers, but this was big. And they wanted a specialist; they wanted guarantees, and from what I hear, Hinton Allard was as close as you could come—legally. We're not sure exactly what the case was, we're going back tomorrow, but I think it had something to do with the class action suits being filed by the estates of cancer patients."

Bingo! The tobacco connection confirmed. Wait'll I tell Henry.

"Mom," I said, "if I could give you a kiss over the telephone wires, I would. This is great stuff. Thanks."

"I've still got more feelers out," she said. "And don't forget we're going back tomorrow. I'll call you if I hear anything more. Say, Nat, this is fun."

Fun, a word I thought I'd never hear cross my mother's lips again. She was having fun—life does go on.

I was on a roll now. Next I attacked haute couture, doggie

style. And two hours later, the thing was reported, written, and buzzed through cyberspace to Charlotte. So it wouldn't win the Penney-Missouri feature writing prize, who cared? I sure as hell didn't. If they don't get me off this stupid beat soon, I don't know what I'll do. Unfortunately, quitting isn't much of a threat. With all the newspaper shutdowns, buyoffs, and cutbacks, journalism jobs are as easy to come by as honest horse dealers. As one editor likes to remind his grumbling staff, "Just remember, there's a line at least ten deep of qualified reporters dying to work at *The Charlotte Commercial Appeal* for a fraction of what we pay you."

Which isn't much. But it pays the bills and with two horses to support, I've got plenty of them. The second horse being my first horse, Homer T. Horse, the oldest living retiree this side of Boca Raton.

I was glad the fashion monkey was off my back for the week. I had an hour or so left before dark. Cold isn't the only thing wrong with winter. Turning the lights out at 4:30 wouldn't have been my plan if I'd designed the world. I'd have also done away with the colors gray, taupe, beige, and mauve.

I'd thought about going to Laconte's barn to ask Karen more questions and take a good look around. That would be the place where I needed to inhale details. If I was going to write a story about the last day of Josane's life, I'd have to paint a vivid word picture of what the place looked, smelled, and sounded like.

I didn't have time to do it now. I glanced at the telephone, a reporter's best friend. People think reporters run around all day, getting their trench coats dirty chasing reluctant interviewees, just like Billie on *Lou Grant*. The closest our newsroom comes to that television show is Torkesquist, our photographer who makes the show's crazy shooter, Animal, seem like a button-down gray flannel suit. Me, I spend at least eighty percent of my time with a telephone growing out of my right ear.

And that's how I spent the rest of the afternoon.

I watched the sky turn darker and drearier shades of gray until any hint of color got sucked into the blackness. The clock on the wall said 4:43. Not even five o'clock, and it was time-for-bed dark outside.

Since Lannie had known less than Karen about Josane's divorce, I needed another way to track down the lawyer and find out why Josane was so happy the day she died.

I'd let my fingers do the walking. How many lawyers could there be around here? I found the Fauquier-Loudoun counties Yellow Pages and turned to L. This lawyer joke was on me—five full pages of one lawyer after the next clamoring for clients. "Is your child the victim of birth trauma?" "Had an accident?" "Your pain, your gain . . ." I'd be there till sunrise, calling them all.

I was stuck. I had to call Reenie and I didn't want to. Not only because I didn't feel like talking to her, but because I had to charge it to my phone and then hand the bill in at the end of the month and hope the chain hadn't tightened us out of reimbursements.

"Reenie? It's Nattie Gold," I said. I filled her in as briefly and economically as possible about who I'd talked to so far.

"I can't talk long, so let me just ask you one question. Was Josane about to be divorced? How come you didn't tell me?"

Silence. And more silence. I knew the question would throw her for a loop, because it's not as if marriage is a small detail you might forget. But I didn't want her spinning into orbit on what could easily turn out to be my dime.

"Reenie, are you there?"

Finally, words. "I didn't want you thinking bad about Josane."

"For getting married?" I said.

"For getting a divorce. We never had anyone in our family get a divorce; our church doesn't hold it to be right. Our pastor says when you get married, the Lord has chosen your mate and you don't go against the Lord's plan for you. Josane just up and got herself married and called us afterward, saying she didn't want a big fuss. There was no arguing with her either way. Ever since she was little, when she got to getting her mind fixed on something, that was it, there nothing that would make that girl budge. Not an eighteen-wheeler. Not anything. She never did bring him down to meet us. I met him once up to her house. But they were pretty near splitting up by then."

I could tell Reenie was about to go off into the long story of Josane's marriage. I needed the short story now. I could flesh out the rest in my office, on *The Appeal's* phone bill.

"Reenie," I said. "You should've told me or at least the police. The ex-husband is always the first suspect."

"He wouldn't have done anything to her," Reenie said. " 'Sides, it wouldn't have done much good to tell anyone. Only thing it'd done would make people think poorly of Josane, make them think she was something she wasn't."

"Look, Reenie, my parents got divorced when I was ten, and I didn't think any the worse of my mother. Would you mind telling me his name so I can talk to him?"

"Wouldn't have done any good to tell the police or you his name."

"How's that?" I said.

"No good at all," Reenie said. She was starting to drift back into outer space.

I could hear Bell Tel's cash register jingling with every passing, quiet second.

"Why? Reenie," I pressed, "what harm would it do for me to talk to him?"

More silence. I wanted to reach through the wires and shake the answer out of her. I know she's a grieving mother, but still . . .

Finally. "No harm at all, now. I guess. But you can't talk to him. No one can. The only one talking to him nowadays is the Good Lord. He died about a year after what happened to Josane, crashed up his car real bad. Her lawyer, a real nice man by the name of Snowden Cox, called me to tell me."

Another dead young body. That made six, between the two stories Henry and I were working on: (1) Josane (2) her unnamed husband (3) Jim Benson (4) the little girl on the pony (5) the pony (6) and Josane's horse, Rita. Had Henry and I been a little less lucky today, we might have been numbers seven and eight.

The bodies were growing exponentially. I was starting to feel as if I were in an Agatha Christie mystery—"And then there were . . ." At least her bodies went only to ten. There was no telling where this might stop.

CHAPTER 24

"Oh, my God, oh, my God, what it this? I can't believe it, I just can't believe someone could be so sick. . . . MOTHER, BRIDGE!!!"

"Calm down. Let me take it, here, give it to me. Just sit down."

I jumped out of my chair and ran to the front door, where I heard the commotion: a blanched Annie holding her shoe in front of her as if it were a test tube full of Ebola, and Henry trying to settle her down.

It wasn't working.

"MOTHER!!! Where are you? MOTHER!!"

Henry looked shaken too. But obviously not about Annie. The second he saw me he rushed up and grabbed my arm to get my attention. "What's wrong with the boys? Is Chet or Hank hurt? There's no answer at Martha's and the phone's been busy here. You said it was urgent."

"Oh, that," I said. "Nothing's wrong, everything's fine. Hank had a bad feeling something happened to you, that's all."

Henry's shoulders relaxed and his hand dropped from my arm. Annie, meanwhile, had settled herself down and onto a very expensive-looking tapestry chair in the foyer, still holding the offending shoe in front of her.

I turned my attention to that crisis. "Annie, what in God's name was that all about? And what's wrong with your shoe?"

She looked at her shoe and it must've registered she was still

210

holding it. It dropped from her fingers and clattered to the heart pine floor. When it landed, I saw why she wasn't keen on slipping it back on. The sides of the black suede were acting like Velcro to some kind of oozy goo.

"Ecchh," I said. "What'd you step in, roadkill?"

Henry meanwhile had dashed off to the kitchen and come back with a roll of paper towels and then went outside to the front step.

"I don't know what I stepped in," Annie said. "Whatever it was was right out there on the step. Poor Henry happened to be coming in the door just as I was. I'm sorry I acted like an idiot, all that screaming. As you can see, I'd never have been a candidate for medical school."

She laughed and the tan started seeping back into her face.

"Okay, okay," I said, "so you didn't go to medical school. I thought you liked majoring in economics, as much as anyone could like economics. Would someone mind telling me what all the hollering was about?"

Annie pointed a long, slender finger. I followed it to the returned Henry and his hand. Yuck. He was holding something a little too organic for my tastes.

"I stepped right in that," Annie said. "These shoes are gone."

I looked at them: Bruno Maglis. Neiman's, knowing Annie's shopping habits. She wasn't a T J Maxx kind of gal like me. $250 gone in one squishy step. I'd have cleaned them, but then, if I ever paid that much for a pair of shoes, I'd have been wearing Baggies around my feet for protection. Safe steps.

"Someone tell me what this is all about," I said.

Annie cleared her throat. "If we knew, we'd tell you. I came home, walked to the door, and felt something soft and wet under my left foot. I looked down and saw that thing under my shoe. By then it was too late. I'd squashed it and it got all over. As I said, Henry happened to be coming in—really barreling in—at the same time."

"The telephone message," Henry explained.

"Got it," I said. "Why were you screaming for your mother?"

"When I looked down at my foot, I saw a piece of paper or an envelope or something on that thing that said 'Mr. and Mrs. Duncan.' "

"One second," I said. I went outside and the cold air smacked me square in the face. I looked down on the step and saw a dark puddle of something. I leaned in and smelled. Eighth-grade biology with Mrs. Brackett and her bottled frogs. I looked around for the paper or whatever it was Annie had seen. I didn't see anything. The cold was starting to bite into my bones when I saw it, faceup on the frozen dirt near the landing. It was a Christmas card, no envelope. On the back it said "Mr. and Mrs. Duncan." I flipped it over to a Santa with cranberry cheeks and a big ain't-life-terrific smile. I opened it. In merry green print it said, "Bringing you all the joy this ho-ho-holiday season!!!!"

Underneath that in not-so-merry black typed letters:

MR. DUNCAN—THIS IS WHAT YOU DID TO HIM. YOU HAVE TO PAY. YOU ALL HAVE TO PAY.

TODAY WAS JUST THE BEGINNING OF THE END FOR YOU. I HOPED IT WOULDN'T KILL YOU, THAT WOULD BE TOO FAST. JUST SCARE YOU. SCARE YOU THE SAME AS IT SCARED HIM THE DAY THEY TOLD HIM. THEN HE HAD TO SPEND THE REST OF WHAT HE HAD LEFT KNOWING HE'D BE DYING SOON. JUST LIKE YOU DO NOW.

WHEN YOU CRASHED, DID YOU SEE THE FACES OF ALL THE PEOPLE YOU KILLED? DID YOU HEAR THEIR SCREAMING, THEIR CRYING, THEIR MOANS? DID YOU HEAR THEM BEGGING TO DIE BECAUSE IT HURT SO BAD?

IT DOESN'T SEEM FAIR FOR YOU AND YOUR KIND TO DIE FAST AND WITHOUT HURTING BEFOREHAND LIKE HE DID. BUT THAT'S ALL I CAN MANAGE, LORD, TELL HIM THAT'S

ALL I CAN DO. I'M TRYING, TRYING MY BEST FOR YOU AND HIM, BUT IT'S SO HARD.

I carried the card inside and tried to hand it to Henry, who really didn't have any hands left between the paper towels in his right hand and the wacko's innard-dropping in the other.

"Oh," I said, and took the paper towels from him. I sure as hell wasn't going to touch the other. I unrolled a couple sheets of the paper towels and made a landing pad for the whatever.

"Drop it," I said, pointing to the paper towel on the floor. Henry bent down and placed it carefully on top. Me, I'd have let it splatter.

"Look at this," I said. "Your pen pal is getting very creative. What's next, boiled house pets in the kitchen? Now let's see Duncan deny his brake lines were cut."

Annie stood up and walked, lopsided, to Henry. She still was wearing the right shoe. Being closer to his genetic makeup than I, she could look over his shoulder, whereas the best I could do was to peek through his underarm.

"This is about that tobacco business you were talking about last night, isn't it?" Annie said.

I nodded.

"I thought so. I hope you weren't buying his act last night. I know Bridge well enough to know Henry was making him uncomfortable with those questions. After I showed you to your rooms, I passed by the library and heard him talking on the telephone. I don't know whom he was talking to, but I'm sure it was about Henry and those letters. I clearly heard him say, 'I thought you were going to put a stop to this whole mess. I told you this could mean real trouble for us. That's the reporter who sent Jim Bakker to jail.' Then he saw me looking at him and hung up the phone. He was very angry I'd heard what he said."

"How do you know that?" I said.

"Well, he rushed past me without saying good night," Annie said, looking at me as if that explained everything.

In my family, anger—which I'm sure occupies at least the top half of all our DNA helixes—comes with a sound track, chase scenes, and special effects. Screams, shrieks, hollers, slamming doors, crashing apple juice bottles, Benihana blade acrobatics—you name it, we've done it. It's a wonder no one in my family has been jailed yet. Once I watched my grandmother chase my grandfather around their apartment with a ten-inch butcher knife because he refused to carve the corned beef the way she told him to do it—with the grain. And she was only a little bit angry. My stepfather David used to call our flash floods of emotion the Polnyakoff curse, that being my grandmother's maiden name.

"He didn't say good night?" I said. "What do you guys do when you really get mad, refuse to say please and thank you at the dinner table?"

"Very funny, Nattie," Annie said. "I've been at your house and seen how you deal with anger. I don't know which is worse, your hysteria or our denial."

I was waiting for Henry to weigh in and cast a vote for His People. I turned toward him, but he wasn't there. Then I saw him out of the corner of my eye, hunkered into the telephone I'd become one with this afternoon. I didn't need to be a betting woman to know who he was talking to.

And I wasn't going to say Topping.

He was talking to Hank. I could tell by the way he melted into the cradle of the telephone and the goofy smile on his face and the sweet tone in his voice. A woman can tell when a man's talking to his children, especially when she's watched this particular Daddy moon dance before.

"So is Hank all settled down now?" I said as Henry came into the room.

"I don't know," Henry said. "There was still no answer."

It's a good thing I'm not a betting woman. I'll leave that to my mother and her $5 slot machines in Vegas. So much for my deductive and intuitive skills.

"Oh," I said, and didn't have much else to add besides, "got your dinner plans all squared away?" Amazingly enough, I held my tongue. Maybe these last three years of therapy with the Good Doctor Grass were doing something other than making my insurance company apoplectic. Though that was reason enough to keep going, even if I did sleep through half the sessions.

Or maybe I was just grossed out enough by the piece of performance art on the floor to get back to the subject at hand. Someone or something's body part and its liquids staining Annie's pre–Civil War floor.

"What do you think it is, the obvious?" I asked, and looked down to the offending spare part. "The only thing I can remember from biology is the lock and key theory of enzymes—western yin and yang. By the sound of things, Annie, you either screamed or got sick through your classes. So what about you, Henry, did you ace your way through or at least pay attention to human anatomy?"

"I got a B plus—in high school," Henry said. "That was too many years ago to remember anything. I don't know, let's take a closer look."

Henry and I got down on our hands and knees and got up close and personal with It. Annie refrained.

"If you don't mind," she said, "I'll let you two do the examination."

Nestled on its paper towel bed was a slab of what looked a cross between congealed coffee ice cream and provolone cheese.

Henry pushed it down with his finger.

"It's firmer than it looks. I'm no pathologist, but given the letters so far, my guess would be with yours. Go with the obvious, it's probably a piece of a—"

"Lung."

Henry and I both turned around. It was Outerbridge Duncan standing by the door, his lips curled up in repulsion as if he'd spent the night sharing a railroad sleeping compartment with a bloated Giardia sufferer.

"It's a lung, for heaven's sake," Duncan said. "I've gotten enough propaganda from the cancer and lung associations to spot a lung from across a stadium. You wouldn't believe the things they bombard the American public with."

"They send you lungs?" I said. "For Christmas? How merry."

Duncan wasn't smiling. "Of course not. Pictures, drawings, papers. It's enough to make one invest in a paper shredder."

"As if you didn't have a Pentagon-sized one already," I muttered to myself.

"Excuse me?" Duncan said.

"She said, 'Can you tell if it's a human lung?' " Henry said, and glared at me.

Duncan bent down and looked at the lung, pushing it back and forth with his Montblanc pen.

"Human, certainly," Duncan said. "God forbid they desecrate an animal. These fanatics seem to have a professional courtesy system going for each other's ridiculous causes. It's a diseased lung, of course. One can tell by the consistency. A healthy lung would be far less firm, more like bubble packing. And these cauli-flower growths in the middle are a dead giveaway. Lung cancer. *They'll* blame it on cigarettes. But it was more likely asbestos or possibly a genetic predisposition."

"*Who* will blame it on lung cancer?" Henry said.

"The fanatics. The PETA-types who throw blood on innocent women for wearing fur coats. Every industry has them, including, unfortunately, ours."

If Henry hadn't still been glaring at me, I would have said, "Well, you do kill three million people a year, you know."

Duncan turned toward Annie. "Now, let's get this cleaned up

before your mother comes back. She would not be happy finding something like this here." He called into the kitchen, "Rosalita, come in here with a bucket."

"Has this happened before?" Henry said.

"No, this is a new one," Duncan said. "Must be the holidays. All that eggnog gets everyone going."

"How's the car?" I said.

"Not as bad as one might have expected," Duncan said. "Once they hammer out the dents and reconstitute the air bags, I'm assured it will be good as new. Better, in fact, since they've gotten this brake business worked out. My mechanic said this particular model has had trouble with its brakes."

Henry handed him the Christmas card. "I think it was more than that, don't you?"

Duncan opened the card. By the time he finished reading it, his cheeks were coloring up to the cranberry of Santa's cheeks.

"Rosalita, where are you?" Duncan called out. He tucked the card in his breast pocket.

"As I said before, the holidays get everyone unpleasantly stirred up. Now, if you'll excuse me."

He started to turn and leave, but Henry put his hand on Duncan's shoulder.

"Sir," he said, "if I could just ask you a few questions."

You could practically hear the wheels whirring in Duncan's head, weighing and measuring his options. Not to talk and get Henry even more dogged. Or talk and bet he was a wilier chess player than Henry.

It's a good thing I'd already sworn off betting. I'd have been at a loss as to who to put my money on. They don't come much better than Henry, but Duncan was a professional liar.

"All right, I have about ten minutes," Duncan said. "Join me in the library for a drink."

Duncan completed his turn, Henry followed him and so did I.

I was about to say, "No more alcohol for me, thanks," when Duncan said, "Excuse me, Nattie, but I think this conversation is best said between Henry and myself, if you don't mind."

Of course I minded. But I smiled sweetly, as if he were my best friend's stepfather who'd never pressed his rancid mouth against mine.

"I completely understand," I said. "And I don't think I'll need any clarification later, thanks just the same."

He gave me a Dr. Mengele look and walked out. That just left me, Annie, and the thing in the foyer.

"Rosalita, I asked you to clean that mess up now," I heard Duncan say. Then I got it, why he and his people didn't need the fireworks, the screams, or the knife tossing. With the tone of his voice alone he could instill more terror than a thousand shrieks. It was clear if she didn't hotfoot it out there in two seconds, she'd be hotfooting it out the door permanently. I heard Rosalita apologize and scurry into the kitchen and back our way.

Annie stood up and walked over to me. Level, this time. She'd taken off the right shoe.

"Did he make a pass at you?" Annie said. Her face was tight and she was angry. I'd seen that look before. When her father showed up at our dorm room, unannounced, uninvited, and unfunded.

The last thing I wanted to do was wear my welcome any thinner. But I sure wasn't going to lie to protect that jerk.

"How'd you know?" I said.

"He's done it before. I thought I'd made it very clear what would happen if he didn't control himself. Not clear enough, I see. I never said anything to Mother, because she seems fairly happy with him for the moment. And I can't take another one of her weddings. You remember the event of the century she made my wedding into. Hers are just the same. Possibly even more involved. The flowers, the guest lists, the caterers. It goes on and on. I think she keeps getting married because all that planning gives her a purpose in life for a few months."

Just then Rosalita came in, carrying a bucket and a plastic bag and looking very distraught.

"Here, Rosalita," Annie said, "let me do that. Don't worry about him. Just stay out of his way."

The woman started arguing with Annie about cleaning up the mess. Annie prevailed and sent Rosalita back into the kitchen.

"Not only is he a would-be philanderer, but he treats the people who work for us like slaves," Annie said as she slipped her hand in a plastic bag. She closed her eyes and reached for the lung and tossed it, along with its paper towel bed and her shoes, into another plastic bag. I took the sponge from the bucket and wiped away the spot.

"Let's go out for dinner," Annie said. "I can't face looking at him tonight."

I started to hesitate. The smell of Rosalita's garlic concoction was as thick as a Minnesota accent, plus I didn't have a spare twenty-five bucks. Between my mother's Hanukkah gift and George's riding clinic, I'd blown my discretionary spending wad.

"You pay when I come to Charlotte," Annie said. "This one's on me."

I wasn't going to argue or act proud. First of all, I'm not, and secondly, Annie's great-great-great-grandfather had been Cornelius Vanderbilt's number two guy, which would be akin to being Bill Gates's number two guy, who from what I read is now worth more than half the national debt.

CHAPTER 25

"**Y**ou have mail."

Like I said, I'm a cyberjunkie. I hadn't even brushed my teeth or cleared the sleep from my eyes, but here I was, plugged into the electronic collective consciousness and ready to download at least an hour before the sky was ready to upload.

I clicked on the cheery mailbox.

Six messages. Two from my equine cyberpals (Naglady and Whinney); one from Jean, the painless dentist/editor; one from my L.A. friend, and the last one from someone I didn't know. If there's a choice between new and old, those of the classic hysteric personality traits always go for the new. Proving the Good Doctor right in this one arena only, I chose mystery door number six: an357@anon.penet.fi.

Yet one more reason to install a little more obsessive circuitry in my brain. I should have gone for door number 1, 2, 3, 4, or 5. Then maybe I'd have been awake enough to have my life threatened.

NATALIE GOLD—JOSANE ASHMORE IS DEAD. LET HER STAY THAT WAY. FOR YOUR GOOD AS WELL AS THE GOOD OF OTHERS. HAVE A SAFE AND HAPPY HOLIDAY.

Great, last time around my answering machine played bearer of bad news and death threats. This time it looked as if I hitched a bum ride on the cyberspacial highway. There are some people who should just stay away from electronics, and it was becoming increasingly clear I'm one of them.

I may be a cyberjunkie, but that doesn't mean I know anything more about cyberspace than clicking on my mailbox icon to get my messages or stumbling my way to the horse list serv. I had no idea what this return address meant or how to find it. If that was even possible. Surely whoever sent me that happy holiday greeting was smart enough to cover his or her electronic tracks. However, just in case I was dealing with a dimwit who threatened me directly from his or her pod, I e-mailed the mystery address, along with a help-me-please message to Margot, *The Appeal*'s Julie Krome of cyberspace, who can find anything or anyone in the netherworld of rams, megs, and bytes. Then I remembered—she worked the graveyard shift at *The Appeal* so I wouldn't be hearing from her for at least another twelve hours.

Whoever it was either knew me personally or had the eyes or strong glasses to read the agate in *The Chronicle of the Horse*. No one else could have figured out my nom-de-space: Brenda Starr.

It wasn't exactly a you'll-be-dead-tomorrow threat, but close enough to make me wonder if fashion writing wasn't such a bad thing. I could write whatever I wanted to about Calvin Klein or Ralph Lauren and be reasonably assured they would never try to mow me down with a truck. Though I'm not as sure I could say the same for the buyers, fashion consultants, and owners of Coplon's, Dillard's, or Belk—Charlotte's version of Macy's, Bloomingdale's, and Saks, all of whom I've irritated a great deal over the last three years with my columns. Irritated them enough to send them running into Richards's office crybabying about my negative "attitude." Or, as they say in my hometown, Philadelphia, att-EEEEE-tood.

When it comes to fashion, I follow the writer Kingsley Amis's advice: If you can't annoy somebody, there's little point in writing.

I read the rest of my e-mail. Jean wrote to tell me about her annual dinner at Candace's. ONCE AGAIN, KIWI FRUIT GARNISHES ON EVERYTHING. THEN THIS ROAST THING WITH FRILLY LEG

CAPS THE SAME COLOR AS THE KIWI. AND SUGARED FRUIT ON KIWI-COLORED PLATES. I FELT LIKE I WAS IN A MARTHA STEWART NIGHTMARE.

As they say in real estate, Candace showed well, both on and off her person. She had a pretty enough face, though she had that kind of skim milk complexion that looks one coat shy of a finished paint job so you end up watching the blue of her veins pulse as if she's some kind of living anatomy lesson. She was slim and tall enough to not look totally ridiculous in her big and unfashionable shoulder pads and wore her dark brown hair in a power coif that didn't dare get out of place. Coordinated from head to toe by her personal shopper, she was always pulled together in OUTFITS. So it came as no shock that her dinner parties were more matchy-matchy than a Myers Park matron.

JEAN, I messaged back, WHAT, NO TOMATO FLOWERS? HOW'S IT LOOKING FOR ME TO GET AN EXTENSION ON THIS STORY? LOOKS LIKE I BIT OFF MORE THAN I CAN CHEW—NAT.

My horse friends were writing with the latest gossip: a certain blond, beautiful, and temperamental trainer we knew who recently broke up with another beautiful, but not blond or temperamental horse trainer was getting married. The surprise was, he was marrying a woman. Maybe he'd been seeing my shrink. The Good Doctor's weird take on sex extends to preference; he thinks homosexuality can be "fixed"—by him, of course.

The last message was from my film friend, who turned out to be well connected enough in LaLa Land to have heard something about Christopher Carey.

"NATS, BABY, HOW'D YOU HEAR WAY OUT THERE IN THE LAND OF COTTON ABOUT CAREY AND HIS MAIL PROBLEMS? CELEBRITIES GET WEIRD LETTERS A LOT. YOU KNOW THAT LINE BETWEEN FAN AND STALKER CAN GET PRETTY DAMN THIN. BUT THIS LATEST THING I HEARD ABOUT GOES BEYOND WEIRD. SOMEONE SENT CAREY A BODY PART. MY SOURCE DIDN'T KNOW EXACTLY WHAT KIND, BUT

SOMETHING INTERNAL. JUST WHEN YOU THINK YOU'VE HEARD THE
SICKEST THING, ALONG COMES SOMETHING WORSE."

This was good enough to wake Henry for. But I decided to
give him a little more time in the sack. It was purely selfish on my
part. I didn't want to deal with a grumpy Henry today. He'd
gotten in late the night before, not that I was waiting. A big guy
like him on old wood floors makes enough noise to wake a light
sleeper like me.

I was dying to know what Duncan said to Henry after he so
rudely dismissed me, and I was dying to tell Henry about my
mother's Nancy Drew work. Also, I wouldn't have minded hearing
about the Mundell manse and anything he cared to share about
Topping and her father. I figured I'd give Henry another half hour
or so of sleep before I came knocking.

I went down to the kitchen, where Rosalita was already up and
cooking. She offered me coffee. I accepted and tried my pidgin
Spanish on her. *Gracias* was as far as I got. She smiled and went
back to work—making biscuits that looked good enough for me to
disturb the elimination phase of my body.

I got dressed and gathered my things for the interview with
Flip Nilson. Since I am a sprinter, I was finished in less than ten
minutes. I had to kill some time, so I picked up the stack of magazines I'd lifted from Bladstone's place. I'd finished the Demi issue
of *Vanity Fair* last night, no sense in keeping it. I walked over to
the trash can and gave it the heave-ho, when I saw the Bladstone
annual report tucked inside—I'd used it as a page marker. I hadn't
looked at it before and grabbed it from the circular file. Annual
reports are a hoot, with all that Pollyanna copy and those badly
posed photographs. I think of them as American folk art, our version of Mexican Virgin Mary and Baby Jesus shadow boxes. I
flipped through the thing, looking at the, in fact, badly posed
photos and skimming the euphemized cutlines. See, Nattie, I said
to myself, there is something worse than fashion writing; you could
be writing this drek.

The pictures were goofy enough. L. M. and his kin everywhere. With the twenty-year-cigarette roller, Rufus White, on page 3; the marketing manager, Stanley Burns, on page 7; and the white-coated scientist, Peterson Scott, on page 10.

Double take. Peterson Scott? My brother's mad botanist client who rearranges plant DNA?

I read the cutline. "L. M. Bladstone confers with the renowned Dr. Peterson Scott, formerly of the Massachusetts Institute of Technology, at the Richmond research laboratory of Mundell International Enterprises, a subsidiary of Bladstone, Inc. 'We're always looking for ways to make a smoother tasting cigarette,' Mr. Bladstone says, 'even smoother than nature herself could have done.' "

Mundell Enterprises? As in Santee and Topping Mundell? So that's the Mundell tobacco connection. I wondered if Henry knew yet, and I wondered if my brother, Larry, had any idea what his mad botanist client was up to. I looked at the clock. Oh, what the hell, Henry could catch up on his sleep later, this was too good to let him sleep.

I slipped into our adjoining bathroom and knocked on his door. I heard a muffled "Come in," and I did. There was Henry, nuzzled neck-deep in the down comforter.

"Wait'll you hear what I've found out. You're going to owe me big-time," I said, and marched over to the side of his bed and plopped myself next to him.

"And a good morning to you too, Nattie. What number cup of coffee are you on?"

"Number one—and it's decaf. You're just grumpy because you got only twenty minutes of shut-eye last night. It's not my fault you were out until the owls went to sleep. You'll never guess how Topping's daddy fits into the tobacco picture."

Henry shut his eyes and started to turn over. "Mundell International Enterprises runs a research laboratory in Richmond for Bladstone."

"Oh," I said, and turned him back toward me. "Okay, so you know that. I bet you didn't know this."

I told him what my mother found out about Hinton Allard and his lawyerly tobacco connection. "And for my finale," I said, popping up the screen on my laptop, "take a look at this."

I showed Henry my L.A. friend's e-mail and he sat straight up to take hold of the computer. As he sat straight up, the comforter slipped straight down, far enough for me to catch a peek at what Henry wore to bed. Nothing. And far enough for me to see what was on the top of his left butt cheek. Something.

"Henry," I said, more shocked than I'd been in a very long time, "a tattoo? On your rear end? A rose on your butt? You? Henry B. Goode, Henry B. Prim and Proper?"

Henry's face became one with his alma mater—crimson.

He grabbed for the comforter, covering the aforementioned decorated body part, and cleared his throat.

"Oh, that," he said. "What's the matter, you don't see me as the tattoo type? Maybe I also dress up in leather jackets on Friday nights. Are you the only one allowed to have outbursts?"

"Outbursts are one thing," I said, "letting some Harley guy jab needles full of ink into your flesh is another. Okay, so how drunk were you?"

He laughed. "The most drunk I'd ever been in my life. First and last time. It was the night Martha took the boys and left. Les Restenbacher—the cops reporter who sleeps in his car or the men's room, depending on the temperature outside—found out about it and came over that night. He'd just gone through a divorce himself, which is why he's been living in his car since then. He took me to a bar on Independence, a fairly sleazy place. I should've left, but I didn't want to be alone. We drank. And we drank. I couldn't even stand by the time we left. Neither could he. Somehow we made it to Sunny's Tattoos. He got the snake, I got the rose."

"I'll be damned," I said. "Too many surprises in one morning.

225

My fragile system can't take it. A tattoo on Henry Goode's rumpus, well, glory be. I give, why a rose?"

Henry looked at me for a minute and with a sad, remembering smile said, "When Martha left, she said she couldn't stand living anymore with someone who never took time to smell the roses."

"Oh," I said. Now it was my turn to be quiet.

Henry broke the silence.

"So much for roses," he said. "I'm going to call your mother and thank her. Allard's tobacco connection is intriguing. I'd like to find out more about that class action suit."

"She could track it down for you," I said, "she's got the connections and she said it was fun. That in itself is worth more than a Pulitzer to me. So, you still think Allard was just another holiday drunk driver who bit the dust? And what about Carey's organ donor?"

Henry looked at the laptop screen again.

"Damn, this is a bigger story than I thought," he said. "It makes me think I have to stop and think good and hard about what it means. To the story and to the people on the list. I probably have an obligation to contact the rest of the people and tell them they're at risk. It also means it's a hell of a story. And it's a hell of a story a lot of other journalists would like to have."

He took a deep breath and shook his head. "I've got to think about this for a while."

Of course he had to think about it for a while. He'd been a coffee percolator in his last life.

"What about the police?" I said. "You going to call them?"

"Probably," Henry said. "First I'll call *The Appeal*'s lawyer, ask him for advice. The last thing I want is to become an arm of law enforcement. But there have been two deaths associated with the list so far. I think at this point I have no choice. If we do work with the police, this story has the potential of making the six o'clock news before I'm even close to publishing. This is a tricky one. In the meantime, why don't you call the one you know on the list, the artist? Find out what kind of mail he's been getting and see if you can make any connection between him and tobacco. I guess at this point we'll have to tell him about the list. Can he be trusted?"

"With anything but my heart," I said.

Henry looked at me and got the gist of things surprisingly fast.

"Oh," he said, "I didn't realize. Would you rather not?"

"No, I can handle it, and besides, it's time to stitch up this wound once and for all."

I looked at the clock. I had twenty minutes to get to The Plains to meet Flip.

"So who won the chess game last night, you or Duncan? Give me the condensed battle plan, I've got to leave in a few minutes. And feel free to add a few tidbits about Santee Mundell if you don't mind."

I'd call the talk between Henry and Duncan a draw. Apparently Duncan admitted he'd been the target of attempted murder, but denied any connection to the others on the list. Henry isn't one to give a shortened version of anything, so by the time he finished telling me about his ten minutes with Duncan, ten minutes had passed. I had to leave, or be rudely late to my meeting.

"Tell me tonight about Mundell," I said as I started to hurry out the door.

"Nattie, wait a second," Henry said. "I didn't think you'd mind, I told Toppy you were working on a story about Josane Ashmore. She's very interested and wants to do whatever she can to help you. She was very close with Josane. She'll be home all morning and said to stop by after your interview with Josane's boyfriend. Apparently she lives not too far from where you're going, she's on the Halfway Road, next to Duvall's place. You'll see the Mundell sign."

CHAPTER 26

The Plains.

An odd name for a town in the rolling hills of Virginia.

Kansas, Indiana, Nebraska, North Dakota, Florida—now, they know from flatlands. The Plains in Virginia? Who was I to quibble?

The story goes that the town's original name was The White Plains because of all the white rock in the Bull Run mountains. And I thought White Plains meant vast undifferentiated stretches of white concrete shopping malls.

I drove down the Halfway Road, where I did see long, sweeping, flatish fields that I guess some heartsick midwesterner could say resembled home, if he or she were homesick or near-sighted enough. This was another one of those high-dollar horse-country roads Annie was telling me about. I passed Burnleigh, Robert Duvall's estate, and looked for signs of life. It was deader than Jim Benson. Duvall wasn't in, and his tango-teaching wife had long gone—with the pool guy. Next farm was Topping's. I squinted and saw the mansion in the distance.

With a few minutes to spare, I arrived in downtown The Plains, a half-block of businesses punctuated in the center by a multiarmed signpost announcing THE PLAINS. LONGITUDE 38. LATITUDE 77. POP. 382 and mile-marking distances everywhere from Paris, Virginia (14) to Shanghai (7,396).

Of course parking the boat near the Rail Stop was a problem. I sure wasn't going to try to parallel-park 154 feet of sheet metal, so

228

I kept driving until I found a place I could pull into that didn't involve backing.

I hotfooted it to the restaurant and went inside. The Rail Stop had obviously been just that, a rail stop. There was an old-time ticket booth for the cashier's stand and hand-painted murals of trains and hounds and foxes on the walls.

I saw Flip standing by the cash register–ticket booth.

"Hi," I said, "thanks for meeting me."

He said something, but I didn't hear, because I near about jumped into his arms. The Rail Stop indeed. The insistent choo-choo of a train came roaring into my ears, and for a moment I couldn't figure where it was coming from.

Flip pointed up and I saw it, a toy train circling just below the ceiling. I'd been so focused on getting there in time and finding Flip, I hadn't seen the elevated train tracks.

We sat down by the bay window, exchanged a few weather pleasantries, then ordered. I don't know if I was hungry or nervous; whatever it was, I ordered more than coffee. A cheese and onion omelet with rye toast. The hell with this Fit for Life stuff. My stomach was complaining and I was tired of listening to it whine.

By the time the coffee came, Flip and I had gotten pretty chatty. Not about Josane, but I had to start somewhere. Like his name. A childhood nickname from his brother who couldn't pronounce his real name, Philip. And what he was doing in Middleburg, hanging around horse people. He worked for the family business: Winner's Circle Farm Products, a company that made and distributed everything from alfalfa cubes to horse liniment.

"I've been here all my life," he said. "Born, raised, and schooled here. I used to think about moving someplace new, start over fresh, you know, a clean slate. Then I realized it would just be a diversion. Wherever I went, I'd still be in the same place. The slate might look a little different, but the writing'd be the same."

A do-what look washed over my face. I of the extra-long-

adventure gene—the particular DNA structure that makes a person impulsive, exploratory, fickle, excitable, quick-tempered, and extravagant; I, who worship not only at the altar of color, but newness, had a difficult time understanding.

"Jumping around from place to place is just a way of jumping away from yourself," he said. "It's taken me a long time to understand that."

Well, call me Grasshopper.

Our food came, two fluffy omelets and real home fries. I speared one and popped it into my mouth. Ahh, home. I know, technically this was the South, but gastronomically speaking, we were in rye-bread land. I hadn't sunk my teeth into a real home fry in three years. Those matchstick things you get instead of grits don't count.

I noticed that Flip wasn't doing any diving into his food. He ate calmly; everything he did, he did calmly, which made me nervous. I'd have used the word serene to describe him. Until I brought up Josane.

"Well," I said between bites, "since this is a story about Josane, would you mind telling me about the last time you saw her?"

I saw his hand stiffen.

"We had words."

"What kind of words?"

"The wrong kind to have before someone dies. The kind you wish every day of your life you could take back. The kind that when a reporter asks, looks bad. But I'll tell you this, I didn't come back to hurt her or follow her when she went out riding, or anything else you or her mother might be thinking. I'll be the first to admit, I've been stupid—really stupid—with women. That day, Josane's last day, was my wake-up call, even though it took me a while to hear it afterward. I'd never been so angry in my life, and yes, I could've killed her. But I didn't. I stormed out instead and went to the studio."

"Studio?" I said.

"Seven Mountains, a kung-fu place I'd heard about in Leesburg. I'd been doing karate since I was six, winning tournaments, getting more belts, learning everything about the martial arts except the real purpose. I used think it was funny I could kill a person with my hands.

"For years a guy I know who sells horse trailers has been trying to get me to go with him to Seven Mountains. He studies with the sifu there. I guess he saw something in me everyone saw but me. I'd talked to him just that morning and he brought it up again, going with him to the studio. It must have been in my mind, because after I left Josane's, that's what I thought of. I didn't want to go the way I was—I was too mad—so I drove around for a couple of hours to cool off. When I got there I met Tom, my friend's sifu. He changed my life. Not right away. I mean I didn't come home that night a different person. I came home a person who knew he needed to be a different person. Tom opened the door and pointed out the path. But I was the one who had to take the walk."

Flip took a sip of coffee and stopped talking. Empty spaces in conversation make me want to fill them up. I forced myself not to jabber. A cup of coffee later, he started talking again.

"It's been a long walk and I know I've barely started. The problem is, it's easy to get lost, real easy. Especially for me with women. Women, that's always where I take the wrong turn."

He looked up from his coffee cup and gave me his killer smile. I can imagine how many eager young lovelies he'd felled with that grin and those baby blues. He was a gorgeous man and I didn't envy his looks one bit. Beauty like that is a curse. I'd watched a college friend of mine succumb to her astounding beauty—she was a smart girl, but no one including herself took her seriously because no one could get beyond her face. Thanks, but no thanks, I'll keep my long, crooked nose and wandering left eye.

"If you met him, Tom, I mean, you probably wouldn't notice anything about him. He's an unassuming, quiet guy. But he's there, not that he talks or brags about it. You can tell by his peacefulness. He found the way for himself, through meditating, kung fu, and just living. He says it's no big deal; all of us know it, the irony is, we start out there.

"Maybe that's so," Flip continued. "The trouble is, Tom's opening the door for me came too late to help with Josane. I came back that night and she was dead. Like I said, it took me a while to hear the wake-up call. All I did for the next three weeks was drink myself into trying to forget about her. That's why I took all her things to the dump—I'm sure her mother told you about that—I was trying to forget everything. Everything.

"I know this is part of my journey, but knowing something doesn't make you feel better. Knowledge is as intoxicating as women. Another easy way to get lost. You get fooled into thinking knowledge gives you answers. It gives you answers all right, but to the wrong questions."

Flip's head sunk to his chest and he cried. He didn't try to wipe away the tears. I watched them spill onto his omelet. He looked up and said, "Questions, everyone's got questions. Have I answered yours?"

I've got shelves full of metaphysical books and would have loved to hear more about his mystical meanderings, but now was the time to get him to talk about that final day with Josane.

"Flip," I said softly, "what happened that afternoon that got you so upset?"

He looked at me. Bloodshot whites against the bright blue of his eyes.

"What happened?" he said. "What happened? I walked in on Josane at the wrong time. She came to the door in a robe, a robe I'd given her, and nothing underneath. I could tell by the look on her face what she'd been doing. I tried to get into the bedroom to see who it was. I could've killed him. Josane stopped me. 'What's the point?' she kept saying. I could've gotten past her, but that crazy girl from the store came by."

"Lannie?" I said.

"Yeah, that's the one. She rushed in like she was Superwoman or something and started screaming for me to leave. Then she pulled a gun from her purse and threatened to use it on me. A gun! A deranged person like that can carry a concealed weapon in Virginia. Stupid legislators. She would have used it on me too. I don't know why she came carrying a gun, especially since she'd told Josane she'd stopped by to drop off a bottle of something she'd made up for Rita, Josane's horse. I left and never did find out who Josane had stashed in her bedroom."

"What about Lannie?"

"*What* about her? Man, she's a nutcase. I kept telling Josane to get rid of her. But that wasn't Josane's way. Josane felt sorry for Lannie, thought it was her godly duty to help her. And look what happened, Lannie helped herself to Josane's money. That really surprised me. Lannie worshiped Josane. I used to think it went beyond worship. I thought Lannie was a dyke, until one time Josane fixed her up. We all went out together. It was one weird night because you could tell Lannie had it bad for the guy. And I don't think the feeling was mutual. When we drove him back to Warrenton, Lannie kept asking if he'd call her again and when. Finally Josane had to say something to Lannie before she'd let Snowden out of the car."

"Snowden?" I said. "Snowden Cox the lawyer?"

Flip nodded. "Yeah, you know him?"

"Not yet," I said. "But I'm not leaving until I do. Josane's mother told me he was handling Josane's divorce."

"That's the one. He's supposed to be a good lawyer, but he was sure taking his sweet time on the divorce. I used to think that's what was holding up Josane and me getting married. Now I know it was me that was holding up things. I don't know how she found him or why she was using him, but the price was right. He and Josane had worked out some kind of deal so it hardly cost her anything."

Some kind of deal, indeed. She'd spent the morning with him and I wondered if it hadn't been Snowden Cox with whom Josane had spent her last afternoon. Maybe Flip had walked in on something other than legal briefs.

I slipped into my even more delicate mode and asked as gently as possible if Snowden Cox could have been the mystery man in the bedroom.

Flip's face fell, and so did my heart. It's not fun watching anyone hurt, even a possible murderer. Flip's tale of his newfound spiritual journey could've been just that—a tale. It was possible everything he'd just said to me had been a lie and that he did follow Josane on the trail and beat her to death. If that was the case, he was a damned good liar or a psychopath who metamorphosed his fictions into fact.

"Yeah, sure, anything's possible," he said. "Any man would've jumped at the opportunity to be with Josane. Snowden Cox? Could be. If that's the case, maybe it wasn't a riding accident after all. As crazy as Lannie was about Snowden, and as crazy as she was to start with, the combination of finding him with Josane and then Josane firing her might've been enough to send that looney tune over the edge. She could've easily found Josane on those trails, she knows them like a bloodhound."

Flip pushed the plate of half-eaten omelet and uneaten home fries to the center of the table.

"Oh, man," he said, "rehashing this stuff makes me sick. I can't stop thinking about that day, asking myself why Josane had to die. I go over and over it in my mind, thinking if I hadn't been such a hothead or if I'd done something different, maybe she'd be alive. It's like a cement mixer in my gut, churning and churning at me.

"It got to the point I couldn't think about anything else. That's when Tom suggested I meditate on the question of suffering; but if I wanted to find out why the suffering, then I also had to ask why the joy? I've been asking those questions for almost four years. . . . He says I'll find peace someday. I'm still waiting."

Me too.

CHAPTER 27

Yin and yang. Flip Nilson and Topping Mundell. Going from the seemingly spiritual to the certainly spiritually void.

So I thought, or wanted to think.

It turns out Miss Topping Mundell wasn't the empty, but gorgeous vessel I expected. Nor was she my greatest source of intimidation: the prototypical horse show snootball, one of those thin-thighed, Foxcroft-schooled, condescending, rich-kid in girls who make me feel like I'm back in ninth grade. That was the year I, the new kid from the poor inner-city school, walked into the girls' room of the oh-so tony Bala Cynwyd Junior High to find Randy Zoloff and all her in girlfriends in their in-girl outfits of Lady Bug A-lines, Peter Pan–collared shirts in miniature heathered florals, Aigner fisherman purses, and Weejun loafers making fun of everything about me, especially my knockoff version of all of the above.

Nope, Topping, I hate to say, was all right. And not only because she told me about fifteen times how wonderful a horse Brenda is.

I got to her house around 9:30. She, not a maid, met me at the door. It was a big house, but not nearly as grand as Annie's. Actually it was a little long in the tooth and peculiarly floored. Unlike Annie's house, with gymnasium expanses of perfectly restored heart pine, the Mundells' entire first floor was a checkerboard of black and white linoleum squares. It made me want to tap-dance.

"Come on in the kitchen," Topping said, "I'm baking a cake. It's Daddy's birthday. Coffee?"

I was up to number four, and they all hadn't been decaf.

"I'm vibrating already," I said. "I could be my own sex toy."

Topping laughed. "Henry and Karen both told me you were funny. I'm glad you came. Not only because I could use a good laugh, but I'm interested in this story you're doing on Josane. Everyone here thinks it was a riding accident, but if you think it was something more, I'll be happy to help you in whatever way I can. Josane was my best friend, she was like an older sister to me. It's still hard to believe she's gone. But don't get me started on that now, I'll start crying into this cake, and it's supposed to be a happy cake, not a sad cake."

She poured melted chocolate into the bowl, then added flour and buttermilk, turning the batter a fawny brown. Over the whir of the beater—not a Williams Sonoma faux-pro three-digit kind, but an old suburban Mixmaster from the '70s—she said: "This is going to sound strange, but one of the things that makes Josane's death even more difficult to accept was that she was too alive to die. Do you know what I mean, or do I just sound crazy?"

I didn't want to get into my tales of woe, but I knew exactly what she meant. Some people seem too big to die, David had been one of them.

"You don't sound crazy to me," I said. "And yes, I know what you mean." I choked back my tears.

Topping was looking at her watch, timing the beater. "It sounds kind of Hallmark-cardy, but Josane really lived her life. Every time I saw her she was happy. She was amazing that way. Nothing could get her down. I know it sounds strange, but if I ever get blue, I feel like she's still here with me, trying to perk me back up.

"Finished," she said, and turned off the beater. "So who else have you talked to besides Flipped-out Nilson?"

"Flipped-out?"

"That's what we call him since his 'rebirth,' " Topping said, flicking her two index fingers down around the word. "Rebirth, as if he's changed one iota. I don't believe his journey talk for one minute. Especially after meeting his guru, or master, or whatever it is Flip calls the man. If he's so enlightened, then how come he could hardly wait for his wife to leave the room before he came on to me? They're two of kind, Flip and Tom, that was his name, wasn't it? All it takes is a short skirt or tight jeans and Flip's up to his old tricks."

Topping shook her head. "People never really change, do they? Anyway, I understand you were planning to talk to Lannie? How'd that go? Boy, between Flip, Lannie, me, and Annie you'll probably leave Middleburg thinking we're all either crazy or too rich for our own good or both."

The thought had crossed my mind, but that's where I commanded it to stay.

I told her a little about my meeting with Lannie. I didn't go into detail; I didn't have to. Topping, like everyone else around, thought Lannie was two flakes short of a bale.

"Nuts, the woman is totally nuts," Topping said. "But I don't think in a dangerous way. She's more pathetic than anything. I know Lannie pretty well. I suppose you know she was a groom at the barn. She was the kind who took the spiders outside rather than kill them. I can't see her possibly hurting anyone, especially Josane. Josane was the best thing that ever happened to Lannie and Lannie knew it. Now, Flip, he's another story. I've always thought that man was dangerous. I'd seen Josane come to the barn many times with bruises. You can't fall off a horse *that* much. She finally told me about it, that he'd hit her and push her around. It didn't take much to set him off either, the wrong kind of look or too big a smile to another man. Once Flip roughed her up for thanking a gas station attendant too enthusiastically. Of course, Josane didn't help things much; she was the most accomplished flirt I've ever seen.

But that doesn't excuse Flip's behavior. I tried to make her take out a restraining order, but she didn't want anyone to know about it. She kept telling me she was going to handle it her own way. Just the day before she died she told me she was going to tell Flip it was over between them."

Topping took a fingerful of cake dough. "My favorite part, want a lick?"

"Sure," I said, and stuck my finger in. She was my kind of cook, not overly concerned with germs. "Delicious—German chocolate?"

She nodded. "Daddy's favorite. He loves it when I double the frosting recipe. I don't know if Henry told you I told him this, but you have the cutest mare. You're lucky you found a horse like that. I think you get one horse like that in your life—I'm still looking."

She laughed. "And looking and looking. I'm like that little pink Duracell rabbit in that way. It's probably the same thing with men. You know, a lid for every pot, you just have to find it."

Now I laughed. "Some pots are too odd-shaped to have a lid," I said. "And I think I'm one of them. Thanks about Brenda. I lucked out when I found her. I should be so lucky finding the lid to my pot."

"You just have to keep looking and looking," Topping said. "I told Josane the exact same thing. Flip wasn't for her. You know, I hadn't thought about this before, but maybe Josane told Flip that morning. Maybe that's what happened."

I sat back down at the kitchen table. "What do you mean?"

"If too big a smile made Flip mad, imagine what telling him it was over did to him. Flip knew Josane rode every afternoon around that time and he knows those trails as well as anyone."

Topping dipped her finger in for seconds. "Mmm, Daddy'll love this. You know I often think if Thrill hadn't lost a shoe that morning, I'd have gone out with her that day. And maybe then she'd still be alive."

I knew the horse Thrill. When the Mundells bought him,

he'd been the number-one junior hunter in the country. I heard they'd offered an extra $90,000 to the $150,000 price if Topping could have the horse before the big indoor show circuit. In an amazing act of integrity, especially considering the world in which it was committed—the horse show world—the trainer/owner turned down the extra bucks because the kid who'd ridden the horse all year worked so hard to get him qualified for the indoor shows and it was her last chance to show as a junior since she was aging out of the division. In the end, it really didn't matter when Topping started showing Thrill, because that union didn't last much longer than her fix-up with Rox-Dene. Topping couldn't ride one any better than the other. She sold him after crashing him through an in and out and getting the poor horse wedged between the two fences. That made my in and out story seem like a bad hair day.

She wasn't the best rider around and I had to give her credit in a way—her stick-to-itiveness. Topping did keep plugging no matter what. I sort of felt sorry for her; all the money in the world to buy the best horses and she still could barely get around a course.

"Josane should have never gone out on the trail alone with that horse," Topping said. "But I'm sure you already know about trying to change Josane's mind. We used to call her Mule around the barn because she was so stubborn."

"When did you find out about the accident?" I asked.

"Charlie called me at home early that evening. I knew something was wrong right away, he was frantic, Rita had come galloping back to the barn wild-eyed and without Josane. He wanted to know if I'd heard from Josane. I hadn't and I rushed out to the barn to help look for her. We couldn't find her and it was getting dark. Everyone was panicking. Especially Charlie. Finally we found her near a tree. Her helmet had come off and it looked like she'd hit her head."

"Her helmet came off?" I said. "Wasn't she wearing one with a harness?"

"No, she hated that kind," Topping said. "The only bad thing I could say about Josane is that she was a little vain. She said the regulation kind looked like a football helmet."

Regulation for juniors. Not for adults. That's why she wasn't wearing it, she never had to. In the ASHA's penultimate act of stupidity, the governing body of horse shows requires only junior riders to show in hunt caps with chin harnesses. Adults are allowed to wear the brain buckets—those thin shells of fiberglass with an elastic chin strap everyone cuts off.

Topping poured the batter into three parchment-paper-lined cake tins and slid them carefully into the oven.

"You know," she said, "Henry's favorite cake is also German chocolate cake. Isn't that funny?"

"What a coincidence," I said.

Henry and Topping, it'd slipped my mind. Well, he could do worse, I suppose. She was friendly and turned out not to be the idiot I'd thought. On the contrary, as she showed me around the house I saw her college diploma on the wall of her father's study. Magna cum laude from Brown. It wasn't Harvard, but it wasn't far off.

We walked up the staircase to the second floor; at the top of the landing was a life-sized oil portrait of Topping and an older man seated in front of her. Slate-gray hair edged with white, one of those straight Upper Wasp half-noses and eyes that made you feel like saying yes, sir; Daddy Mundell was one handsome old goat. Between her mother, the gorgeous French twist I'd seen at the funeral home, and her father, who could've beat Ben Bradlee in the Mr. Senior Hunk Pageant, Topping had hit the looks lottery.

"Nice painting," I said.

"You think so?" Topping said. "Some days I like it, others I think he got Daddy all wrong. Oh, well, come on up to my room, I'll show you some pictures of Josane."

Topping led me down the hall to the room at the end. Hers. It was a time warp. Was everyone in Middleburg loony? It looked like an eleven-year-old girl lived there. Baby-doll pink walls, white provincial canopy bed, frilly lace curtains, stuffed animals on the shelves, and horse show ribbons strung around the room.

She saw me looking around, zooming in on the fluffy Jemima Puddleduck on her pillow.

"Oh, this room," she said, "isn't it something? Daddy keeps promising we'll redecorate, but he's been so busy."

"It's something all right," I said. "Makes me want to slip into patent leather Mary Janes and white anklets. But, I have to admit, I'd have killed for a room like this—and someone down the hall called Daddy—when I was a little girl."

"Where was your father?" she asked.

I gave her the abbreviated version of my fatherless childhood, sparing the gory details that the Good Doctor likes to go over and over.

"Oh, my God," Topping said. "That's really horrible. You know what therapists say, there's no one more important to the development of a young girl than a father. I don't know what I'd have done if I'd been you."

You'd have built walls, I thought, the same as I did, that's what you'd have done. Walls you hope no one can crumble.

"I made it in one piece. But if you look closely, you can see the glue marks. Most people think they're wrinkles," I said, and laughed. You build walls and learn to laugh when it hurts the most.

"Nattie Gold," Topping said, laughing with me, "you hardly have a line on your face. I hope I look half as good as you when I get to be your age."

Ouch. It's not as if I were old enough to be her grandmother.

She's twenty-seven, I'm thirty-seven. Ten small years between the two of us.

She opened a drawer and fished around inside, finding a stack of photos bundled together with a rubber band. "Here," she said, "I think these are some I took at the barn right before Josane died. I keep them buried here because it makes me sad to look at them."

I skimmed through the pile. Sure enough, they were of Josane and Josane and Rita and Josane and Topping. "Can I borrow them?" I said. "I don't know why, but it helps me write when I can get a really good mental picture of the person I'm trying to write about. You never know what you'll see in a photo, a gesture or a certain way of smiling. It all adds up to more details, which makes a more complete story."

"As I said earlier, anything I can do to help," Topping said. "Take them, just put them in the mail or give them to Henry when you're finished. Oh, my God, speaking of Henry, I forgot to tell you he called and asked you to call him at Annie's. I'm so sorry I forgot."

"No problem," I said. "He probably wants to go over our record-checking plans in the bowels of the Loudoun County courthouse. I can't tell you how excited I am about spending a day with a stack of dusty books taller than Henry, trying to find out who sugar-daddied Josane's business. Topping, I'll be your best friend for life if you could tell me who it was. That'd spare me the drudgery of reading all that agate."

"You know," she said, "I've often wondered that very same thing myself. Josane was very private about her affairs. I think she was afraid Flip would find out. But I'll be more than happy to ask around for you, see what I can come up with. Let's go downstairs, use the phone there so I can go check the cakes."

Topping opened the oven. Inside I saw pouffing tins of German chocolate cake. She closed the oven doors and said, "A few more minutes."

I reached around to the phone and dialed Annie's number. No sooner did it start to ring than I heard a crash. I turned in time to see a red tabby cat knock a bowl off the counter.

"Goddammit," Topping screamed, but the cat screamed louder after Topping threw it halfway across the black and white checkerboard. "Stupid idiot cat, I bet those cakes fell because of you."

Topping opened the oven door and sure enough the cakes looked like someone let the air out of the tires. She slammed the door and looked around, presumably for the cat, when she saw me looking at her.

"Sorry about that, Nattie," Topping said. "I guess I don't have to tell you about a redhead's temper. It's just that I wanted the cake to be perfect. Well, maybe I'll—"

"Duncan residence," I heard in my other ear. I held my finger up to Topping and mouthed, "Just a minute."

"Oh, hi, Rosalita," I said. "Is Henry still there?"

"Gold, I was just giving up on you," Henry said. "Having a good interview with Toppy? Admit it, she's not what you thought she'd be, right? Anyway, call your landlord. He tracked you down here, says it's important."

Oh, shit, my rent check. I bet the damn thing bounced. Not again. He was a nice guy, so he never tacked on the twenty-five-dollar returned-check charge. This was getting embarrassing. I'd better start recording what checks I write.

"Jim?" I said. "Hey, it's Nattie. Look, I'm really sorry about the check. Just run it through again and I promise it'll never—"

"Hold up a minute, Nattie. Your check's fine. I wouldn't call you up there for something like that. This is important. The man who lives in the apartment below you called me this morning because he heard some banging around in your place late last night. He knew you were out of town, so he called me. I didn't want to go in there until I talked to you first."

Oh, I groaned. Another break-in. A love offering from my anonymous e-mailer, or just the random crime of city life? I can't say I hadn't been warned. After the first break-in, Tony had practically jumped up and down, trying to get me to pop for the most expensive dead bolts, but I cheaped out and went the Hechinger's budget bottom-of-the line route.

"I can't take another break-in," I said to Jim. "Yeah, go in. Here's the number where I am. Call me from my apartment, just please don't tell me if my plastic horses got smashed up again."

CHAPTER 28

"Lou," I shouted into the phone. "Put your goddamned hearing aid in."

It'd been Lou in my apartment. Jim called back and said a strange man was snoring on my bed, had to practically hit him with a shovel to wake him. "Claims he's your father and all that banging last night was him doing something called the twenty rites of rejuvenation, where you close your eyes and spin around in five different positions."

Jim wanted to call the police, but when I heard about the rejuvenation rites, I told him everything was fine.

I heard the high-pitched whine coming closer.

"Okay, Nattie, it's in."

"Lou, what the hell are you doing there?" I said. "I thought you were in Stonehenge with Mrs. Flock."

"Machu Picchu," he said. "We got back yesterday."

"Then why aren't you there? I thought you were moving in next door with her so you could keep me supplied with carrot juice forever."

I heard him giggle. Uh-oh, trouble. My father always giggled when he got nervous.

"What's wrong, Lou, she kick you out?"

"Not exactly," he said, and giggled. I guess she had. "She didn't like a painting I wanted to hang. She didn't like the energy coming from it."

"What painting?"

"That poster I got in Copenhagen with you. The Munchkin one."

"You mean the Edvard Munch? The little guy with his mouth in an O, screaming? I don't blame her, it gives me the willies too. You broke up because of a poster?"

"Maybe a few other reasons too." A few more giggles and I knew it was really over between the two of them. I just hoped he hadn't pissed her off badly enough so she stopped talking to me. She had been—up until her intercontinental tango with my father—a friendly and helpful next-door neighbor.

"How long you planning to stay?" I said.

"I could go back to Father Divine's or Lemon Grass if it's a problem."

"No, no, pull up your futon and stay as long as you want. It's okay. You can scare off the burglars." Imagine, a seventy-year-old guy who divides his living between Father Divine's rest stop for the homeless and the Lemon Grass House, aka the enema institute of San Diego.

I hung up the phone.

"I thought your father was gone," Topping said.

"He's back—with a vengeance," I said.

"Well, that's great," Topping said. "Lucky for you."

"Yup, lucky me," I said. I wondered how lucky she'd think I was if I told her about the last conversation I'd had with my father when he tried to pay my way out to his enema institute.

"I've got to go find myself a murderer," I said. "And try to catch Charlie and Karen at the barn before the funeral. Thanks for taking the time to talk. Call me at Annie's if you find out anything."

Topping took the cakes and dumped them in the trash. "Oh, well, might as well start over," she said. "You're going to the barn now? You know, you could have spared yourself breakfast with

Flip—I know eating with that caveman couldn't have been much fun—and talked to him at the barn. He works there, on the machinery, in the late mornings. By the way, are you going back to Annie's before dinner?"

"I can't imagine why not," I said. "Why?"

"Would you mind giving Henry something for me?" She walked out of the room and came back carrying a CD with an envelope taped to the front of it.

"Be happy to," I said, and slipped it into my coat pocket.

"See you at Paper Chase," Topping said as I started to leave.

"Huh?"

"At George's clinic. Henry told me you were riding in it. So am I. Maybe we can eat lunch together."

"If I'm up to eating," I said. "Let me see what kind of shape I'm in after the morning with George."

I got in Annie's Suburban and started the engine. The CD was biting into my hip, so I tossed it on the seat next to me. Some shot I am, it landed on the floor, pulling the envelope off as it went down. I reached to pick it up and saw the title.

Wham, a direct hit to the emotional solar plexus.

I guess Dorothy was right, I had it for Henry more than I wanted to admit. It knocked the wind out of me when I saw Seal's face on the cover, because I knew what was on the back. Sure enough when I flipped it over I saw Miss Topping Mundell's handiwork; underlined in bright, lipstick red with a little heart next to it was the song title "Kiss from a Rose."

The rose. It seems I wasn't the only female to discover Henry's floral arrangements in the last twenty-four hours. I looked at the envelope. It wasn't sealed. Should I or shouldn't I? I tossed that around about as long as it took me to say it. What the hell, just more karmic debt to pay off.

Carefully, I slid out the note. Her penmanship was as gorgeous as she was. *Dear Henry, I* thoroughly *enjoyed last night. When you listen to this, think of me. Love, Toppy.*

I don't know who the faster operator was, him or her. I could feel my guts churning and I hated feeling this way. It's easier going through life as the ice queen—the Good Doctor's nickname for me fully suited in my man armor—hermetically sealed from this kind of hurt. The rational side of me knew Henry was entitled to do whatever he wanted with whomever. But when has my rational side ever had hold of the reins? I looked down at the steering wheel; I was white-knuckling it the way Henry had yesterday when he'd been fighting for our lives. Then I looked at the speedometer: eighty miles an hour. And this was no straight ribbon of road I was careening down.

I was on my way to killing myself or, worse, someone else. Calm down, I ordered. Fat chance, the little man in my head snarled back.

I'll show you.

"Ohmnahmahsheviya, ohmnahmahsheviya . . ." I chanted over and over, driving his obnoxious little voice back into the deep corners of my unconsciousness. Every once in a while my father comes up with something that really works—not that I've ever even considered trying his gospel according to high colonic. But such was the case with his wild yam pills that keep him, me, and even my skeptical brother on a happy keel and also, this cocka-mamie chant. I don't know why it works, but it does. I loosened my death grip on the wheel and slowed down to forty-five, a reasonable speed on a curvy road. I stopped thinking about Henry and Topping and started thinking about where I was going.

To the barn. Josane's barn. Now was the time to inhale the details.

"Look for the white fencing, you can't miss it," Karen had told me yesterday.

She wasn't kidding. The farm looked like Tara from the road with its miles of starched white four-board and white-columned mansion on the horizon. SUMMER RIDGE FARM, a handsomely painted royal blue and white sign announced. I drove down the long drive, under a towering alley of skyscraping elms that could rival Charlotte's Queens Road spectacle, past the horse-show-sized sand ring chock full of fancy horse show jumps, by the lima-bean-shaped pond, to the front of the barn. Barn, now, that would be a stretch of the dictionary definition to include what was in front of me; it'd be the equivalent of calling The Plaza a motel.

I pulled to the side parking area and docked next to a white dually truck. On its door was a sign with the same tasteful royal blue logo as the one out front: SUMMER RIDGE FARM. Another white truck. I leaned against the driver's-side window and saw a set of keys in the ignition. Another white truck waiting for any crazed lunatic to take it on a killjoy ride.

I walked to the front of the barn. Someone sure had money to burn when they built this place. Though I prefer the charm of an old barn, I could be happy here even if it was a bit of a mixed metaphor. While the house looked to be pure Scarlett O'Hara, the barn was a study in Henry the whatever with neo-Tudor everything. Heavy white stucco walls cross-beamed all over the place with big, dark wooden rafters and gables everywhere you turned.

It was big and surprisingly airy inside, the aisles wide enough to get three horses by without one pinning his ears back in protest. The floors were long, level stretches of shiny new black macadam striped down the center with wide walkways of grooved black rubber mats. The horse blankets, so clean you could put a fresh-born baby to sleep on them, were carefully folded on brass racks hanging from the front of each stall. Next to the blankets were nameplates of the residents inside, handscripted in fancy white calligraphy on a wash of royal-blue-stained wood.

"Hello," I called out. No answer. I walked down the aisle. I'd come to horse Hollywood. All the big boys and big girls of the horse show world were here, munching their perfect flakes of perfect alfalfa in their perfect stalls. Trump Card, Brass Ring, Fritz and Bill, Camden Yards, Savoy: all here; fat, shiny, and poised to blow away the competition.

In horseflesh alone, there was enough money here to take a chink out of the national debt. Despite his run of bad luck, Charlie Laconte still had a string of high-dollar clients who bought the best and paid the most to keep them that way. Between training, grooming, and showing, each owner must have been shelling out at least four to five grand *per* month *per* horse, and most of these people had two or three horses. Then next month that figure doubles when everyone heads south for the Palm Beach circuit.

I knocked on the office door. No answer. I turned the doorknob. It was open and I went in. Regardless of how fancy the barn was—in this case, as fancy as I'd seen in a while—it was still a barn in one regard: It was cold as a politician's heart, and those gloriously gabled ceilings didn't help matters. My hands and feet were starting to numb up and I knew the office would be heated. They always are, to keep the horses—and Jack Russells—from freezing.

Like most show barns, the office walls were covered with winning photos of their horses and riders. Glossy eight-by-tens in shiny black frames. After all these years I still love looking at horse pictures as much as I love the smell of a sweaty horse. When I was in the hospital having my leg bolted together, I made Gail bring a stack of *Practical Horseman* magazines and the dirtiest horse brush she could find, just so I could stick my nose deep into its sweat-stained bristles and pull out that intoxicating smell. When you're addicted, you're addicted. They don't call heroin horse for nothing.

I climbed over a tangle of heavy black hose and past Tastycake's royal blue doggie bed, piped and embroidered in white, to the far wall of photos. I began examining each one, first studying the horse, then the rider. There wasn't a dangling knee in the equine bunch; they were all jumping like jackrabbits, which explained the border of tricolor championship ribbons circling the room. The riders were another story. With the exception of Charlie and Jim—both of whom rode with textbook perfect equitation even George Morris couldn't criticize—the other riders bore testament to the generosity of their mounts. Elbows were flying, heels were up, knees pinched, eyes down, backs roached. What a collection of bad riding, frozen by the photographer like an equitation dos and don'ts hall of shame.

I saw Topping there, flinging her body over Thrill's neck as the big bay horse tried valiantly to carry her over the fence. There were a few more of Topping on various horses. A few of a guy I recognized on a tall chestnut. This guy, as I recalled, was a good enough rider, but had the bad financial sense to pay Charlie $75,000 for a horse that refused to switch leads for anyone but Charlie. Every time I saw the guy at the horse shows, he was in tears. Last I heard, he took a $65,000 hit and sold the horse back to Charlie for $10,000.

I recognized the next horse. God, was she ever a beauty. It was Rita, sailing over a big brush fence. Charlie was on her back and both of them were in such perfect form, it made the hair rise on my arm. The picture next to that was also of Rita; it looked like the same show. I looked at the striped awnings of the booths and the big trees in the ring. Upperville, it was Upperville. Josane was holding Rita, who wore the tricolor championship ribbon on her bridle. I leaned in close to the picture to see if I could make out the writing on the streamers. I squinted hard.

UPPERVILLE GREEN CONFORMATION CHAMPION.

Green conformation? Odd. I thought that mare couldn't show conformation because of the bumps on her legs.

I went back to looking at the pictures, and that's how Karen found me.

"Oh, hey," I said. "Hope you don't mind. I love looking at horse pictures."

"That's why you came?" Karen said. "To look at the pictures?"

"That, and look around, ask you some more questions," I said.

"God, you're as persistent as a cold," Karen said. "I can't think of anything else to tell you, but ask away."

So I did. First about Lannie and why she hadn't told me she'd worked at the barn.

"You never asked," Karen said. "And I didn't think it was my place to tell you. I figured if she wanted you to know she worked here and got fired, she'd tell you."

"Fired?"

"Oh, she forgot to tell you that part, huh? Big surprise. Ask her yourself. She should be here sometime in the next couple hours delivering feed. Yeah, I fired her ass off this place. I saw her smack a customer's horse in the head one too many times."

"I thought Lannie was a troubled but gentle soul," I said.

"Yeah, who told you that, her mother? She slammed the horse so hard with the chain of a lead shank, it left a scar on the mare's head. What was she thinking? A scar on a conformation hunter? That customer could have sued *our* asses off."

"Who'd she hit, Rita?"

"Are you kidding? That was Josane's horse. She'd have never done anything to piss off Josane. Besides, Rita didn't go in the conformation divisions."

I pointed to the picture.

"One time," Karen said. "And one time only. The only reason the mare won was that Josane found some kind of magic potion shit that brought down the bumps on the mare's legs. Trouble was, it stopped working."

"What'd she use?" I said. Brenda had a few bumps I'd have liked to get rid of, even temporarily.

"Some kind of DMSO mixture is all I know. And the only reason I know that is because I had to rub it on the mare's legs. Yecch, that stuff is disgusting. I was tasting rancid garlic and bad oysters all day."

Yecch is right. I knew the stuff firsthand; I'd used it on Brenda a couple times back when it was the veterinary thing to do. DMSO, it stands for dimethyl sulfoxide. Though it's approved only as a veterinary liniment, it was also the rage a while back for human aches and pains. You can still get it at drugstores or hardware stores—no kidding, it doubles as the Incredible Hulk of chemical elbow grease. The downside is the second you touch it, you're tasting it—for a long time.

"Didn't you wear gloves?"

"There was a little hole in them that I didn't see. That's all it takes and that's why I don't mess with it. She might've gotten it from Lannie. She's quite the junior chemist with all her bottles of homemade herbal horse remedies. I think they even sell some of her stuff over at the feed store where she works. But then again, Lannie usually messes only with herbs and soy sauce, or whatever that brown shit is she uses. Josane could've gotten it from anyone. She was obsessed with getting those bumps off Rita. I think she went through a carton of Preparation H and Saran wrap trying to sweat the damn things off. Maybe Charlie knows more about it or where Josane got it from. I'll ask him myself, if you want me to."

"That'd be great or better yet, I'll ask him myself, if he's around."

"Forget it, sister," Karen said. "He's a basket case. Can't get past one word without crying. Leave him alone for a while. He can't tell you anything I haven't. So just back off on that one, okay?"

"No problemo," I said, and held up my hands. "Just a couple more questions and then would it be all right if I looked around?"

"Fire away and stay as long as you like. You could feed for me tonight if you're really wanting to camp out."

"What happened to Josane's riding stuff?"

Karen laughed. "This is what I meant about her people being weird. Her daughter's dead and the mother starts ranting about Josane's things being missing. I mean, who would care? Apparently Josane's mother. She couldn't wait to get her hands on Josane's saddle. I guess she knew how much Josane paid for it. Can't hardly find a saddle that cost more than a Butet. I'm sure she sold it before the ground froze back over Josane's grave. I think she's got Josane's bridle and boots too. Not the helmet. Her mother didn't even want to see it, not that I blame her. But there's nothing wrong with it. I put it up in the hayloft, in deep storage. I thought if some kid we were taking to a show forgot her helmet, I could always dig up that one for her. It wasn't cracked or even torn, and you know Josane, or I guess you didn't, but it was the best money could buy."

"How could a kid ride in a helmet without a harness?"

"What are you talking about?" Karen said. "Josane's helmet had a harness. As many times as Josane came off that mare, Charlie would've never let her ride in anything but. I'll show it to you, be right back."

A few minutes later Karen was back with a white box in her hands.

"Mind if I borrow it for a few days?" I said.

"I have a better idea. You don't look like the kind to spook at ghosts. If it fits, it's yours, a gift from the beyond. We'll never use it. Hope your head is big, though. Seven and a half, I think this is."

I lifted it out of the box. It looked brand new. I piled my hair on my head and put it on. Perfect fit.

"Hey," Karen said, "I've got an even better idea. You train with Rob, right? Knowing Rob, he makes you ride all his horses, even the stupid ones. So I know you can ride. And Peggy Eames had a lot of good things to say about how you brought your mare around from a wild child. In my book, if you pass the Queen Peggy test, you're okay. I got to go to this goddamned funeral, and it looks like poor Charlie can't stop crying long enough to shorten his reins. I've got a couple of horses that have to be ridden today. If they go any longer, they'll kill their owners when they come out for their Sunday rides. What d'ya say? Want to ride one or two of them? I think I can even scrounge up a pair of chaps that might fit."

I've never been one to turn down a ride. Especially on one of these million-dollar babies. Karen found me a kids' pair of chaps that sort of fit.

"You can flop around backward on him, ride on his neck, whatever, he won't mind," Karen said, pointing to the gray in the first stall. "He can take a joke. He has to. You should see what he puts up with. If you've got the time and the inclination, you can ride the mare next to him. She doesn't have quite the sense of humor as the gray, but she won't hurt you. I don't want to be rude, but I gotta go. Shit, I like going to funerals about as much as I like cleaning sheaths."

"Just a second," I said. "One more question before my horse fix. Do you drive that truck by the side of the barn?"

"Another car question?" Karen said, "Jeez. Nope, I drive the black Beemer out back. That's the farm truck."

"Are the keys in it all the time?" I said. "And who can drive it?"

"I never take the keys out," Karen said. "That way they never get lost. Who can drive it? Anyone with a license, I guess, sometimes even without one. The barn help uses it sometimes, the boarders, some of the kids' mothers, whoever wants to take it can. Another theory brewing?"

I told her about my and Henry's near death experience of an automotive kind yesterday and what the gas station attendant said about a light-colored truck zooming by.

"Well, shit," Karen said, "that's about as helpful as an ice cube in winter. I know of at least five light-colored pickups without even sitting down to think, and that's not including Nilson and his old man's entire fleet of them. By the way, ride in the indoor, you won't get hit with the wind as bad."

I saddled up the gray gelding in the first stall. Moonstruck. I'd heard of him; he was always in the blues in the children's hunter division, packing around any squirmy kid they put on his back. I rubbed his face and blew into his nose.

"Ready, boy?"

Well, he didn't say no. So I led him down the ramp and into the indoor. I sunk up to my ankles in the soft footing. I reached down and ran a little of it through my fingers; ground-up running shoes, maybe? Whatever it was, I knew it would feel like riding on a pillow.

And it did. Between the luxurious footing and Moonstruck's air-ride trot, I felt like I'd gone to horsey heaven. Ahhh, I needed this. It'd been too long since I'd been astride; four days is pushing it for me. After that I get so unbearable, even I can't stand being with myself.

I trotted around the ring in circles and half-turns. All I had to do was lay my leg gently on his side and my wish was his command—the definition of a well-broke horse. These people may have been paying more each month than I earned a year in my first newspaper job, but at least they were getting something for their money. It takes a lot of work to get a horse this responsive.

His canter was smoother than his trot. I rocked around the ring, getting that good horse feeling. So what about Henry and Topping? So what about Candace? So what about the nasty e-mailer? So what that Lou'd just moved in with me forever? So what about anything? I leaned forward, eased both legs against his sides, and stretched him into a hand gallop. I felt the air whoosh by my face as the pace picked up. I'd have liked to be outdoors in a big grassy field with no possibility of groundhog holes; then again, I'd have also liked to have thighs about six inches longer and ten pounds lighter. I was on a horse and my legs worked. That was good enough for me.

Moonstruck seemed to be enjoying his gallop as much as I was. His ears were pricked and he needed little encouragement to march forward. We rounded the turn and his ears rotated back, then forward, then back. Horse radar, always scanning for bobcats or mountain lions or whatever predator considered them dinner way back when in the wilds. Even though horses have been domesticated for thousands of years, their fear-flight mechanism remains firmly coded in their DNA. Which is a fancy way to say a horse will spook at its own shadow or just about anything else.

"Easy, boy," I said, and slid my hand up and down his neck to take his mind off his ancestral foes. I sat a little deeper in the saddle, just in case my reassurance wasn't enough. It was. He settled down and I whoaed him into a trot, then a walk. I fed him the reins and let him stretch out his neck.

"Good, good, boy," I said, stretching out the words as I leaned forward and stroked his neck. We turned the same corner that had troubled him earlier. I started to sit back again, but before I got there, we both saw something out of the corners of our eyes. A piece of black plastic flapping by the window. Hard to believe a pricey place like this uses trash bags for storm windows.

I, as a human being, know plastic can do me no harm unless I wrap it around my face. Moonstruck didn't share my optimism. One good flap and it sent him flying into a major spook, which usually ends in a buck, or many a buck. I might've stayed on, but the wind must've picked up, because the flapping got louder. It didn't sound anything like a mountain lion to me, but who knew what was going on in Moonstruck's instinct-driven mind? He cracked his back and went straight up. So did I. That's where we parted company.

As usual, it took about three hours to hit ground. When you get dumped from a horse, your brain sends you into slo-mo. Three hours to wonder what body part you've broken this time. But instead of wham, it was more whoosh. That glorious footing. I tumbled onto the cushioned ground. Moonstruck, meanwhile, was still bucking around, beating back the imaginary mountain lion clawing at his throat. I stood up and, much to my delight, nothing hurt.

"Whoa, boy," I said. Right, whoa, boy to a bucking bronco. I watched his rodeo impersonation for another few minutes. Finally, he settled down and I caught him. I walked him over to the offending window to meet his plastic bag/bogeyman. To his relief and my surprise, it was gone, blown away to terrify another creature.

I led him back to the mounting block and got back on. Yes, I got back on. That's what horse-crazy people do, they get back on even if it means they'll be gliding through life in a wheelchair.

The rest of my ride was uneventful. Moonstruck was so tuckered out from his little outburst, he hardly wanted to trot, which was fine by me. I looked at the clock on the wall and it was later than I thought. As much as I wanted to, I couldn't spend my day riding. The humorless mare next to Moonstruck would have to wait for another jockey. I wrote a note to Karen, thanking her for the ride. "You were right about Moonstruck, he's quite the jokester. Thanks again, Nat."

I made sure everything was perfect—no saddle marks on Moonstruck's back or wisps of hay in the aisle—and then walked back to the Suburban. I opened the door and what did I find? A black plastic trash bag draped around my steering wheel with a note.

Horses spook over the stupidest things, don't they? Let Josane rest in peace or the next time, it won't just be a little fall. People can get killed riding, but you know that already, don't you?

CHAPTER 29

I should've been scared. But here's where the Polnyakoff curse comes in handy. I was too mad to be scared.

I got in the car, wadded up the black plastic, and threw it on the floor next to Henry's rosie tape.

Annie's wasn't far away, and I needed a shower and change of clothes. Plus I needed to sit down and come up with a plan before I wound up sharing the cold earth with Josane.

First thing to do, contact Margot, *The Appeal*'s cyberjock, and tell her things were getting serious up here and I really needed to track down my mystery e-mailer fast. I stormed in, slammed my purse on the foyer table, and headed for my laptop. It was on the bureau in my room, where I passed by a mirror. I was wearing a faceful of ground-up sneaker smudge, thanks to my tumble. I wiped my arm across my cheeks and walked down to the living room to plug into the telephonic umbilical cord.

Who should I find there, but Henry in his newsroom coverboy pose: phone planted to his right ear, fingers Fred Astairing across his keyboard.

"Huh?" I said. "Why aren't you cavorting in the musty, dusty archives of Loudoun County?"

He smiled, held up his index finger, and said, "Just a second, Nat."

Judging by the next thing I did, I'll be paying the Good Doctor half my discretionary earnings for the rest of my life.

"Gold delivery service for one Mr. Rose," I said, ignoring his ongoing conversation. "It's from your gardener."

I threw the CD in his lap and plunged myself down on the same chintz chair in which I'd done such a fine job with my mouth the first night.

I heard Henry wrapping up his conversation and then saw him hang up the phone. He picked up the CD and read the attached note.

His face reddened, about the same shade of rouge as his tattoo.

"What are you so angry about?" he said. "Did you see me throwing CDs around when you spent the night at Tony's?"

"That's different," I said.

"Oh, what's so different about it? Did you ever consider nothing happened between me and Toppy either?"

How'd he know Tony's "dawg wouldn't hunt" that night?

"Tony told you?"

He nodded. I thought guys only talk about football or gadgets. Certainly not the intimate—or, in this case, the would-be intimate—times of their life.

"Tony didn't want me to think he was standing in the way of the two of us. Little does he know you do a pretty good job of that yourself."

I leapt up from the chair. "What are you talking about, *I* do a pretty good job? What about *you*?"

"What *about* me?" Henry said, his face getting even redder. "What do you mean, what about you? Did I pick a fight with you on the way up here about whom I should interview? Did I trample on your story? Did I try to castrate you with a flying CD? So you tell me, Nattie, what about me? Never mind. Just forget it, forget I said anything. At least Toppy's agreeable."

"Yeah, so are guinea pigs," I said. If I'd really wanted to start World War III, I'd have added, "With about the same sexual appetite and rapidity—they screw anything that moves: brothers, fathers, gullible reporters."

But I shut up and slumped back into the chair, wishing I were any other place but here, sitting next to the most irritating man in the world.

Neither of us spoke, two stubborn mules dug in deep, until I, obviously the more actualized of the two, sliced through the silence.

"So what *are* you doing here?" I said finally. "And just for the record, what you did or didn't do with Topping Mundell isn't my business. For your—and Tony's—information, that's not why I'm so angry . . . at least not entirely."

"Candace again?" Henry said.

"I hadn't even considered that possibility," I said. "Unless Middleburg's our newest key penetration zone, I can't see her leaving her throne—even to murder me, which I'm sure is high on her wish list, right below the annihilation of *The Appeal*'s entire chain of command so she can assume control."

Henry walked over and sat down on the sofa next to me, his long legs skimming the edges of my knees. I'm not normally an aura seer, but a blind man could've sensed the charge dancing between us.

"Nattie," Henry said, "did someone try to hurt you? Is that what you're in such a rage about?"

I nodded and fished the note from my pocket. "Read this," I said. "This idiot made me fall off the horse I was riding. . . ."

"Riding a horse?"

Oh, man, I didn't want to go into it for that reason. I knew Henry thought I had better things to do than ride, and I didn't want to hear him say it again. But old Henry surprised me on two counts. One: After I told him how the ride came to be and he didn't say anything but "That's too bad someone spoiled it for you." And two: He expressed concern for my safety. *He was actu-*

ally worried about me. Unbelievable. Except up until that moment I hadn't been worried. If Henry was worried, I worried that I really had something to be worried about.

"You're obviously making someone very nervous with all your questions," Henry said. "Let's be careful. All right? From now on let me know where you're going and when you plan to be back."

"Henry," I said, "you're sounding like an editor."

"I'm sounding like your friend," Henry said as he leaned forward and brushed his fingers across my dirty cheek. "Like someone who cares about you more than you're willing to have someone care about you."

"You're right about that," I said, and caught his hand in mine. I held it against my face, and with my other hand I reached for him and brought him close to me.

Then I kissed him, slow and soft. I think it shocked both of us—literally and figuratively. I saw the surprise in his eyes and kissed him harder. The gold glitter was really swirling through me now. I felt like one of those snow globes. Henry was shaking me up pretty good, and judging by his reaction, he was pretty stirred himself.

Still kissing, I moved from the chair and pressed myself next to him. He leaned into me and slid us down onto the couch. We kissed and kissed and kissed and kissed. I hadn't been this steamed up in years. We were in our own little snowstorm, whited out from the rest of the world.

"Excuse me."

I was so disoriented, not only did I not know where I was, but whose voice that belonged to.

"I'm terribly sorry."

I caught my breath, opened my eyes, and remembered. Annie's. I was at Annie's and I knew whose voice that was.

"Mr. Duncan," I said.

"Bridge," he said.

"Bridge," I said, and paused long enough to get myself back into a normal breathing pattern so I didn't sound exactly like a panting dog in heat, and long enough to figure out what to say next. "Has the wind stopped? Still cold out?"

Henry, being a man, had other problems to worry about than breath. He sat back upright on the sofa, shifted around a little, and put his laptop on his lap, creating a new use for portable computers that even Bill Gates hadn't thought of.

Henry got himself all arranged and then said, "Bridge. Nice to see you. Nattie and I were just going over the principles of CPR."

Henry laughed and slipped into a surprisingly good Maxwell Smart imitation. "So you don't buy that. Would you believe that's how reporters talk to each other in North Carolina?"

Bridge chuckled or leered, depending on your perspective. Mine was leer. "Sorry to have interrupted your 'conversation,' " he said. "I'll just be a moment, then you can resume your 'talk.' "

I stood up. "Don't rush out on my account. I've got to get this grime off me."

I wobbled out on jelly legs to my room and blasted the cold water in the shower. That brought down my mercury pronto and got me thinking clearly again. What had I just done? How could I be so stupid? It's Henry and Topping, not Henry and Nattie. Digest that, Miss Act-First-and-Think-About-It-When-It's-Too-Late.

CHAPTER 30

"Okay," I said. "Back to the original question, why *are* you here and not there, in Leesburg, getting eyestrain, going over the books for clues?"

Henry was back in his reporter's pose; I was showered, grime-free, and cooled down; and Bridge was gone, probably to spread more propaganda about the benefits of smoking to third world countries and American children.

"Changing priorities," Henry said.

"All right, I'll bite, what do you mean by that?"

"I thought I'd postpone the record checking until tomorrow and look into these lung pieces," Henry said. "It's probably not that easy to get your hands on human organs. I'm hoping they can lead me to Benson's killer."

"You seem so sure he was killed by your wacko. What about that little girl's father? Karen said he was dangerous."

Henry took his reporter's notebook from the table. "Dangerous only to himself. That's where I went this morning, after I spoke with you. Here, listen to this." He scanned his notes and found the quote. " 'Most days, I can't even get out of bed. Then when I do, I go to her room and sit there. I start out when the sun rises and then it sets. I'm still there. I've got nowhere else to go now. I never will.' Nat, he didn't kill Jim Benson; he's incapacitated by his grief and he has a solid alibi—he was in the hospital recovering from a suicide attempt. He just got out yesterday, but I wouldn't be surprised if he's back there soon. Maybe you can get that man in touch with your contact from Compassionate Friends. I've never seen anyone suffer like he is. As a parent, I can't even imagine the pain. . . ."

"Don't," I said. "Spare yourself. At Compassionate Friends meetings the sorrow is so thick, you're choking on everyone's tears. Give me his name and I'll call Christine Motley today and ask her to call him."

"Thanks, Nattie."

I stood by the chair, Henry on the other side of the room by the telephone. That old, awkward silence. Someone had to bring IT up. Under the beating needles of icy water, I'd sworn to myself I'd undo what happened between Henry and me.

"Henry," I said. "About before. I got carried away. I guess if Bridge hadn't come in when he did, we'd be even sorrier."

"Sorry?" Henry said. "Why're you sorry?"

"For starters, we got caught acting like a couple of over-hormoned teenagers on Daddy's couch. Then there's that little matter of you and Topping Mundell. Then there's the even bigger matter of what could have happened. We can hardly let a paragraph pass between the two of us without you correcting me or me getting mad—and we were about to, about to . . ."

"Say it, Nattie, we were about to make love on the couch."

"Yes, that," I said. "I might not have put it so delicately."

"Well, what do you think we should do about it?" Henry said.

"I don't know," I said. This wasn't going in the direction I promised myself I'd take it. I could hear my resolve crackling. "I don't know."

You do too. Just tell him to zip it up and forget about it.

"I don't know," I said again, and completely forgot my script. I started winging it, talking first and, once again, not even thinking about it, completely forgetting any and all lessons I'd learned through life about why that's such a stupid way to operate. "Maybe we should go someplace for dinner and explore our options."

Henry smiled and was about to say something. Then he nodded his head backward and whispered, "Damn."

"Nattie," he said, "I would love to go to dinner with you, but—"

The big *but* I learned about in est.

I held up my hand. "Don't even bother to finish. Let me. *But* you promised *Toppy* you'd paint her windows or take out her garbage or show her your rose again."

"Nattie, just a second."

"Forget it, Henry. Just forget it. I have a job to do. And I can't forget I promised I'd help you with yours, now, can I?"

I stormed out of the room, back to mine. There was nothing to do there but brood. I went down the hall to Annie's room and knocked. She wasn't there and I went in to use her phone. Christine Motley picked up on the fourth ring.

We exchanged pleasantries.

"Nattie," she said. "Is anything wrong? You sound off or upset. Anything I can do?"

That put things in perspective. This woman had lived through the worst kind of pain and she was asking me about my little heartache.

"No, I'm fine," I said, and forced myself to mean it. Then I told her where I was, what I was working on, and about the man with the dead daughter.

"Give me his number," Christine said. "I'll call him as soon as we hang up. Then I'll call the chapter organizer up there and tell her about him. Nattie, don't expect much. Some people can never be reached. I worry that Reenie Ashmore might be one of them. I think it's wonderful of you to look into her daughter's death. Maybe an answer might help her find some peace. You never know what's going to help a person. . . . So how do you know this man?"

I told her I was here with Henry Goode and it was someone he'd met on a story.

"Henry Goode?" Christine said. "The reporter from the Bakker story? You're up there with him? How come? You two teaming up again?"

"Not likely anytime in the next century. We'd kill each other if we worked together on another story. And we might just do that anyway. No, this is Henry's gig."

I swore her to secrecy and told her about the list and the lung pieces.

"That's really creepy," Christine said. "Sending organs to people. Grief makes people do crazy things. In a funny way, grief is a lot like love: Both are enough to drive a sane person mad."

"Did you ever hit the nail on the head with that," I said.

"I thought that's what I heard in your voice," Christine said. "It must be Henry—you two hitting some bumps?"

"Bumps, that's an understatement. Try roadblocks the length of the Great Wall. Men, I just don't know if they're worth the effort."

Christine laughed. "Well, they are infuriating at times, but take a lesson from me, it's all worth the effort, every last second of every day. It's taken me years to realize that. When I lost Landon, I thought my life was over. I was right, in a way. Part of it was and always will be. There's a hole in my heart and I had to learn how to live without that piece of me. It took a long time and I almost killed myself and my marriage. I know it's one day at a time, but you also can't forget that one day there won't be another day after that. You know what I'm saying, Nattie? Or do I need a sledgehammer? Don't let the stupid things get in the way. Okay, I'll get off my soapbox now."

"Christine," I said. "You can get on your soapbox anytime you want with me. What you say is true, but you might need that sledgehammer to get it past the nasty little man in my head who keeps fouling me up."

Christine laughed harder. "Oh, you mean Jesse? I've got him too. I call him Jesse because he's a crafty cuss and every bit as nasty as our good senator. Just shout him down, Nattie."

She was right, and it was almost enough to make me go down-stairs to talk things over with Henry. Almost, except *my* Jesse had the floor and he was filibustering his sour little soul out.

When in dismay, distract. I focused my attention on work. Still to do: track down the e-mailer; interview the nurse at the hospital who saw Josane, and while I was in Warrenton, drop in on Josane's lawyer-possible-paramour Snowden Cox; call the feed store to see if Lannie was delivering feed to the barn when the plastic bag flapper sent me nosefirst into the dust; ditto for Flip, see if he was there then; find out why Topping told that little fib about Josane's helmet; and, if I started feeling a little more magnanimous toward Henry, call my brother, Larry, to find out what his mad botanist client does for a tobacco company; and finally, find my old boyfriend John and ask him how an artist can be tangled up with the tobacco industry.

Distractions, nothing better—other than being on a horse—to soothe the tormented soul of the love lost.

I called work. No luck, as I knew it would be. But it was worse than I thought: Margot not only wasn't due in for another four or five hours, but was taking a couple of vacation days. I hooked up my laptop and tried to find her in cyberspace. She hadn't e-mailed back to me yet and I sent her another message labeled URGENT, MIGHT BE GETTING IN OVER MY HEAD HERE.

There was a small blessing, I had no e-mail waiting. Seeing me sploosh in the indoor must've quelled my anxious murderer for the moment.

The man at the feed store said Lannie couldn't come to the phone, that she was delivering grain. "Where?" I asked as inno-cently as possible.

"Over around The Plains, Aldie, and Middleburg. I think Summer Ridge, Plain Bay, and Woodhall farms are on today's route."

Summer Ridge, she'd been there. The question was, when? When I was riding? The question was the same for Flip. I called the barn and let the phone ring for what seemed forever. I knew Charlie and Karen were at the funeral. Finally someone picked up; it was Flip's voice. I hung up and hoped he didn't have call tracking.

Either of them could've done it. Or neither of them.

I called the hospital; the nurse wasn't due in for another hour. The same for my brother, Larry. And I didn't feel like talking to Topping at the moment. Nothing left to do, but THE call.

John and I hadn't spoken since that night at Northern Lights in New Paltz, many years—and tears—ago. I called his number— yes, I still remembered, it was tattooed in my memory—and an old man with a thick Spanish accent answered. He could barely speak English, so he had no idea who or where John Osborne was. Next, I called a mutual friend of ours who told me John had moved to New York City a few years ago and gave me his work number.

"Work as in studio?" I said.

"No, work as in work. Office, tie, showing up at nine and saying 'How high?' when they tell you to jump. Here's his number."

It didn't sound like the John I knew. I called and an efficient voice answered announcing a long string of names. John's wasn't one of them.

"I'd like to talk to John Osborne, please."

"One moment, please." I wasn't sure if I was talking to a human or a machine. A few seconds later it came back on. "Mr. Osborne is in our Washington office today, the number is . . ."

He was in Washington D.C., the nation's capital, a mere fifty miles away. That's the closest we'd been to each other since I moved south. I called the Washington number and I swear the same voice answered, announcing the same long string of names.

"John Osborne," I said.

"One moment please."

What to say to someone with whom the last conversation you had ended in a blubbering, embarrassing, humiliating cry?

"John Osborne."

"So it is," I said. "Guess who this is? I'll give you one clue: I threw out the turquoise scarves."

"Nattie? Is that really you?"

"Me, in the telephonic," I said.

"Damn, I loved those turquoise scarves. I've never had a night like that since—"

I'd shot myself in the foot enough for one day, so I didn't tell him he should have thought about that when he told me we'd lost that magic tingle.

"That's why God invented memory," I said. "So how've you been?"

We gave each other abbreviated rundowns on our lives. I told him I was in Upperville trying to find a dead woman's murderer. He didn't go into his job, so I led him there.

"John, you know me, I'm not one to dance around. Let me ask you flat out: What the hell is your connection to tobacco? I thought you were going to be the next Edward Hopper."

Silence. No retort on his part. Finally he said, "Nattie, you do cut right through the bullshit. How could I forget that? I'm glad to hear you stayed on your track—chasing murderers, that's impressive."

I hadn't told him the fashion part.

"Only impressive on the right days," I said. "Back to tobacco. Last time I knew you, you were a painter."

"I was, you're right," John said. "Then I started looking at forty and forty didn't look too good poor. My car—remember that car you forced me to buy so at least I'd have something to show for what little money I made?—was falling apart. I was still living in that same little duplex in Plattekill . . . I don't know what happened, I got tired of living that way. . . . Look, I've got a meeting in

271

a few minutes and I'm not close to ready. You're in Upperville? Isn't that just outside Middleburg? How about dinner tonight? I'll come get you. How's seven-thirty?"

The other little man in my head—the one who thinks he's protecting me—was bounding off the insides of my skull walls screaming, "No, no, no!! What are you, a certified lunatic? Think I'm going to sweep up the bloody mess when he rips you apart again?"

I pushed him back to let him duke it out with Jesse.

"Seven-thirty's fine," I said, and gave him the directions.

CHAPTER 31

Next to beige and taupe, I hate confrontation more than anything in the world. So I slipped out the side door, closing it
silently behind me.

As I backed away, Henry came out the front door. He didn't
make a dash for me, and I wouldn't have stopped if he had.

I looked in the rearview mirror at Henry standing there. I
wasn't so far that I couldn't see the deep wrinkle of his brow. What
was it that was making him look like a shar-pei: hurt, confusion,
surprise, anger, or all of the above?

Later. I'd find out later, when we'd both cooled down. I'd
already planned my route, a sure sign something was wrong with
me. Looking at a map and plotting my course was one more distraction I could pile atop the others, one more way to avoid the
obvious: I was acting like a stupid idiot.

After a couple of wrong turns—so much for planning—I
found my way to Warrenton. I still had time before the nurse
showed up for duty, so I headed directly to Snowden Cox's office,
hoping a small-town lawyer might be in his office with no clients
crying about missed child support. I drove through Warrenton's
imitation of New Jersey, a run of suburban strip development on
either side of the highway, wondering when the charm was going
to kick in. I'd heard Warrenton was beautiful. So far, only to a
developer. Then I saw the signs to the old town Warrenton and
pointed the nose of the Suburban that way. Things were looking
better: old, gracious homes lopsided by time, hugging the sides of

the narrow streets; towering trees arching to the heavens and front porches so welcoming, I could taste the sweet tea. I could see Reynolds Price, who as far as I'm concerned perfected the art of writing, growing up here, learning the beauty of life.

I found Cox's office easier than I'd imagined. It was around the corner from the old Warrenton courthouse.

I parked—hallelujah! there was a space big enough right in front—and walked across the brick courtyard to Cox's office. If Henry were here, I'd have to eat crow. I made a big fuss about this being the North, though technically the South. I stand corrected. I was in the South. Here's why: "What can I do to help you? You want to see Mr. Cox? Well, just sit down one second. I'll see if I can't get you in right now. Can I get you some coffee or something?"

It was Snowden Cox's secretary and I felt like I was taking a first-class ride on the Concorde—or at the Harris Teeter checkout line on Randolph Road in Charlotte. I don't know if it's in the water or what, but southerners take this graciousness stuff seriously. Even my grandmother—the original red-haired hot-tempered Polnyakoff—hadn't been able to pick a fight with anyone when she'd come to visit me. I think it was the first time in her life she'd gone through a day without threatening to get someone fired or screaming, "Your wife should be a widow."

I declined the coffee. I didn't want to be jangling when I talked to Cox. In less than a minute she was back, leading me into his office, a standard lawyer's office with the standard mahogany leather high-back armchair behind the standard desk and in front of the standard bookshelf filled with the standard law books. He could've used my stepfather David's touch. David used to decorate showrooms at the High Point furniture market and did the same for my mother's law office. By the time he'd finished, everyone was talking about it so much, *North Carolina Lawyer* ran pictures of it in their Christmas issue.

"What can I do for you, Miss Gold?"

Snowden Cox was sitting in his chair, but I could still tell he was a tall man, very tall. I'd guess six-three or better. He had dark, curly hair, a long face, long nose, dark eyes, and the longest set of eyelashes I'd ever seen on a man. He had no gray, no lines, and no sagging jowl. I'd put him in his late thirties to early forties, possibly older if he was sporting a good set of genes.

I could see what Josane saw in him, especially in contrast to Flip, who with his white-blond hair and glacier eyes was all hard edges and right angles. Snowden Cox seemed to be a man smoothed down with a fine-grade sandpaper, from his soft hot-cocoa voice to his deep brown corduroy eyes.

"I'm a reporter for *The Charlotte Commercial Appeal*," I started to say, and then launched into my spiel, ending with the official *Appeal*'s I'm-doing-a-story-about . . .

"Josane Ashmore," he said. "Now, there's someone I think about often. Her poor mother, how is she?"

"Not very well," I said. "She's having a hard time getting over Josane's death and thinks maybe her daughter was murdered."

"I know, I know," he said. "I even looked into it myself. Thought I owed Josane at least that much. I'm afraid it's a pretty straight call: riding accident, head injury. I wish I could help you more."

"Mr. Cox, would you mind answering a few questions?"

"Call me Snowden, please. I've got about ten or fifteen spare minutes before my next appointment, they're all yours." His smile was as soft and reassuring as his eyes. He must have seemed like a warm blanket to Josane—which I didn't get into right away.

I asked about Josane's husband and the divorce. Any acrimony? Fights over money, split property, jealousy? Anything?

"No, the hardest part was arranging around his schedule. He traveled a lot for his job; as I recall, he sold sports equipment. There was no acrimony between them, just the opposite. They'd started out as very good friends, and that's how they ended up. He wouldn't have hurt her, if that's what you're thinking. I think it was he who planted the murder idea in Josane's mother's mind. Just a few days before his death, he called to tell me he had some new leads he was pursuing. Funny, I remember what he said, 'I'm really onto something now, I think this is it.' Naturally, that piqued my curiosity. He told me he hadn't told Josane's mother about it because he didn't want to get her hopes up until he was sure, but he was close to sure. He didn't want to go into it on the phone and he couldn't come in that day. He said he had to go to Richmond, I assumed on business. Then the next thing I heard, he died in a car crash."

I could see the goose bumps rise on my arms. Another damn body. This was turning out to be my own private Vietnam. When was the count going to stop?

I got the necessary details about Josane's husband—name, address, etc.—and moved on to Lannie Post.

"That double date? I did it as a favor to Josane," Snowden said. "At first it was fun, she was a pleasant-enough woman. But it went quickly downhill toward the end when it got embarrassing. Then the telephone calls started and the visits to my office and my house. I did feel sorry for her, but after a while she got to be such a nuisance, I didn't know what to do."

"What stopped her pursuit of you?"

Snowden looked down at his desk, at his hands held together, his fingers entwined. He raised his two index fingers and started tapping them against each other. I half expected him to say, *Here's the church, here's the steeple, but where are all the people?*

"Snowden," I said. "Does this have anything to do with the morning before Josane died?"

That shifted his gaze in a hurry. His steepled fingers froze and he looked up at me.

"How do you know about that?"

"It made sense, a lucky guess, whatever," I said. "Flip told me about coming in on Josane and someone. He didn't know who that someone was."

"Getting involved with a client, well, it wasn't the smartest thing I've ever done," Snowden said. "The thing about Josane was, she was irresistible. Everything about her. She was a remarkable woman. I often think if she hadn't died . . . No sense in that. Anyway, that morning Josane came to my office, we went for coffee, then back to her house. We were there for about an hour when Flip came. Josane knew by the knock on the door it was him. She made me promise to stay in the bedroom. She didn't want a fight to start. Flip's somewhat of a hothead and we were in a, well, a compromising situation. I also didn't think it was necessary to rub Flip's nose in our business. Josane had told me she'd just ended her relationship with him, primarily because he'd become too possessive. She and I had commiserated about that, because I recently ended a similar relationship."

Snowden stood up and walked to the window. I was wrong; Henry was six-three and it looked like Snowden had a couple of inches on him.

"What about when Lannie came?" I said.

"All hell broke loose," Snowden said. "Lannie was screaming at Flip, threatening to kill him right there if he hurt Josane. Finally Flip left. That's when I came out. At this point Lannie was calling me five or six times a day, so you can imagine what happened when she saw me coming out of Josane's bedroom. She was uncontrollable, shrieking about being betrayed. I wanted to call an ambulance and have her sedated or something, but Josane wouldn't hear of it. She got her calmed down by agreeing to have dinner with Lannie that night. Finally she left."

"Was Josane upset?"

"No, not really," Snowden said. "Josane had a—what would be the best way to describe it—a buoyant personality. I stayed for another hour or so. By the time I had to leave, we'd entirely forgotten about the intrusion. Both of us were very happy. I'm sure it would have been the beginning of something that could have lasted. . . . We made plans to spend that weekend at the Inn at Little Washington. . . ."

That explained Josane's giddy mood at the barn. Karen, the barn manager, had been right. So Snowden Cox was the new man in her life. Too bad for her, he could've been a keeper.

"I know you think it was a riding accident," I said. "But given the dramatic outbursts—Flip marching around like a banty cock and Lannie doing her *Fatal Attraction* imitation—don't you think it's possible one of them could have been angry enough to kill Josane? What makes you so sure it wasn't murder?"

Snowden walked to the chair next to mine and sat down. "Nothing makes me so sure of anything. I specialize in family law—divorce, custody, things like that. I can't tell you how many distraught people I deal with day in and day out, screaming, threatening, and the like. In fifteen years, no one has yet to carry through on a threat. People get swept away in the heat of the moment and say anything. Haven't you ever done that? Does that mean you're capable of murder?"

Was he reading my mind? How'd he know about me and Henry?

Snowden continued. "I suppose it is possible that Josane could've been murdered. But it's unlikely, given the autopsy report and facts of the case. That's what I've told her mother repeatedly. She just doesn't want to hear that answer. I'd be very surprised if I were wrong. But let me ask you this, is it going to bring Josane back to life? Is it going to give me that weekend with her that we planned, or maybe even a life together? Is it going to make her mother stop crying?"

"No," I said.

Snowden looked at his watch, and I knew my ten or fifteen minutes were coming to a close.

"Two more questions," I said. "Then I'll be out of your hair. Do you know who put the money up for Josane's store and bought her horse? Did she ever mention a rich, appreciative older man?"

Snowden shook his head. "No, she never did. I always assumed she came from a wealthy family. She had that demeanor and she traveled in very rarefied circles. She had a Christmas card on her mantel from Prince Albert of Monaco. It said something like 'Dear Josie, thanks for the gift, I'm looking forward to seeing you at the spring races. . . .' And money was never an issue in her divorce. She didn't even ask for alimony or split property. But since her death I've heard the same rumors. Everyone from Jack Kent Cooke to Paul Mellon was supposed to have been her secret lover who gave her unlimited funds. I'm sorry, I don't have any answers for you in that area."

"If you hear anything, let me know," I said. "Investigative Journalism 101: Follow the money. Anyway, one more thing. Do you know a woman by the name of Topping Mundell?"

A surprised look washed over his face. "Of course I do. I met Josane through Toppy; we used to be engaged."

She does get around, that Topping. "Really?" I said. "What happened? A mutual parting of the ways?"

"Mutual? In retrospect, probably. Though at the time Toppy might not have agreed. We ended our engagement about six or nine months before Josane died. We weren't getting along well, there's a fairly large age difference between us, and though Toppy's a wonderful woman, I think she needed to grow up a little more, maybe be on her own some, before she married."

"How'd you two leave it? Friendly?"

"Of course," Snowden said. "I see her at the Middleburg Hunt Club Ball. We dance. We talk. Share a glass of wine. Then we smile and move on to the next person."

CHAPTER 32

Back to New Jersey, or Warrenton's imitation of it. I left the old part of town and made my way to Fauquier Hospital, named after the county of. A strange name, given to adolescent giggly mispronunciations. Being many chronological years beyond adolescence, I stifled my giggle when I first heard it pronounced by someone with enough of a drawl to make it sound like the two words I said more than any other two words the year before my mother got remarried. The two words that got me kicked out of camp and several F's in citizenship.

Fauquier Hospital sits atop a large hill that erupts with no warning straight out of the flatland below, looking like an aggravated and swollen pimple on a fifteen-year-old's face. At the peak is a redbrick collection of sharp right angles and glass. It would be easy to mistake the place for a Holiday Inn, with its rectangular drive-under portichere and motel-modern architecture.

Sarah Carpenter, the nurse in question, still worked in the ER. And this being the South, the nurses couldn't have been nicer when I came in looking for her.

"That's her there, hon," one of them said, pointing down the hall, where a tallish woman with a pear-shaped figure stood. She had dark brown hair, pale skin, large wire-rimmed glasses, and an easy smile. I'd say she was in her early thirties.

I introduced myself.

"Josane Ashmore?" she said. "Was that that real pretty girl

they brought in here? Must be four years or so ago. A riding accident, right?"

"That's what everyone says," I said. "Good memory you've
got."

"Well, we get lots of riding accidents. Broken bones, mostly. So
when someone dies that way, you tend to remember it. And that
girl, she was hard to forget. Lord, she was pretty. I think someone
said she was a Miss something in the Miss America Pageant."

"Miss Connecticut," I said. "Do you also remember her
mother? She probably looked a lot like her daughter. Do you
remember her talking to you about Josane's death?"

"Sure I do," Sarah Carpenter said. "Working in the emergency room, I deal with a lot of grieving parents, and I haven't forgotten one of them. Seeing a person in that kind of pain stays with
you. I think it's the biggest reason nurses shift to other floors. I've
about had it myself. Yes, I do remember that girl's mother. And
you're right, she did look a lot like her daughter. She came in a few
days later, asking me questions about what her daughter's body
looked like and was she hurt anywhere else but her head. She
didn't want to accept the fact that her daughter was gone. I see that
all the time and I can't blame them one bit. Not one bit."

I could see why this woman went into nursing. She was calm
and soothing and compassionate. Too bad she hadn't gone to
medical school. The world could use a few more doctors like her.

"Josane's mother said you mentioned a funny smell?"

The nurse scrunched her mouth on one side and looked up.
"A smell, a smell, hmmm. Let me think. She was asking so many
questions, she seemed so desperate for anything. A smell? Oh, I
remember now. Her mother asked if anything, anything at all,
seemed odd. The only thing I could come up with was a faint,
peculiar odor. But I told her mother, it could've come from the
blanket she was wrapped in or even another person, maybe one of
the EMTs who was working on her daughter."

"Do you remember what the smell was?"

"It's going to sound silly. But I thought she smelled a little like my grandmother."

A grandmother smell? For me that would be brisket and Joy and peppermint Chiclets. Who knows what her grandmother's peccadilloes were. Maybe she'd been a hard drinker and smelled of Johnnie Walker Red. Or maybe she just had that sad-old-lady nursing-home smell: part decay, part talcum powder, part denture cream, part dried tears.

"Was there anything more specific about the smell?" I asked. "A kind of perfume, a specific odor? Or a mustiness?"

"My grandmother was a very fastidious woman," she said. "Her house was immaculate and so was she. But she smoked occasionally. And even though everything she wore was fresh pressed or freshly dry-cleaned, she always had a faint ashtray odor to her, mixed with whatever perfume she wore. She'd be mortified to hear me say it, but it's true. You know how smells sometimes make you think of people or places? Well, when I leaned over Josane, for some reason all I could think about was my grandmother. It wasn't until a couple days later, when her mother came to talk to me, that I realized why."

So Josane had smelled of cigarettes. Not a big deal if she was a smoker. I thanked Sarah, gave her my card, asked her to call me if she thought of anything else, and then found a pay phone.

"Snowden," I said. "Thanks for taking the call. Just one quick question. Did Josane smoke cigarettes?"

He laughed. "Josane smoke? Hardly. She was a rampant anti-smoker and thought cigarettes should be banned. She hated cigarette smoke. She refused to let Lannie smoke in her store and made Flip stand outside of the car when he smoked."

So Flip and Lannie were both smokers. Figures. They both had access to white trucks too, along with half of Middleburg. No one said this was going to be easy, and I'd been a fool to promise Candace a story by the end of the week.

CHAPTER 33

I'd have liked to walk around the old part of Warrenton, possibly hit a tack store or two. But it was dark and I wanted to find my way back to Annie's in time to at least change and at most make myself as irresistible as God-givenly possible. I didn't want John, or at least didn't think I did, but I wouldn't mind him wanting me.

Henry's car was gone, so was Duncan's. Annie was rushing out and I was rushing in.

"I'm going out to dinner with an old friend, don't know when I'll be back," I called to her.

Annie smiled wide. I knew that smile, it was her hot-man-on-a-hook smile. "Me too," she said. "Except I know when I'll be back—tomorrow. See ya. . . ."

I ran upstairs, figured out what to wear, and plugged in. "You have mail."

I held my breath and looked at the return addresses. Finally a turn for the better. Two notes from Margot.

NATTIE, I HOPE YOU KNOW HOW TO SWIM. AFRAID I CAN'T HELP MUCH WITH YOUR NASTY E-MAIL. IT CAME THROUGH SOMETHING CALLED AN ANONYMOUS REMAILER, ALSO CALLED AN ANONYMOUS SERVER. THESE SERVICES LET YOU SEND ELECTRONIC MAIL TO A PERSON WITHOUT THE RECIPIENT KNOWING YOUR NAME OR YOUR E-MAIL ADDRESS BY STRIPPING AWAY YOUR REAL NAME AND ADDRESS AND REPLACING IT WITH A DUMMY ADDRESS. THEY'RE SET UP

FOR LEGIT PURPOSES—MAYBE YOU'RE POSTING ON A CON-
TROVERSIAL BULLETIN BOARD OR WANT TO BE A WHISTLE-
BLOWER, WHATEVER. SO FAR THERE'RE ABOUT A DOZEN
PUBLIC REMAILERS ON THE INTERNET. YOURS CAME BY WAY
OF THE BEST-KNOWN ANONYMOUS REMAILER, A SERVICE
RUN BY A GUY NAMED JOHAN HELSINGIUS WHO'S PRESIDENT
OF A HELSINKI, FINLAND, COMPANY THAT HELPS BUSI-
NESSES CONNECT TO THE INTERNET. YOU CAN TELL YOURS
CAME THROUGH HIS SERVICE BY THE ADDRESS; HIS ALL END
WITH @ANON.PENET.FIR.

I KNOW YOU, NATTIE, AND I KNOW YOU'RE SITTING
THERE ASKING WHY SOMEONE WOULD RUN THIS KIND OF
SERVICE. THEY OBVIOUSLY CAN'T CHARGE FOR IT, SINCE
EVERYTHING IS ANONYMOUS, SO LET ME PASS ALONG
HELSINGIUS'S QUOTE FROM *WIRED* MAGAZINE:

"IT'S IMPORTANT TO BE ABLE TO EXPRESS CERTAIN
VIEWS WITHOUT EVERYONE KNOWING WHO YOU ARE. . . .
LIVING IN FINLAND, I GOT A PRETTY CLOSE VIEW OF HOW
THINGS WERE IN THE FORMER SOVIET UNION. IF YOU ACTU-
ALLY OWNED A PHOTOCOPIER OR EVEN A TYPEWRITER
THERE, YOU WOULD HAVE TO REGISTER IT AND THEY
WOULD TAKE SAMPLES OF WHAT YOUR TYPEWRITER WOULD
PUT OUT SO THEY COULD IDENTIFY IT LATER. THAT'S
SOMETHING I FIND SO APPALLING. THE FACT THAT YOU
HAVE TO REGISTER EVERY MEANS OF PROVIDING INFORMA-
TION TO THE PUBLIC SORT OF PARALLELS IT, LIKE SAYING
YOU HAVE TO SIGN EVERYTHING ON THE NET. WE ALWAYS
HAVE TO BE ABLE TO TRACK YOU DOWN."

I GUESS HE'S YOUR BASIC ULTIMATE LIBERTARIAN AND
HE DOES HAVE A GOOD POINT. AMERICANS ARE GETTING
BASHED PRETTY BADLY THESE DAYS ON THE INTERNET
WITH OUR FIXATION ON CONTROLLING THINGS. HOWEVER,
IN OUR DEFENSE IT SURE WOULD BE NICE TO BE ABLE TO

TRACK DOWN THIS LOOSE CANNON FOR YOU. SORRY, I
TRIED, MARGOT.

Margot, take two.

NATTIE, HI, IT'S ME AGAIN. I JUST HEARD FROM A CYBERBUDDY
IN DENMARK WHO KNOWS HELSINGIUS AND WILL TALK TO HIM
ABOUT YOUR MESSAGE. MAYBE HE CAN GET US A PARTIAL TRACK.
I'LL LET YOU KNOW TOMORROW. I HOPE YOU'RE AT LEAST
HALFWAY THROUGH THAT STORY YOU'RE WORKING ON, BECAUSE
CANDACE HAS ALREADY PROMISED IT FOR PAGE ONE ON SUNDAY.

It looked as if I might have to make an emergency beg-call to
Gary Stockwell the ME. But that was tomorrow's issue. Tonight's
was getting through dinner without doing myself further psycho-
logical damage.

One more electronic umbilical hookup and I'd be ready. I
punched in 1-800-555-6459, *The Appeal*'s toll-free line we've been
told over and over costs fifty cents a call and aggravates our general manager whenever we use it. I hit the retrieval code for my
voice mail. Maybe my stalker was branching out into new media.
Also as *The Appeal*'s official fashion arbiter, I had to see what
fashion questions someone couldn't live without having answered
pronto. I'd already spent a couple hours tracking down the fashion
show wedding finale burner submitted to me on Christmas Day
from our reader in Gastonia. All the designer houses agreed with
the gum popper who answered the phones at Isaac Mizrahi:
"Symbolism, honey, a new beginning, start of something special.
Ha, special. Weddings, marriage, whoever thought that up, sending brides down the runway at the end of the shows, has never
been married, I'll tell you that."

There were no fashion questions awaiting me this time. I guess
everyone had their outfits picked for New Year's Eve. But I did

have three messages. The first from Gail, who was the giggliest I'd ever heard her. What did Allie do, the perfect lead change?

"I miss you, Nattie, and so does Brenda, and believe it or not, even Rob has mentioned your name. Good luck at the clinic with Georgie."

Georgie? What drugs was she on? Then I found out.

"By the by, guess who I've been going out with? Or more to the point, staying in with."

Now, that, as they say in the South, caught me upside the head in a hurry. I knew what high she was on. This drug was more exhilarating, more powerful, more addictive, and more dangerous than anything a chemist could cook up: the love drug. And when Gail got hooked, she got spectacularly hooked. Oh, boy, oh, boy, who this time?

"Give up?" she said. "I'll give you a hint. Click, click. Still can't get it? One more hint—he may be missing a finger, but he knows how to use his other nine just fine."

Wham, upside the head again. Torkesquist! She was messing around with Torkesquist, *The Appeal*'s crazy shooter. This would either end in a double murder or God only knows what. Speaking of, take care of her, would you?

Next came Henry's voice on the phone. "Nattie, this is ridiculous. We're acting like children. I agreed to go to Topping's house for dinner because she said her father had more to tell me. It's business. About the CD, I *told* her about the tattoo. Told, as in words. She asked me what was the stupidest thing I'd ever done and I mentioned the tattoo. Can we get past this now? Okay? Interesting news on the lung. Apparently human organs are not that easy to come by. The sender's probably involved in the medical profession, most likely pathology. Either a doctor or an autopsy technician, uncharitably known in the business as a deiner. It comes from the German word 'to serve.' And after hearing what they do, I can see why. Once the pathologist finishes, the deiner takes over, removing the organs, sewing up the body, and cleaning up the whole mess afterward. This should narrow things down considerably. If I don't see you tonight, which I hope to, then I'll see you tomorrow at the Loudoun County courthouse."

Like Scarlett said, tomorrow is another day. Maybe then I could act close to my age, and if not that, then at least half of it.

I hit the button for the last message, praying it wasn't a death threat. A person can take only so many assaults in one day. Whew, it was from Christine Motley.

"Hi, Nattie. Well, I spoke to Henry's man who lost his daughter. I wish I had better news to report, but he's in a bad way. We'll do our best, though sometimes that's not enough. That's not the only reason I'm calling. Something popped in my mind that might interest Henry. I have a friend whose father died of lung cancer last year. She used to talk to me about grieving. I suppose I've become something of an expert in that area. I remembered something she told me, a story about someone contacting her, asking her to join a group for families of lung cancer victims. At that point they were pursuing legal retribution, a big class action suit. Then about six months later she told me she dropped out of the group because it turned ugly. She said there was too much anger and finger-pointing for her and she didn't like being in the same room with some of the other members. I distinctly remember her using the word *dangerous*, that two in particular seemed dangerous. Anyway, maybe this has something to do with that list. If Henry wants, I'll call her and see if she'd be willing to talk more about it to Henry. I hope things have gotten back on track with you two. God bless."

Between Henry's deiner theory and Christine's news, maybe, just maybe, he'd be catching himself a killer. I should be so lucky.

I still had some time before I saw John. Rather than pace or sweat, I pulled out the pictures Topping gave to me. I looked at the smiling Josane. What a waste, all that beauty rotting in the earth. I flipped through the photos. Josane had a bod, all right, and she wasn't shy about showing it. In one picture she was wearing a lime-green scoop-neck shirt small enough to wrap around her curves, which were considerable.

"Talk to me, Josane, tell me what happened. Give your poor mother some peace."

Great, now I'm talking to pictures. You know what they say about desperate times demanding desperate measures.

"Come on, Josane."

I listened hard, hoping for a celestial whisper. What I heard was the wind blowing the trees outside. Heavenly Morse code? Hardly. I was about to put the pictures away, when I saw something that hadn't registered before. In the green-shirt photo I saw something gleaming around her neck, a few inches above her cleavage. A necklace. I brought the picture up close and looked harder. I couldn't be sure without a magnifying glass, but it looked an awful lot like two horseshoes hammered into a heart with a glittering something inside, an awful lot like the exact same necklace that had been dangling around Lannie's neck.

CHAPTER 34

"Country Cookin'? We haven't seen each other for more than three years and we're eating here, at an all-you-can-eat mashed potatoes and gravy bar in Warrenton?"

"I thought you liked kitsch?"

"On my budget, kitsch is great. On your budget, the Inn at Little Washington would be nice. *I* don't work for the biggest advertising company in the free world, I work for the cheapest newspaper chain in America."

"Next time, the Inn at Little Washington. I promise."

"What next time? There's not going to be a next time. This is your basic catch-up-with-our-lives and let-me-grill-you dinner. Our next times ended three years ago, remember?"

Twenty minutes together, and we were fighting like, well, like Henry and I fight. Lest anyone think me an argumentative type, let me say in my defense, this isn't how it was back when between the two of us. We didn't fight because we just didn't have that much to talk about. I don't know why the love bug bit me so bad for this guy, but it had. Given our few mutual interests and sparse conversations, it was just as well we'd gone our separate ways. It took me only three years and about $13,000 in Good Doctor bills to reach that conclusion.

John had given me a big hug when he saw me at Annie's. And I'm glad to report I felt not one tingle, not even a hint of the old let's-skip-dinner-and-move-right-to-the-bedroom business that once ran our lives. It was like hugging my brother. John looked pretty much the same: tall—I always go for tall men; good bones—I always go for good bones; and put together from the Mayflowerian genetic pool—I always go for Wasps.

"Okay, we're sitting at the restaurant of your choice," I said. "Can you tell me your tobacco connection now, or do I have to eat a plate of greens first?"

John started to talk, but the waitress came over. We ordered— the vegetable bar for me, a sirloin for him. The place was so crowded with people milling around the buffet line and waiting to get a table, we had to shout our order.

"Let's get a salad," John said. "I'll tell everything while we wait in line."

Judging by the length of it, he could read me *War and Peace.*

We got in behind a lady with big blond hair who was squeezed into a tight purple sweatsuit with gold appliqué flowers all over it, proving my theory that the yentas of Miami Beach and country folk were separated at birth. The only real difference was how they came by their matching wardrobes: The country folk made theirs in Thursday night craft class at MJDesigns, whereas the yentas bought theirs at Burdine's.

"I'm waiting. . . ." I said.

"God, Gold, I forgot how relentless you are. Listen, this isn't something I'm especially proud of. Twenty years ago, if someone had told me I'd be doing this, I'd have punched him in the nose. I know it's my fault, it's just that life has a funny way of taking strange turns. . . ."

"John, skip the mea culpa preamble and just tell me. How bad could it be? You're not designing propaganda for the Moral Majority, are you?"

He hung his head and muttered, "Worse than that."

I put my arm around him—in a sisterly way only. "Come on, John, I won't judge you, just tell me."

"Paul Polar."

"Huh?" I said.

"Paul Polar. Polar Lights. Seen him on any billboards, buses, scoreboards lately? Sure you have. He's that ultracool polar bear trying get everyone to try Polar Lights, the number-one selling cigarette in the eighteen-to-twenty-five-year age group. It's probably the number-one selling cigarette in the ten-to-eighteen-year category, but we don't track that age group. Why would we? *Our campaign is not designed to lure in young smokers.* Sure, they told me to draw a comic book character because they were going after the mature smokers."

"You?" I said. "You draw that? What a slimebag you've become. Just so you can drive that fancy Lexus around and feel like an Important Guy? Jesus H. Christ, John, have you no conscience?"

"Nattie, two minutes ago you said you wouldn't judge me."

"That was two minutes before I found out you'll be personally responsible for more than three million deaths a year when these kids age up in the lung-cancer-candidate category. I suddenly lost my appetite. I'll see you at the table."

I sat back down. John was right. Life does have a funny way of taking strange turns. I couldn't believe I ever shed a tear for this guy.

A while later John came back carrying two plates.

"Here," he said. "I think I remembered what you like."

I didn't look at him. Instead, I watched the waitresses trying to get trays full of food to the tables while stop-and-go weaving their way around clumps of people. It was like watching traffic in New York City. Surely the food would be cold by the time they made it through the gridlock.

"I've been wrestling with this since I took the job," John said. "Some days I'm ready to quit. But it's the old velvet handcuffs . . . Come on, Nattie, haven't you ever compromised your journalistic goals. Just a little?"

That got my attention. I hadn't told him about my other

newspaper hat—the frivolous chapeau of fashion writer I wear on most days.

"All right, all right," I said. "I'll talk—and eat. Thanks for the plate. Even I have to admit, the vegetables look good. So, gotten any weird mail lately? Possibly a hunk of human lung?"

John dropped his fork and it clattered to the floor.

"I'll take that as a yes, then," I said.

"How'd you know?"

I filled him in on Henry's list and the other murders.

"Oh, shit," he said. "I could be next."

I shook my head. "Probably not. You're lucky this person seems to have a strong anal retentive side. So far he or she seems fixated on alphabetical order. Last I heard, the nutcase was up to D. But you never know."

Just then the waitress came. "Sorry it took so long, I could barely get to y'all."

She placed John's steak and mashed potatoes with a heavy dose of gooey brown gravy in front of him. "Enjoy your meal," she said.

"Right," I said.

John dug into his food like a starving man, gulping down the bites so he'd have something to do other than talk to me.

Just like old times—we had nothing to say to each other. But this time it wasn't for lack of a topic. He came up for air once to say, "I never tasted sweet mashed potatoes before. Boy, do they put sugar in everything in the South?"

I shrugged. I wasn't about to chitchat about the culinary peculiarities of the South, not when we had some real talking to do.

Finally, when his plate was clean, he talked. "I wasn't really hungry, but eating seemed to be better than looking at your accusing eyes."

"It's not my finger-pointing you have to live with," I said. "That's your soul, or what little's left of it, squeezing at you. So, how much money are we talking, and how did you even get the job?"

John took a few sips of ice water and then told me the story. I started to feel bad that I'd been so hard on him. It would have been a big chunk of change for anyone to turn down, especially someone like John, who never had money and didn't come from a family used to a surplus of the stuff.

"You started at *$175,000* a year?" I said. "An unknown artist getting almost a quarter of a million dollars? That doesn't sound right, John."

"It wasn't exactly a quarter of a million, then, though it's considerably more now and I wasn't exactly unknown at that point," he said. "I'd been doing some freelance work just to pay the rent until a deal I'd been waiting for came through. A guy who liked my paintings was about to open a gallery in Key West, said he was going to do a one-man show for me. But his financing fell through. You remember that old story. I had to do something to buy groceries. So I took these little advertising jobs. I didn't think much about them, until something I drew—a talking sofa—won a big national advertising award. Not being in that world, I had no idea of its importance. The next thing I know, all the ad magazines are calling me up, asking for interviews. All of a sudden I'm the new wunderkind of Madison Avenue. Albeit at thirty-nine, the oldest wunderkind in history. I'm sure you see where this is going. I had four or five agencies bidding against one another to get me to join their staff. I picked the highest bidder."

John took a few more sips of ice water.

"Is it hot in here, or is it me?"

"I'm the wrong person to ask," I said. "I frost over in October and don't thaw till March. Did you know going in what you'd be working on?"

"No, stupidly, I didn't ask about their client list. But to be honest, Nattie, and I'm tired of lying to myself, I don't know that it would have mattered had I known. They were offering $50,000 more a year than anyone else. At that point $50,000 was a lot of money."

"Still is to me," I said. "It's more than I make a whole year."

John loosened his tie—a cobalt blue Hermès—and unbuttoned the top button from his smooth white cotton shirt. I didn't know the label, but it oozed high dollar.

"Damn, it's hot in here," he said. "All these people . . ."

"Too early for menopause," I said. "Not to mention the little problem of your being the wrong sex. Maybe your conscience has kicked back in and is burning a hole through you."

"Very funny, Nattie. So what would you have done, Ms. High-and-Mighty?"

While I was thinking, John was getting whiter and whiter, which given his northern European heritage, was pretty white to start with.

"John, are you all right? You don't look so good."

"I don't know, Nattie," John said. His voice sounded worried, verging on panic. "Something's not right. My heart's racing and I'm burning up."

He put his hand to his chest and started gasping. "I'm burning up, Nattie, and I can't breathe. I can't breathe, I can't breathe."

Flashback to David. Those were the exact words he'd used right before he died.

I stood up and screamed, *"HELP, SOMEONE CALL AN AMBULANCE!!!!!!"*

All sound stopped in the restaurant save the sickening sound of John gasping for air. I saw someone rush to a telephone. John, meanwhile, fell facefirst on his empty plate.

"HELP, SOMEONE, HELP!!!! PLEASE. DOESN'T ANY-ONE HERE KNOW CPR?"

This anyone sure as hell didn't. I'd been meaning to take the course, but I was always too damn busy with my horse. Damn my selfishness. Dammit, dammit, dammit. John was fighting for his life, and all I could do was shriek like a banshee.

Finally someone came up. And damn if it wasn't the purple sweatsuit.

"Step aside, honey, let me see what I can do."

In no time she had John on the floor and was kissing life back into him.

"Is that ambulance here yet?" she said between breaths. "Call them again and tell them to hurry their butts on up here before they got themselves two bodies to work on."

Practically on cue, the EMTs came rushing in and pushed me aside. They were working furiously, poking and sticking and prodding him.

"Can I ride in the back with him?"

"You his wife?"

I shook my head.

"Sorry."

The woman in the purple sweatsuit stepped next to me and said, "I'll take you on up to the hospital. It's not but less than a mile from here."

"Do you think he's going to be okay?" I said.

She looked at me. I could tell by her face what the answer was. "If'n I were you, I'd start asking Jesus for a favor right about now." Then she looked closer at me. "Or whoever it is you like to send your prayers to."

There it went again, that old southern Jew-dar.

As they wheeled John away she said, "Pray hard, honey. This boy could use the kind of help a doctor can't give him."

CHAPTER 35

By the time Halsy Cantrell—the lady in the purple sweatsuit—got me there, John was gone.

Gone as in not where I was. Not gone as in dead. I could hear the commotion and the frenzied medical talk jabbing its way down the shiny corridors. I could tell it was really serious, life-threateningly so, because no one bothered me with forms to fill out or insurance questions.

Halsy put her arm around me and was there-thereing me pretty good. I'd have liked to bury myself in the crook of her arm and fall asleep for six months, or for however long it took all these messes to resolve themselves.

"What do you think's happening back there, Halsy? Do you think he's going to make it?"

"I think it's in the Lord's hands, honey, and I wouldn't presume to know what his plans are for this boy."

Oh, no, I groaned. Were they up there playing Monopoly again? Someone land on Boardwalk with three hotels? Just as I was about to think myself some really blasphemous thoughts, I saw a nurse slip through the door. It was Sarah Carpenter. She saw me and did a double take.

"Miss Gold?" she said. "Is that you? Are you with him?" She pointed to the door she just came from.

I jumped up and rushed to her. "Is he all right? Is he going to live? Was it a heart attack?"

"Take it easy, Miss Gold. He is alive, but he's got a rough night ahead of him. The doctors are still trying to determine the problem."

I sank to my knees and whispered, "Thank you."

"Are *you* all right? Do you feel as if you're going to pass out?"

I looked up at her worried face. "No, no, I'm fine. Can I stay here? Can I go where they take him?"

"Certainly you can. I'll keep you posted on how he's doing. We're doing our best for him."

She turned and started walking down the hall. Then she came back to me. "You probably shouldn't tell anyone I told you this, but the funny thing is, when I leaned over to draw blood, I smelled that same smell on him that I was telling you about when you were here this afternoon."

"Smell?" I said. "Your grandmother's ashtray smell? John doesn't smoke, and we were in the nonsmoking section of the restaurant."

"Funny, huh?" she said.

I nodded dumbly and walked back to my chair next to Halsy. "Cigarette smell," I muttered to myself.

"What's that, honey?" Halsy said.

"Oh, nothing, I'm just talking to myself. That nurse said he had a little bit of a cigarette smell to him, and John doesn't smoke."

"Oh, I hate that smell. My daddy never smoked a day in his life, but Lord if he didn't smell like something horrible and spoilt when he came in from his garden. He used to make himself up a potion out of chewing tobacco and some kind of liquid and spray it all over his tomato plants and roses. He said nothing worked better than that, no insecticide you could buy or anything. He learned that from his granddaddy back when that's when they used nicotine for bug killer. His granddaddy used to buy it in bottles to spray on his crops. 'Yes, sir,' he used to say, 'there ain't nothing that can kill a bug—or a human—like that nasty stuff.'"

"Oh, my God, Halsy, you're a genius. A goddamned genius."
I jumped and pounded through the swinging double doors, where
I saw John lying on the gurney with what seemed every doctor in
Fauquier County working on him.

"Nicotine poisoning," I said loud enough to get someone's
attention. "He's got nicotine poisoning."

One of the doctors looked up at me. Thankfully he didn't dis-
miss me as a crazed lunatic wandering the emergency room halls.

"How do you know that? Did something happen, did you see
something?"

"It's too long a story to go into now. Just trust me. Test his
blood or whatever you check for nicotine levels. I bet he's got
enough in him to kill an elephant."

The doctor was about to ask me another question, when a
loud, shrill beep went off.

"We're losing him again," one of the nurses shouted.

The doctor whirled around. "You'll have to leave. I'll check
the nicotine."

I backed away and watched as they paddled enough electrical
juice into John's chest to melt his fillings. There was a lot more
STAT talk, and I stood there frozen with my back to the swinging
doors. No one noticed me, they were all too busy scrambling
around trying to bring John back. It wasn't until I heard the
rhythmic beeping of the monitors resume that I backed out the
doors and set myself down next to Halsy.

"He's still alive," I said to her. "But barely."

"Praise the Lord," she said.

I wasn't ready to be praising anyone just yet. A while later
Sarah pushed out through the doors and came by my side.

"They're moving him to Intensive Care. You and your friend
can wait in the waiting room near the ICU."

Which is how I spent the rest of my night—shuffling between
the vending machines, the ICU waiting room, and a hard metal

chair by John's bed for five minutes every hour on the hour. John looked bad; he had that dirty-carpet gray color people get when they're hooked up to every medical machine ever invented. He moaned in and out of consciousness, but never really came through clear enough to talk. I held his hand and told him I was by his side.

Though I tried to convince Halsy to go home, she stuck to me like new Velcro. "Honey, I got a vested interest in this boy now."

So we sat through the darkness together. Sometimes talking, sometimes not. I'm sure she was praying during those times, because I could see her hands clasped together and her lips moving. I was having my own discussions with Whomever. I'd already bargained away my foul mouth and hot temper. I'd gotten to the just plain begging stage, when Sarah tapped me on the shoulder.

"I think he's out of the woods now," she said, and smiled so kindly at me, I wanted to kiss her. "But he'll have to stay in the hospital for a while yet. Maybe a week, maybe more."

"Oh, thank God," I said, and meant it. "What about the nicotine? Did they find out if that was it?"

"Unofficially, yes. But I'm supposed to let the doctor tell you. Wonder how that happened?"

So did I. It had to have happened at the restaurant. As best as Halsy and I could figure, someone must've doused his potatoes or his gravy with a dose of nicotine when the waitress was making her way through the crowds. John had been so keyed up by our topic of conversation, he probably would've eaten a fried shoe put in front of him. Someone had been following him. And I knew who that someone was. Henry's wacko.

Henry. Oh no, Henry. I looked at the clock on the wall. Ten-twenty. I'd forgotten all about meeting him at the Loudoun County courthouse.

I found a pay phone and called the courthouse. The clerk

hadn't seen any tall reporters from North Carolina yet. I called Annie's. Henry answered. His hello alone sounded like his pet dog had died.

"Henry, this is Nattie, what's wrong?"

"Nattie, Nattie, is that you? Where are you? Are you all right? Where've you been? I thought you were dead."

What's this, a Henry and Nattie personality exchange? "Calm down," I said. "I'm okay, but my friend John, Mr. O on your list, is in critical condition." Then I filled him in on my night at the Fauquier Hospital and how I got there.

It turns out Henry spent the night awake and pacing also. In my hysteria about John I'd forgotten Annie wasn't there last night and couldn't tell anyone where I'd gone. I didn't leave a note for Henry, because at that point we weren't speaking. Apparently he got home around ten and found an empty house. Annie was with her latest beau, the Duncans were spending the night in Washington, Rosalita was off, and I was nowhere to be found. By midnight he'd called Flip, Lannie, and Karen, all of whom said they had no idea where I was. By two A.M., around the time John was wheeled to the ICU, Henry had called the police looking for a dead redhead.

"I'm alive," I said. "Can't get rid of me that easy. Darn, Henry, it looks like your psycho's losing control. I think we're really in trouble now."

"What do you mean by that?"

"O for Osborne isn't anywhere near D for Duncan. Your person's out of order, alphabetical order. I think that's bad, maybe a meltdown or something. Maybe he or she feels trapped and wants to take care of business, all of it, right now."

"I hope you're wrong, but just in case you're not, I've got Margot running computer searches on autopsy technicians and missing human organs. *The Appeal*'s lawyers contacted the police this morning, and I'm fairly sure they're notifying everyone else on the list, telling them about the other deaths. So I've got to work fast and get this story in before every journalist in North Carolina jumps on it. How's your mother coming with that information on the class action suit?"

"Oh, shit, I mean shoot—sorry about that," I said, and looked upward. "I forgot to tell you about Christine Motley, you've got to call her this second. I think she's got a friend who may be on to something. Here's her number. . . ."

Henry seemed reluctant to hang up. "I'm all right, Henry. Really I am. Go, go call that lady. It's our turn for some luck now. Oh, one more thing. I was a total idiot yesterday, I'm sorry."

"Dinner tonight?"

"I'd like nothing better," I said, and hung up.

I felt a tap on my shoulder. It was Halsy, wearing a smile brighter than her sweatsuit.

"He's conscious and he's asking to see you."

CHAPTER 36

I left the hospital after John himself told me he was okay. He didn't look it or sound it, but at least he could say it. And his doctor concurred: a week in the hospital, assuming his HMO approved the stay, and he'd be good as new.

Halsy was still sticking to me like new Velcro and insisted on driving me back to Country Cookin', where I picked up John's Lexus. He'd given me the keys. Hypocrite that I am, I popped myself right into that smooth taupe leather bucket seat and started her up without even a third thought that this dream machine was bought with death money. Halsy had hugged me hard before I left, but not as hard as I hugged her. I couldn't begin to thank her, and when I tried, she held up her hand and told me to hush.

"You take care and keep in touch with me—and the Lord," she said as she walked to her car. "See what a little faith does?"

I was so tired, I could barely see the road, let alone the big picture. I blew her a kiss and waved.

The car was a real princess-and-the-pea drive. I could have zoomed over a crater and not felt it. Henry was waiting by the door and threw his arms around me when I walked in.

"Nattie, you scared the hell out of me, did I tell you that?"

"About fifteen times," I said. "So how was the cake?"

"Cake, what cake are you talking about?"

"German chocolate, your favorite, remember?"

He didn't know what I was talking about. A good sign. Some

healthy part of me was screaming to shut up and let it drop. For once, I listened.

"It's good to see you too," I said, and leaned into his hug.

"I owe you, Nattie," Henry said. "Christine's friend turned out to be a winner. She told me all about that group she was involved with. The first meeting she went to, the focus was on legal retribution. They met with a lawyer, talked legal strategies, and planned their class action suit. But by the sixth meeting the focus had completely shifted to finding their own form of retribution. Apparently one of the new members convinced the rest of the group that they were just spinning their wheels going the legal route, that 'the American judicial system was controlled by the tobacco cartel conspiracy.' Christine's friend stopped going after a while because all they talked about was this so-called conspiracy, a conspiracy to cover up everything from the way the tobacco industry is infiltrating America's elementary schools, to how they lace their cigarettes with superpotent forms of nicotine to addict smokers. She thought they were paranoid, until it came out a few months later that the tobacco companies were in fact spiking cigarettes."

"This is great stuff, Henry," I said. "What else did the group think the 'cartel' was doing?"

"You name it, they thought it. Some of it's too crazy to consider—for instance, that elementary school thing that involved altering the genetic structure of the tobacco plant so it has a sweet, candylike taste, but a couple of the other things sound possible: advertising campaigns directed at the less educated, misinformation smears of well-known antismoking advocates, buying congressmen—such as Mr. G on the list, Booker Greene, the New York congressman originally from North Carolina. It turns out that he sponsors so many tobacco bills, they call him the Marlboro Man in Congress. Apparently the tobacco companies are the only industry to take any financial interest in his constituents, who are amongst the poorest in the country.

They sponsor athletic events, street parties, anything where they can hang their advertising banners."

"Wait," I said, remembering John's comment about the sweet mashed potatoes, "Go back to the tobacco candy thing. Did they have any proof, anything to back up their allegations?"

"Christine's friend thought they were crazy. But she did say one woman, one of the more rabid of the bunch, claimed a tobacco company research botanist who manipulates DNA had contacted her and told her about his experiments because he felt guilty."

"Research botanist who manipulates DNA?" I said. "How many of those could there be? Henry, the gods are smiling upon us today. I'll bet you anything it was Peterson Scott, my brother's crazy, mad botanist client."

"That would certainly be convenient," Henry said. "This man, hopefully Peterson Scott, had heard about the lawsuit—and that woman's loss. It was her son who'd died. Apparently when she started going to the meetings, she started out a normal sort of person, though consumed with grief and, according to Christine's friend, guilt."

"Let me guess," I said. "The woman was a smoker, right? And she thinks she killed him with her secondhand smoke? My mother's still in denial; she's convinced herself all the research that proves secondhand smoke is more deadly than firsthand smoke is a smear campaign against the tobacco companies."

"You've got part of it," Henry said. "That woman was a smoker, and her son grew up breathing her smoke day in and day out. But that's not all of it. After he'd grown up and left the house, she had a cancer scare herself and stopped smoking. By that time her son was well into years of smoking two or three packs a day himself. Apparently she'd sit and cry through some of the meetings, blaming herself for getting him started smoking and then not forcing him to stop. As if you could force a thirty-year-old man to stop smoking. That's how old he was when he got lung cancer.

From what I've learned, if you start smoking early enough, it's not as rare as you'd think to get lung cancer at that age."

Another dead body. Even if it was his own damn fault, it didn't make it any easier to stomach. My heart went out to his mother and every other tortured soul in her group.

"She's your girl, Henry," I said. "I know it. Think, here's this woman racked with guilt and anger. It's a lot easier to act on the anger than the guilt, and as one who was spawned on anger, let me tell you, it can take over. Couple that with grief, and you've got the perfect recipe for the Mr. Hyde in us to make himself known. Even Christine said it, 'Grief makes you do crazy things,' and there's no grief greater than a parent's. Henry, I know it in my bones. It's her. You've got to find her quick. Because I'll bet you anything she'd just as soon be dead and that makes her all the more dangerous."

"You're probably right as usual, Ms. Gold," Henry said. "I'm already working on tracking her down. I hope you're also right about who the botanist is. Maybe he can make things happen faster. First I have to get the woman's name and then find out her occupation. Christine's friend didn't know what she did, but knew she wasn't a doctor. If she turns out to be an autopsy technician, I'm sure we've got ourselves a match."

"Well, good luck finding her, even with the mad doctor's help," I said. "Too bad one of Larry's clients hasn't invented special glasses that turn our society's invisibles visible. It's a sad but true fact of life: there ain't nothing more invisible than a middle-aged woman. I'll call Larry right now and ask about Scott."

Henry looked at me. "Nattie, don't take this wrong, but you look terrible. After you call your brother, go get some sleep."

He was right. I looked almost as bad as John. But sleep was the last thing I could get. I still had a story to do. Not that there was any chance of writing it before the clinic with George Morris tomorrow and meeting Candace's deadline. I had to find out who sugar-daddied Josane's life before the courts closed.

"No rest for the weary, Henry. Or have you forgotten? We've got a date with some books."

Henry took my hand and led me upstairs. "You've got a date with the bed. I'll do the books. It'll take only a few hours. I owe you at least that."

Who could argue? Not me. Not the new, reformed, clean-talking, levelheaded Nattie Gold.

I called my brother; he wasn't in, but his secretary gave me Scott's home and office numbers. I handed the slip of paper to Henry and then got horizontal. Talk about sweet dreams: Henry tucked me in and kissed me good night. I'd have grabbed his hand and pulled him next to me. But I could barely manage to close my eyes before I fell asleep, let alone get my fire stoked up.

The next thing I knew, someone was tapping my shoulder gently. I reached up to take his hand in mine. "Henry," I said behind closed eyes.

Then I opened my eyes. "Mr. Duncan, get out. I thought I told you to—"

He put his finger on my lips. "Shhhh," he said. "I'm here on business. Damage control. I just heard about your friend, John Osborne. I understand he's going to live. This person, she's got to be stopped."

"Okay," I said. "So we agree on one thing. How'd you know it was a she?"

"I could tell you her name if that would be useful."

I sat straight up. "You know her name? I suppose you know her address too?"

He nodded.

"What else do you know and why're you telling me? What's in it for you?"

"Very perceptive. I like a smart woman."

"Cut it out, just cut it out right now. And start talking before I start screaming."

"Her name is Susan Hancock. She lives in Greensboro, where I believe your mother lives, right? Your mother's an attorney specializing in family law, correct? Mrs. Hancock is, as Henry has probably guessed by now, an autopsy technician at Moses Cone Hospital. Isn't that where your stepfather, David Wolfe, passed away not too long ago?"

"What've you guys got, your own personal CIA? Yes, yes, and yes," I said. "Go on."

"We knew all about Mrs. Hancock's little tragedy," Duncan said.

"Little tragedy? Her son died a horrible death. That's a little tragedy to you?"

"If you look at the big picture, yes. Tobacco is one of the biggest industries in the United States. If it fails, the country fails. Think of the jobs lost, the unemployment compensation, increase in welfare, food stamps. It could bankrupt this nation. Mrs. Hancock was instrumental in forming a group, as you know already from Christine Motley, right?"

"Enough. I get the picture. Your net spreads wide. Just keep talking and get to the part why you're telling me, a reporter who thinks you're two steps lower than dirt, all this."

He cleared his throat. "There's no need to be nasty. Mrs. Hancock's group originally was interested in pursuing legal channels. They filed a class action suit against all the tobacco companies on behalf of all the victims of lung cancer. Their opening gambit was for ten billion. It sounded ridiculous at the time and some of us got a good chuckle out of it.

"Then things took a turn for the worse. We knew well in advance that the nicotine spiking story would be breaking, though we could do nothing about it."

"But you sure gave it your best, didn't you?" I said. "What'd it cost you in lawyer money to try to make Bladstone's increased nicotine studies go away? One mil? Two?"

"Suffice it to say, our effort wasn't successful. Between that and the growing discontentment toward the tobacco industry, suddenly Mrs. Hancock and her little group's class action suit didn't sound so ridiculous. In fact, one of our leading attorneys investigating the suit, Hinton Allard, the late Hinton Allard I'm sorry to add, told us we were heading for trouble. Ten billion dollars is a lot of money. Possibly enough to bankrupt the industry. We had to do something."

"How come you didn't just kill her? Take her out right then. A single bullet through the head. Maybe you could have gotten one of your NRA buddies to do it, for free even, as a professional courtesy or just a good time."

A tight smile edged across Duncan's face. "As I was saying, we had to do something. So we decided to refocus the group's attention."

"How's that work? Brian implants, secret drugs?"

"Much easier. We planted someone in the group, someone to stir them up, someone to remind them of the inefficiency of the American judicial system."

"You mean someone to turn them into vigilantes."

"I guess you could put it that way."

"Who'd you hire? Tim McVeigh? Oh, I forgot, he's in jail."

"Well, unfortunately, that's not far from the truth, though we didn't know it at the time. We found a man with, how shall I put it, antigovernment learnings. We thought he was just a strong John Bircher type. We didn't know about his connection to the Leaders of the White Way Militia until the idiot blew up himself and a few of his fellow minutemen last month while mixing a vat of fertilizer with gasoline. He was, unfortunately, smoking at the same time."

"I guess that net of yours has a few holes in it. So what happened? Did he arm your group with M-16s and teach them survival skills?"

"Not everyone. Just Susan Hancock. We didn't run a psych

exam on him and we should've. According to one of our psychia-trists, Mrs. Hancock developed what's called a 'shared paranoia' from him. No one could have predicted it. Yes, she was upset, but so was everyone else in the group. All we wanted to do was distract them from their legal suit. We had no idea it would turn into this. We unfortunately underestimated this woman's passion."

"There's that word from you again. You must truly be a demented soul in the sack. It's not passion that poor woman feels. It's utter hopelessness, a grief so great, a monster like you could never understand. Cut to the chase, Duncan, what do you want from me?"

"We can't find her. We know she's near. She's cut off contact with everyone from the group. We think the only person she's talking to is Dr. Peterson Scott. Peterson Scott, your brother's client. We think he'll talk to your brother, tell him where she is. It's now in everyone's interest to stop her."

"Everyone's interest? You mean your own and the rest of the slimcballs on thc list? Maybe I'll just go back to sleep and let her pick you off one by one."

CHAPTER 37

I listened as Duncan's footsteps carried him down the stairs. Then I slipped into Annie's room and called the Loudoun County courthouse, once again looking for Henry. This time the clerk had seen a tall reporter from North Carolina.

"Nattie, what's up?" Henry said.

I told him. "I'll be right there," he said.

"Wait, wait," I said. "I hate to be selfish, but I've got a story to write too. How's the sugar-daddy search going?"

"Gone, done, and finished," Henry said. "Want to hear now or when I get back?"

"Henry, instant gratification isn't fast enough for me. Jack Kent Cooke?"

"Nope, he's got his hands full with his South American sweetie. Sitting down? It was none other than Santee Mundell, Topping's father."

"Well, I'll be. I wonder if she knows. She sure didn't act like it yesterday. Hey, wait a minute. Reenie Ashmore mentioned an older European man, said something about an accent."

"Ever hear anyone talk in very thick Charleston low country? You'd think they were from someplace other than the United States too. Mundell's an old-line Charlestonian and he's got as heavy a low-country accent as I've ever heard. This low-country talk is interesting, it comes from when—"

"Henry, I know you love history and I really want to hear exactly how the low-country talk came to be, but tell me here, at

Annie's. I've got to find my brother, okay? And thanks for finding Daddy Warbucks."

So it was Santee Mundell who bought Josane that store, her life, and her horse. Now all I had to do was figure out a polite way to ask Topping if she knew Daddy was schtupping her best friend.

I dialed Larry's number in Houston again, told his secretary it was urgent. It didn't matter how urgent it was, he still wasn't there. My brother was up in the wild blue yonder, loop-de-looping his plane. My poor mother, she's got one kid who jumps horses, the other who flies planes. No wonder she lives every day expecting a catastrophe. However, she always has; she was such a worrier when we were growing up, I guess subconsciously Larry and I decided to give her something to worry about.

"Tell him to call me the second he gets in," I said. "Tell him it's life or death."

I've been wanting to say that my whole life. And this time it was true.

I hung up the phone and it rang the second it nestled in the cradle. Without thinking where I was, I picked it up as if I were in my home.

"Nattie, it's me. I'm here."

Click. Who else talks to me in the monosyllabic but Rob? I can't believe I'd completely forgotten Brenda. I was supposed to meet Rob at Paper Chase Farms during my lunch break from my day of record checking. I scribbled a note to Henry: *Be back in a couple hours, BRENDA'S HERE, YIPPEEE-I-O!!!!*

I rushed out the side door, bypassing contact with Darth Vader, aka Outerbridge Duncan. In less than ten minutes I was as happy as I'd ever been in my life. Brenda was by my side, nuzzling my hand for more carrots.

I wrapped my arms around her long, coppery neck and hugged and hugged and hugged.

"Nattie, you're going to kill that mare."

"It's good to see you too, Rob," I said, and hugged him next.

"Make sure she gets a bran mash," Rob said. "It was a long drive and it's cold. Also, make sure she's got two water buckets. If she doesn't drink enough, she could colic."

Veterinary Science 101, we go over this every time he takes her someplace for me. As if I didn't know how fragile a horse's stomach is, as if I haven't spent many a night camped by Brenda's stall, walking her around, waiting for her to poop so I knew she wasn't obstructed. All it takes is some cramping to get a horse rolling around, doing the watusi on the ground. That's why you've got to spot colic—a fancy name for stomachache—early. Every time a colicky horse tries to sink to his knees, you've got to yank him back up. It sounds heartless and cruel, but the alternative is excruciating and often fatal. Let them roll and twist and they can kink up their intestines pretty good. If they get a kink in the tubing, whatever goes in can't come out—we're talking obstruction, blockage, internal blowouts. Imagine filling a balloon with water and leaving on the tap. You get the picture, and it isn't pretty.

"Don't worry, don't worry," I said. "I'm not leaving until she drinks something." Then I started to blather on and on about how nervous I was, riding with George Morris.

"Suppose he calls me stubby or chubby or hates the way I ride?"

"You're as good a rider as anyone here," Rob said. "You'll do fine if you show up looking normal. But if you walk in with dirty tack or your hair sticking out or wearing one of your magenta shirts, I won't know you. I don't care what excuse you've got. Your period, someone tried to murder you, I don't care. If you can't get here clean, neat, and normal, don't come."

With that he turned around and walked back to the horse trailer.

"See you tomorrow morning," I called out to him. "I'll be the 'normal' one with red hair."

I led Brenda around the indoor ring just to show her there were no mountain lions or goblins lurking in the corners. Not that this horse is much of a spooker, but you can never be too careful. Then I put her in her stall and started hunting for the feed room to find bran. A woman with short dark hair took me there, helped me make the mash, asked me if I needed anything else. She was being so nice, I half expected her to offer to clean my tack.

"Hey, Jan," someone called to her. "Phone."

Jan. Jan Neuharth? That was the devil's daughter? I couldn't believe it. I don't know what I expected, but I certainly didn't expect the Welcome Wagon. She owned the barn; she being the daughter of the man who changed the complexion of American newspapers: Al Neuharth, the father of *USA Today*. I hadn't even wanted to ride in the clinic when I first saw where it was. But I couldn't really blame him for the televisation of American newspapers. He'd just been a shrewd old cocker who realized way before anyone else that our collective attention span had shrunk to that of the fruit fly.

Paper Chase Farms was some operation, 112 acres of high-dollar Middleburg real estate; three barns, 55 stalls, 70 horses, an indoor ring, an outdoor ring, a lunging ring, a cross-country course, heated bathrooms with showers, and a heated office with Mr. Coffee ready and waiting. Though it was big and clean, it didn't shout MONEY the way Summer Ridge, Josane's barn, did. Paper Chase wasn't a show barn that catered to millionaires; this place made its mortgage teaching people how to ride, more than a hundred of them every week paying anywhere from twenty-six to fifty dollars a pop. Though the board seemed high to me—five hundred a month—I bet they weren't pocketing much of that. Any horse person knows there's no better way to lose money than operating a boarding business, between the cost of feed, hay, field maintenance, and barn help. The big money to be had in horses is in the buying and selling, but it's always a gamble. It's just as easy to lose big-time as it is to win, some might even say easier. The steady money's in lessons. Slow and sure, but it pays the feed bills.

I carried the warm mash to Brenda's stall, or at least tried to. What looked like a small hairy pony was sitting in front of the door.

"Oh, sorry about that. Come here, girl," said a woman about my age, but, of course, not my height. At a barn it's a given everyone's taller than me, except sometimes the youngest short-stirrup kids.

"Golly," I said in accordance with the new clean-mouth legislation I ratified last night. "That's the biggest dog I've ever seen, especially here in the kingdom of Jack Russell."

"Irish wolfhound," she said. "A real dog. My name's Amy Benjamin, I'm riding in the second session, how about you?"

"Same," I said. "Except my name's Nattie Gold. This is Brenda Starr."

She pointed to the gray horse in the stall next to Brenda's. "That's Gertie. So, are you as nervous as I am? I've showed, hunted, and timber-raced this mare, but I'm more worried about George Morris watching me ride than I was going on my first date."

"Ditto," I said. "I don't want to be on the receiving end of his Veg-O-Matic mouth either. But if it's any consolation, I hear it's worth it, that you come out practically riding like Margie Gold-stein, or as close as a human being can come, since I'm convinced she's not of this planet. Don't you think she and Michael Jordan are really alien hybrids? How else do you explain it? Ever seen her ride? It's like finding religion. So, how'd the date work out?"

"Don't even ask."

We talked as we groomed our horses. It turned out Amy had shipped down from Philadelphia, where she actually worked. How refreshing, another rider who needed a weekly paycheck to pay the bills. She was a social worker who specialized in child welfare.

"Child welfare?" I said. "Do you do anything with therapeutic riding?"

"You bet we do," she said. "It's an amazing program. I try to get all my kids, especially the most troubled ones, involved."

"Troubled as in emotional problems?" I said. "I thought it was for physically handicapped kids."

"I don't want to sound callous, but that's because they make the best poster kids. These programs are always scrambling for funding, so they make sure they come up with the most compelling fund-raising campaigns. You've seen those pictures, they tug at your heart, don't they?"

I had to agree with her.

"But the kids with emotional problems need it too, maybe even more so. Lots of them are abused and have grown up not being able to control any aspect of their lives. Then, when they get on a horse and find they can make that big twelve-hundred-pound animal do what they want it to do, well, without sounding overly dramatic, it's a life-changing experience. The self-esteem that comes from it is immeasurable."

She wasn't asking, but I had a birthday coming up and my grandmother usually sent me a few hundred bucks. I could easily part with some of it. "What's the name of the organization? Address, too, if you've got it."

"I don't have the address on me, I'll give it to you tomorrow. But it's the Mid-Atlantic Therapeutic Riding Program."

"Oh," I said, "I know that one. Topping Mundell runs it, right?"

Amy gave me a funny look. "Topping Mundell, the woman who rides with Summer Ridge?"

"Yeah," I said. "Tall, red-haired, ridiculously beautiful, that Topping Mundell. I heard she was a big mover and shaker with Mid-Atlantic Therapeutic. If my information's correct, she started the program and administers it as well."

"Nattie, I'd check your source if I were you. She doesn't run the program, and she sure didn't start it either. I've seen her at a couple of fund-raising events, but that's the extent of her involvement."

Maybe I'd misremembered the name of the group, or maybe she'd been lying. I made a mental note to ask Henry in a nonconfrontational manner.

"Wouldn't be the first time I had my facts wrong," I said. "I'll be back in a few minutes, I've got to make a phone call."

Between John's major nicotine drama and Outerbridge Duncan enlisting me in his little reconnaissance operation, I hadn't had time to focus on my murder story. The necklace—I had to find out how Lannie came to be wearing Josane's necklace. I wished I had time to drive to Marshall and ask her in person, but I didn't. I'd have to practice my phone skills and figure out a nonthreatening way to find out if she took the necklace from Josane's jewelry box or off her dead body.

I held the phone a few inches from my ear, preparing for the worst.

First bit of luck: Lannie was in. "Hi, Lannie," I started. "I didn't mean to upset you the other day or imply anything. I'm just trying to help Josane's mother. You loved Josane, so you can understand how upset she still is."

"What do you want?" Lannie said. Second bit of luck: She hadn't hung up on me yet.

"Please don't take this wrong, but Topping Mundell gave me some snapshots of Josane and in one of them I noticed she was wearing the same necklace you were wearing yesterday and I was just wondering . . ."

"Wondering if I stole that too? Maybe ripped it off her neck after I killed her? Sorry to spoil your little theory. I bought that necklace before Josane died and I've got the receipt to prove it. I bought it from the same jeweler who made Josane's; I had him make me one just like it. Ask him yourself, he'll remember because he didn't want to do it. He's one of these *artist* types who doesn't like to do the same thing twice. But everyone's got a price. He said he'd make one more, and that was it, then he was throwing out the mold. If you don't believe me, he's on the main street in Middleburg. Cogswell Jewelers."

"Thanks," I said. "I guess I just missed you yesterday at Summer Ridge Farm. Weren't you delivering grain there in the morning?"

"No," she said. "I didn't make it there till the afternoon, anything else?"

That was real swift, Nattie. Guess the CIA will be knocking on my door any second with recruitment papers. What'd I expect her to do? Come out and say "Yes, I was there delivering grain and while I was at it I waved a black plastic bag around to get you dumped"?

"Actually," I said, "there is something else and it has nothing to do with the story. This is speaking as an owner of a horse with too many bumps on her, I hear you're quite the kitchen wizard. Got any more of that stuff Flip said you brought by Josane's that morning? Wasn't it supposed to be a miracle bump remover of some kind?"

I heard a sharp intake of air from her end. "Flip's a goddammed liar. I didn't make anything for Josane's mare. I didn't bring anything by her house. If something was there, he brought it over; he's in the horse products business, not me. I don't know what you're talking about. I've got to go, a customer just walked in."

Click. Must be a second cousin to Rob.

This was getting worse by the minute. Everyone was lying about everything. I'd need a troughful of sodium pentathol to sort this thing out.

CHAPTER 38

So much for my romantic night with Henry. So much for our quiet dinner and whatever followed later at the Ashby Inn, the most romantic place this side of Paris.

Guess where I spent the second night in a row away from a bed? On a lawn chair bundled up in a dirty horse blanket in front of Brenda's stall. That's the bad part. The good part: Henry was right next to me.

Brenda wouldn't drink, and do I ever know firsthand about leading a horse to water. I'd promised Rob I wouldn't leave until she drank and I wouldn't have been comfortable leaving even if I hadn't promised. An eight-hour trailer ride in the cold weather is asking for colic, and not drinking water afterward is just like saying pretty please.

Though Brenda seemed fine. She was chewing hay, doing her best to ignore me and Henry.

"Maybe she's just not thirsty," Henry said.

"Maybe. Probably. But maybe she's not drinking for a reason, like her stomach hurts. I know this stinks, sitting in a cold barn, but I can't take the chance. Why don't you go on back to Annie's?"

I sort of meant it. No reason Henry should have to suffer through the night. She wasn't his horse.

"I'm staying," he said. "Wait'll I tell the boys about my night with the horses. They'll get a big kick out of it."

Boys, my butt. He was worried about the mystery flapper flapping on over to Paper Chase. I could tell by his face, but neither of us said it.

Despite all that horse heat, it was cold in the barn—which wasn't so bad in a way. Henry and I scrunched up against each other and talked our way through the night. Without one fight.

I told him about my trip to the jeweler in Middleburg. Finally someone had been telling the truth about something. The goldsmith confirmed he'd made an exact copy of Josane's necklace, down to the 1.3 carat diamond in the center. He never made another like it; he, as Lannie said, threw out the mold. I even got him to tell me what the necklace cost: $2,500, about the same amount Lannie had stolen from Josane's cash register. No wonder she'd gotten so testy about whether she'd stolen the necklace. Technically, she had.

"She had this thing about dressing like Josane," I said to Henry. "I guess down to every last detail, including her pricey jewelry. The jeweler told me he'd offered to use a zirconium instead of a diamond and cast it out of a different metal. But Lannie refused. She told him it had to be *exactly* the same."

"She sounds disturbed to me," Henry said. "Disturbed enough to kill Josane when Josane rejected her?"

"Possibly," I said. "Too bad she and Flip can't stand each other. They could go off into the sunset and obsess happily ever after about Josane. I just can't think about this anymore tonight, Henry. I keep coming up more confused than I start when I try to figure it out. Keep an eye on Brenda, I'm going to call Larry again. He can't still be in his plane."

I tried his office, no answer. I left my life-or-death message on his machine. I tried his home. Got my nephew, Jordan, who wanted to talk about his latest Peewee baseball victory. I didn't want to warp his little mind, so I didn't give him the life-or-death message. "Just have your daddy call me at this number," I said. I called his cell phone, got another answering machine.

"Larry, Larry, this is Nattie. Where the heck are you? CALL ME. I am not joking around with this life-or-death stuff. It's about Peterson Scott; he might be needing you for something other than getting the FDA off his back. Try the FBI. I think he's got something to do with a crazy woman who's picking off tobacco people. There's two dead bodies so far and she almost got John Osborne. Remember him? My old boyfriend? CALL ME NOW!!!!"

I didn't even get back to the stall, when the pay phone started ringing.

"Larry?" I said.

"How do you know about Scott?" he said. No hello, how's life, how's the job? But my brother never did have the best phone manners.

I told him everything: the list, the lung, Hinton Allard, Jim Benson, the sweet nicotine on John's potatoes, and Duncan's sordid role in the whole stinking mess.

"Nattie, get out of there, you're in over your head. These guys mean business, and they're not going to let anyone stand in their way."

"Larry, I'm not getting out of here. So forget it. Just forget it. We're not kids, you can't boss me around. Tell me, where is he?"

Silence.

"You're with him, aren't you? That's where you went flying today, isn't it? You're in Richmond? Scott's probably sitting right next to you. Ask him where Susan Hancock is. Tell him she's melting down. She's got to be stopped before she kills again, or gets herself killed. I know she's somewhere in the area. Ask him where. Please, Larry."

He put his hand over the phone. I heard muffled talking.

"I'm telling you this because Scott says she won't hurt you and he's extremely worried about her. I can't fly us up there because it's sleeting in Richmond and it would take us too long to drive there. Apparently she called just before I got here. Scott says she sounds desperate, that you're right, she's falling apart and someone's got to get to her quickly. He's been trying to convince her to stop this revenge thing and get on with her life, but that lunatic your friend's stepfather hired was like Svengali. Apparently he pushed her into the murder plan and helped her break into Scott's office to steal some of his nicotine experiments. Then, when he blew himself up, she became convinced he was murdered by what she calls the tobacco cartel. Scott's the only one she talks to now. He's become a sort of lifeline to her, which, as you can imagine, puts him in a precarious legal position."

"Larry," I said, "where is she?"

"How far are you from Warrenton?"

"Fifteen minutes, twenty tops."

"The Rip Van Winkle Motor Lodge, Room Four. Call me when you get there. Nattie, I'm not asking. I'm telling you, call me when you get there. Let her talk to Scott."

I hung up the phone without saying good-bye and ran to Brenda's stall.

"Did she drink?" I said.

"I heard some slurping sounds. I think so," Henry said.

I looked at one of the water buckets. It was down by a quarter. But the best part was a fresh pile of steaming green manure. I felt like doing a victory dance around the little circles of refuse. Like I've said a million times, horse people are crazy.

I grabbed Henry's hand. "Let's go. I found her."

For the third time in two days I was heading back to Warrenton.

"There it is," I screamed. "Over there on the right. Great neon."

Rip Van Winkle rendered in orange, red, and green tubes of free-flowing electrons of whatever it is that makes the neon fly.

"Number Four," I said. "That must be her car, the blue Taurus with North Carolina plates."

Sure enough, pasted to the back window was a Moses Cone Hospital parking sticker.

We hopped out of the car and knocked on the door. I could hear a television going in the background.

"Mrs. Hancock," I called. "This is Nattie Gold. Peterson Scott sent me here. He's really worried about you."

I knocked again. No answer.

"Mrs. Hancock, please. We're here to help you. Open the door."

Henry tried the knob. It was locked. I pulled my Harris Teeter card from my purse.

"What're you going to do with that?" Henry said.

"Open the door, what else? I've seen it done a million times on television."

He started to object on legal, moral, and journalistic grounds.

"Henry, she's killed two people. Let's not discuss the morality of the situation."

I slipped the card between the lock and the door and slid it down. The knob remained steadfast. I did it again. The knob wouldn't turn.

"So much for the educational value of television. Let's go use our persuasive techniques on the night manager."

It took a lot of doing, but we finally did it: convinced the lady in the motel office to open the door for us. What got her to say yes was me bragging about Henry breaking the PTL story. She'd been a silver card holder herself and lost half of her retirement money.

"I shouldn't be doing this, but if you say she's in trouble . . ."

We assured her she was. And was she ever.

The woman slid the key in the door and pushed it open. The smell hit me first. Susan Hancock was faceup in a pool of her own vomit. Her body was jerking in a way a body jerks when it's in trouble, bad trouble.

"Call an ambulance. Quickly," Henry said to the motel manager as he rushed to the bed. Susan Hancock stopped moving. Henry put his fingers on her neck.

"There's a pulse, but it's faint and jumping around. She's not breathing, Nattie, get a towel."

I did. Meanwhile, Henry reached in her mouth and pulled out more vomit. I wiped her face and Henry leaned over her and started blowing air in her mouth. I guess he'd made the time in his life to take a CPR course.

While he blew, I found the bottle; an amber-colored prescription vial on the floor by the bed. Empty.

"Elavil," I said to Henry. "It says the prescription was for thirty pills."

He kept blowing until the ambulance arrived. Talk about déjà vu, for all of us.

"Didn't we see you last night?" one of the ambulance attendants said to me.

I said yes and handed him the bottle. He looked at it and then at the woman on the bed. "I don't think this one's going to be so lucky."

They whisked her out and into the ambulance. "She's going fast," I heard one of the attendants shout to the driver.

The motel manager hadn't come back yet, so Henry and I did a quick search of her room. He found the note in the Gideon Bible.

Lord, bring me home. I tried, you know I tried. but I don't deserve to live. Thomas should be the one alive, not me.

I did some of your work, didn't I? Got rid of some of the enemy? I thought that would make me more worthy to live, but nothing could do that. I can't do it anymore. It just hurts too bad to wake up each morning. The Lord giveth and the Lord

taketh. Take me now. please. I've been a good soldier, I've done
my duty. But it's time for you to take me home. take me home
to see my Thomas again. Let me see my boy, please Lord.

"Ohhhhh, boy," I said. "That poor woman. I hope someone
has mercy on her soul."

Henry put his arm around me and we stood there. Silent.

CHAPTER 39

Susan Hancock died before the ambulance turned up the hill to Fauquier Hospital. And I think it was the most merciful thing that could have happened. When I get some time, I plan to spend it meditating on the joy/suffering question. Because right now to me, between Susan Hancock, Reenie Ashmore, Christine Motley, and my mother, there seems to be a lot more of the latter and not enough of the former.

Henry and I waited at the hospital until my brother, Larry, and Peterson Scott arrived. Scott had been crying, I could tell by his eyes. My brother—his lawyer—tried to shut him up, but Scott wanted to talk and didn't mind one bit doing it to a couple of reporters. He went on record with the whole story, plus his DNA tobacco tinkerings. Yes, he'd developed a more addictable cigarette; yes, he'd developed a candy-sweet nicotine. Hell, he said, he could do anything with the stuff. He even brewed up a time-release nicotine, but the tobacco companies weren't interested. They wanted something that hit hard and fast, so smokers reach for the next cigarette before the first one goes out.

My eyes were starting to close on their own. The clock said two. I had to be at Paper Chase in six hours. If I didn't get some sleep, I'd fall off Brenda. Henry needed to keep talking to Scott for his story, because Outerbridge Duncan sure wasn't going to be telling it on the record. He gave me the keys to his car and I drove back to Annie's.

Guess whose bed I slid into? The giant pouf. I figured Henry probably wouldn't be using it, and if I was wrong, so much the better.

The alarm grabbed me out of my dream, something too convoluted to even remember. Darn, I'd been right. Henry was still with Scott.

Reluctantly, I moved from my cocoon and made myself as normal as possible for a type B personality slob. I had a date with George Morris, the rider of my dreams—and nightmares.

CHAPTER 40

"You look normal," Rob said to me. "So does Brenda."

Normal—it'd taken me an hour to get her that way. Normal to me for a horse in the winter is furry, dirty, and caked in mud. Normal to Rob is ready to step in the ring at Madison Square Garden.

As I'd been normalfying Brenda, a woman walked up to me. She looked familiar, but I couldn't place the face. Time to up the ginkgo. My memory was slipping at age thirty-seven and eleven-twelfths and my father convinced me to turn to his herbal cure. The only reason I relented is that he can remember the color his kitchen floor was when he was four years old.

"Nattie?" she said. "I'm Diane."

Diane, Diane, Diane. I scanned my memory for the name and face and came up blank.

"Candace's sister," she said.

That's why she looked familiar. She unfortunately looked like her sister. We shook hands.

"I'm the one doing residency at G.W. Candy told me you'd be here, so I thought this'd be a good chance to meet finally. And I wouldn't mind watching George Morris teach. I've read his book three times. Do you mind?"

She wasn't ordering me around. Maybe her sister was a genetic fluke. Maybe their parents did breed human beings after all.

"No, no," I said. "Stick around. Join us for lunch. I'd love to hear a psychiatrist's interpretation of the morning events."

I led Brenda into the indoor ring, now crammed with a course of jumps. I looked at the big, ugly oxer in the center, and cringed. Now was as good a time as any to get over my oxer-phobia. We got on and started warming up. Within minutes Brenda was as flexible as a ten-year-old Romanian gymnast, bending this way and that, arching her neck and coming down onto the bit.

I patted her neck. "Good girl," I said. Her radar ears peri-scoped around to me. "Yes, that's right, good girl. You're the best."

As we cantered, trotted, and walked around, the ring filled with other riders. A flea-bitten gray cantered by my side. I did a double take. Could it be who I thought it was under that helmet?

I pressed my outside leg on Brenda and she moved to a canter. I came on the inside of the gray horse, cranked my head, and took a good look. It was.

"Lannie?" I said.

She turned her head to me. *"You?* What're *you* doing here?"

"Same as you," I said. "Riding in the clinic."

She tried to turn away from me but was too close to the wall. By swinging her horse like that, she threw his haunches—the firing end—into Brenda's face. Brenda is a very good-natured horse, but even good-natured horses have their limits. Another horse's butt in the face was hers. She bit him and he bucked a kick at her, sending his hoof into Brenda's chest and Lannie into the air.

It was a square landing, flat on her rear. I started to apologize, though I'm not sure what for, she'd started it. I didn't even get out the sorry part before she cut me off.

"Just shut up and leave me alone," she said. "And stay away from me. I'm not answering any more of your stupid questions. Write whatever the hell you want, I'm sure you will anyway."

Nothing like beginning the clinic on a happy note. I steered

Brenda to the other end of the ring and clear of her. I scanned the other riders, looking for Topping, but didn't see her. I did see George Morris striding into the indoor arena as if he owned it. He was wearing tight black dress boots, tight blue britches, an even tighter blue knit shirt, and not an ounce of fat. The man was pushing—or had pushed—sixty, but you couldn't tell it from the neck down. Or from the neck up. Most horse people look like a pair of old boots by the time they hit fifty, given all those hours under the sun. But not George. He had some wear on his face, but so did I, and I was young enough to be his daughter.

"Everyone, ride into the center, please. Face me, no talking." Then he launched into the Morris theory of riding and what we'd be doing in today's clinic. He spoke in a grand, theatrical manner accentuated by his strange accent, an usual combination of 1940s society talk marbled with West Virginia backcountry. Imagine Walter Brennan with Southampton lockjaw projecting at Carnegie Hall.

I looked at my fellow riders. Most of them were tall and slim. But there were a couple of chubbies in the bunch, Lannie being one of them, and one woman for whom chubby would be a euphemism. I steeled myself for the worst; George Morris was famous for pointing out weight problems. As he was talking, I saw out of the corner of my eye someone rush into the ring on a big chestnut horse.

"Sorry, George. Karen couldn't get Paladin loaded."

It was Topping. George Morris turned her way and said, "Topping Mundell, if you want to ride in this clinic, be on time. Now, as I was saying, when you trot, you should be how many degrees forward?"

He called on me. Thank God I'd been listening when he told us, so I knew the answer. "Five," I said.

"Correct," he said. "Now, let's ride. Spread out, everyone.

You on the little bay, that's exactly where your leg should be. Everyone look at her leg position. It is EXXX-cellent."

To my surprise, the woman on the little bay was the heavy one, the one I expected him to slice and dice.

For thirty-five minutes we walked, trotted, cantered, circled, serpentined, and halted. He learned our names and called out to each of us—in a mind-bogglingly polite manner—as we went by.

"Nattie, those knees. Do not pinch. Stretch your legs down, don't grip. Streeeeeehtch tall. Very nice.

"Topping, carry your hands higher. Go with the horse's head. With the horse's head. Yes, go with the horse's head. Lannie, ride him into the corners. Into the corners."

This isn't to say he was nice to everyone. He took after one rider, a fourteen-year-old girl named Kelly with concentration problems.

"That's what's wrong with your generation, you've got no discipline. No discipline. Kelly, listen to me when I talk, I told you five times to let go of his head. Let go of his head. Amy, don't forget your back. Nattie, knees. Topping, hands. Kelly, discipline. Discipline, discipline. Do I have to spell it for you?"

Little Kelly may not have had discipline, but she sure had stamina and steel nerves. Nothing seemed to bother her, not even George Morris ranting about her generation's free fall into adulthood.

As The George was lecturing Kelly, I noticed Lannie and Topping exchanging words. Lannie had the same look on her face as when she'd hissed to me earlier. They didn't even notice me as I trotted by slowly.

". . . What're you so worried about?" Topping said. "What do you mean she found out—"

Topping looked up and saw me. "Oh, hi, Nattie," she said. "Lannie thinks George has been picking on her. I actually think he's in a remarkably benevolent mood—so far."

A voice boomed to us from the back, "Ladies, if you want to talk, there is an office. I suggest you do it there."

The jumping phase started and we began with a simple brush box. The little bay horse was a little jerk. He'd jump one fence, then refuse the next. His rider was almost in tears. I expected George Morris to say something snide about her weight, such as that being the reason the horse wouldn't jump.

Here's what he said and why I wanted a full list of the vitamins he was on. I could have used a few of those personality-altering tongue dullers myself: "You're a very good rider, just keep trying. This horse is a cheat. And here's how we're going to fix a cheat."

Darn if he didn't fix him. Within five minutes the little bay was doing everything his owner asked.

Brenda couldn't have been better. She cantered to every fence in a long and low stride. It'd be hard not to love her. Even George Morris said something about her.

"Watch this horse go," he said. "She has a beautiful head and neck carriage."

Topping wasn't having such a good day. Paladin was being a pig about his lead changes. This was the horse Charlie had bought back from his client, the guy who was always in tears at the shows because he couldn't get the horse to change leads either. I don't know why Topping bought him, but I'd bet she paid a bundle.

"George, I can't get this damn horse on its right lead," she said.

He walked over to her, said something quietly enough so no one else could hear, and moved back to the center of the ring.

"Now we'll do the in and out; the vertical in, the oxer out."

I groaned. That ugly oxer as part of the in and out. Nothing like confronting your demons head-on.

The woman on the little bay went first. Perfect. He jumped it like a jackrabbit and she'd gotten him to it like Anne Kursinski, who's got enough Olympic metal to fill the teeth of every one of us in the clinic.

"Very good. Now, Amy, did you see her body position? Which is not acceptable: ahead, behind, or on the vertical?"

Amy hesitated, and George's stabilizers must've been slipping. "Come on, come on, I know you're a blonde, but you can get it right."

Amy shot him a dirty look and said, "Forward."

"Very good—for a blonde. Now go jump it."

She did. Perfectly. Score one for blondes.

My turn next. My heart was beating hard. "Stop it," I said to myself. "Jump the jump and have fun. That's why you're here. These are your entertainment dollars."

I put my leg on Brenda and pressed her into a forward canter. She stretched out and took me there like I was riding a cloud. Five strides away I saw the spot. We were dead on the money. Whooosh over the first one, I was flying just like my brother. Down and on the ground for one stride and whooosh in the air again. This time longer and higher, over that big ugly oxer.

"Very nice, Nattie. Good job. This girl has a system that works for her. We all need a system. Topping, your turn."

She pushed the horse into a canter and he picked up the wrong lead. I don't know why she kept coming to the jump, but she did and she couldn't have gotten there any worse if she'd planned it. The horse popped in a half-stride before the first fence and tried to jump it anyway. Topping was way ahead of the vertical to start with and flopped forward on the horse's neck while grabbing at his mouth with the reins. The horse landed on its knees, scrambled to its feet, and tried to fit in the next stride before the ugly oxer fence. But Topping was still yanking on his head and the poor horse had nowhere to go but down.

George Morris ran over to the splayed horse and rider. Topping and the horse stood up, both shaken but uninjured. "Are you all right?"

She nodded.

"This is what happens when you do not let go of your horse's head. You cannot forget to release his head. Crest release. Do you remember what that means? Your hands go up the horse's neck. Up his neck to let him do his job. Up his neck and plant them there and grab the mane if you are unsteady, Topping. Do you understand? If you continue to have problems, you should consider riding in the two-foot-six-inch group tomorrow."

Her face flushed red. "The beginner group? You're not serious? I've been riding all my life, I'm not riding with beginners. You can't treat me like a child who knows nothing about riding. This horse has done nothing but give me problems all morning, and what have you done about it except tell me to work it out or ride in another group? You're the Great George Morris, you get on him and get him through the in and out. You get him to switch his leads. I don't care if you trained the entire Olympic team. That was a hundred years ago. What are you now? Someone who writes a monthly column in *Practical Horseman*? You take this horse; here, you take him."

With that, Topping threw the reins at him and stormed out of the ring. We were all stunned. All but George, who knows the show must go on.

"Jan," he called, "could you please take this horse. Let's get back to crest releases. For a green horse or rider you go all the way up the neck, all the way up the neck, for a . . ."

Unbelievable. This man was unflappable. After an assault like that, I would've hauled off and flattened her. We continued our class as if nothing happened. Brenda sailed over the in and out three more times and I think I finally licked my oxerphobia.

To my surprise, Henry and his boys walked in right before my final flight. I knew he had them for the morning, but I thought he'd planned on taking them to the Manassas battleground. He waved my way and the boys started running around. George Morris shot him a withering look and Henry gathered up his troops, holding them in place by the collars.

I pointed Brenda toward the fences. Again we nailed the spots and I heard two little voices cheering. This time George Morris smiled and asked us to gather in the center of the ring, where he went over everything he'd taught. He complimented us all, thanked us, and said, "See you tomorrow, same time."

I led Brenda to her stall, where I was joined by Henry and the bouncing boys.

"Daddy, I want to learn to ride, please, can I, please?" It was Chet.

"If he gets to ride, I get a Sega." Hank the younger.

"I get a Sega too."

"Do not."

"Do too."

In no time flat there was a tangle of boys rolling on the macadam.

"Chet, Hank!!!"

He separated the boys and threatened dire consequences—no computer for a week. That shut them up.

"Henry," I said. "I've got about fifteen minutes' worth of work to do with Brenda—wrap her legs, clean her water bucket, etc. More et ceteras than you'd be interested in. Why don't you walk the boys around the barn or get them something to eat at the snack bar."

The mention of a snack got their attention. Before Henry left, he put his arm around me, leaned close, and whispered in my ear, "Dinner *tonight*, then? The boys are spending their last night with their mother."

"Ohhhh, look at Daddy, kissy-face with Nattie!!!"

"Okay, enough, boys," Henry said, and led them away. From

the back he looked exactly like a groom leading a couple of fractious colts.

I put Brenda in her stall because I wanted to find Lannie before she left. I might as well ask her what she was so worried about. What was the worst she could do? Then I remembered. Well, she wasn't going to kill me in front of George Morris.

I wove my way around Paper Chase, looking for a flea-bitten gray and matching rider. I wonder if she beamed out there, because I couldn't find her anywhere.

It looked as if I'd have to make that call to Gary Stockwell, *The Appeal*'s managing editor. I wasn't much closer to breaking this story than when I'd started. What did I have? Everything. And nothing. A dead girl who smelled of cigarettes. A jealous, woman-bashing boyfriend with lethal-weapon hands who's found Buddha. An obsessed friend who makes Selena's killer seem normal. And a spoiled-rich-girl best friend with a 450-degree Fahrenheit temper who's lying about everything but her name. For all I knew, that too.

Like I said. Everything and nothing.

I reluctantly walked to the phone and punched in the *Appeal*'s 800 number. Take that Miami, 50 cents off your 29.5 percent return on the dollar.

"Gary, this is Nattie. I'd rather have my teeth filled than ask you for this, but . . ."

I sketched out my predicament and he painted in his.

"I hear you, Nattie, but Candace's already promised it for page one on Sunday. She's going to flip when I tell her it's not going to happen. I don't know, I just don't know, let me think about this. Give me the number where you are now, I'll get back to you."

Not a good sign. Gary was afraid of Candace's fury. I guess it was true what they said about her: She had the biggest balls in the newsroom.

I could kiss my measly seven rating down the tubes. So what, I'd just ridden with George Morris, learned more about riding than I thought was humanly possible, AND he loved my horse. Life was good.

Diane was in the stall with Brenda, rubbing her head. "She's a terrific horse, Nattie."

"Don't I know it," I said. "I must have done at least one good thing in my last life to deserve her. What'd you think of George? Amazingly subdued, huh? Even when provoked."

"That was some display," Diane said.

"You couldn't tell with the helmet," I said, "but she's a red-head. As another redheaded female, I can personally attest that it's true what they say about chestnut mares: We're a bunch of hot-heads with tempers the size of Montana."

"If yours is Montana, then hers is the former Soviet Union," Diane said. "Or maybe she's crazy—a raging borderline—and the red hair is incidental."

"You know Diane, after three days in this place I'd say any-thing's possible," I said. "Borderline, what's that, on the border between neurotic and psychotic? Some days I'm a bit of a fence straddler there myself. No offense, but that sister of yours is about to push me right over."

"She's a trip, isn't she?" Diane said. "I think I went into psy-chiatry so I could understand her. But what I've learned is, some people defy understanding."

I decided right there: Diane would be a good addition to the barn. Maybe she could even analyze Rob into talking to me. "My barn is February Farm, a stall's just come up, the trails are not to be believed, and the care couldn't be better. Okay, what was her nickname?"

Diane looked confused for a second. "Oh, now I remember. I promised I'd tell you Candy's nickname. She'll kill me, but so what? We called her 'Leaky' because she'd cry whenever she didn't get her way."

Candace "Leaky" Fitzgerald. Hmmm, when and where do you use this?

"I'll get us a couple of sandwiches, okay?" Diane said. "Meet me in the snack room."

My legs were throbbing. This new southern development on my body had seeped down into my calves, which were sausaged into a pair of custom riding boots I'd bought ten pounds ago. I gathered up my boot pull, sneakers, jeans, and a magenta turtle-neck and made my way to the bathroom to change.

To my surprise, Topping was there, covered in mud and also changing.

"Hey, Topping," I said as I peeled off my tasteful Polo shirt in boring beige, one of three acceptable colors to Rob.

She said hello, but there was definitely a frost in the air and the room was heated. I guess she was still upset from her exchange with George.

"Is everything okay with you?" I said. "I've got the same temper, so I know what it feels like to lose it. I don't know about you, but when the hormones start mixing with my genetic coding, I become a screaming mcemie. I've got the perfect thing. It's this homeopathic PMS stuff called Natural Phases. It works wonders for me. One minute I'm ready to kill someone, I let a couple of the pills dissolve in my mouth, and a few hours later I notice my hands aren't clenched anymore and I'm not planning my boss's murder. I think I've got some on me."

Topping did in fact have her fists clenched. "No thanks," she said. "You can keep your little pills to yourself."

Whoa, what'd I do? I hate it when people other than my employers are mad at me. It makes me start blathering even more like a puppy looking for a petting.

"Topping, I don't know what your plans are now, but why don't you join us for lunch? I think you'd—"

"I *had* lunch plans with Henry. But I guess I don't now, thanks to you and your 'kissy face' display. Is that the reason he went home early the other night and couldn't even stay for the cake? More 'kissy facing'?"

She'd been watching me and Henry. That sent me for a loop.

I started to stutter. "T-T-T-Topping, look, I-I-I ahh don't know how to answer this. I-I-I . . ."

"Then don't," she said. She pulled her arms and her turtleneck up over her head, where the collar got stuck for a moment. And for that moment I was staring at a lacy white bra filled to the max with two big globes of flesh, atop them a gold chain burrowed into the Y of her cleavage. She slid the shirt over her head. As her arms lowered, so did her chest. Up went the chain and I saw what was dangling on the end: two gold hammered horseshoes in the shape of a heart with a big diamond in the center.

Just then Amy Benjamin walked in, gushing about the clinic. "Was that the most awesome morning you've ever spent, and what'd you think about that woman who lost it? What a nutcase."

Topping slipped on a blue silk shirt and turned to face Amy.

Amy started apologizing, and I was still trying to get a word in. Finally, I just plowed through Amy's words.

"Topping," I said. "Where'd you get that necklace?"

"Daddy gave it to me. Why, do you want that too?"

She stormed out of the bathroom and slammed the door.

Amy looked dazed. "What was that all about?"

"Maybe a lot more than it seems," I said, and started throwing my clothes back on so I could chase down Topping.

"God, she's certifiable, isn't she?" Amy said. "First she takes after George Morris, then that woman on the ugly gray horse."

"A flea-bitten gray?" I said. "The woman's about my height?"

"That's the one. They were just going at each other outside like two cats. Someone should have poured a bucket of water on the both of them to calm them down. I'm usually not one to eavesdrop, but it was pretty riveting."

"Did you hear what they were fighting about?"

"Sort of, but it was hard to make any sense of it. The shorter one kept saying something about how Topping tricked her. Topping called her pathetic and told her Josephine or someone with a name like that was just using her like she used everyone else. Then there was more screaming, mostly Topping trying to get the other woman to leave and stop ranting before everyone found out something. She never did say what that something was. The other woman was pretty upset, kind of crying and screaming at the same time and saying something like 'You made me do it. It's your fault.' Then she actually shoved Topping into the mud. Can you believe that?"

I didn't know what to believe at this point. All I knew is that I had to find Topping. Quick.

"Amy," I said. "I gotta go. Leave your number on my stall door and I'll call you tonight. If I'm right about what I think, it's you who's not going to believe it."

With that, I rushed out of the bathroom and smack into George Morris.

"Ah, Miss Gold," he said. "I'd like to talk to you about your horse and that story you wrote about Wally Hempstead. He was a scourge on our profession and I think . . ."

Unfortunately he thought a lot. I stood there nodding my head, smiling, saying thank-you, and wishing he'd be finished so I could find Topping. I was torn: be rude to George Morris and cut him off mid-sentence—name me a basketball fanatic who'd kiss off Michael Jordan, especially if the Air Man wanted to talk about that person's basketball skills—or keep smiling.

Okay, yes, I'm horse crazy. I did what any other horse-crazy person would've done in that situation. I kept smiling. And nodding and interjecting the appropriate "Really? How interesting" while letting what could have been a homicidal maniac get away.

Five or ten minutes must've passed before another rider in the clinic came up to us to ask George some questions. My entry for an out. I took it and ran to Brenda's stall, making sure this wasn't a repeat performance of the last time I'd tracked down a killer. No matter how crazy people are—and I'd say you have to be pretty crazy to take a life—they're not so befuddled in their thinking that they don't know my emotional Achilles' heel—Brenda. Poor Brenda, owned by a reporter who can't be happy stalking fashion trends.

I whisked open her stall door, expecting to find a drooling Topping with a crowbar in her hands. Brenda was alone, quietly eating her hay.

I raced around the barn, looking for Topping, and cursed the place for being so big, though I used no foul language, even in thought. A promise is a promise.

I don't know how long I ran around looking for her. Finally, I went to the snack bar to find Diane.

"Grilled cheese. You're a vegetarian, right? Sorry, it's cold," she said.

"Diane, forget the food. The borderline thing. Wasn't that the official movie psychiatrist's diagnosis of Glenn Close's character in *Fatal Attraction*?"

Diane nodded. "Yup, you've got it. In residency, sometimes we don't even call it borderline, we call it Close-line."

Just then a smiling Henry walked in with Hank.

"Hellowww, darlin', " he said in his best country-western voice. I could tell he was feeling mighty chipper, having spent the previous evening with the very loquacious Peterson Scott, the mad botanist who'd just indicted—on the record—the biggest industry in the Carolinas.

"Diane Fitzgerald, meet Henry Goode and his boys, Hank and—" I looked around.

"Chet? Chet? Henry, where's the poet? His son writes amazing poetry," I explained to Diane.

"Lucky him," Henry said, still in his Randy Travis voice. "He scored himself a rahhhhd on a little pony led by one fine-looking cowgirl. I'll bet he's singin' her some sonnets right now. I'd sing her a few myself if I weren't smitten with you."

"Oh, Henry," I said in an even thicker Dolly Parton. "Well, fancy that. I'm smitten too, as smitten as a mama tick at a blood bank on National Give Blood Day. Now let's talk English. What're you saying about Chet? They don't give pony rides here. Who'd Chet finagle into giving him a ride?"

Hank jumped in. "I told him not to go, but he wouldn't listen to me. No one listens to me 'cause I'm the youngest. But I told him not to go with *her*. I didn't like that lady and I told Chet that. But Daddy told me to be quiet or else he'd take the computer away."

I bent down eye level to Hank, which wasn't too far down.

"What lady, Hank? I'm listening."

"That lady who has the same color hair as you. But she's not funny like you. Or nice."

I turned to Henry. "Did Topping Mundell take Chet? Did you let her take him?"

"Yes, why? What's the big deal? She said she had a meeting at the barn where her therapeutic riding program meets and she'd give Chet a ride. The stable is about a mile from Martha's parents, so I thought I'd pick him up in an hour or so when I drove Hankie home."

"Oh, no, you didn't. Topping's nuts. She's a loose cannon waiting to explode."

Henry gave me a funny look. "We're not getting into this again, are we? I told you I'm not interested in her. Come on, Nattie, what's it going to take to convince you?"

Hank jumped in again. "I told Daddy not to let him go. I told him. I told him. But he never listens to me. Never. He always tells me I have a pro-action imageration, whatever that is."

"Overactive imagination," Henry said, and hugged the little

boy. "And there's nothing wrong with that. It's part of what makes you my Mister Hank-man. Nattie, let's stop this, you're scaring Hank."

I pulled his shirtsleeve and took him four steps away. "Could I talk to you privately for a second, then?"

"Hankie, here's a dollar, get yourself a soda. No Coca-Cola though."

"Yeah, yeah, yeah," the little boy said. "I know, no caffeine."

"Look, Henry, this has nothing to do with jealousy," I said, and then downloaded my Glenn-Close-Topping-killed-Josane theory, ending with the necklace.

"She's the ultimate Daddy's girl from hell," I said. "Look at it from Topping's view and see if it doesn't make sense in a sick, twisted kind of way: Daddy's been all hers since her icebox mommy shivered out of her life years ago. It's just Toppy and Daddy in that big house with funny floors. Enter Josane. Beautiful, gregarious, sexy Josane. Suddenly Daddy's got someone else on his mind, someone young and pretty just like Topping. But she's not Topping. He's buying this other someone presents, paying her rent, even buying her horses—just like he did for Topping. Josane's stolen Daddy right out from under her. As if that weren't unbearable enough, Josane adds another man to her collection. In Topping's mind, another one of *her* men: her recently exed fiancé of whom she'd been overly possessive. That's not enough to convince you? Don't forget her temper. I saw her make a fastball out of her cat and pitch him across the room just because her birthday cake for 'Daddy' fell. And you should've seen her temper tantrum with George Morris."

Henry wasn't buying it. Not yet.

"The necklace. That's when I knew. She's wearing Josane's custom-made necklace. I spoke to the jeweler myself, remember? He swears he made just two and threw away the mold.

Lannie bought one and Santee Mundell the other. He even had Josane's initials inscribed in it. I saw Josane's necklace not fifteen minutes ago, bobbing around Topping's considerable bosom. She told me 'Daddy gave it to me.' Baloney, the only way she got that was from Josane's dead or almost dead body. You can't blame that on a 'pro-action imageration'; can you? Ask Diane. She's a shrink, she saw Topping explode in the clinic. She was the one who joking around first called her a borderline personality. Borderline as in Glenn Close in *Fatal Attraction.* Remember what she does in the movie after she boils the pet rabbit? She takes the kid."

I could see Henry going into a sped-up version of his normal cogitative state. We were talking about the safety of his child, and that cranked him up.

Hank came back with his soda—a Sprite. "Hank," he said. "We're going to drive to that barn now and get Chet. I'm going to show you he's fine and you've got nothing to worry about."

"I told you he shouldn't've gone with her. She's a bad lady, isn't she, Nattie?"

I looked at Henry and then back at Hank. "I don't know if she's bad, Hank," I said. "I don't really know anything for sure yet except I'm sure Chet's having a great time riding. Why don't we go find out, huh?"

Diane offered to wrap Brenda's legs and I gratefully accepted. If she stood unwrapped overnight, Rob would take her away from me.

As we were walking to Henry's car we ran into Lannie, unfortunately, literally. Hank was walking backward and slammed into her.

"Will you watch where you're going?" Lannie said to Hank. Then she saw me.

"Just stay away from me," she said. Her eyes were Easter-bunny red.

"Henry, Hank," I said, "go on up to the car, I'll meet you in a second."

Henry looked at me. "Nattie, make it quick, please."

"This shouldn't take long," I said to Henry, but looked directly at Lannie.

"Okay, Lannie, no more fun and games. I know Topping killed Josane; the missing piece is you. What'd she trick you into? What'd she make you do? And what was the wrestling match about between the two of you?"

Lannie started to walk away. I grabbed her shoulder and spun her around.

"Look," I said, "I don't care if you hate me, hate my profession, or hate my mother. You're going to tell me and tell me fast. That nutcase just took Henry's kid, and if she hurts one hair on his head, I'm coming after you. You think Topping's got a temper? You haven't seen mine."

It looked like someone let the air out of her, or what little life remained.

"Henry?" Lannie said. "Henry Goode, the other reporter from *The Appeal*? Topping's new boyfriend?"

"Is that what she told you?" I said. "She's crazy. I mean really crazy. As in killing-people crazy. But you already know that, don't you? Lannie, what'd she trick you into doing? This has something to do with Josane's death, doesn't it?"

Lannie was shaking her head and the waterworks started again. I didn't have time for tears. I grabbed her shoulder and shook her. "Come on, Lannie, Topping tricked you into what? Killing Josane because she couldn't do it but wanted her dead? Is that it?"

Lannie was off in outer space, responding to her own set of questions. "This morning Topping told me she could get you off my back because her new boyfriend worked with you and he'd tell you to stop. No one would ever know. She promised. The next thing I know she's screaming at me, blaming everything on me, saying no one will believe me, they'll believe her."

"Lannie, I don't have time for twenty questions. Just tell me."

"She promised me nothing bad would happen. I know you won't write it like that, but that's the truth. She told me it wouldn't hurt Josane bad. It'd just make her a little sick and I could go to her house that night and take her to the hospital. Like a rescue thing. And I'd be the one doing the rescue and then she'd like me again. We'd go back to the way it was before I took the money. To the way things were."

"Lannie," I said, "what're you talking about?"

"I didn't know Topping wanted her dead, I swear I didn't. I didn't know anything about Topping's father and Josane. That night I went to Josane's and waited for her, like we'd planned. We were supposed to go to Mosby's Tavern for dinner. She never showed up. It wasn't like her to do something like that and I started getting worried. I didn't know what to do. I waited for three or four hours and finally went home. The next day Topping told me there'd been a 'riding accident.' That's when I saw it. The necklace around Topping's neck. Our necklace. Mine and Josane's. Around Topping's neck. It wasn't right, taking it off Josane. And I told Topping that. She laughed in my face. Imagine that, she laughed in my face with her best friend not dead a day. That's when I knew that riding accident story she told me about Josane wasn't true. Topping and all those people finding Josane, how could she have taken the necklace without anyone seeing? When I asked her, she laughed more and called me a stupid fool. Then she started talking crazy about how Josane deserved to die for stealing her father. I tried to take the necklace from her, I wanted to send it to Josane's mother, and Topping went nuts. She was screaming that it was her necklace, she'd found it in her father's drawer and thought he'd gotten it for her as a birthday surprise. Then a week later she saw it on Josane. Now it was hers again, she said. No one was going to take it because she'd worked so hard to get it back. When I asked how she took the necklace with everyone watching, she called me an idiot again and told me she found Josane hours before anyone else, lying on the ground, dying because of me. Because of me. I loved Josane and I wanted to call the police and tell them everything. But Topping got even crazier and told me she'd make it look like I killed Josane on purpose. Then she told me if I just shut up about it, I'd have nothing to worry about because she'd fixed everything to make it look like a riding accident and who wouldn't believe it with that crazy horse of hers? She said she took Josane's helmet off and put her head on a rock, so it looked like she'd fallen on it. I didn't want to go along, I didn't know it would hurt her, I swear I didn't. Topping promised me that stuff would just make her a little sick and I could take her to the hospital. Then it would be like old times."

I shook her shoulders. "The bump medicine for Rita, is that what you're talking about?"

She dropped her head and nodded it. "I didn't know it would kill her. I swear I didn't."

"What was in it?" I said.

"I don't know for sure," Lannie said. "She gave me a bottle of it to mix with DMSO. Something from her father's laboratory, something like that cold medicine, Contact. A time-release something."

Man, how could I be so dense? Of course, Peterson Scott's time-release nicotine. He works for Mundell Industries. Topping probably helped herself to a few bottles of the poison and had Lannie mix it with DMSO. That stuff acts like the Concorde, supersonic-jetting whatever's mixed in it straight into your bloodstream. That explains the cigarette smell on Josane and why it kicked in when she was way out on the trail.

Lannie was crying. "I didn't think it would kill her. Topping said it would just hurt her a little."

"You better pray that kid's okay," I said, and ran to Henry's car.

That was the longest ride of my life. And the traffic on Route 50 past all those strip malls didn't help much. Stop and go. Stop and go. I wanted to scream, but I forced myself to stay calm for Hank's sake, who kept muttering, "I told them not to go."

We got to Rock Creek Parkway and zoomed up the twisty road. I didn't know what Henry was thinking, because he was talking to Hank, promising him everything was fine and Chet was probably having the time of his life. I saw the brown and white sign: MID-ATLANTIC THERAPEUTIC RIDING PROGRAM HEAD-QUARTERS. Henry pulled right in front of the Quonset-hutty-looking building. Didn't look for a parking space, didn't check if he was between the lines.

"Hank, stay in the car. I'll lock the doors and—"

"I don't want to stay in the car. I'm not staying in the car alone."

Henry knew he wasn't going to win that one no matter how many computer days he took away. "If you come with me, you have do exactly what and when I tell you to do. No arguments, no tantrums. Deal?"

Hank nodded and we tried to walk calmly into the arena.

"I'm sure he's right in there with a big smile on his face," Henry said.

"She seemed icky to me, Dad. Icky scary, kind of," Hank said.

I breathed easier when I saw the arena. There were ten or twelve kids being led around on horses. I was hoping I'd over-reacted and that Chet would be one of them.

Not being a parent, I don't have parental radar, so I started picking though the group, looking for Chet. Before I'd gotten to the second kid, Henry, whose voice was edging into panic, said, "He's not here, Nattie. Let's find the office."

It was in the barn, about a hundred yards from the arena. A young woman was behind the counter, reading a Dick Fran-cis book.

"Do you know Topping Mundell?" Henry said.

"Yeah," she said. We were in the North again.

"Have you seen her? Was she with a boy about five feet tall?"

"Yeah," she said, and turned the page.

Henry leaned over the counter and grabbed the book out of her hands.

"This is important," he said, overenunciating each word as if English were her second language. "When did you see her? And where did she go with the boy?"

"Jeez, no reason to act like a butt-hole about it. She put the kid on Hazel Nut and took him for a trail ride."

"Is she on a horse too?" I said.

"Yeah, she took out Blaze. They headed back that way, you know, toward the monument graveyard."

"What monument graveyard?" Henry said. "What're you talking about?"

The woman gave Henry a bored look. "You know, where they ditch all the old pieces of the monuments and statues and junk like that. There's piles and piles of it stacked up. I don't know what they're keeping it for. Old broken pieces of statues, hunks of buildings, parts of columns; it looks like that last scene in *Planet of the Apes*. That movie comes on cable all the time."

The woman went back to Dick. Henry leaned over the counter and pushed his face in hers. "How do I find it?"

"Calm down, would ya. God, you're just as nuts as Topping. What's up? You two have a fight or something?"

"Just tell me how to get there," Henry said.

The woman stood, reluctantly, and walked us to the door. "See that trail over there on the right? Follow it and turn right at the fork. Keep going, looking for broken cement body parts sticking out of the ground."

We tried to run, but the ice had scabbed over the ground. So we walked as fast as we could and still stay vertical. I know it wasn't the time to sightsee, but the sights to be seen were beautiful. It felt like we were walking in the middle of the Henry David Thoreau poster I'd hung on my freshman dorm wall. We were winding our way through the park. Still no sight of Chet and Topping. Hank was starting to cry and Henry was doing all he could to keep going and stop the boy from all-out hysterics.

We turned a bend and I caught a flash of something.

"Way up ahead," I said. "See it? It could be just a deer."

"Chet," Henry boomed across the park. "Chet, is that you?"

Despite the ice, we ran. All three of us took turns taking tumbles. As we got closer, we saw it clearly. It wasn't a deer. It was Chet on a chestnut pony with a flaxen mane and tail. Topping had the pony's reins in her hands.

She walked her horse faster.

"Topping, wait up," Henry called to her.

She picked up the pace. "Wait up for what? For lunch? It's a little late for that, isn't it? I thought you wanted me. Not her. Me. Do you hear me?"

"Daddy," Chet called. "She's acting weird and going too fast. Make her stop."

"Topping," Henry said. "Just let Chet go. He didn't do anything to you. I'm the one you're angry with."

"Not you, her. She's just like Josane but not as pretty. Couldn't wait to get her claws in you and every other man around. I saw her staring at Daddy's portrait. And Snowden. Don't think I don't know about that, just like Josane didn't think I knew about her and Daddy and then her and Snowden. Don't think I didn't know. Come on, Chet, let's go for a gallop."

She kicked her horse and he took off, dragging poor Hazel Nut behind.

"Daddy, help!!!!" Chet screamed.

We watched in horror as the horses started galloping down the path away from us. I broke out into a flat-out run, and so did

Henry and Hank. I don't know what kept me on my feet, maybe my guardian angel.

"Daddy!!!!" We heard it and saw it. Hazel Nut took a spectacular fall, her feet slipped out from under her, and she landed on her side. On Chet.

"Chet!!!" Henry screamed as loud as a human being can scream and ran so fast I could see only a blur. By the time Henry and I reached Hank, he was by Chet's side, cradling the boy in his arms, crying and rocking him. I thought he was dead.

Then I heard a little voice. "Hey, you're holding me so hard, I can't breathe."

Henry was crying into Chet, "Thank God you're alive."

I looked around and saw why. Miraculously, the horse had landed in a big drift of crusted snow, cushioning her fall onto Chet. Where she was now, however, was anyone's guess.

"You take Chet back, make sure he's okay, no concussion or anything," I said. "I can't believe that idiot let him ride without a helmet. I've got to find Hazel Nut. She could be hurt."

Henry started to argue with me. But I was hopping mad. Beware the Polnyakoff temper. I really wanted to find that lunatic Topping. She wouldn't kill me, she obviously didn't have the guts to do her own dirty work. She had to set Lannie up to do that.

I stormed ahead.

I didn't hear or see anything of Topping or Hazel Nut, so I trudged farther. Then, up ahead, I saw her. Hazel Nut. Her reins were caught, snagged in the broken bones of a concrete hero. I wove my way around the remains and freed her up.

She was panting and shaking. "Easy, girl," I said, and hated Topping even more for not only terrifying a kid, but this poor, dumb pony. "Easy, girl."

I put the reins over her head and got on. Before I turned to leave, I looked around. The monument graveyard. Broken pieces of America, right there before my feet.

"Bitch."

It didn't come from me, since I wasn't cursing anymore.

I spun Hazel Nut around. "Topping," I said. "How'd you do it? Follow Josane back out on the trail and smash her in the head once she was dead to make it look like a fall? Is that it?"

She didn't answer, not that I was expecting one. But she did run her horse right upside Hazel Nut and smack my mount hard across the butt with a whip. Like any horse, Hazel Nut took that as a sign to gallop—again. Around and over the bits and pieces of America with Topping right on my tail. I tried to pull her back, but even Anne Kursinski couldn't have avoided what was staring us smack in the face a half-stride away. I don't know whose nose it was, but it was big. A big jutting nose rising from the earth.

I heard George Morris's voice in my head. ". . . Crest release. If you're unsteady, plant your hands in his neck and grab mane. . . ." Unsteady wasn't the word. I dug my hands so deep into Hazel Nut's neck, I was giving her a free Rolfing session and my fingers became one with her mane. I kicked her and she flew over whoever's nose it was. My hands were planted, so I wasn't going anywhere but with her.

Topping, on the other hand, was going places. She tried to turn away, but as usual was way too far forward on her horse, once again ahead of the vertical—the wrong place to be. Her horse popped straight up in the air and she did the same thing she'd done in the clinic, flopped forward and started grabbing at his mouth. Once again it had the same effect. He toppled down to the ground.

She landed shoulder-first on a slab of white limestone. I heard it snap, crackle, pop—her bone, not the entablature, probably the same one she'd broken from her tumble off Rox-Dene.

"Ahhhhhhh," she screamed.

I looked down at Topping writhing around on the hunk of history. In case anyone thinks whoever's in charge of things down here doesn't have a sense of humor, here's what Topping was doing the slow grind on, I swear it's true. Carved deeply into the white stone, all in capital letters were the words *DEPART-MENT OF JUSTICE.*

I walked Hazel Nut closer to Topping and said: "Crest release, Topping. You should have listened to George. But you always were a lousy rider."

CHAPTER 41

Candace got her page-one story out of me and I pushed deadline by only forty-five minutes. I thought that was pretty good, considering. "Leaky," on the other hand, didn't. She told me it was going in my review that I "cavalierly pushed deadlines" and it would slip me down to a six on the old one-to-ten scale.

As for my romantic dinner that night with Henry—and whatever afterward—it wasn't to be. Henry spent the night zonked out on his marshmallow bed while I tapped away late into the stars to make Candace happy, which I've finally realized is impossible.

My old boyfriend, John, had another five days or so left to go in the hospital when I left Middleburg. Every time I called his room, Sarah Carpenter, the friendly nurse, picked up the phone. I made him swear he'd either do nothing or do right by her, none of this "I lost the tingle" baloney. He said the doctors have told him he'll be okay as long as he never tries to smoke a cigarette and steers clear of secondhand smoke. The last time I talked to him, he was still wrestling with his future. After riding in his Lexus, I can't honestly say I know what I'd do in his high-dollar Italian shoes.

Chet turned out to be just fine. Rattled and scared of horses probably for a lifetime, but fine. I don't know what the district attorney's planning to do about Lannie. She spilled her guts to the cops: that she gave Josane the DMSO she'd laced with Topping's time-release nicotine. I asked Tony, my sheriff buddy, to put in a call to his friends up in Middleburg and see what he could do to help Lannie walk.

Topping they carted off to the hospital and up to surgery. But before they did I asked Sarah Carpenter for one more favor—to call a nurse friend of hers at the hospital and get me the necklace so I could give it to Josane's mother. I was right about the Rice Krispies sound: Topping had pulverized her shoulder pretty good and it took a railroad track worth of pins, bolts, and plates to put it all back together. After recovery it's off to jail for Daddy's little girl, even though my horse friends swear she'll never serve time, that Daddy'll buy her way out. But they'd been wrong about George Lindemann, the rich little slimebag who killed his horse for insurance money he didn't need because he didn't want to admit he couldn't ride the horse. He got the maximum sentence: thirty-three months in prison plus a $750,000-dollar fine, with Judge George Marovich concluding: "No case in recent memory has troubled me to the extent that this one has. . . . It's time for me to find personal peace and accept that there are things that make no sense at all. . . . I ask you to ask yourself the question that I cannot answer: 'Why the hell did you do this and why were you so unconcerned about the consequences of your actions?' I think I've given you enough time to do that."

Too bad Topping's not going to be tried in Marovich's Chicago court.

As for the rest of the clinic with George Morris, the second day was even better than the first. Partially because we were two riders down: Topping and Lannie. But more because George was brilliant; in fact, I'm going to name my first child after him if I can ever get far enough in a relationship to consider that a possibility.

Speaking of. Henry. Sweet Henry. Notice I don't say irritating, annoying, nitpicking Henry. An argumentative word hasn't crossed our lips since he scooped his little boy out of the crusty snow. I'm not saying it'll last, but almost losing the most important thing in the world to you has a way of jump-starting a person into prioritizing what's important in life. And I guess Henry decided I must be one of those things.

I, too, have changed. As Flip's guru suggested, I've been meditating on this joy/suffering issue. I haven't gotten the answer nailed down yet. But I've had glimpses. Rides through the woods. Seeing Henry with his boys. Writing the perfect story. Hearing my mother laugh again.

I know it'll come eventually. Nana Greenburg told me so in that weird dream where she's waving to me in the beauty-queen way and singing in a strange language that I could suddenly understand. I didn't know it then, but I'd sung the answer along with her. "There will be an answer, let it be, let it be."

So I'm letting it be for now. Or as Tom, Flip's travel agent to nirvana, calls it, letting be.

I wish I could say the same for the dead girl's father that Henry interviewed. The last I heard, Charlie Laconte found him wandering the fields his little girl used to gallop her pony across. Wandering, lost in his tears and memories.

Reenie Ashmore is faring a little better. A little. She still talks about Josane in the present tense, but says she going to start going to Christine's meetings regularly and start talking there about Josane, the daughter she lost.

All these tears. It seems like there's a river of them out there, half of them from me. Just when I thought I'd cried enough, I started crying some more. But these, thank goodness, were happy tears.

The night we got back to Charlotte, Gail and Torkesquist were waiting by my door, entwined in each other.

"Gold," Torkesquist said. "I gotta break your heart here: Looks like you'll have to get your rug burns from someone else. Gail and I are getting married tomorrow and she says she won't do it without you there."

Gail started crying, threw her arms around me, and that's how we stayed—locked together in happy tears.

Lou heard the commotion and came outside. When Gail told him the news, he ran into my apartment and brought a present for the happy couple: a matching set of Superman-strength magnets to synchronize their energy fields.

The wedding was at Tork's Turf, attended by me, Henry, Rob, Lou, and Allie and Hap—the two horses Gail and Torkesquist rode in on. As fashion writer, I feel I should comment on what Gail wore: an exquisite antique-blue brocade sidesaddle outfit with a long, flowing skirt and a nipped-in jacket.

"Wait," I said just as she was about to mount. "You're missing one thing. Something borrowed." I pulled out Dorothy's happy man wedding necklace. It was the exact blue of her dress.

"Legend has it once Torkesquist sees this on you, he'll never look at another woman. But why would he? He's got you. Gail, you look gorgeous."

We hugged and the waterworks started again.

"It's time to get hitched," she said through her tears.

The ceremony was delightfully brief, and when they kissed we cheered, and when we cheered, that must've annoyed Hap the ugly Ap's sensitive ears. Just as Torkesquist locked lips with his new bride, his horse locked teeth with the groom's leg.

"Yiiiiikes," he screamed.

Lou walked over to the horse and started circling his hands around Hap's face.

"No wonder, his chi's all blocked up," Lou said. "That's the problem."

Then Lou poked his fingers along Hap's neck and down deep into his ears. My mouth fell open. I couldn't believe Hap hadn't kicked the brown rice out of my father. Most horses won't let you near their ears, let along perform digital penetration. Hap not only tolerated it, but was leaning into Lou like I'd leaned into Henry that night on the Duncans' couch. Finally my father'd found his soul mate.

For the rest of the afternoon Hap refused to let Lou out of his sight, even when he went to my car to fetch the gallon of special celebration juice he'd made fresh that morning in his ear-deafening Champion juicer. Ear-deafening only to me, since he couldn't hear a thing because he took his hearing aid out.

Lou came back with Hap plastered by his side and poured a round for everyone.

"To forever," he said, and we all clinked our glasses of ruby-red juice together.

ABOUT THE AUTHOR

JODY JAFFE has long experience in both the worlds of journalism and horse shows. For the past twenty-four years she has been riding and showing hunters. She spent ten years as a feature writer for *The Charlotte Observer* and is the author of *Horse of a Different Killer*. She makes her home in Washington, D.C., with her husband, Charlie Shepard, and their sons, Ben and Sam.